THE
MAN WHO
WAS THERE

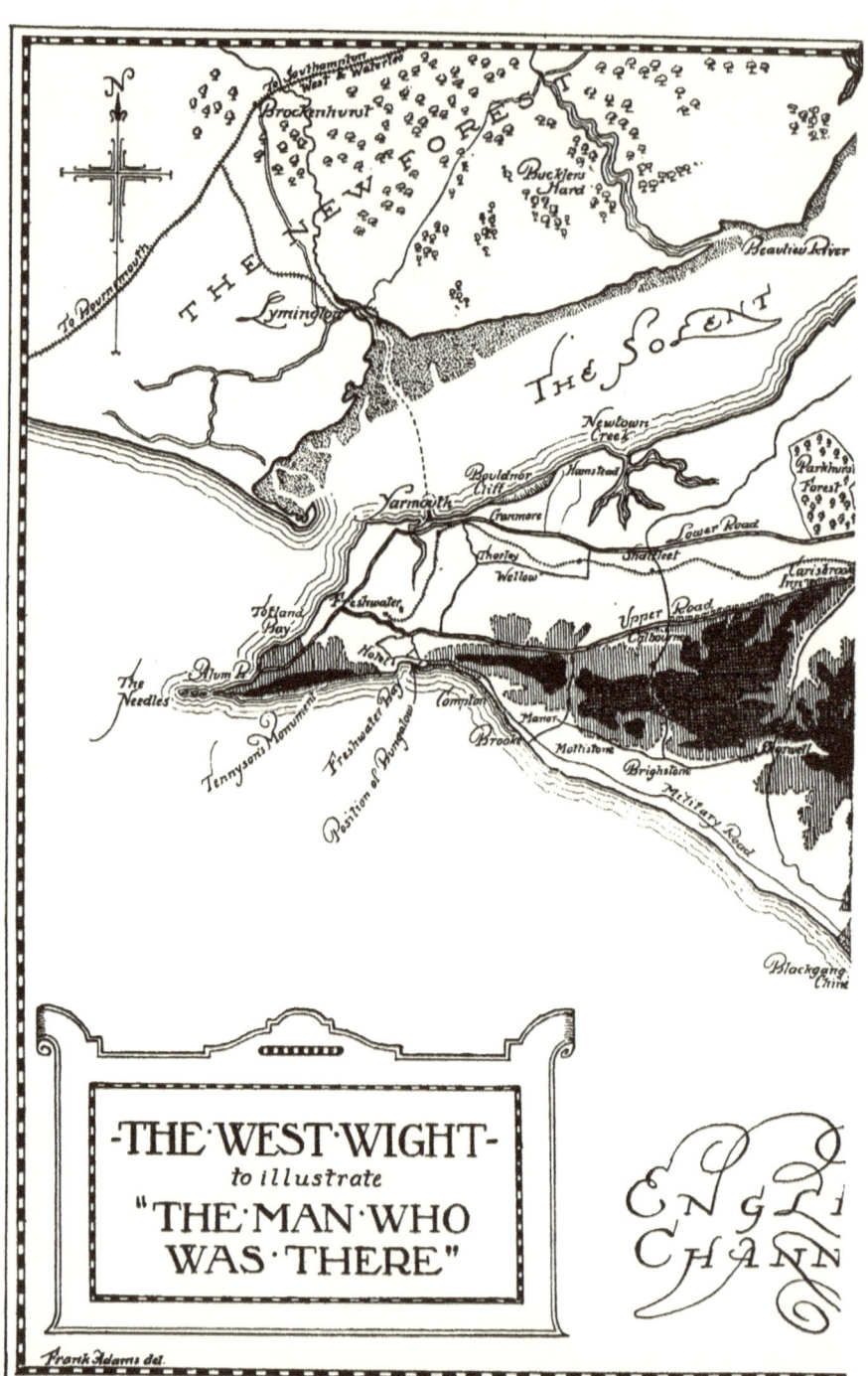

-THE·WEST·WIGHT-
to illustrate
"THE·MAN·WHO
WAS·THERE"

Frank Adams del.

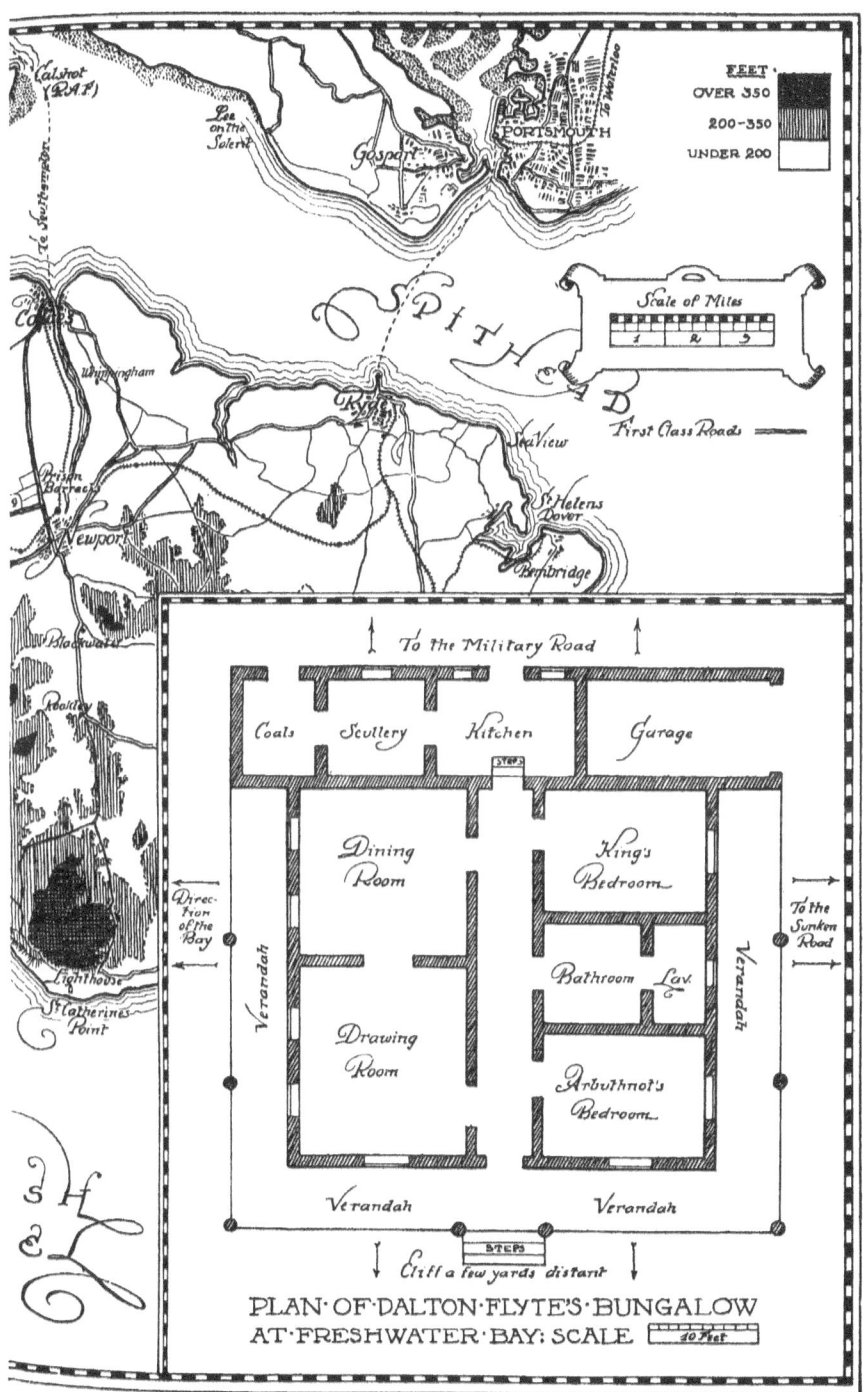

FEET
OVER 350
200-350
UNDER 200

Calshot (R.A.F.)

Lee on the Solent

Gosport

PORTSMOUTH

To Waterloo

SPITHEAD

Scale of Miles
1 2 3

First Class Roads

Whippingham

Ryde

SeaView

St Helens

Dover

Bembridge

Prison Barracks

Newport

Blackwater

Rookley

Lighthouse

St Catherines Point

To the Military Road

| Coals | Scullery | Kitchen | | Garage |

STEPS

Dining Room

King's Bedroom

Direction of the Bay

Verandah

Bathroom Lav.

To the Sunken Road

Verandah

Drawing Room

Arbuthnot's Bedroom

Verandah

Verandah

STEPS

Cliff a few yards distant

PLAN·OF·DALTON·FLYTE'S·BUNGALOW
AT·FRESHWATER·BAY: SCALE   10 Feet

THE
MAN WHO
WAS THERE

N. A. Temple-Ellis

COACHWHIP PUBLICATIONS
Greenville, Ohio

The Man Who Was There, by N. A. Temple-Ellis
© 2026 Coachwhip Publications edition

First published 1930
Neville Aldridge Holdaway, 1894-1954
CoachwhipBooks.com

ISBN 1-61646-631-6
ISBN-13 978-1-61646-631-2

Foreword

I was obliged to be absent from England while this book was in preparation, and I did not see it till it had reached the proof stage. Bearing in mind the scrupulous fidelity with which, on a previous occasion, Mr. Temple-Ellis had compiled from my materials an account of one of the investigations of my friend Montrose Arbuthnot, I had not hesitated in this case to give him a free hand. I am bound to say that he has interpreted his instructions very liberally.

The close acquaintance which has existed between us since I originally arranged with him to collaborate in producing the record which was eventually published under the title of *The Inconsistent Villains,* led me in the course of conversation to relate to him much which might be considered extraneous to the end in view. It is on this point that he has sacrificed discretion to the writer's instinct to make the most of his material.

Let me make it clear that I do not accuse Mr. Temple-Ellis of any divagation from the truth. Far from it. He has only used detail of a personal nature to invest with the air of fiction a story whose bald outlines are already familiar to the public, and in so doing he has assigned to me an undue prominence which I deplore.

I did not seek to interfere with the book at the last moment beyond inserting this prefatory note, for I am well aware of the homicidal emotions roused in publishers' breasts by authors' last-minute corrections. If there is trouble to come, I have no doubt it will fall, as usual, on the broad back of

Edmund King

1
Events of Saturday, May 26th

On the dining-room floor of the little bungalow lay a man with a bullet through his heart, and on the veranda outside another man sat in a deckchair, placidly reading *Palgrave's Golden Treasury.* This, in a sentence, describes a situation unique in my experience. It remains to be seen how we came to be in the picture.

It was an abominable spring that year, and just as the weather made a belated attempt to improve I fell a victim to influenza. My friend Arbuthnot, diligent delver into the more obscure and questionable doings of men, who shares my Kensington flat, was openly scornful but actually, I hope and believe, a little concerned. At any rate, when I was still shaky about the knees and regarding my usual brand of tobacco with unqualified aversion, he carted me off to recuperate in the Isle of Wight. Hence it was that late May saw us at Freshwater Bay, a little, quiet seaside place at the western end of the island, and here we took up our abode in a modest hostelry on the very edge of the bay itself, a long, irregular building that at its seaward end almost exposed its very walls to the buffetings of the Channel.

Arbuthnot from time to time while we were there took great pains to explain to me the geological and other circumstances that had produced a corner of the world so

peculiarly full of charm. I can't say that I understood much
about it when he had finished, and I rather resented having
the glamour of what is almost a lost land (for the sea eats
into it year by year) explained in a jargon of anticlines,
consequent drainage and marine erosion. I will therefore
be content to say in plain language that the bay is almost
a perfect semicircle bitten out, as it were, from a long expanse of chalky coast, so that its low shores are flanked on
east and west by great white cliffs which rise almost sheer
from the sea. Above the cliffs are smooth, rounded downs,
and in the bay itself stand massive rocks, carved into curious shapes by the fretting of the waves which beat upon
them when winter brings up its southwesters.

When we were there the splendour of a wonderful season lay like a presence over the land, a healing power that
rapidly brought me back to vigour. Then we tramped here
and there where cliff and down and cove and chine and
inland vale were always presenting something fresh and
delectable to the eye. And here, as I have said, we walked
into tragedy in its baldest and extremest form.

It was hardly more than half-past six one glorious morning when Arbuthnot roused me for a round of golf. I was
nothing loth, and by seven o'clock we had passed along
the road that runs just behind and parallel to the sea-front
and were mounting the farther slope that leads to the no-
ble down where the golf-links are situated. At that early
hour no caddies interrupted the tranquility of the scene
and we seemed alone in the world. Nevertheless, though
it sounds foolish, I had begun the day with a feeling that
things were about to go wrong. To begin with, the maid
who had grown accustomed to our habits had left two days
previously, after a tiff with the manageress, and her substitute was a fool who stowed my belongings in all sorts of
impossible places and had apparently spirited my safety-
razor blades away into thin air, so that my shave with a

dulled blade had been anything but happy. In addition, the morning tea was only lukewarm, and I had discovered a split in the shaft of my favourite mashie. Altogether I was prepared to look upon the world that morning with a jaundiced eye, and said as much to Arbuthnot.

It was at this very moment that a wild scream of terror pulled us up in our tracks. It came from a woman who was rushing towards us across the turf. She ran cow-like, and but for the wild panic apparent in her shriek I could have laughed.

"She must have come from that bungalow," said Arbuthnot, pointing to a low, white building which lay not more than two hundred yards from us and near the edge of the cliff.

"A case of burglary, very likely," I said. "She has just discovered her loss."

"No, King, a case of murder, more probably," answered my friend. "People are stupefied by a robbery but appalled by a murder. On the other hand, it may be merely a mouse in the pantry."

"Help!" gasped the woman, arriving with an uncertain step and holding a hand over her heart.

"What kind of help?" asked Arbuthnot.

"He's dead!" she cried inconsequentially.

Judging by her appearance, I had decided that she must be some kind of domestic servant.

"In the bungalow?" queried Arbuthnot.

"Yes, sir," answered the woman, taking a better grip of herself in our reassuring presence. "It's my master, Mr. Flyte. He's lying in the dining-room, and I think he's been shot, for there's blood on his chest."

"And who are you?" inquired Arbuthnot.

"I'm the housekeeper, sir, but I don't stay here at night. I live in Freshwater and come here to work first thing in the morning."

"I see. We'll walk back with you and make sure that he's dead. Then the police will have to be fetched."

"I daren't go into that room again," she protested, over-come by a violent fit of shivering.

"You needn't," said Arbuthnot kindly. "Walk back with us and you can wait outside while we have a look at things." With a shrug of his shoulders and a remark about a bus-man's holiday, he led the way back to the harmless-looking red-tiled bungalow that had so suddenly assumed a sinister significance. I followed, gazing at the golf-clubs hanging from Arbuthnot's shoulder and thinking of the butterfly and the skull and such-like incongruities.

We entered by the back door, which faced landwards and led directly into the kitchen. The house was built to an exceedingly simple design, and the plan I have given in this book should make everything clear. Beyond the kitch-en the woman declined to go. A door with glass panels was opposite the one by which we had entered, and from this door she resolutely kept her face averted.

"Where is it?" asked Arbuthnot.

"In the dining-room. Through the passage and the first door on the right."

"I presume there is no one else in the house?" he went on.

"No, Mr. Flyte lived all alone. Unless—my God!"

She was making for the door by which we had entered and I realized the thought that had suddenly entered her head. Arbuthnot stepped between her and the exit.

"Surely," I said soothingly, "you can see that if your master has been murdered, the murderer is not going to remain here in the house till he is arrested. You are per-fectly safe."

"Sit down," said Arbuthnot, "and compose yourself. If you run screaming all over the place and collect a crowd you will hamper the police in the execution of their duty and perhaps impede the course of justice." She was evidently impressed by this and consented to sit down, while my friend favoured me with a grin.

"Come on," said he to me, dumping his clubs in a corner and motioning me to do likewise. He led the way into the passage, which was in semi-darkness for part of its length. Light streamed into it at one point from an open door on the right. It is, I think, one of the nastiest feelings in life to be going to meet a corpse, nerving oneself against what one may see and yet not properly aware of what that something may be like.

Arbuthnot stepped into the room and I peered over his shoulder with a catch in my breath, for whatever one may have seen in war one can never become completely inured to crimes of violence in times of peace. Opposite us were two windows, the left-hand one screened by a white curtain, and through the curious way in which one part of the brain will work on its own, I found myself wondering how it was that no light came through a white curtain. The curtain on the other window had been drawn aside and the clear daylight shone on a rich dark-red carpet. I took a pace forward. Then I saw the body. It lay between the dining-room table and the outside wall of the room, with its face upturned and its feet towards us. Arbuthnot went down on his knees.

"Dead," he announced, after a very brief examination. "He was shot through the heart at point-blank range. There are the marks of the powder from the charge on his waistcoat."

"Then he may have shot himself?" I asked.

"That remains to be seen."

The man whose body I surveyed must have already reached middle age when he died. His hair was thin, but what there was was carefully disposed to conceal incipient baldness. He had rather heavy lips and a thin nose marked at the sides by the regular use of pince-nez; his pale blue eyes stared at the ceiling from beneath inadequate eyebrows. He was of average height, and his body showed the disposition to rotundity which sometimes comes with the approach of fifty. On one of his thin white fingers glittered a magnificent diamond ring.

"Look at the ring," I said. "It can't be a case of robbery with violence."

Arbuthnot was not paying much attention to me. He moved to the other window, drew aside the curtain, opened the window, and unbolted the shutters which protected it on the outside. Then I realized why the window had previously admitted no light. The heavy, white-painted shutters were more characteristic of Mediterranean houses than of an English bungalow.

"Quaint idea," I said. "Reminds me of the Riviera."

Arbuthnot retraced his steps to the kitchen. I followed.

"Did you open the window in the dining-room?" he asked of the woman who sat there nervously fingering her dress.

"Yes, sir. It was all dark when I went in, and I opened one window and threw back the shutters, and was just going to the other window when I trod on his foot. Tell me, sir, is he really dead?"

"Absolutely," said Arbuthnot. "Was he a good master to you?"

"Always. Never a bit of trouble. And now, this happening, what shall I do?" She threatened hysteria.

"Answer me a question," said Arbuthnot curtly. "Did you find the back door locked when you arrived this morning?"

"Yes, sir, just as usual. I have my own key and let myself in every morning."

At this he turned and went back to the dining-room and began a methodical survey. Apart from the dining-table and the usual quota of chairs, sideboard, and so forth, there were two articles there, rather unusual in such surroundings, which showed that the occupant had also used the room as a study. A large, roll-top desk stood open in one corner behind the dead man's head, and in the adjacent corner was a massive safe. Arbuthnot stepped to the latter article, took the handle in his hand, and the door swung open. There was a vision of empty shelves. Arbuthnot looked at me with his eyebrows raised.

"Whoever committed the crime took the dead man's keys, cleared the safe, and decamped," I said. "That's as clear as the multiplication table."

"In that case," responded my friend, "a time-table is even more important than the multiplication table."

"How so?"

"Why, if one has the temerity to commit a crime in an island one must consider ways and means of getting away from it."

"Pity we haven't one," I cried.

"I have," said he, pulling a little yellow-covered booklet from his pocket. Arbuthnot has a knack which is almost uncanny of being always provided with something or other which becomes suddenly essential.

"The shooting presumably took place at night when the escape of the sound would have been largely prevented by the shutters, and when every one else in the district was probably asleep. Hence the murderer, if such there be, could not leave by any regular route until the first boat this morning?"

"When does that leave?" I queried eagerly.

Arbuthnot flicked over the pages.

"It leaves Ryde at 7.15 and arrives at Portsmouth at 7.45," he said. "As the time is now 7.40, we are rather late in the field. If the man has reached Portsmouth he is as good as lost so far as stopping him *en route* goes. I don't imagine that he would travel on to Waterloo, for that would allow two more hours for the police to get on his track."

I conceded the justice of his statements.

"However, we don't know that he left by steamer. He may have crossed by motor-boat and landed inconspicuously in any one of those little creeks that come down from the New Forest."

"Moreover," I said, "there are also boats from Yarmouth and from Cowes, and both are nearer this place than Ryde is."

Arbuthnot turned over the pages again. "The first boat from Cowes is at eight o'clock," he answered, "and the first from Yarmouth at 8.25. This in itself renders it unlikely that either of these routes would be used. There is another point to consider. The early boat from Ryde carries back to Portsmouth a large crowd of week-enders, amongst whom our hypothetical criminal would be much less likely to be remembered if inquiries came to be made later. Still, it is rather waste of time going into these matters at this stage. For all we know the man may be sitting in the drawing-room listening to all we are saying!"

I gazed uneasily over my shoulder at the open doorway that led into the room he had mentioned. That room, like the rest of the house, lay in semi-darkness, and I presumed that shutters were an adjunct to all the windows of the building except those of the back premises. At that precise moment the silence of the house was broken by the distant sound of a loud sneeze. I spun round as if shot.

"Was that the woman in the kitchen?" I whispered hoarsely.

"No," said Arbuthnot, "we should have heard her more plainly. The sound seemed to me to come from outside. It may be some perfectly innocent stranger wandering round the house. However, we'll have a look."

He darted into the passage and made for the front door. It was locked and no key was to be seen.

"Back through the kitchen," he said, and we retraced our steps. The woman jumped up as we passed through.

"I'm not staying here alone," she cried.

"Wait outside the door. We're only going round to the front."

Outside the kitchen we turned to our right, passed along at the foot of a raised veranda, which apparently surrounded the house except for the back, and so came upon that puzzling sight to which I referred at the very beginning of this account.

We stopped dead in our tracks. The man sat comfortably in a deck-chair, with a book on his knees and a rucksack and an ash-plant on the ground beside him. He was looking in our direction, for evidently we had made some noise sufficient to attract his attention. He stood up as we appeared and I saw a boyish face under a somewhat battered hat. I have seen too many things in my time to attach undue importance to looks, but otherwise his clear grey eyes with their steady look, his firm mouth and athletic frame would have impressed me favourably.

"I must apologize for what would seem an intrusion," said the unknown, removing his hat as he spoke. "As a matter of fact, I am on a walking tour, and last night I rather lost my bearings on the downs—indeed, I had to sleep under a gorse-bush—so when I spotted this place at dawn I thought I would wait till some one was about so that I could make inquiries." He passed his hand over his unshaven chin with an apologetic smile, while I had time to remember Arbuthnot's dictum, "If a person prefaces his remark with the gambit 'As a matter of fact', it is more than an even chance that he is going to tell you a lie."

"Please don't apologize," said Arbuthnot with a laugh. "We are equally trespassers. We came in the hope that the secretary of the golf club lived here."

"Indeed? I naturally thought you came from the house. I had been dozing, but some little time back some sound awakened me and then I thought I heard people stirring inside."

"Do you find reading on an empty stomach very inspiring?" asked my friend lightly, with a keen glance at the volume the other held in his hand.

"Not as a rule, but the *Golden Treasury* always goes with me on these jaunts."

"Ah!" Arbuthnot sniffed the morning air. "I wonder if old Wordsworth found anything in Elysium to console him for the loss of a morning like this:

Earth has not anything to show more fair."

"Quite so," returned the other. "We might add

Never did sun more beautifully steep
In his first splendour valley, rock, and hill.

But we are rather divorcing the lines from their context, you know."

"This won't do," said Arbuthnot. "Here are we discussing all manner of things and you've had a night in the open and must be pining for a wash and some food. Come along to our hotel down below and we'll fix you up with pleasure."

The other hesitated, glanced at the shuttered window behind him, and finally said, "That's very kind of you, but as I've had the cheek to occupy some man's veranda since early dawn, perhaps I ought to stay and explain. Some one may have seen me sitting here."

"Loitering with felonious intent," suggested Arbuthnot smilingly. "However, I don't think there's much point in waiting to interview the occupant."

"Why not?"

"You won't get much satisfaction from him."

"How's that? Is he some old curmudgeon? I thought you said just now that you didn't know him?"

"I met him for the first time a few minutes ago."

"And he would have nothing to do with you?"

"Nothing at all."

"How was that?"

"He was dead."

"Oh!"

I was watching the man intently, and I knew Arbuthnot was doing the same, to judge if his surprise were genuine or counterfeited.

"Dead! You don't mean murdered, do you?"

"That's exactly what I do mean. Moreover, if you'll excuse my suggesting it, the man's carelessness in allowing such a thing to happen has put you in a rather peculiar position."

"What an extraordinary affair!" murmured the other. "Why, I've only been back in England a bare twenty-four hours and I suppose by to-morrow morning I shall be in all the papers as 'the mysterious man on the veranda.' Good thing I've no relations to worry about me. But tell me how you chanced on this business."

"We were on the way for a round of golf, when the housekeeper, in a panic-stricken condition, accosted us and brought us here to see what she had found. The man has been shot through the heart and his safe has been rifled."

The other man whistled. "That's odd. I hope you don't imagine that the contents are in my rucksack," he said with a whimsical smile.

"Hardly," said Arbuthnot; "but, joking apart, I think it would be wise on your part to remain here and answer any questions the police may like to ask you. For example, as you arrived here at early dawn, your evidence will help to narrow down the time in which the crime could have been committed."

"That's certainly sensible. I've no objection to remaining. Fortunately my time's my own. That reminds me that I ought to introduce myself. My name is Rodd—Thornton Rodd, civil engineer."

"Mine is Arbuthnot, and my friend here is King."

"Your name seems somehow familiar," said Rodd, knitting his brows. "Why, of course—" His face twitched momentarily as if he had received a shock. "You don't mean to say you've been called in on this business already?"

"No, as I told you, my being here is entirely fortuitous. Even the police know nothing of the affair so far."

"I see. By Jove, I'm certainly hungry. What's the time? My watch stopped in the night."

"It is ten minutes past eight," I said.

"Is that all? This sleeping out gives one a colossal appetite. What do you propose to do now? Can I see the scene of the crime?"

"I think," said Arbuthnot, "that we will send the housekeeper for a policeman—she will find one most easily—and in the meantime we might have a look round."

Rodd gathered up his belongings and we returned the way we had come. We found the housekeeper clutching the handle of the back door and looking fearfully around. She recoiled with a shriek when she saw the third man with us.

"Is that him?" she called tremblingly.

"If you mean the murderer, it's not," said Arbuthnot. "Don't be frightened. This is only a gentleman who joined us a few minutes ago. Now I know you don't like staying here, and some one has to fetch the police, so I think you had better go. Bring them here at once and don't mention the business to anyone else. We will stay here and keep an eye on things."

She needed no second bidding and hurried away with shaky steps and her shawl well drawn over her head.

"I suppose this sort of thing is jolly interesting to you?" said Rodd to Arbuthnot.

"Not necessarily. Most crime is merely sordid. More-over, a great deal is badly bungled. A clever crime requires a first-class intelligence, nerves of steel, and an absence of conscience. Fortunately for us, this is a rare combination."

"And this particular crime?"

"I'll tell you in half an hour whether it's worth my attention."

Together we went back to the dining-room and allowed Rodd to inspect the corpse. We were both on the *qui vive* for any expression of emotion, but he surveyed the dead man with nonchalance.

"Do you know who he was?" he asked.

"Beyond that his name was Flyte we know nothing," answered Arbuthnot.

"The flight of a soul, eh?" Then he must have felt that we took his witticism as a mark of bad taste, for he added apologetically, "I've seen some dead bodies in my time; in the war, of course, and once after the bursting of a dam, and I'm afraid I'm a bit callous. Is that the safe that was robbed?"

He took a step towards it as he spoke and Arbuthnot gave me a little push to follow him. Glancing back I saw my friend drop on his knees, and bring out from under the table a little white card, which he glanced at and thrust into his pocket with an expression as near surprise as he ever permitted himself.

"Don't touch anything," said he, "or you may destroy thumb-marks."

"And incidentally leave our own," remarked Rodd. "No, thanks, I'm quite deep enough in this case as it is."

Arbuthnot led into the drawing-room and threw open the windows. In this room everything appeared to be in order, apart from needing the attentions of the house-keeper. There were the ashes of a small fire in the grate, but this was not surprising for, despite the season, the nights had been distinctly chilly. Arbuthnot scrutinized the ashes carefully for some time.

Meanwhile Rodd and I prowled round the room without reference to each other's doings, and it was purely by chance that I should have glanced at his face at a moment when he was not looking towards me. I caught my breath. He was glaring through the open door that led from the drawing-room into the hall and his face was frozen into a grinning mask of pure horror! As skilfully as possible I sidled round behind him. What I expected to see I do not know, but what actually met my gaze was an ordinary oak hall-stand with a mirror, a couple of brushes, a salver, and a clump of walking-sticks and umbrellas. Then he gave a little sob in his throat and turned elsewhere. I bent aimlessly over a revolving bookcase while my brain worked at fever speed. *Something* had looked through the doorway and Rodd had seen it. Then why had he not raised the alarm? There was only one answer, and it left me gasping.

"Arbuthnot," I said, "do you think there is any chance that the criminal may still be lurking in one of the rooms?"

"I don't," he said, and became interested in an ash-tray lying on an occasional table. Here were the stubs of half a dozen cigarettes. Some, I could see at a glance, had the oval shape characteristic of most Oriental brands.

"'Narkundas'—an expensive brand," said Arbuthnot. "And here, in addition, we have two ends that belong to one of the cheapest varieties of the genus Virginia."

"Clearly," said Rodd, "the late Flyte smoked the expensive brand and the criminal soothed his nerves after the event with the Virginias. But as both brands are well known I don't see that they afford any clue."

Nothing else in the drawing-room, which was furnished in a comfortable but uninteresting style, seemed to interest Arbuthnot. We returned to the dining-room. "I hardly like to interfere with the corpse before the police have seen it," said he, "but I think I should be justified in gently examining the pockets." Without more words he commenced a systematic search. The only results were an unmarked linen handkerchief and a silver cigarette case of a common pattern. Arbuthnot snapped it open and showed us three cigarettes with 'Narkunda' in gold lettering upon them. Then he replaced the articles he had abstracted.

The drawers in the desk were not locked and contained nothing but stationery and some files of receipted bills for household accounts. Evidently the deceased had kept everything of importance in his safe. Then Arbuthnot went and raked in the cupboards of the sideboard and drew out a box of cigarettes.

"These," he said, "ought to be Narkundas, but they're not. They're Ambrosias—a kind of scented cigarette."

"Is the box a new one?" I asked.

"No, it is half empty."

"That's peculiar."

"Maybe it is, but one can hardly start theorizing because a man happens to have two brands of cigarettes in his house. Let's have a look elsewhere."

In turn we visited the two bedrooms and the bathroom. I was not sorry to get away from the vicinity of the body, for its vacant stare ceilingwards was not pleasant to look at; but despite Arbuthnot's conviction I was thoroughly alarmed at the possible presence of some unknown in the house. I reasoned it out thus. The criminal was not a homicidal maniac. He had murdered for plunder. He would not

seek to add another crime to his account but rather would
try to elude us by slipping from room to room. There was
no danger from him unless he were cornered. In that case
we were unarmed and he had a revolver, besides the prob-
able assistance of one of our party. If only I could get a
word alone with Arbuthnot! But that seemed impossible.

Each bedroom possessed a single bed. Neither had been
slept in. All the windows were shuttered. We threw them
open.

"A most methodical man, this Flyte," said Rodd. "Here
he has all his daily papers preserved in a filing cabinet."

"And yet," replied Arbuthnot, "his methodical nature
seems to have deserted him as recently as a week ago. The
last paper here is a copy of the *Morning Post* dated May
17th."

"That's very curious," remarked Rodd. "We might have
a look round and see if the others are lying about anywhere." He went out of the room and I had a moment to
decide whether I should follow him or seize the opportunity to tell Arbuthnot what I had seen. I chose the latter
course.

"Arbuthnot," I said in a whisper, "Rodd saw something in
the passage just now that nearly scared the life out of him."

"Where in the passage?" he asked briefly.

"He was looking through the drawing-room door."

"Did you see anything?"

"No, it must have gone by that time. But there was the
fear of death on his face. Do you think there might be
some one concealed here?"

"We might see what the fellow is doing," said Arbuthnot in low tones.

We met him in the passage, carrying his hat, stick, and
rucksack, which he had previously laid down in the dining-
room.

"Not a sign of a newspaper anywhere," he said. "I vote we go outside. This house is beginning to get on my nerves."

"I am going to look at the garage," said Arbuthnot. Nevertheless he stopped at the door leading from the hall to the kitchen.

"It is abundantly clear," he said, "that the late Flyte was either an inordinately timorous man or else he had special reasons for apprehending that his peace was likely to be disturbed. You notice that this door is fitted on the hall side to receive three cross-bars which can be fixed in position by means of iron pins passing through these side rings and secured by a hinged cap to which a padlock can be attached."

"That accounts also for the shutters," I said.

"Precisely. And here we have the door fixings." He was fumbling in a recess in the wall as he spoke. "Two padlocks, two pins, and three narrow iron cross-bars. Hullo! That's funny—there are only two cross-bars here. Really, that's the third most interesting thing I've seen since I've been in this house."

Rodd looked as if he would have liked to ask a question but considered it wiser to forbear. We went outdoors and found the garage locked.

"That's distinctly annoying," said Arbuthnot. "I should very much like to know whether the car is at present inside there."

"We don't even know that he had a car," said Rodd. "He may have used the place as a fowl-house."

"Obviously he had a car. Look at the marks of oil on the ground outside the door, and see here the wheel-tracks across the turf." The house was not approached by any regular road, but traffic across the smooth turf had gradually produced a track which served the purpose.

"Here are the police," I said. Two men in blue, accompanied by a woman, had appeared on the slope.

"Well," said Rodd with a light laugh, "you've had your half-hour. Do you find the case interesting enough to pursue?"

"I rather fancy I do," replied Arbuthnot.

2
Further Events of the Same Day

As the little party advanced towards us I could see that the police-officers were a sergeant and a constable.

"Good morning, gentlemen," said the former as he came up. "This is a fine tale Mrs. Morris has told us. If half of what she says is correct, it's above my head. I've sent for a doctor, who should be along in a minute, and I've telephoned to Newport for an inspector to come along."

"It's certainly a case of murder," said Arbuthnot.

The sergeant removed his helmet and mopped his brow. "It's years since we had such a thing in these parts," he said. "Well, I suppose we'd better have a look round while we're waiting, though others will go over it all again, I've no doubt."

Arbuthnot leading, we re-entered the house in single file, but beyond the kitchen Mrs. Morris refused to go. Arbuthnot walked on, but the sergeant hesitated.

"I can take down your statement as well in the kitchen as anywhere else," he observed, "but I'll need you to identify the body."

"Give me a minute to settle myself and I'll come," she promised. "I won't mind it when the doctor's here. It'll seem more natural-like having a doctor about."

I hardly followed her reasoning, but we left her to compose herself and went into the dining-room, where Arbuthnot was already standing.

"A bad business," said the sergeant, looking round at us alter he had inspected the body. "Hullo! Where's the other gentleman gone to?"

I turned hastily, only to see Rodd entering the doorway.

"Hope I didn't keep you people waiting," he said. "I was finishing my cigarette outside. It hardly seems decent to smoke in here."

I admired his casual manner, for I was coming to think that Mr. Thornton Rodd was far more concerned in the affair than he wished us to know. However I considered it, it was a bewildering business.

"I think, gentlemen," said the worthy sergeant, "that I'd better take down your statements first. After that we'll have a look round, if the inspector is not here by then to take charge."

It was a somewhat lengthy business transferring all our statements to paper, and he had barely finished interviewing us one by one when there were sounds of a car outside.

"Sorry I'm a bit late," said the doctor as he entered. "I had a case I couldn't leave. It seems a morning of arrivals and departures," he added as he dropped on his knees beside the corpse. His examination took him barely a minute.

"There is no doubt whatever about the cause of death," he said as he rose to his feet. "The shot has gone clean through his heart. Death must have been instantaneous. I suppose you'll want a post-mortem to recover the bullet?"

"We certainly shall, sir, but I'm not having the body moved until the inspector's seen it."

"How long has he been dead?" asked Arbuthnot.

"Between ten and twelve hours I should say. *Rigor mortis* is nearly complete," was the answer, and with that the doctor prepared to go.

"Please stay a minute, sir. Mrs. Morris is afraid to face the corpse and we need her to identify it. She thinks if a doctor were present it would be easier for her."

"Oh, very well. Bring her in."

Mrs. Morris was brought in shrinking and supported by the constable. After some persuasion she pulled herself together and gazed intently at the dead man.

"That's him," she said, and backed away. "That's Mr. Dalton Flyte, who was my master."

"Are you prepared to swear that?" asked the sergeant.

"Yes, of course I am—but let me get out of this. I'm going to faint."

And she promptly did so, which made me realize her point in demanding the presence of the doctor. We found some brandy in the sideboard, and when she had been restored to consciousness the doctor departed.

"Now I'll have a look round," said the sergeant.

"Make it a brief one," suggested Arbuthnot. "None of us has had any breakfast yet."

"I'm sorry about that, sir, but I'd be obliged if you'd wait."

So once again we went hither and thither in the house, while Arbuthnot indicated what he had already noticed. I don't think the sergeant had gathered anything from the name my friend had given, but he was a sensible fellow and made copious entries respecting various things Arbuthnot pointed out.

"Now," said the latter finally, "I think you've seen everything there is to see except the hats and umbrellas in the hall."

"Why, you don't suppose that the murderer carefully put his hat and stick in the stand before proceeding to commit the crime, do you?" asked Rodd with a laugh.

"I'll see everything," said the sergeant. "It's better than getting my knuckles rapped for neglect."

"Perfectly right," said Arbuthnot, and we all proceeded through the hall, which was really little more than the passage I have sometimes called it in this narrative, the sergeant leading and Rodd bringing up the rear behind me.

"Bowler hat, sold by Tate, Piccadilly; soft hat, maker's name Thatch, Oxford Street; umbrella, two silver-mounted walking-sticks, no particular marks; one malacca cane, one ash-stick— Hullo!" The sergeant stopped abruptly in his catalogue.

"Something interesting?" queried Arbuthnot.

"Here's initials on this handle—been carved by somebody. Look here, sir, 'T.R,'" as plain as you like."

There was a loud laugh from behind me.

"Good heavens! That's my stick," called out Rodd. "I absent-mindedly stuck it in the stand when we were walking round. It's a good thing these gentlemen here can testify that I had an ash-stick when they saw me outside first thing this morning."

"Did you see Mr. Rodd with this stick?" asked the sergeant, looking rather bewildered.

"I saw him with a stick of that kind, and he certainly hasn't one with him now," said Arbuthnot.

"Well, Mr. Rodd, if you'll excuse my saying so, it might have looked rather funny if this gentleman hadn't been here to verify your statement. You can't be too careful in a case of this kind."

"That's very true," said Arbuthnot approvingly. As for me, my mind was in a state of chaos and I gasped and said nothing.

"It's about time some one was along from Newport," remarked the sergeant.

"It's about time we had breakfast," replied Arbuthnot. "We're staying at the Stagrock Hotel, and Mr. Rodd, I hope, will come along to breakfast with us so that you will know where to find us all again if you want us."

"Very good, sir. I've no doubt you'll all be wanted again. It's a good thing you're on holiday, so that it'll be no inconvenience having to wait for the inquest."

We passed out, Arbuthnot stopping to say a few words to Mrs. Morris, the purport of which I did not catch, as we left. Outside a small crowd had already assembled, including several boys whose comments when they saw us did more credit to their ingenuity than to their knowledge of facts.

"Since we all have to stay here, why not put up at the same place as us?" suggested Arbuthnot to Rodd.

"I'd like to very much, presuming you've now got over your initial suspicion of me when you said you were looking for the secretary of the golf club."

Arbuthnot laughed. "I admit your presence struck me as peculiar," he said, "but you saved the situation by being able to cap my quotation."

Breakfast was waiting for us when we reached the hotel, and I could see by the way we were received that the news had spread. The little foreign waiter remained assiduous long after any need for his attentions had ceased. For his pains he had the pleasure of listening to Arbuthnot discoursing on golf, relativity, and potato-growing, and the privilege of fetching additional pots of tea. In spite of his boasted hunger, I did not fail to notice that Rodd drank more than he ate, and at times seemed to attend to the conversation with an effort.

After breakfast we lighted pipes in the drawing-room, whose windows directly overlooked the sea.

"Crime or no crime, it's great to be in England again," said Rodd, gazing out where a thousand little waves were dancing into the bay and lapping round the scattered rocks that the ebb tide had disclosed. "I've just done two years in Canada as engineer to a hydro-electric power enterprise up country from Quebec, living in a world of trees and rushing waters and with nothing but wilderness between one and the Pole, and this calm of the English country is what I've been dreaming of half the time."

"Wait till the newspaper correspondents begin to arrive," said Arbuthnot. "You're liable to find your calm suddenly disturbed. Are you on leave or is your power scheme complete?"

"I'm really on leave, and though I'm keen in a way to go back and see the thing through, there are other factors. For one thing, I've been lucky enough to come into a little money, or I should never have been able to afford this holiday."

"I thought the exile invariably made for London on his return?" I suggested.

"I suppose he generally does, but after two years in the backwoods I felt too rusty for an immediate plunge. So when I came off the *Mauretania* yesterday I dumped most of my baggage with Cook's, dashed up to town for a necessary interview with my solicitors, and then came straight away here."

"Know this part well?" I asked.

"I used to be brought here for seaside holidays when I was a little kid," he explained. "It's at that time of life one gets one's really strong impressions of places, 'when every common sight is apparelled in celestial light,' you know. Later in life you feel that you saw things then as you can't see them now."

I nodded.

"I think I'll take my pipe for a walk," he added. "Care to come?"

I looked at Arbuthnot. He was gazing into space and absently rubbing the bowl of his pipe against his left palm. It was an old signal between us, the left hand denoting refusal and the right the reverse.

"No, thanks. I've had enough exercise for one morning. I wouldn't advise you to go on the down. Look there." From a side window we could see the distant slope stippled by the black dots that indicated the advance guard of sightseers.

"No fear. I'll be careful to avoid the down."

"And don't go manufacturing evidence against yourself," said Arbuthnot grinning.

"That again is good counsel. I'll be most discreet," answered Rodd, returning the grin, as he went out.

I lay back in my chair with a sigh of relief. "I'm feeling a bit breathless," I said. "Events seem to have been moving a little too rapidly for me."

"And you would like to sit still and take stock of recent occurrences?" returned Arbuthnot. "That's all very well, but as I've told you before, what to do often has to take priority over what to think. Come upstairs; we shall be less likely to be disturbed there."

I obediently followed, confidently expecting to settle down and listen to Arbuthnot's opinion on the affairs of the morning. Instead of having anything to say, however, he gathered a pair of prismatic binoculars from the table and took up a position in the eastward-facing window. From this point of vantage one could see the sweep of the bay, with the downs above it and the two colossal detached rocks that mark the eastern end of the opening. The cliff-top was still alive with people, but the part of beach we could see was deserted. That end is almost exclusively composed of large pebbles, disappears almost entirely at high tide, and is very little used.

"There goes our friend Rodd," remarked Arbuthnot. A figure in a sports jacket and flannels had appeared on the little esplanade that ran beneath our eyes. Arbuthnot pulled me farther from the window. Together we saw him reach the end of the paved walk, jump lightly to the beach, and continue his steps away from us along the edge of the waves.

"What does our friend do?" murmured Arbuthnot, taking his glasses into use as the figure receded gradually into the distance. "He stoops and picks up something—he repeats the action—perhaps 'gathering pebbles on the shore of the vast ocean'—he drops his walking-stick—he doesn't seem capable of looking after a stick—he picks it up. Now he leaves the water's edge and continues his walk at the foot of the cliff—it is rough going on those big pebbles—he nears the corner of the bay—and disappears." One must imagine these comments spread out over the quarter of an hour or so that it took Rodd to reach the eastern point.

"If he goes farther," I said, "he is asking for trouble. Once round the point there is next to no beach, even at low tide. If what I am told locally is correct he would not be the first to be cut off there with an unscaleable cliff behind him."

"He's probably interested in those caves at the point that we explored the other day," he answered. "Local legends have it that they were once used by smugglers. I suppose that story is tacked on to every cave that exists along the south coast of England, but in this case it may have a basis of truth, for I noticed when we were there that some points seem above the level of wave-action."

"That seems hardly possible unless they were artificially made so," I said.

"Not a bit of it. When in a storm a big wave momentarily blocks the entrance the air inside is instantaneously compressed and then released. This makes it act as a kind of explosive, shattering down rock which is beyond the reach of the waves. Hullo! Our friend reappears." To my unaided eyes he was little more than a black dot moving against the dazzling white of his chalky background.

"Still gathering pebbles," remarked Arbuthnot, whose interest in the movements of Thornton Rodd seemed to be on the wane. "Since the man is so energetic I suggest you take him for another stroll later on to-day."

"Certainly. After lunch?"

"No, not earlier than seven o'clock this evening if you can arrange it so."

"I'll try. Any particular direction?"

"Yes. Walk over the western downs to Alum Bay."

"What about dinner?" I queried doubtfully.

"Rodd isn't the sort to let that kind of trifle worry him. I'll arrange that some food is kept for you."

We went downstairs and sat in deck-chairs in the sunshine, and for a good half-hour I suppose neither of us spoke to the other, each busily occupied with his own thoughts.

"Arbuthnot," I said at last, speaking what was uppermost in my mind, "it's difficult to believe anything wrong of young Rodd, and yet I can't feel altogether satisfied about him. Of course he *may* be a perfectly innocent person. The look of agony I chanced to see on his face may have been due to something totally unconnected with the crime we were investigating."

"A severe spasm of toothache, for example," suggested Arbuthnot with the mock interest he sometimes assumes to annoy me. "Suppose," he continued, "that it was the sight of a walking-stick in the hall stand that moved him to terror?"

"No," I said, realizing that my wits were on trial. "If he had been connected with the crime and made the mistake of taking the wrong stick from the stand last night he had ample opportunity afterwards to make the exchange, when he left us to look for the missing copies of the *Morning Post*. Instead of this, his own stick was actually found in the stand some time after. And yet, as I say, I'm not satisfied. Supposing he is guilty, a man capable of such an amazing bluff would be capable of anything. He may have decided to leave his stick there and claim it when occasion arose, as he actually *did*, rather than risk being caught making the exchange."

"True, O King. But in that case what became of the stick he had with him when we met him first?"

"I think," I said after some reflection, "that he probably dumped it in some corner of the house. A plain ash-stick standing in some corner, where a careless bachelor might easily have placed it, would never excite comment."

"A very fine hypothesis. But I fear an interruption to our conversation."

He pointed with his pipe-stem across the bay. On the slope of the distant downs the red-and-white bungalow that shrouded such tragedy was the gayest thing in view. A big car was just leaving it and heading downhill.

"This, I fancy," said Arbuthnot, "means a visit from the higher authorities." We watched the car approach. As Arbuthnot had foretold, it swung round the corner and drew up outside the hotel. Our friend, the sergeant of police, was the first to alight.

"Captain Bernard, superintendent of police, wishes to see you gentlemen," he announced as he came up. We stood up and were greeted by a tall, soldierly-looking man.

"Of course, I recognized your name as soon as I saw it on your statement," he said to Arbuthnot as he shook hands, "and thought what an odd chance it was that you, of all people, should be on the spot. I'm much obliged to you for the assistance you gave to my sergeant."

"Not at all," replied my friend. "I'm afraid I did very little. I was very anxious to verify if the car had been taken, but I had no authority to break into the garage. It was clear, however, that whoever had the keys of the bungalow would look on the car as the easiest means of getting away."

"He did," said the superintendent, "and that fact was the cause of the affair coming to a satisfactory conclusion—satisfactory, that is, for us, although most unfortunate for the people concerned."

"Then I take it the mystery is solved?"

"A few things remain to be cleared up."

"And the criminal?"

"His body is at present lying in the mortuary at Newport."

"That's interesting."

The superintendent looked at his watch. "I want to see Mrs. Morris before I leave," he said. "Would it be possible for me to see her here? She had been allowed to go home before. I arrived as she was feeling rather upset."

"Certainly," said Arbuthnot. "We are the only guests in the hotel to-day. There is another party staying here, but they have gone for an excursion in the New Forest."

"Then I'll send Sergeant Rogers in the car to fetch her, and in the meantime, if you like, I'll tell you what we know about the case. We owe you that much."

"I should very much like to hear it."

Orders were issued to the sergeant and the car moved away, while we went inside the hotel.

"Lunch is ready," remarked Arbuthnot. "Why not join us?"

"With pleasure."

At that moment the door of the dining-room opened and Thornton Rodd walked on. He stopped abruptly when he saw a stranger with us. Arbuthnot beckoned to him.

"Come in, Rodd. This is Captain Bernard, superintendent of police." He turned to the superintendent. "This is Mr. Rodd, who followed close on the footsteps of crime this morning. I take it there's no objection to his joining our symposium?"

"None at all. I must ask you all to be discreet in your remarks for the next day or two, that's all, for although there is no doubt we have found the actual criminal, there may be a gang involved."

"So you've got him!" said Rodd rather breathlessly and, so I thought, with his voice pitched a little higher than usual. "That's quick work."

"It's very gratifying," said Arbuthnot, "except to King here, who has been cherishing a hope that he might add you, however temporarily, to his visiting list of notorious criminals."

"Oh, shucks!" cried Thornton Rodd rather inelegantly.

"I beg your pardon?" I said.

"It's a word I learnt the other side," he said. "I mean, you *really* didn't think that of me, did you?"

"Forgive my little joke," said Arbuthnot. "Here are we wasting time when we are all keen to hear of the other half of this morning's events."

In between the ministrations of the waiter, the superintendent of police had a curious tale to tell.

"I was roused very early this morning by a telephone message from Calshot. It appears that the officer of the watch on board an incoming trooper which was steaming up the Solent this morning spotted through his glasses what appeared to be the burnt-out remains of a car lying near the foot of what is called Bouldnor Cliff. You probably know that large ships using the Solent entrance to Southampton hug the island side where the deeper water lies. Thinking it a peculiar sight he had the information wirelessed to Calshot, who sent on his message as I have said. I at once sent Inspector Farrell out to look into the matter.

"Not so many minutes later came the message from Freshwater. Thinking that the West Wight was suddenly looking up in the matter of thrills, I decided to come out myself. I went first to the scene of the car wreck. I suppose, by the way, you haven't a local map? It would be very useful."

Arbuthnot had a map. I have never known an occasion when he hadn't. He spread it out impartially over plates and dishes and we all bent over it.

"You see there are two main roads from Newport to Freshwater," continued Captain Bernard.[1] "I came by the more northerly one, which is generally distinguished as the lower road because it keeps away from the downs. Here you see a small by-road branching off nearly at right angles to the main road and running northward. It passes this little place called Cranmore, and beyond that point is very little used. There was at one time a brickfield farther on, but that has been abandoned for some years. The road remains, though it is not much more than a track. Here, you notice, it bends to the right to reach the shore by avoiding Bouldnor Cliff. I call it cliff, for that is the general name for it, but it is not particularly high and is composed almost entirely of clay. One might best call it a very steep slope.

"It was easy to discover that, at the point where the road came nearest to the cliff on its left, there were wheel-tracks showing that a car had left the road at that point and travelled toward the edge of the cliff. I followed these tracks and found that the car in question had indeed gone over the cliff. I went over after it, scrambling down through the bushes clinging to the slope, which showed signs of having withstood the passage of some heavy body. Then I came upon the scene of the catastrophe.

"The driver of the car had apparently kept her in equilibrium for a little distance after her downward plunge, for as I have said the slope cannot really be called a cliff. What finally brought him to disaster was his encounter with a tree. The car must have turned a complete somersault, throwing the driver out and clear. Then it had evidently burst into flames, for it was a charred ruin when I got there.

---

[1] See map supplied with this volume.

"My inspector was standing a little way off and at his feet was a body. The man was dead beyond doubt. The top of his skull was crushed in and it looked as if when the car struck the tree he must have been flung forward against the upright of the wind-screen. This I verified later by finding traces of dried blood on the right-hand upright, which had escaped the flames by catching against the tree-trunk.

"At that moment, of course, the affair was nothing more to me than a tragic accident, and I was in a hurry to get on to Freshwater, so I asked my inspector for his report. He had very little to tell me. He had found nothing on the corpse by which to identify it and neither of us recognized it as anyone we had known. It was dressed in a badly-fitting suit of brown tweeds, and had been a slim, fair, clean-shaven man of from thirty-five to forty years of age, as far as I could judge, with almost effeminate features."

"No hat?" asked Arbuthnot suddenly.

"None has been found. Possibly it flew off his head as the car plunged downwards and may be picked up some-where near the scene of the accident. The only contents of the man's pockets were a bunch of keys. The back num-ber plate of the car had been scorched to the point of obliterating the figures, but the inspector had found the front one only damaged by collision with the tree, and had succeeded in making out the number to be DL 9942. As this was a local number I stopped at the call office in Yar-mouth on my way here and rang up Newport to ascertain the owner's name. You can picture my astonishment when they told me that the number belonged to a car registered in the name of Mr. Dalton Flyte of Freshwater."

"Ah!" said Thornton Rodd, leaning forward with a quick intake of breath.

"Yes, it was an amazing situation to have seen the Nemesis that had overtaken the murderer before one had actually seen the body of his victim. I immediately did a right-about turn and made my way back to the scene of the accident to obtain the bunch of keys I had left in the inspector's charge. Then it occurred to me further that the dead motorist might have had an accomplice and this accomplice might have survived the disaster. Farrell, who was still on the spot waiting for the stretcher he had sent for, and I quartered the clayey ground carefully for any footprints besides our own, but found nothing. Now the message from Freshwater spoke of robbery as well as murder, so, as the corpse had nothing of value on it, we made a careful examination of the ruins of the car on the chance of finding coin or jewellery, but without result. Some ashes we found which might have been those of bank-notes or valuable documents of some kind, and now that I am aware that the safe was completely emptied I think it very likely they were such. Then I came on here hell-for-leather to find my sergeant getting alarmed at the lack of response to his urgent message."

"Do you think it possible that any articles of value were stolen from the car after the accident by some person otherwise unconnected with the crime?" asked Rodd.

"No. It would be a most unlikely thing for the country people to do, and besides, there was the absence of any footprints."

"Quite so."

"What were the keys you found?" inquired Arbuthnot.

"There were several—the keys of the front and back doors, of the garage, of the safe, of several cupboards in the house, and of various boxes and trunks."

"The complete set in fact?"

"Exactly."

"It can't be often," said Rodd, "that a case winds itself up so promptly."

"I wouldn't say it was wound up," returned the superintendent in courteous tones, which somehow or other nevertheless suggested that Mr. Rodd was discoursing of matters of which he was profoundly ignorant. "Several points remain to be cleared up before we can consider the case disposed of. There will be two inquests, for example."

"Have you considered," asked Arbuthnot, "how the murderer came to take the path that led to his death? I take it we can put aside the possibility that in remorse or terror he aimed at suicide."

"It was easy to leave the road at that point without noticing it," said Bernard.

"Yes, but it is not quite so easy to explain how he came to be on that road at all."

"Quite right. I have been thinking over that point very carefully. I think we can assume that the criminal was not a local man and that he therefore was probably operating by the map. I asked myself first how he would attempt to escape out of the area. He was very unlikely to use the Yarmouth-Lymington route because comparatively few people travel that way and any peculiarity in his appearance might be noted and remembered. Moreover, having the car in his possession made it easy for him to reach Cowes or Ryde before dawn. I decided that he would probably make for Cowes." Here Arbuthnot threw me a glance that made me remember some previous remarks of his.

"You see," went on the superintendent, "the farther you drive a car the greater the chance that some one has noticed you and will remember something about you. To reach Ryde he would have to pass through Newport, and the police on duty in the streets at night would almost certainly have made some note of a car passing through in the small hours. Now look at the map." Once again the invaluable one-inch sheet of the Ordnance Survey came in for our scrutiny.

"You notice that it is possible to reach Cowes from Freshwater without passing through Newport, if you take the by-road that branches off to the left at right angles to the main road just past the village of Shalfleet. This I believe is what the murderer intended to do."

"Then what do you think happened?" I asked.

"I am inclined to think that he took the wrong turning. See, here is the road from Freshwater to Yarmouth. A branch goes off to the right at right angles near Thorley, continues through Wellow, and joins the main lower road to Newport near Shalfleet. This road is less frequented than the main road and therefore would appeal to him. After his turn to the right the map would tell him that he must take the first turning to the left, which would be his by-road to Cowes."

"Carry on," said Arbuthnot.

"I think that the man missed his turn to the right at Thorley, continued till he met the main road coming from Yarmouth, turned to his right *there*—it is also a right-angle turn—and *then* taking the first turning to the left found himself on the road that led to his doom."

I had followed things carefully on the map as he was speaking and it all seemed very logical.

"Very ingenious," said Arbuthnot.

As he spoke there were sounds of a car pulling up outside.

"That will be Mrs. Morris," said the superintendent, preparing to rise from his seat. "That reminds me that there is still some work to be done before we can consider the affair concluded."

"When you are dealing with the remaining points, perhaps you could spare a little consideration for the one that should interest me most?" suggested Arbuthnot.

"Why, certainly," said the superintendent, looking a little puzzled.

"It is this," said my friend withdrawing something from his pocket. "I found it," he added, "on the floor of

Mr. Dalton Flyte's dining-room." He threw the object on the tablecloth as he spoke and our eager heads nearly met over it.

It was one of his own visiting cards.

3
Events up to Monday, May 28th

"That's an exceedingly peculiar thing," said the superintendent, regarding it with a considerable degree of amazement.

"Aha!" said Rodd *sotto voce* to me. "I only put my stick in the stand; I didn't throw my visiting card on the floor. Who's under suspicion now?"

"You cannot tell, of course," went on the superintendent, "whether it is actually one of your own cards, or one that has been prepared by some unauthorized person for his own private ends. Yet I think it sheds some light on the affair. Quite possibly the murderer used it as a blind to secure admission to the house. Your name is pretty well known in these days."

"It *is* one of my own cards," said Arbuthnot.

"How can you possibly know that?"

"I'll let you into a little secret. If you look very carefully indeed at the crossing of the final 't' in my name you will see that the stroke is not continuous but is divided into two portions, separated from each other by an extremely narrow white line which would pass unnoticed except under the most careful scrutiny." He handed a pocket lens to Bernard and in turn we verified what we had just been told.

"I've found that little dodge useful more than once," said my friend, "but this is not the time to talk of them. Mrs. Morris is waiting."

The police sergeant appeared at the door.

"I would suggest that you interview Mrs. Morris in the adjacent drawing-room," said Arbuthnot. "You will be quite private there."

The superintendent hesitated.

"It is irregular," he said, "but under the circumstances I should be very pleased if you were present at the examination. I'm afraid I can't ask these gentlemen as well. Mrs. Morris would have every right to object."

"I'm going to lie down," said Rodd promptly. "I had precious little sleep last night under that infernal gorse-bush."

With that he walked out. The superintendent looked rather relieved.

"I take it that Sir Edmund King is generally in your confidence?" he asked Arbuthnot.

"Invariably," was the reply.

"Then I don't see why both of you should not be present. As you came to Mrs. Morris's assistance this morning I don't suppose she is likely to object."

When the party assembled in the drawing-room, I could see that the good housekeeper, after past tearfulness, had acquired some composure. I felt sympathy for her, for, apart from the shock she had sustained, she had also lost an obviously comfortable livelihood.

"You are Mrs. Lucy Morris, widow of the late Charles Morris?" asked the superintendent, referring to the notes the sergeant had taken in the morning.

"Yes, sir."

"And you live at Bramble Cottage, Schoolgreen, Freshwater?"

"Yes, sir."

"Very well. The statement you made to Sergeant Rogers this morning is quite clear as far as it goes, but I should wish to put you some supplementary questions."

"Yes, sir."

"How do you get into the house when you arrive in the morning?"

"I have my own key of the kitchen door."

"Is it in your possession at present?"

"Yes, sir." She produced it and passed it to him, and he in his turn gave it to the sergeant. "We had better retain this for the present. You have no personal possessions in the house that you wish to remove?"

"No, sir."

"May I ask a question?" said Arbuthnot.

"Certainly."

"When you came to work in the mornings could you get from the kitchen to the rest of the house?"

"No, sir. The door leading from the kitchen to the passage was always barred. When Mr. Flyte heard me moving about in the kitchen getting his morning tea he would come out of his bedroom and unbar the door."

"And how did you find that door this morning?"

"It was open."

"What were your hours of duty?" asked the superintendent.

"I used to have to get there by seven in the morning, and I generally didn't get away till after nine o'clock at night when I had washed up the dinner thing's."

"Those were rather long hours?"

"Yes, sir, but the pay was good, and besides, those were only the hours when Mr. Flyte was at the bungalow."

"Then he wasn't a regular resident?"

"He was here every week-end."

"Do you know where he spent the rest of his time?"

"Yes, sir. He used to go up to London every Monday morning and would come back here either Thursday afternoon or Friday afternoon, and once in a way not till Saturday."

"What were your duties when he was away?"

"I had to go to the bungalow once a day to see that everything was all right."

"Tell me," put in Arbuthnot, "was the door leading from the kitchen to the passage barred on these occasions when Mr. Flyte was away?"

"No, sir, it was always open then so that I could go anywhere in the house."

"I see. Do you ever remember noticing any signs that an attempt had been made to enter the house in your master's absence?"

"No, sir."

"How did you know when Mr. Flyte was returning?" inquired the superintendent.

"He always sent me a telegram."

"From?"

"It used to be marked 'Waterloo', and I'd get it about three hours before he came himself."

"Did he employ a chauffeur to fetch him from the station in his car?"

"No, sir, he always took a cab."

"Did you understand that Mr. Flyte was in business in London?"

"No, sir; he always seemed to me to be a retired gentleman. I think he used to go up to London for a change. People about here used to say that he had made a fortune overseas and come home to spend his last days in England."

"He never told you that himself?"

"No, it was only talk I heard from folks."

"Had he any friends in Freshwater?"

"No proper friends. At least none ever came while I was there. The rector used to call now and then in the way of duty, and people sometimes came to get subscriptions out of him."

"He had a reputation for generosity?"

"He always gave when he was asked."

"You never saw any callers whom you did not recognize as local residents?"

"No, sir. Mr. Flyte said to me once, 'I'm too old to make new friends now'."

"Was he well thought of locally?"

"I think so, sir. He used to go to church most Sunday mornings and he belonged to the golf club, though he didn't play very often. People took him as they found him. He never did no harm to anybody."

"You do not recollect any person coming to the house at any time who aroused your suspicions?" inquired Arbuthnot.

"No, sir, we don't get tramps in the Isle of Wight, and I can't call to mind anybody of the kind you mean."

"Did your master suffer from any kind of illness?"

"Not to my knowledge."

"I believe, however, that he had very bad eyesight?"

"Yes, he was almost as blind as a bat unless he wore glasses. He could see very well with them though."

"Now, Mrs. Morris, we needn't worry you much longer," said the superintendent. "Will you tell us at what time you left the bungalow on the night the crime was committed?"

"I didn't, sir."

"You didn't? You remained there during the night?"

"No, sir. I mean that I wasn't at the house at all yesterday."

I sat up and became interested. The monotony of question and answer was suddenly broken.

"Will you kindly tell me how it was that you were not at the bungalow on that occasion?"

For the first time in her evidence Mrs. Morris became confused. She flushed, stammered, and fell silent again.

"Is it anything you would prefer to tell to another woman?" asked the superintendent gently.

"No, sir."

"Then you must tell us."

"Well, it was like this—it was crab," she blurted out.

"Crab?" I echoed involuntarily.

"Go on," said Bernard.

"Well, Mr. Dalton Flyte came down from London on Thursday this week—got here by the ten-past one train, in fact—and when I got home that night I found that my niece who keeps house for me had bought two goodish-sized crabs cheap from a woman at the door, and being fond of crab, both of us, the truth is we sat down and polished off one each, crab being the sort of thing you can't keep long. We shouldn't have eat so much, I admit, all the same. Next morning—yesterday that is—we were both properly laid up. I woke up in the night feeling that bad you'd hardly believe. And my niece was no better. It wasn't till this morning I felt fit enough to come out of the house."

"So Mr. Flyte had no servant yesterday?"

"No, sir. Once or twice before when I've been poorly I've sent my niece to do for him, but I couldn't do it this time. But Mr. Flyte was very kind-hearted. Two or three times he's given me the day off without my asking, saying he'd fend for himself, like when the Mothers' Union had their outing."

"I am afraid your indulgence in crab may have assisted to do your master a very bad turn," said Bernard. "You see, the house wasn't broken into. Most likely the murderer, finding the coast clear, managed to creep in and secrete himself somewhere in the house early in the evening."

"I know—I know. It's been on my mind ever since I saw the body. It'll be a lesson to me." She burst into tears. "I've had my share of trouble lately," she sobbed. "First my niece's husband being in that accident on the warship and then my house being broken into, and—"

"Your house burgled, you say?" broke in Arbuthnot sharply.

"Ah, yes," said Bernard, "I remember that. About a fort-night ago was it not, Sergeant Rogers?"

"Yes, sir. We never traced the person who did it. Nothing was taken, and we came to put it down as the prank of some schoolboys or young chaps with time on their hands and wanting some fun."

"Nothing was taken, you say?" queried Arbuthnot. "That was unfortunate."

"It's all very well to joke, sir, but it wasn't no joke to me," said Mrs. Morris, sniffing.

"I mean that if they had taken some things it might have assisted in tracing them," said Arbuthnot soothingly. "You've certainly had your share of trouble recently, and we'll hope the tide will now turn. Meanwhile let me show my sympathy by asking you to accept this trifle."

It was a five-pound note that changed hands, and Mrs. Morris departed in a very much improved mood.

"As to-morrow happens to be Sunday, the inquests will not take place until the following day," said the superin-tendent as he prepared to go. "The inquest on Flyte will be at Freshwater at ten in the morning, and that on the other man will take place at Newport at two on the same day, but they are hardly likely to reveal any new facts. I should say that had Fate not stepped in and disposed of the crim-inal we should have had a big job on in running him to ground. He was certainly no fool. For example, we cannot find any finger impressions anywhere in the bungalow."

"And yet you found no gloves in his possession?"

"We did not. He may have discarded them before he met with the accident."

"And you suppose that he did the same with the weapon with which he committed the crime?"

"I presume so, since it wasn't to be found at the scene of the accident."

"The man can't have been a bridge-player," said Arbuthnot, with his usual grin.

"I don't follow you."

"Or he would have realized that the bunch of keys you found in his possession should have been his first discard."

"Quite right. But fortunately for the police all murderers seem to make at least one mistake. A very curious affair," he mused. "The case is virtually over, and yet we don't know who the murderer was, we know next to nothing about his victim, and we don't know what was stolen from the bungalow." With that he bade us good-bye and we watched his car disappearing up the road that led to the village of Freshwater.

"Feeling energetic, King?"

"Tolerably. Are you thinking of going for a walk? I suppose I can consider my trip to Alum Bay this evening cancelled?"

"You may consider nothing of the sort. But at present I propose to take the car that is available here for hire and make a trip to the scene of the motor accident. It will probably be waste of time, and yet it is an opportunity I should not wish to neglect."

I was willing to accompany him, and within twenty minutes we were heading northwards, with Arbuthnot at the wheel.

"I was rather impressed by the superintendent's theory as to the accident," I remarked.

"Bernard seems an intelligent sort of chap," was the answer, "but his theory is useless."

"It fits the facts," I said. "You can't ask more than that of any theory."

"Quite true. But if there happen to be five theories that equally well fit the facts the chances are four to one against any one of them being correct. The error lies in theorizing without sufficient facts. Moreover, I think he has made a mistake in supposing that a man escaping in a car would choose to travel on narrow, unfrequented roads. It's just on that sort of road that the passer-by would take note of the unusual appearance of a car, especially if he had to jump into the hedge to avoid it."

"Have you an alternative theory then?"

"Wait till we get there," was the only answer he would vouchsafe.

After five and twenty minutes' steady going we slowed down, swung left up a little lane, passed two or three cottages and a larger house, mounted a gradual slope and half a mile farther on came to a standstill. By that time the road we were following had degenerated into a grass-grown track.

"This is where the road changes direction," said Arbuthnot, getting out. "On our left is the edge of the so-called cliff."

We had little difficulty in scrambling down through the bushes and reaching the scene of the accident. On duty beside the wreck of the car stood a stolid constable and on a knoll a little way off sat a youth with a camera.

"Can't allow you to touch anything, sir," said the former as we approached.

"Quite right, officer," was the gracious reply. "We have really come here to admire the view."

The officer grunted as if he felt the remark bordered on impertinence, but in truth the outlook from where we stood was delightful. Below us lay the placid blue of the Solent, with two little red-sailed yachts cruising easily in the slightest of breezes. Beyond them the outline of the restful green of the New Forest was broken by the grey hull and red funnels of an outward-bound Union Castle liner, cutting a bright swathe of foam in the quiet water.

Arbuthnot approached the youth. He knew how to speak charmingly when he liked.

"I imagine you've heard all about this affair?" he said.

"Well, rumour has been pretty busy to-day. I have heard that the man who was killed here had previously robbed and murdered some one at Freshwater."

"Do you live anywhere near here, by any chance?"

"A little way down the road by which you must have come."

"Then it is possible you heard this car passing last night."

"I did."

"That's interesting. But it's not fair to cross-question you like this without explanation." He briefly introduced himself and then me.

"I'm not meditating any crime at present except the murder of certain examiners," said the young man with a smile, as he recognized my companion's name, "so I can face your questions with a clear conscience."

"About what time did this car pass?" asked Arbuthnot.

"About midnight. I had stayed up late swotting and was just going off to sleep when I heard it. I thought then that some one had mistaken the road for the one leading to Hamstead, and I supposed I should hear the car return. Then I fell asleep."

"I see. I suppose you haven't seen a hat lying about here anywhere?"

"What kind of hat?"

"Any kind of hat."

"I'm afraid not, but if I do find such a thing I'll let you know, if you like."

"Thanks very much. We are staying at the Stagrock Hotel at Freshwater Bay. Now, King," he continued, "let us look at the position for a moment. You have been waiting for a theory of the accident."

"Let's have it," I said.

"Suppose then that our criminal wished to escape from the island. He chooses this lonely road, which but for a slight error of judgement would have led him to the shore. The cliff behind would shield him from observation from the land side, and, moreover, this is one of the loneliest parts of the whole coast. Further, it is faced by the quietest part of the Hampshire coast. Chances of interruption from any direction would be nearly nil. When he reached the shore an accomplice was to have some small vessel waiting, probably a motor-boat which could come right inshore. Any marks on the sand caused by the embarkation would soon be obliterated by the next tide. They would have crossed the Solent and in all probability entered the Beaulieu River, landing somewhere near Buckler's Hard. There you are, King. Of two theories always choose the simpler."

Standing there on the spot I could not fail to realize the simplicity and reasonableness of the plan.

"Yes, your theory is the better one," I conceded.

"It's a brilliant idea," cried the youth, who had been closely following the argument.

"As for me, I don't believe a word of it," added Arbuthnot suddenly, and nodding to the youth he turned away, leaving us regarding each other in some confusion. Then he came back and said with a smile, "Even my natural modesty does not prevent my seeing you would like to use your camera."

"It would be awfully good of you."

"Do you want my friend in it as well? You do? Let's make it a family group. Come along, officer!"

The constable seemed to have had sharp ears. He joined in with alacrity. "And if you happen to find a hat lying about here anywhere let me know at the Stagrock Hotel and you won't lose by it," said my friend to him as we finally left the scene.

"Quite a pleasant—and useless—afternoon," he added cheerfully as we drove homeward. It was later than half-past five when we reached Freshwater. Arbuthnot was clamorous for tea. As it was brought in Rodd joined us, proclaiming that he had slept like the dead.

"Your epithets are altogether too topical," I growled, for try as I would I could not altogether rid myself of suspicion of that young man, however ridiculous it seemed under the circumstances.

"Who could think of crime on an evening like this?" he cried gaily. He was right there. The seaward-facing French windows were open and a little south-west breeze stirred pleasantly in the curtains. The tide had commenced to retreat and here and there curious rocks stood revealed, breaking the never-ending succession of ripples that came shorewards and lapped gently against the sea wall below us. The farther cliffs, lighted by the low sun, were almost blindingly white against the empyrean above them. "It's all marvellous to me," he continued more quietly;

> "—*the broad sun*
> *Is sinking down in its tranquility;*
> *The gentleness of heaven is on the sea.*"

"More tea!" shouted Arbuthnot in a voice of thunder.

I lighted my pipe and settled down in an arm-chair. A feeling of lassitude that occasionally came over me to remind me of my recent illness made me disinclined to move. Arbuthnot sat on, pouring out more tea. Rodd had lugged his book of verse from his pocket and was absorbed in it. Then a sparkle of light caught my eye. I looked out of the eastern window and saw that the sun's rays were catching some pane of glass in the bungalow upon the cliff. After that, try as I might, I could not get the day's happenings out of my mind. I told myself angrily that both the protagonists were dead and that further inquiry into the affair was of the nature of an academic exercise. Nevertheless a corner of my brain worked busily.

"Arbuthnot," I said eventually, "why were you so interested in that fireplace this morning?"

"I looked to see if any papers had been burnt there."

"Had there?"

"No."

"Peace, you vultures!" grunted Rodd from behind his book.

"However, I did note one thing of interest. The hearth had been swept."

"I don't see the point. I noted the brush there. Why shouldn't the hearth be swept?"

"I was thinking," he said in a dreamy tone, "of Sarah Battle. Confound you, Rodd! What the devil did you do that for?"

The crash had made me jump. The little tea-table was lying on its side on the floor and the teapot was rolling in a semicircle spouting its precious amber fluid along its course. Beyond was a vision of shards. Rodd burst out laughing.

"I've got cramp," he said. "I'm sorry I kicked over your tea. It's all due to getting lost on those beastly downs last night. I believe I've got a cold coming as well."

"What with your destructiveness and King's inquisitiveness I shall never finish my tea. For goodness' sake go for a walk."

"Shall we?" I asked Rodd.

"Good idea," he answered.

"If you're late I'll tell them to keep some—crab for you. Order some more tea as you go out, will you?" remarked Arbuthnot, and with that we went forth into the evening sunshine.

"How about going to Alum Bay?" I suggested. "It's a five-mile walk altogether, but well worth it, unless you're feeling too tired."

"Tired!" said Rodd scornfully. "I've had to depend on my feet for the last two years, and they're not likely to let me down on a five-mile walk. Come on."

We set off at a brisk pace, past the old battery and round the edge of a little cove beyond it, and then slowed down at the steep ascent to the down that carries Tennyson's monument. When we finally reached the massive stone cross I was glad to sit down for a brief rest. Rodd sat on the edge of the cliff and swung his feet in space five hundred feet above the sea.

"I take off my hat to old man Hudson," he said. "But for him I should now be scratching mosquito bites in a shack on the edge of the Height of Land."

"Indeed?" I said, but he needed no encouragement to go on talking.

"Yes, he left me two hundred thousand Canadian dollars when he died last month. Only a small fraction of his whole fortune, of course, but a godsend to a penniless engineer."

"I gather that he appreciated your services."

"Well, it was like this. He was the contractor for the power scheme. You know the Hudson and Banks Company of Montreal?"

I didn't, but I preferred to conceal my ignorance.

"Well, about eleven months ago we had a very bad wash-out. Unusually heavy rains—kind of cloudburst in fact. The flood water got bottled up somewhere up stream from us, and when it did come it came with a hell of a rush."

"Yes?" I said encouragingly.

"Well, I happened to chip in and save the situation as far as that was possible. Can't explain it in non-technical language, I'm afraid. Anyway, the old man was grateful and, as I've said, turned up trumps in the end. So the first moment I could safely leave the place I got leave and dashed across here to freshen myself up." He shook himself as if some incubus burdened him. "The forests and the waters," he murmured, "both lovely things—and yet they wear away a man's soul. Come on."

We swung downhill at a good rate towards Alum Bay, making desultory conversation, and I found myself unwillingly revising my opinion of Rodd. The trace of aggressiveness I had noticed was quite a natural attribute of a shy man returning from the backwoods to civilization. Moreover, it was pure nonsense in view of all that had happened to suspect him of complicity in the crime. A man with the equivalent of fifty thousand English pounds does not need to assist in murder in order to enrich himself. I did not doubt that he was telling me the truth, for he must know that his statements could easily be inquired into. Yet Arbuthnot had insisted on my taking him for this walk! I decided eventually that my friend had simply wanted us out of the way in order to have freedom to attend to some matter probably in no way connected with Rodd. Having worried this out I warmed to the fellow, and we reached the hotel after our walk on much friendlier terms. We sat down to our belated dinner in peace, and Arbuthnot told us that the New Forest picnic party had returned and retired to bed exhausted by their outing. Rodd punctuated his repast with occasional sneezes.

"To-morrow," said Arbuthnot, "we shall have the Press down upon us. Two or three of the more go-ahead papers will send down a man; the others will depend on local reports. It will make a good column in Monday's issue, and

that, I hope, will be the end of it. I will interview them
if they come. You fellows can keep out of the way. You,
Rodd, would do well to take a day in bed and get rid of
your cold."

Arbuthnot was as good as his word and sent the press-
men away satisfied. The only liberty he permitted himself
was to explain my absence (I was away over the downs
towards Calbourne) by stating that I had shut myself up
to write an article on 'The Influence of Natural Beauty on
Human Passions with Special Reference to Homicide' for
the *Hibbert Journal*. One 'daily' printed this invention,
and to my annoyance it was commented on in the following week's *Charivaria*. However—

About nine o'clock on Monday morning Bernard paid
us a visit. He did not seem so pleased with life as when we
had seen him on Saturday. It happened that Arbuthnot and
I were alone at the time, and he took the opportunity of
telling us what was puzzling him.

"After I left you on Saturday," he said, "I rounded up
the manager of the local branch of the Capital and Coun-
ties Bank—dug him out from his afternoon's gardening, in
fact. Bank managers are canny individuals, who are specially trained to refuse information by alleging that the
bank's duty to its customers prevents their giving it, so
what I wormed out of him you must consider confidential
for the present."

"Certainly," said Arbuthnot. I nodded.

"It seems that Flyte opened a current account here
about three years ago, when he took the bungalow, giving his landlord's name as reference. He deposited a fairly
large sum in cash. The only operations on the account
after that were the cheques drawn to pay local bills and
so forth and occasional deposits, always in cash. Speaking from memory, the manager believed that there were at
present over a hundred pounds to the dead man's credit.

For a long time he was suspicious of the account and used to watch carefully to see that no cheques were missing from the series presented for payment, which might indicate that they had been improperly used elsewhere. After a time, however, he got used to it. Bankers, like doctors, see the curious side of human nature, and many people are as secretive over their finances as they are over their diseases."

"Certainly the late Flyte doesn't seem to have courted publicity," remarked Arbuthnot.

"Then I went on and saw Williams, a local speculative builder and the owner of the bungalow, and here again I ran up against an almost blank wall. It appears Flyte took the bungalow immediately after it was built. The owner had intended to sell, but the rent offered was enough to tempt him and he let the place to Flyte, who paid down six months' rent in advance, in cash. Then it appears he told the landlord that it would save him some correspondence if he could give the landlord's name as reference to the local bank. He gave the impression, though Williams naturally does not recollect the actual words, that he had no friends in England and that the bulk of his money was out of the country. Flyte had the shutters, bolts, bars, and so forth put in at his own expense, but with the landlord's sanction. He made some remark to the landlord about not being able to live in the East for twenty years without making some enemies."

Arbuthnot chuckled. "A time-worn expedient," said he. "Did you find out how Flyte got into touch with Williams?"

"That's about the only useful thing I did do. It appears that Flyte wrote first from London saying that an acquaintance had mentioned the bungalow to him."

"Did you see the letter?"

"Yes. Williams had filed it. It was written from the Brompton Palace Hotel, so I'm afraid it doesn't help much.

I am hoping that when the news of the tragedy appears in the London Press this morning we shall hear from some relations or solicitors."

"Nothing has been ascertained about the other man, I suppose?"

"No. His finger-prints have gone to Scotland Yard. If he is a known criminal he will be identified without doubt."

"And you haven't found his hat?"

"No. A search was made by my orders, but with no result."

"That's a pity. I should like to have seen his hat."

"We don't even know that he was wearing a hat," remarked Bernard.

"All murderers wear hats," said Arbuthnot.

4

Events up to Tuesday, May 29th

The inquest on Dalton Flyte was of very little interest. The jury returned a verdict strictly in accordance with the evidence. The bullet which had done the damage was produced. It was a .32, such as would be fired from a small revolver or an automatic pistol, but, as Arbuthnot pointed out to me, there are so many makes of weapon which would take such a bullet that it could not be considered as being of any great help in the investigation.[1] We saw Bernard after the proceedings.

"Are you taking Mrs. Morris to the other inquest?" asked Arbuthnot.

"Why should I?"

"It is just possible that she might recognize the body as that of a man whom she had seen about the place previously."

"Yes, it is possible, though hardly likely. Still, we'll accept your suggestion. Are you coming yourself?"

"Yes. I have nothing better to do."

By the kindness of the superintendent Arbuthnot and I were allowed to accompany Mrs. Morris and him in their

---

[1] The bullet was embedded in his spine and so damaged as to give no hope of distinguishing marks.—M. A.

visit to the mortuary. She shook her head when she saw the corpse. "Never seen him in my life," she declared.

"His clothes don't fit him very well," remarked Arbuthnot.

"No; it would appear to be a suit purchased for the occasion," answered Bernard.

"Your late master hadn't a suit like that by any chance?" inquired Arbuthnot of Mrs. Morris.

"No, sir, not to my knowledge."

"You have found none of his clothing or other possessions missing?"

"No, sir. I was there most of yesterday with the police checking things. I can't be quite certain about clothes because he would take suits to London and sometimes bring different ones back, but I never saw him with a suit like this one."

The Newport inquest was even less productive of information than the Freshwater one. The medical officer who had viewed the body about ten in the morning of the day it had been discovered assigned a maximum of twelve hours for the period that had elapsed since death. Before we set out westward again a curious piece of news came to hand. We were getting into our hired car when Bernard came up to us with a telegram in his hand.

"This sounds more hopeful," he said and read out:

"Dalton Flyte lived Brompton Palace Hotel intermittently past three years left Thursday,

"We hardly imagined that Flyte would still be using the hotel from which he wrote to his late landlord three years ago, so on Saturday we simply addressed an inquiry to the London police by letter, and this is their reply," explained the superintendent. "We shall now ask for all available details, supposing the necessary information has not already come to hand in some other way."

"There doesn't seem much stuffing left in this affair," I remarked, as we drove off. "That last piece of news clearly indicates that the late Flyte was some harmless retired fellow who, lacking friends, oscillated between an hotel life in London and a hermit's existence in the Isle of Wight. Judging by what we know of his financial habits he probably kept a large sum of money in his safe, and that led to his brutal murder."

"There will be another brutal murder presently," growled Arbuthnot.

"Indeed! Whose?"

"Yours."

"You've no better theory," I retorted, stung by this last remark.

"Very likely. The basis of all scientific inquiry is the patient accumulation of facts. The world is too full of arm-chair theorists."

"And careless drivers," I said maliciously. "You've taken the wrong turning."

"Not a bit of it. There's more than one way of getting to Freshwater."

The road we were on led almost imperceptibly upwards through a valley that ran right into the heart of the chalk downs. Finally we came to the crest, had a moment's vision of the Channel, and dipped rapidly down wooded slopes to the peaceful village of Shorwell. Here we swung to the right, passing other little villages—Brighstone, Mottistone—and ever drawing nearer to the sea. At Brook, Arbuthnot turned the car coastwards and we came out on a narrow, ill-kept road that closely followed the edge of the low cliffs.

"This is the military road," said my friend. "I believe it was built in connexion with coast defence. It traverses the whole of the south-west coast of the island but is very little used. I don't think that any military importance attaches to it nowadays."

The road led on and up. Soon we were climbing a steep gradient that led to the downs. On our left front the chalk cliff rose white and immense. Then it went out of sight as we rose to its level. The road entered a cutting in the convex seaward face of the downs. On our left, could we have seen over the top of the cutting, was the edge of the cliff only a few yards away. A child running carelessly down that slope would have plunged to death before it could have arrested its movement. Like many people born in a flat country I have a kind of horror of cliffs. I sometimes see them in my dreams and find myself poised on an edge that gives on to nothingness; in my waking hours I take care to avoid the edge, for if I dare to look over a kind of vertigo comes upon me, especially since recent happenings.

We emerged from the cutting; the road ran on a downward slope; Freshwater and its western downs came in view, and so did a policeman on a bicycle. Arbuthnot slowed down as we approached him. "It's our friend Rogers," he said, and stopped the car.

"Fine afternoon, gentlemen," said the sergeant, dismounting and looking enviously at us.

"Too fine for cycling," said Arbuthnot, as the last speaker wiped the perspiration from his face.

"You're right there, sir."

"Can we give you a lift anywhere?"

"I have to go over to Brook," said the sergeant dubiously. "Seeing you've just come from there it isn't likely you'll be wanting to go back."

"All roads are the same to us—we're on holiday," said Arbuthnot. "Jump in and we'll take you."

"But what will you do with your bicycle?" I asked.

"I'll just leave it here."

"But some one might steal it," I objected.

"Who?" asked the sergeant, and as I felt this question to be entirely unanswerable I made no further protest.

"Still on the Flyte case?" inquired Arbuthnot as he swung the car round and we headed eastward again.

"No, sir. I've just had a telephone message from Brook that the village idiot's gone and shot himself."

"Killed?" asked Arbuthnot.

"No, sir. Shot in the foot they say."

"A case of father's shotgun and the stray cat, I suppose?" I hazarded.

"No, he did it with a pistol, they told me."

"Pistol, eh?" said Arbuthnot.

"Yes, sir, and it did cross my mind to wonder what law-abiding folks in Brook wanted pistols for."

A few inquiries in the village soon brought us to a cottage where a tearful woman opened in answer to our knock. The young experimenter who had met with such prompt retribution had already departed for the county infirmary, but the lethal weapon with which he had secured his downfall lay on the kitchen table. "And it can stay till doomsday where they left it before I'll touch the thing," declared the woman, who appeared to be the culprit's aunt. Question and answer had not proceeded for thirty seconds before we were hanging on every word she had to say.

"Whose is that pistol?" demanded the sergeant.

"We don't know. That's why somebody telephoned for the police."

"It's a Westfield automatic," said Arbuthnot, taking it up as he spoke and unloading it, while the good lady edged nervously round behind him. He jerked three rounds out on the table. "It takes eight rounds of .32 ammunition," he added.

"I take it the boy found the pistol somewhere?" asked the sergeant.

"He picked it up on the cliffs towards Compton not far from the military road."

"And started playing with it, I suppose?"

"He says he thought it was a toy one some other boy had dropped, and so he pulled the trigger careless-like and it went off all with a rush and shot him in the foot, and he dropped it pretty quick. He made a great hullabaloo, I reckon, and lucky for him there was a man hedge-cutting in a field near by heard him and brought him home, and his father said, 'That'll learn you', but his mother—"

She went on talking, but we had no ears for her any longer; we were all busy with our own thoughts.

"Well," said the sergeant, "boys will be boys, but I don't mind admitting that in this case the boy did a useful piece of work in finding the pistol, though he had no call to go and shoot himself. I'll take possession of this weapon before it does any more harm. Killing one and wounding another's quite enough for a bit. For there's no doubt this is the gun that killed Mr. Dalton Flyte at Freshwater on Friday night."

"Well now, I wondered," she began, but we had no time for her comments. Instead, we obtained her direction to find the hedge-cutter who had rendered first-aid, and he showed us the scene of the accident. It was only a few yards from the cliff and about fifty from the road at a point about half a mile from the village in the direction of Freshwater.

"Clearly it was intended to go over the cliff, but in the dark the man misjudged the distance," I said.

"Very likely," answered Arbuthnot. "It rather knocks on the head the superintendent's theory as to the cause of the motor accident. If the murderer hurled his pistol away at this point he can't very well have gone from here to Bouldnor Cliff by mistaking his road."

"This is a very likely road for him to have taken," said the sergeant. "He wouldn't be likely to meet a soul for miles at night." He examined the weapon. "It's got a number," he said, "and there's a chance, therefore, that it can be traced. Although the man's dead we've got to remember that he was very possibly one of a gang."

We conveyed the sergeant back to where he had left his bicycle, and he mounted it with a glance at me which indicated that he felt that he had vindicated the moral integrity of the district. Rodd was sitting over tea when we returned to the hotel.

"I suppose that now you're free to go you'll soon be leaving this over-exciting locality," I suggested.

"Not a bit of it. I intended to come here, and here I shall stay as long as I like."

"Why not take the bungalow and settle down for a bit?" I proposed. "You'll probably get it cheap. No one will have any particular desire to live there."

"Well, I don't believe in ghosts, but to establish oneself so promptly at the scene of a crime would be like challenging one to put in an appearance. Besides, my leave is limited and although I'm not financially obliged to go back, I guess the ghost of old man Hudson would very rightly haunt me if I didn't, and his would be ten times worse than any Dalton Flyte could put up."

"In any case," said Arbuthnot, "no one can take the house until after quarter day, which is the twenty-fourth of next month, for I have no doubt the rent has been paid up to that date." He turned his attention to the table, drank all the tea he could get, shook the empty pot regretfully and, lighting his pipe, wandered off.

"Is he still interested in this affair?" asked Rodd casually.

"I'm not quite sure. He doesn't say much about it. I should think that after this afternoon's discovery there was very little left to do."

"So you found something fresh, did you?"

"We didn't, but a small boy found the pistol with which the crime was committed and promptly shot himself in the foot with it."

"Hard lines! I suppose he'd been prowling around the scene of the motor accident?"

"No, he found it far from there."

"That's surprising," remarked Rodd, getting up and strolling round the room. "Where did he find it?"

"On the edge of the cliff, going from here towards Brook."

"That's very peculiar. Then if the murderer left here by that road how on earth did he finish up at Bouldnor Cliff?"

"I've heard a theory," I said, "that he was making for the shore near that point, having a motor-boat there to take him across the Solent."

"Does Arbuthnot believe that?"

"I don't know what he thinks," I said truthfully.

"It seems to me," declared Rodd, "that the pistol may have nothing to do with the crime. If the criminal intended to cross the Solent he would have known it to be far safer to drop the thing in the sea."

"It would take the bullet that killed Flyte," I objected.

"So would hundreds of other pistols. I don't see that the finding of that one proves anything." With that he went off and I turned my attention to correspondence that I had neglected during the past few days. Arbuthnot did not return until dinner-time. After that meal he invited me to go for a stroll. We wandered up the road that led to the golf-links.

"I am going up to London to-morrow," said he.

"Having seen enough of this affair?" I suggested.

"Not at all. I am going to the Brompton Palace Hotel. I have spent this evening making Mrs. Morris overtax her memory to recall the days of the week on which Flyte arrived in Freshwater for his last half-dozen or so week-ends. The hotel people will know from their accounts on what dates he left there. If he has led an innocent life in London and an equally harmless one here, one is interest-ed to see if there is any hiatus between his public appear-ances. For example, if he left London on Thursday of one week and arrived here on Saturday we might be inclined to ask what he was doing in the interval."

"Then you're not satisfied with what appears to be the conclusion of a rather ordinary and sordid crime?"

"King, I was never so profoundly dissatisfied in my life. I've been marking time so far. Now I've decided to get a move on. There's a breeze blowing up!"

"I don't feel it," I said, simply enough.

"I don't mean a meteorological one," he said, grinning. Then he glanced to his right where lay the building which still seemed to exercise some fascination for him. "Care to have another look round, King?"

"I wouldn't!" I said promptly. "And in any case it's locked up."

"In my pocket at present is the key of the back door."

"Where did you get that?"

"I borrowed it from the sergeant. It may be only fancy, and yet I've a feeling that there's more in that house than we've seen so far."

"One thing I should like to know," I remarked, as a thought flashed into my head.

"And that is?"

"Whether there is another ash-stick anywhere there."

"Still suspecting Rodd, eh? I thought you had relin-quished that idea."

"I have; and yet I should like to feel sure that there were never two sticks."

"Come on, then."

We had dined at half-past seven and it still needed half an hour to sunset when we entered the kitchen. The air of the house was musty and the light was dim to us on coming in from the golden evening. Some writer has made it a fancy of his that when a house is uninhabited by men, tenants not of this world enter in and make it their dwelling. What would he have said of a building whose occupant had but three days before passed swiftly and horribly into the unknown? I shivered.

Arbuthnot is nothing if not thorough. In turn he subjected the kitchen and the scullery to a most methodical examination. He even penetrated the coal-store that lay beyond the scullery.

"Everywhere," said he, "we have the signs of a normal and carefully-run household. The store is full of coal, which, as you know, is cheapest to purchase in the summer months. And yet, King, the house altogether lacks what one may call the personal touch. I noticed it on our last visit. A bachelor on his way through life notoriously accumulates all sorts of useless trifles to which he is passionately attached: photographs of old friends and old occasions, relics of games he played, expeditions he joined in, and places he visited. Nothing here seems intimately connected with the late tenant. The very books look unread and the golf-clubs new."

We left the kitchen and went into the passage. Although all the windows of the house naturally were closed and bolted the shutters had not been fastened, for who in that quiet and law-abiding community would seek to break in, especially with the doom of the last tenant hanging over the place? The rays of the low sun slanted into the dining-room and the carpet glowed a dull red, which I almost fancied became more vivid at one spot, where Dalton Flyte's life-blood had dripped from his silent body. If I looked long enough there I could gradually see his prostrate form taking shape before me, materializing from the haze that comes before one's eyes when one has stared too long or too intently.

Arbuthnot is not sensitive. "Cut along and look for your theoretical walking-stick," he said genially. I started from my dream and went off to investigate on my own, leaving him to his own devices. My search was fruitless, and I did not enjoy it.

"The house hides its secrets well," said Arbuthnot as he rejoined me and we passed back along the passage. He stopped at the door that led into the kitchen. "King," he added, "even you have not so far devised any theory as to the iron bar that would appear to be missing from this door. Mrs. Morris did not find it when she tidied things up yesterday; I questioned her to-day on that very point. Yet there must have been three. If I put the two that are left into position you will see they form an incomplete safeguard." He stooped down and felt in the recess by the door as he spoke.

"Good God, King, there are *three* here!"

As he spoke the passage grew suddenly dark. This was, of course, only due to the final dip of the sun below the horizon, and yet it seemed to me symbolical of the greater darkness into which we were suddenly plunged.

"Could you have made a mistake in the first instance?" I asked, gazing almost fearfully round.

"I don't make mistakes of that kind," he answered briefly.

I fell silent. There are occasions in life when there is nothing else to do. Some new circumstance comes suddenly within one's ken and the brain cannot in a moment adjust itself to face it. The house, which to me had been a dead husk shrouding a past horror, had instantaneously assumed a fresh significance. Arbuthnot equally had nothing to say, but I could guess that his mind was furiously busy.

"Too dark to see any more," he said finally, and led the way out of the house.

I was quite pleased when the door was closed and locked behind me. We continued our stroll in the direction away from Freshwater, keeping near the edge of the cliff, and presently dipped down into a little cutting that contained a disused road. Arbuthnot turned right along the cutting, and we came to a post-and-rail that barred our way. We climbed it and found ourselves nearing the edge of the cliff.

"If we had gone along this road in the opposite direction we should have found it join the military road," said my friend. "Presumably this was the original road until erosion at the bay cut into it and rendered it useless. Its present significance lies in its being the nearest place where a man could lie concealed and watch the bungalow."

"I've noticed people leaving their cars here while they golfed or walked on the down," I said.

We retraced our steps homewards, walking in silence. Finally Arbuthnot said, "I'm off to London to-morrow morning, as you know. In my absence I want you to take a letter from me to Williams, the owner of the bungalow. Take it immediately after breakfast. He will probably give you some sort of reply. If he should question you, be sure to give him the impression that the contents of the letter are very serious and not to be disregarded on any account."

Back in the hotel sitting-room, which was unoccupied but for ourselves, he sat down to write. I threw myself into a chair and let my thoughts play around the evening's discovery. My failure to find in the bungalow any stick of the type that Rodd had carried had finally eradicated any lingering suspicion of him from my mind. Nevertheless Arbuthnot's attitude toward the crime, backed up by our recent peculiar experiences, forbade me to think that nothing of interest remained in the affair. It was thus that my roving brain came round to Mrs. Morris and stopped. Was there, or was there not, something to question in her conduct in the affair? I began to put small points together. She was a poor woman, and a weak one as well. She had nearly collapsed at the sight of her dead master. She had displayed immense reluctance to return to the presence of the corpse. She had been absent from work the whole day on the date of the crime. Her excuse was incapable of verification or of disproof. It covered her niece as well, who would normally have taken her place. I began to picture the criminal, using some plausible tale that satisfied her limited intelligence, persuading her to remove and hide one of the bars which were Dalton Flyte's chief protection. He would likewise borrow her key, promising to put it in a place easy for her to find when he left after his purpose had been accomplished. He had failed in his attempt on Thursday night, probably because Flyte had noted the disappearance of the bar and was watchful. He had returned to Mrs. Morris, who was now too implicated to withdraw, and warned her to keep away from the bungalow on the Friday. Then, adopting bolder methods, he had very likely entered the bungalow by day, when the inner door was not likely to be barred, and either hidden himself till after nightfall, or more likely, terrorized Flyte into submission until the lateness of the hour made it reasonably safe to kill him. Leaving the key where Mrs. Morris could find it, he had then made his well-arranged exit. Mrs. Morris had seized her first opportunity, when she was working in the bungalow on Sunday, to restore the bar, and very naturally had denied all knowledge of it to Arbuthnot.

"It hangs together," I said, unconsciously speaking aloud.

"So you suspect Mrs. Morris, do you?" said Arbuthnot over his shoulder.

"What do you know about it?" I demanded, somewhat taken aback.

"My dear King, you have an intensely suspicious nature, which acquaintance with me has not improved. When you discovered, rather regretfully, that you could no longer suspect Rodd, you felt obliged to cast round in your mind for another scapegoat. Mrs. Morris was about the only one who presented herself."

"Quite true. But, joking apart, there is something to be said in favour of viewing her with some suspicion."

"Perfectly right. Now you had better listen to what I have written to our friend Williams, for he may catechize you on the subject to-morrow:

> "Dear Sir,
> "My friend, Sir Edmund King, and I are de-sirous of renting for the summer months the bungalow of yours at Freshwater Bay which was, till recently, occupied by the late Mr. Dalton Flyte. Although it might be thought that the bungalow would lose in attractive-ness through having been the scene of a cap-ital offence, I am particularly anxious to se-cure possession of it. Should other tenants or purchasers appear, I would particularly request you to take no steps with regard to their applications until I have seen you on Wednesday, when I return from London. I would urge this on you as a means of pre-venting any further scandal attaching to your property. Kindly treat this letter as strictly confidential.
> "Yours, etc."

"So we are to live there?" I asked, with a shudder of disgust.

"Probably. After quarter day."

"I don't quite see why."

"Neither do I, and neither, no doubt, did the dog in the manger."

At this I shrugged my shoulders and went off to bed, but hardly to sleep. I reconsidered my theory about Mrs. Morris and took pains to estimate its soundness, for if it were otherwise I faced the alarming position that some unknown had had access to the bungalow since the crime. And we were going to live there! I could hardly be blamed for viewing the prospect with acute dislike.

The next morning, which was Tuesday, Arbuthnot departed for the steamer, and I on my mission immediately after breakfast. Rodd joined us at the meal and made jesting allusions to "sleuths", and enlarged on the superior joys of taking a book on the sands which now lay revealed by the falling tide. We tolerated him, knowing that he was, in a sense, fresh to the delights of an English May at its best.

Mr. Williams, burly and side-whiskered, whom I eventually ran to ground in a sort of half-timber work structure called 'Lilac Villa' near Totland Bay, studied the letter I had brought him with great attention. In fact, after reading it once he bethought himself of his spectacles and read it again with their aid. Then he grunted and said, "Well, well," to himself in a kind of semi-confidential growl. Lastly he folded the letter up, placed it carefully in an already bulging wallet, and remarked, "I don't quite get the rights and wrongs of this business."

"Neither do I," I replied frankly, "but I am content to rely on my friend's opinion."

"I thought," he added, "that the fellow who did the act having fallen over the cliff we might call that an end of it."

"So one would think; but in confidence I may tell you that Mr. Arbuthnot as a result of his investigations believes that there is a great deal to come out yet."

"Well, certainly he ought to know."

"You see," I urged, "your last tenant was a man who got what he wanted by having ready money to put down. His money, in fact, was his only guarantee of respectability. Beyond that no one knows anything about him."

"True," conceded Mr. Williams.

"All that my friend means is that in the natural course of events people would be shy of taking a house in which a crime had been committed. Therefore, if some individual not personally known to you came along within a few days and wanted to rent the bungalow in question, it would be on the face of it a peculiar thing, and one to be regarded with suspicion. Not, of course, that anything of the kind is at all likely to happen," I concluded.

"Isn't it! Isn't it!" Mr. Williams burst out suddenly. "If you'll excuse me saying so, sir, your friend knows a long sight more about this business than either you or me. Look here!"

Once more the capacious wallet appeared in sight. From it he pulled out two envelopes and flung them on the table before me. "Came by this morning's post," said he. "Applications to rent the bungalow."

"Two!" I cried, struck with amazement.

"Two," said he, leaning back and inserting his thumbs in the arm-holes of his waistcoat as if he enjoyed the surprise he had given me. And it certainly was a shock. I had not expected there to be any, but I was prepared to believe that one might be received; the appearance of two seemed a definite challenge to the laws of probability.

"In face of this," I said, "you'll be willing to believe there is something in Mr. Arbuthnot's warning."

"In face of this," he replied, "I hope he comes along to see me as soon as he can."

"That will be either to-night or to-morrow morning," I promised.

"Nothing shall be said or done till he comes," added Mr. Williams. "And I'll warrant you now that that bungalow won't be let again unless I know the man who wants it, and his father and grandfather as well. These goings-on may seem ordinary to Londoners, but we've no use for them down here. I'll watch it."

We parted on the best of terms, and I walked back to the hotel pondering what I had learnt, but deriving precious little benefit from my thoughts. When I arrived back a railway delivery van stood outside the hotel and Rodd was supervising the unloading of a large cabin trunk.

"I got this sent over from Southampton," said he, "in order to make myself occasionally more presentable." He eyed his jacket and flannels ruefully. "I'm no advertisement for the hotel at present," he added.

"You're not," I said candidly. "I am assured that tramps do not visit this island, which is a good thing for you, for otherwise you would certainly be mistaken for one."

"I am one," he said with a laugh. "I am a reincarnation of Stevenson's vagabond and a disciple of George Borrow. One of these mornings when there's a wind on the heath your disreputable friend will vanish to fresh woods and pastures new—probably to the New Forest, in fact."

The day passed slowly while I waited for Arbuthnot's return, which did not take place till about half-past eight that evening. Despite what I assumed to have been a busy day for him he invited me to accompany him on a stroll after he had dined.

"Did you see Williams?" he asked, as soon as we were out of earshot of the hotel.

"I did."

"Did he accept my suggestion?"

"Willingly."

"Good. Had he received any application?"

"He had."

"Ah! Pretty sharp work that. Full accounts of the crime only appeared in the London papers for the first time yesterday morning. He did not show you the application?"

"There were two," I said quietly.

Arbuthnot stopped in his walk. "Two!" said he, and then began to chuckle. "Upon my word, King, that's a most interesting piece of news. This affair cuts a little deeper than you thought at first, does it not?"

I admitted the justice of his remark.

"Well, well," continued he, "it is rather too late to seek out Mr. Williams to-night, but to-morrow morning it shall be our first duty to inquire into this anxiety to reside in a house of such evil repute."

"Did your inquiries in town lead to anything?" I inquired.

"I went to the Brompton Palace Hotel. The police had been there before me, of course, but with the exercise of a little tact I obtained all the information that was available. Except for week-ends, Dalton Flyte had lived in the hotel regularly for the past three years, and had a small suite there permanently reserved for him. By all accounts, he led a most innocent life, taking most of his meals in the hotel and rarely being out after ten o'clock at night. Moreover, *if* we can rely on Mrs. Morris's memory, and I grant that's a bit doubtful, he must have gone straight to Freshwater from London for his week-ends. Now supposing the late Flyte were not altogether what he appeared to be, and were concerned in building up a general alibi in case of need, we should expect to find occasional passages of time during which there would be no record of his movements. These I can't find at present."

"How did he pay his hotel bills?" I asked.

"Exactly. That was a very important point. He either paid them in cash or in cheques on his account at Freshwater."

"Another cul-de-sac," I remarked.

"Precisely. I was anxious to see if anything could be traced of the taxi-drivers who drove him to and from Waterloo each week, but I had no time on this visit because I wanted to get back quickly and see Williams."

"So that was the sum total of the results of your investigations?" I inquired.

"Not quite. I held some converse with an affable chambermaid. I asked her about Flyte's eyesight. She said he always wore glasses."

"But we always knew Flyte wore glasses," I pointed out. "Mrs. Morris told us so, and besides the marks on each side of his nose proved it."

"So you are quite satisfied that he wore glasses?" asked Arbuthnot slowly.

"Of course I am."

"Then where are they?"

5
Events up to Thursday, May 31st

"Where are they!" I echoed.

"Yes, where are they? We inspected the body; we inspected the house; we returned there

last night and I carried out another thorough inspection which I admit was mainly in the hope of finding the missing pince-nez. Yet they are not to be found. We have the evidence of Mrs. Morris that Flyte was as blind as a bat without them, and therefore we may assume that he either had them on or close at hand at the time he met his death."

"No doubt the frame was made of gold. The criminal may therefore have thought it worth while adding them to his haul."

"That, King, is pure drivel."

"Why?"

"You really suppose that the murderer troubled to take a pair of pince-nez for the trivial amount of gold in them and left the diamond ring we saw—a ring worth at the very least fifty pounds—on the finger of the dead man?"

"It doesn't seem likely," I admitted. "But what other reason could the murderer have for taking them?"

"What reason have you for supposing that the murderer *did* take them?" returned Arbuthnot by way of reply. "They weren't found on his body. Surely he did not steal them simply to discard them later."

"Yes," I said, "he may have done so."

"Why?"

"He may have stolen them before the crime in order to put Flyte in a helpless position."

"That appears possible."

"Or," said I, "he may have arranged with another person to steal them for him."

"Plausible, King—distinctly plausible, I admit. When your suspicions of a person are aroused you show a remarkable acuteness in seizing on points that may possibly tell against that person."

"Then I take it you don't agree with me?"

"Perhaps not. Yet I recognize that your theory deserves consideration."

"Have you a better?" I asked, but he walked on without replying, and we finished our stroll in silence.

The next morning we set off as early as we reasonably could to interview Mr. Williams. The remarkable arrival of the two letters had been frequently in my thoughts, and I had a suggestion I wished to put before Arbuthnot.

"About these letters," I said. "Isn't it quite a probability that they emanated from the same person?"

"That's certainly ingenious," said Arbuthnot.

"If a sufficiently clever person particularly wanted possession of the bungalow," I went on, encouraged by his remark, "he might consider that the wording of one application might for some reason fail to find favour in the eyes of its recipient. It is difficult to say how any given person is going to be impressed by the form of a letter. Then if he sent a second letter, quite differently worded, it would give him a second chance."

"Very true," said Arbuthnot. "Continue your discourse."

"Moreover," I went on, "such a prompt application after the crime might appear peculiar. Here the arrival of a second apparently independent application would make the first appear much more ordinary."

"That does credit to your intelligence," responded Arbuthnot, and I walked on inspired by his unusual praise till he suddenly added, "but it's probably all wrong, nevertheless."

"This is Lilac Villa," I grumbled. "You'll have a chance to frame a theory for yourself."

Mr. Williams was at home and evidently had been awaiting us. He conducted us into the little room that served him for an office, and I noticed that he treated Arbuthnot with a special measure of respect. The latter went straight to the point.

"My friend tells me that you have already had two applications to rent the bungalow on the cliff."

"That's so, Mr. Arbuthnot."

"For what period do these people ask?"

"For the summer months, they say."

"Both of them?"

"Yes."

"Ah!" I said meaningly to Arbuthnot, remembering my own ideas on the question.

"And the rent offered?"

"One offers twenty-five per cent above what Mr. Flyte paid and the other suggests fifty pounds for the three months, on account of the short period."

"And which is the better offer?"

"They work out to about the same."

"Confirmation," I said to myself.

"Then if I say I am willing to pay sixty pounds for the same period you won't feel that I have any axe to grind in urging you to look with disfavour upon their offers?" went on Arbuthnot.

"They wouldn't get it in any case; you can bet your boots on that," remarked the landlord forcibly. "If you like to take it you can have it at Mr. Flyte's old figure. I'll get a long let or a sale easier in the autumn when the fuss and bother has died down a bit."

"That's a generous offer," answered Arbuthnot, "and I'll accept it with pleasure. Now tell me to whom the furniture in the bungalow belongs."

"To Mr. Flyte, the whole lot of it. But it's got to be out of the house by the twenty-fourth of June. If no one turns up to claim it, it'll be disposed of by order of court."

"I see. Now is there any objection to my seeing the two letters you received?"

"No objection at all. Here they are." He wrestled for a while with his overloaded wallet and finally produced two envelopes. Arbuthnot subjected them to scrutiny.

"Why, you're like a woman trying to guess who's written by looking at the envelope," declared Williams, beginning to chuckle. Arbuthnot joined in the laugh.

"Not quite," said he. "Look at the way these envelopes are addressed. The first one reads,

> *G. Williams, Esq.,*
> *Builder and Contractor,*
> *Totland Bay.*

while the other bears the superscription,

> *G. H. Williams, Esq,,*
> *Lilac Villa,*
> *Totland Bay.*

Are those your correct initials?"

"They are. I'm George Henry, to distinguish me from my father who was Henry George," replied Mr. Williams, enjoying his own humour.

"This," said Arbuthnot to me, "will teach you not to theorize without sufficient facts."

"How so?"

"The first full accounts of the crime were in Monday's papers. I read them all. They referred to 'Mr. G. Williams, builder and contractor, of Totland Bay,' as the owner of the bungalow."

"True," said that person. "I read it myself."

"Hence it is fairly safe to say that one letter is from an individual who took your address from the newspapers, and the other from one who obtained his information from elsewhere."

"There!" said Mr. Williams, slapping his knee, "somehow or other that never entered my head. If you can tell all that front the envelopes, very likely you'll be able to guess the winner of next year's Derby from the insides!" He laughed again, and we joined in.

"This conversation, of course, is understood to be confidential," put in Arbuthnot quietly.

"Sure," said Mr. Williams, and then I saw his face fall as he realized his little joke would not be available for repetition.

Arbuthnot turned his attention to the letters. He read them both attentively without vouchsafing a word. Then he remarked, "The first is from Mr. Herbert J. Parker, of 'The Nook', Ypres Road, Surbiton, whose invalid wife has been recommended to go to the sea-side. He offers fifty pounds for the accommodation, and inquires whether the bee orchid is as common on Freshwater Downs as it used to be, as his chief interest is nature study."

"That's a clever touch," said I.

"Lovely," said Mr. Williams. "It fairly melted my heart when I read it first."

"The second letter, the one addressed to 'Lilac Villa'," went on Arbuthnot, "is from a Mr. Cosmo Edginton, who writes from the Bayswater Court Hotel. He is aware of the crime, but being a member of the Psychical Research Society he rather welcomes the state of affairs."

"Gorgeous," I said.

"Plausible enough," contended Arbuthnot, "if one's suspicions were not awake. Notice that the applicant who admits that he is aware of the possible objection to occupying the bungalow is the one who uses the address that was not given in the newspapers."

"Now," said Mr. Williams, breaking in, "what ought I to do about these chaps—the bee orchard and the other one who isn't so particular?"

"Will you accept a suggestion that can do you no harm and may be of assistance to me?" asked Arbuthnot.

"Sure I will," was the answer.

"Very well. Take a sheet of your business notepaper and a pen and write this." There was a glint of amusement in Arbuthnot's eyes as he spoke. Mr. Williams obediently prepared to write. Arbuthnot dictated.

"Herbert J. Parker, Esq.,
"The Nook,
"Ypres Road,
"Surbiton.

"Dear Sir,
"I beg to acknowledge your offer of the 10th inst., to rent my bungalow. This is receiving my careful and immediate consideration."

"Sign it," added Arbuthnot.

"Is that all?" inquired Mr. Williams, in what seemed to be disappointed tones.

"That's all for the letter," said Arbuthnot. "Now put it in an envelope and address it to Cosmo Edginton, Esquire, Bayswater Court Hotel."

The writer gaped at him for a moment and then burst into a roar of laughter. I myself was not inconsiderably surprised.

"If these people are genuine," explained Arbuthnot, "it can do no harm, whereas if they are otherwise it may give them furiously to think. Now prepare a similar document to be externally Parker and internally Edginton."

Mr. Williams complied with gusto. "Remember," said Arbuthnot, with the little note of command in his voice that might have been resented coming from another man, "these matters must not go beyond us for the present."

I saw that the subtle use of the plural pronoun had inspired Mr. Williams with unlimited fidelity. "You trust me," said he.

"With your permission I'll borrow these letters," added Arbuthnot. "I hope you will let me know if you hear further from these would-be tenants. We shall be at the Stagrock Hotel until we move up nearer to the bee orchids."

Speeded by further laughter from the jovial builder, we departed.

"What do you think of all this?" asked Arbuthnot as we strolled back towards Freshwater.

"I'm not theorizing without sufficient facts," I replied guardedly.

"But surely you noted one remarkable omission from both the letters?" he said.

"I did not," I acknowledged frankly. "What was it?"

"Simply this. Here are two people proposing to take a bungalow, for three months in each case. Yet neither of them raises the question of furniture! Who in his senses would wish to take an unfurnished bungalow and have all the worry and expense of hiring, purchasing, or transporting the wherewithal to furnish it when he was only contemplating three months' residence? It's a case of the pince-nez over again. The most obvious facts are always the ones that somehow escape notice."

"Then what do you propose to do about these letters?"

"I haven't decided," he said frankly. "The man who writes from Surbiton may be only using an accommodation address and the other certainly invites suspicion by addressing his letter from an hotel. It is possible to have them both watched, but I don't think it is worth while my looking into their affairs personally at present. Let us see how they treat the replies I dictated to their inquiries. That will be some help in all probability. Now for a public call-office."

"You're going to telephone?"

"Not at all. It is merely that I find the concentrated atmosphere of the booth assists my meditations. When I have cured you of making that sort of remark, King, you may be quite a tolerable companion."

After that I said no more until we had left the telephone office.

"I rang up the police at Newport," he explained, "and luckily found the superintendent there. They're very concerned over receiving no information about Dalton Flyte. Since the news was published in London on Monday, they expected to hear yesterday, or at latest to-day, from some person or other who was interested in the dead man. Instead there has been a blank silence. Now they are about to advertise and have also asked the B.B.C. to broadcast a request for information."

"I am beginning to think that Dalton Flyte was a myth," I remarked, "and that the name covered the identity of some person who was in hiding from his enemies."

"Why should a man travel to London every week to hide from his enemies?" inquired Arbuthnot. "I am inclined to agree that his real name was not Flyte, certainly, but beyond that any speculations at present as to his past history are a purely Israelitish task."

I spent most of that afternoon in a deck-chair outside the hotel. Arbuthnot had disappeared to write letters, and

I guessed that he was setting on foot inquiries respecting Mr. Williams's peculiar correspondents. The bay had never looked more lovely, but beyond it the empty bungalow seemed to brood like some dark shadow over the scene, and I shifted my chair so that it should not come within my vision. If that place had to be my residence in the future I thought the charms of the district but a poor compensation for the mental discomfort I should feel in living there. When the human brain has been presented with a succession of problems, each one doing a little to increase the mystery of its forerunners, there comes a time when it feels numbed and unable to think. I was in this state that afternoon. Gradually I dropped off to sleep, but it was only to be tormented by dreams.

I moved in a moonless night. My path lay along some dark ridge, and all at once I saw with a ghastly horror that I was but a few yards from the edge of that cliff which flanked the military road. I strove to turn my feet uphill and away from the perilous limit, but, as so often in dreams, they moved under some control other than my own, and I inevitably trended nearer and nearer to the fatal bourn. Then all at once I knew, though I could not see, that some one was behind me. The air seemed suddenly to become like some horribly viscous liquid, against which I strove to move in vain. I clawed against it like a toad seeking to escape from a tank. Then some power was twisting my head round against my will. There leapt into view, gleaming with a bluish luminosity, the face of the dead man in the bungalow. The next instant I was falling. I woke up lying on my back with the faithless deck-chair prostrate beneath me.

I rose ungracefully, anxiously feeling the back of my head, and glared round for a possible aggressor, for it had entered my head that Rodd's boyish exuberance might have led him to descend to the level of practical joking.

But there was no one in sight. I told myself angrily that it was time I pulled myself together, and, collecting a hat and stick, set off, determined to walk myself into a more wholesome frame of mind. I was not successful. Occasionally in one's life dreams come upon one that are not to be dispelled by the return of consciousness. I walked in a world that was simultaneously bright sunshine and the darkest night, and the latter was more real. There was a closeness around my heart as if the clutch of fear was still there, and I cast foolish glances backward on a deserted and sunny path. When I arrived back Arbuthnot sat at tea alone.

"Where's Rodd?" I asked.

"Marking time, I suppose," replied Arbuthnot, reluctantly passing me the teapot.

"What do you mean by marking time?"

"Waiting till he can go."

"He hasn't said anything to me about going," I declared.

"Nor to me."

"I suppose you found out from the hotel people, then?"

"I didn't."

"When do you suppose he's going?"

"To-morrow morning."

"I should like to know why you think so?"

Arbuthnot was engaged in pouring out tea as I spoke. He jerked the spout of the teapot in the direction of the window. I looked out and saw nothing but the bay in the full splendour of early evening.

"Do you mean the bungalow?" I asked.

"No, I mean the sea."

"What about the sea?"

"It is nearly high tide."

"Surely you don't mean he's leaving here by boat?" I said incredulously.

"Hardly," said Arbuthnot, laughing.

"He could have left here any time after the inquest," I pointed out.

"So could we," he replied.

"Then you would suggest that he has an interest in this affair?"

"I suggest nothing. All I would ask is that if at any time to-morrow I should suddenly disappear you will accept my absence philosophically and await my return with patience."

"By all means," I said wonderingly; "but let me tell you my curiosity is aroused."

"Stifle it, King, stifle it. It's a pernicious habit."

I believe I made some pretence of annoyance at this insulting advice, but secretly my heart felt lighter. It was good to realize that Arbuthnot was making a move. My cheerfulness was fated, however, not to be of very long duration.

There were only the three of us at dinner that night, and anyone looking on would have taken us for a gay party. I had cheered up considerably, though every now and again I saw as through a veil my dream of the after-noon. Arbuthnot chose to be conversational and Rodd was in a mood of hilarity. He was prepared to laugh at any-thing, and even went so far as to flick a pellet of bread at me, which act aroused my resentment. I told him so, but he only guffawed.

"I have a theory of my own about this crime," he said suddenly to Arbuthnot.

"Let's have it," said my friend good-humouredly.

"Listen," said Rodd, leaning forward and speaking in confidential tones. "I believe King committed it."

"Confound it!" I said angrily. "There are certain things that shouldn't be made the subjects of wit, and murder is one of them."

"What about de Quincey and his essay on 'Murder as a Fine Art'?" cried Rodd triumphantly.

"The weakness of your theory," said Arbuthnot gravely, "is the absence of motive."

"Not at all. The motive was vanity, which, as every one knows, is the strongest force in human nature."

"And is often manifested in excessive talkativeness," I added.

"I believe," continued Rodd, disregarding my remark, "that the accused had been suffering for years before he committed the crime from what we may call the 'insolubility complex'."

"The what?" said I.

"Proceed," remarked Arbuthnot, who was apparently taking an interest in all this nonsense.

"Long acquaintance with a certain distinguished criminologist had forced him to the conclusion that there was no mystery, however complicated, which the former could not solve. He resented having to think this. Finally he decided that the only way to demonstrate his friend's fallibility was to embark on a career of crime himself."

"Sound psychology," commented Arbuthnot approvingly.

"Moreover, the accused was just recovering from a severe attack of influenza, the after-effect of which is often acute melancholia, which by an easy transition might become suicidal or homicidal mania."

"Things are looking very black against you, King, I am bound to admit," said Arbuthnot solemnly. "But can you indicate how the crime was actually committed?" he asked, turning to Rodd.

"Certainly. It was only too easy in practice. He disguised himself as Mrs. Morris. Certain facial resemblances and a similar habit of speech facilitated his task in no small degree."

Arbuthnot burst out laughing. In spite of my annoyance I was on the verge of doing the same, and I turned away so that Rodd might not perceive that my features were twitching. It was at that moment that I saw the face at the window.

I should explain that the windows of the dining-room looked eastward across the bay. Outside them was a grass plot, a hedge, and then the road that terminated at the sea-front. It was a simple matter for anyone to come up to the windows, and at eight o'clock on a brilliant May evening, when it was still broad daylight, it sounds ridiculous for me to have been alarmed. The obvious explanation was that some inquisitive person, who had been having drinks in the hotel bar and listening to conversation about recent events, had felt an inclination to see three people who were in a measure connected with them. Nevertheless, when one is involved in mystery one is prone to jump to the conclusion that any occurrence out of the ordinary must bear some relation to the main subject of one's thoughts.

As we sat, Rodd and I faced the windows and Arbuthnot had his back to them. The watcher immediately withdrew when he saw my eyes were on him, and vanished from sight. I was perfectly sure it was no face I had seen before; neither could I say that there was anything objectionable in the look of the man, but to be under espionage is always hateful. Neither of the others had seen anything and they rallied me on my distrait expression, Rodd remarking something about "guilty tremors", but I was in no mood for further badinage and rose from the table. As I did so I heard the engine of a car throbbing, and then the sound dying gradually away in the distance. Leaving the others engaged in lighting their pipes I wandered out into the road and strolled along as far as the road junction where the road went off towards the golf-links. Here, as I had hoped, stood a man whose *dolce far niente* expression was in utter harmony with the peace of the evening.

"Did you notice a car come along here a few minutes ago?" I asked.

"Car with two gents in it," he said. "Gents got out and walked along to the hotel. Weren't gone more'n a couple of minutes. Just time for a quick one, I said to myself. This is thirsty weather."

"Did you know them?" I inquired.

"Can't say that I did."

"You didn't happen to notice the number of the car?"

"No, sir, 'fraid I didn't. Thank you kindly, sir. Sorry you missed your friends."

His languor was replaced by a certain briskness as he carried my donation towards the hotel bar.

I returned to find Arbuthnot alone and seized the opportunity to tell him what had occurred.

"It seems a singularly useless thing to do," he said. "All our comings and goings are perfectly open. No man need flatten his nose at a window-frame in order to see what we look like. On the whole, I think it may have something to do with Rodd's trousers."

"Rodd's trousers!" I cried. "His trousers are certainly unique, but I can hardly imagine two men making a journey in a car specially to see them."

"No, not exactly that," replied my friend, using the casual tones he adopts when he is merely speculating on occurrences without a definite assurance that he is right. "Did you notice the flannels he was wearing on the morning we found him at the bungalow?"

"I noted that they were thoroughly disreputable."

"True. And in particular they had a black, oily-looking smear on the inside of the right leg and about a foot from the ground. It looked fresh to me."

"Well, what of it?"

"The *Mauretania* is a goodish-sized ship," he said dreamily.

"So I believe," I answered dryly, for I had a suspicion that my leg was being pulled.

"Yet the passengers hardly need bicycles to get about on."

"Oho! So you think that Rodd was doing his walking tour on wheels?"

"It may be so."

"Then where is the bicycle now?"

"How should I know? If it still exists, the citizens of this law-abiding isle will certainly hand it over to the police when they find it. Why should I worry?"

"Where is Rodd gone?" I asked.

"Upstairs to his bedroom. He probably packs."

"And what are you going to do?"

"I shall sit here, off and on, for hours and hours!"

I also sat down and spent a couple of hours with a book, though I should not have cared to have been asked to give a précis of what I had read. Everything in the hotel was by then quiet, and outdoors there was almost perfect serenity. The mildest of all breezes touched my cheeks as I sat by the open window and the sound of the wavelets on the shore was the merest lisping that I could only hear with difficulty. At eleven o'clock I got up and went to bed. Arbuthnot sat on, nodding me good night as I moved off. I hardly anticipated sleep, and yet I dozed. I was awakened by a creaking on the stairs which I judged to be Arbuthnot abandoning his self-imposed vigil. I fell into another doze, and when I awoke it was daylight. Strangely enough, I was disappointed. I had had an impression, whose origin I could not distinguish, that the past night was to bring forth something that would mark a step towards the solution of our problem. Instead, I had slept peacefully and uninterruptedly, and here was another day of sunshine bidding me get up. Yet Arbuthnot had certainly seemed peculiar in his remarks the night before and had made me feel that he expected some kind of trouble. I was busy thinking over various things as I dressed, and I concluded finally that I was wasting my time. Affairs were too marked by discontinuity; the events of the past few days seemed incapable of being brought into any logical relation with each other. When I was clothed I went downstairs and out, walking briskly in the cool air. I returned with an appetite. Rodd was already seated at breakfast, but Arbuthnot was not to be seen.

"Sleep well?" asked the former.

"Remarkably well," I answered.

"So did I. Have some more tea before Arbuthnot arrives."

"You look more respectable this morning," I remarked.

"Got to be, unfortunately. I'm going up to London to-day. There's a certain amount of legal business to be gone through over old man Hudson's bequest."

"Going this morning?" I inquired.

"Yes. Leaving here by ten-twenty and arriving Waterloo two-twenty."

"I see. Will you be returning?"

"I should very much like to, but I'm not sure. There are two or three old friends I ought to go and see while I'm in England. Anyway, give me your London address and perhaps I'll roll up there some day when least expected."

"Your last appearance came in the category of the unexpected," I said as I complied with his request.

"Yes, it must have been a bit of a shock to you fellows," he said, laughing. "By the way, I haven't an address to exchange with yours, but care of my solicitors, Lord and Randall, Norfolk Street, will always find me." As he was speaking Arbuthnot entered the dining-room.

"Here's a pretty kettle of fish," he said. "I've broken the key of my suit-case. The tragedy is that it contains the only ready cash I have in the world and I want to send off an urgent telegram. You had my last half-crown for tobacco, yesterday, King, so I know you've none either."

"Not a penny," I said, hastily withdrawing my hand from my trouser pocket, where it had gone during the early part of his remarks.

"Lend me your keys. Perhaps one may happen to fit the lock." I handed over my bunch and he went out with them. In a couple of minutes he was back.

"No luck," said he, returning them to me.

"Try mine," suggested Rodd, holding them out to Arbuthnot, "but if they don't work, I'm quite ready to be your banker for the time being. Moderate rate of interest on note of hand only. Strictest privacy guaranteed. No embarrassing inquiries," he added, chuckling.

Arbuthnot took the keys and went out. This time it was some little while before he returned and I sat with about fifteen shillings in silver in my trouser pocket, fearful that at any moment a careless movement might cause it to chink, and in a state of mental confusion over my friend's amazing behaviour. Then the dining-room door opened and Arbuthnot re-entered. His face bore that expression which I was accustomed to see when there was trouble ahead. He returned Rodd his keys with a word of thanks and regret that they had been of no use.

"If you fellows have finished we'll go into the drawing-room," he continued.

"But you've had no breakfast," objected Rodd.

"That must wait," he said, leading the way into the adjacent room. We followed him wonderingly. He carefully closed the door behind us.

"There seems to be a bit of bother on at present," he stated. "The police are here. That's why I asked you to come into this room, so that the hotel domestics might not be in a position to overhear what transpired."

"The police, eh?" said Rodd. "I'm afraid they've got you this time, King." But I noticed that his face had suddenly turned pale.

Arbuthnot reopened the door by which we had just entered. An inspector of police stood in the doorway. Over his shoulder I saw the face of Sergeant Rogers. They advanced into the room and the sergeant closed the door behind him.

"Mr. Thornton Rodd?" said the inspector.

"That's me."

"I hold a warrant for your arrest."

"The devil you do! On what charge?"

"On the charge of being concerned in the murder of Dalton Flyte at Freshwater Bay on the night of the twenty-fifth to twenty-sixth May. And it is my duty to warn you that any statement you make may be used in evidence against you."

6
Events of Thursday, May 31st

"I suppose this isn't by any chance a joke?" asked Rodd, who seemed to have regained composure.

"I'm afraid not," said the inspector dryly.

We must have formed a curious group as we stood there, the officials intent on their duty, Arbuthnot, with the shadow of a grin on his face, standing aloof, Rodd facing his captors in a pose that was not entirely devoid of dignity, and I with my mouth open, as I later realized to my annoyance.

"I hope it won't take you long to establish my innocence," went on Rodd, attempting to laugh.

"That doesn't rest with me," returned the inspector. "I've a car waiting outside, and if you'll oblige us by coming along quietly you'll be treated with every consideration."

"Where are you taking me?"

"To Newport."

"I see." He turned to us. "There's more than one way of spending a holiday," he said. "Would it be troubling you fellows too much to ask you to look after my few belongings until I leave the court without a stain on my character?"

"No trouble at all," I said cheerfully, for while I was in a hopeless muddle mentally, I appreciated that Rodd

was facing with a large amount of courage what must have
been a stunning blow.

"No need, sir," put in the inspector. "His personal possessions will be taken charge of by the authorities."

"Righto!" said Rodd. "Just let me get my hat and a little spare cash I have upstairs and I'm with you. The criminal maintained his iron composure to the very foot of
the scaffold," he added, and Arbuthnot's grin broadened,
while the two officials began to look annoyed.

"Very well," said the inspector gruffly. "But I must
accompany you."

Rodd paused and looked round at us in turn and then
at the bay sparkling in the May morning. "I don't like
the idea of this confinement," he observed. "Neither do I
appreciate the sound of the domestic snuffling at the key-
hole of the door."

Three of us at any rate turned instinctively in that
direction, and with one bound he was through the open
French window and out of the room. A long-drawn shout
of "Gone away" came floating back.

In a fraction of a second the hue and cry had begun. We
all made a wild dash to follow. Sergeant Rogers was first
through the exit, and had he not unfortunately tripped
on the threshold we might have stood a chance of saving
a stern chase. I had a glimpse of Rodd vaulting the hotel
railings, crossing the road outside, dashing across a strip
of waste land that lay behind the esplanade, diving into a
hedge of tamarisk bushes and emerging on the main road.
He ran like an athlete. We pursuers fought shy of the railings and doubled across the hotel garden to the usual way
out. The inspector was first, I was five yards behind, and
the good Rogers, who seemed to have suffered by his fall,
was a poor third. I panted on, wondering what had become
of Arbuthnot, who I knew could run. The loiterer whom I

had rewarded the previous evening stood at the corner. He removed his pipe from his mouth as I passed.

"You'll never catch he," he observed. I was beginning to think so myself.

Rodd was now mounting the slope to the golf-links and the chase was strung out behind in the order I have described but augmented by the hotel waiter and the driver of the police car. There appeared in sight a mixed foursome about to drive off from the first tee. Realizing that the fugitive was gaining on us we raised loud shouts. The golfers stared round, and, seeing the police, must have grasped what was happening, for the men of the party came running to intercept Rodd. One of them was too late in starting, but the other was well-positioned to effect a capture. Rodd ran straight at him. The golfer dropped his driver and sprang in for a tackle. Thinking it was coming to a hand-to-hand struggle we redoubled our efforts to catch up. Then at the critical moment Rodd swerved on his heels—I have seen it done worse at Twickenham—eluded his would-be captor by inches, and ran on. It was then we realized his objective.

A small car, presumably the property of some person playing on the links, stood on the military road. With one bound Rodd was in the driving seat. There was a sudden roar from the engine, a jarring of gears, and the car jumped forward, while the gallant golfer took a flying leap at the back, missed it by a hair's breadth, and fell on his face in the road.

"Back to our own car!" shouted the inspector, angrily turning about, and I saw Rodd look round in his seat and impudently wave his hand in farewell. By the time we got back to the hotel a considerable crowd had assembled, but I did not see Arbuthnot anywhere.

"Rogers," said the inspector sharply, "get on to the 'phone. Let Newport know what has happened and ask

them to warn all stations and especially Ryde, Cowes, and
Yarmouth. Describe what he was wearing. We don't want
the fellow to get away from the island. Are you coming
with us, sir?" he added to me.

"Certainly," I said and dashed into the hotel for my hat
and stick. Honestly, I didn't quite know why I should be
joining in the pursuit with such alacrity, for though it is
the duty of loyal citizens to assist the police in the execution of their duty, there was no compulsion to go rushing
around a whole county in a car, especially after a man
with whom I had lived on friendly terms for some days.
I suppose it was the age-old instinct of the chase which
some people mistakenly call blood-lust. I am sure I had no
desire to shed Rodd's blood, but I thrilled at the prospect
of running him to ground.

"Is your friend coming?" asked the inspector as I clam-
bered back into the car.

"I haven't seen him," I said.

"The gentleman took the hotel car and went out," an
hotel servant informed us.

"Very likely he's already on the scent," I suggested.

The inspector hesitated.

"I don't know the best road to take," he said. "I don't
think the wanted man will follow the military road very
far, for it's very open country that way and it leads away
from where he would want to go. I expect he'll come up
through Brook on to the upper road to Newport, for if
he goes through Brighstone and Shorwell he's bound to
be stopped sooner or later. The news will be all over the
island in quarter of an hour. If we take the upper road
to Newport and are quick about it we might cut him off
where the road from Brook joins it."

"Where the hell is my car?" said an indignant voice on
the outskirts of the gathering, and a perspiring man in
plus-fours thrust himself to the front.

"Been taken by a man wanted on a serious charge," said the inspector. "He can't be at liberty long, though. If you would go to the public call-office thirty yards up the road, ring up the Newport police, and tell them the number of your car it would help. Stand back there!" This last was to the crowd. The car moved forward, swung away from the bay, accelerated, and we were soon humming eastwards.

"We've lost some time," said the inspector, "but he's gone the longer way. Besides, he'll have to stop to open two gates on that road, and there's a steep climb beyond the village of Brook."

Our road ran nearly straight and we made good going, keeping the long line of downs on our right the whole way, until, obeying an order from the inspector, the driver drew up immediately beyond a cross-roads and slowed his car across so as to form a barrier. The officer and I got out and walked the few yards back to where the Brook road joined the main highway. There was no sign of any car.

"We'll get down behind the hedge here," said he. "If he comes round the corner he'll have to pull up sharp when he sees our car across the road. That's our chance to nab him."

"Supposing he's armed?" I suggested.

"We've good reason to believe he isn't," replied the inspector.

"How so?"

"Why, it was his pistol that was picked up on the cliff."

"The devil, it was!" I ejaculated, and all the old suspicions that I had discarded came rushing back on me with tenfold force.

"Bit of a surprise, eh?" remarked he.

"It is. How did you trace it?"

"He'd bought it from a firm of gunsmiths in Piccadilly about two years ago. They had the sale registered in his name. The number was sent up to London from here on

Monday evening, and they'd traced it and informed us by yesterday midday."

"Good work," I said, and relapsed on to my own thoughts, which, I need scarcely say, were all on the subject of the extraordinary conduct of Thornton Rodd.

"And that's not all we've got against him, either," continued the inspector, "but I think we're wasting time here. He either passed before we got here or else he's not coming this way at all. We'll go on to Brook and make inquiries." We drove slowly on, keeping a sharp look-out ahead for a car approaching. The road ran southward, rose gradually as we neared the downs and then dipped sharply downhill. So we came to the village of Brook, and here it was we got our first news of the man we hunted. We met an old man trudging along the road towards us.

"Have you seen a car passing this way?" called out the inspector as we pulled up.

"A smallish car like?"

"That's right."

"I seed such a one 'bout ten minutes ago. Come from Brook it did, and passed me back along the road."

"Who was in it?"

"A youngish fellow was driving. There weren't nobody else in it."

"Was he wearing a soft hat and a navy blue suit?"

"Mebbe he was."

"Then why haven't we met him on our way?" I asked the inspector. "Ten minutes ago we were at the crossroads."

"If it was his car this man saw, he must have branched off to the right and taken the road through Brighstone and Shorwell. In that case I don't think he'll get very far."

We turned the car round and taking the first road on our right drove along the way to Brighstone. Within a mile we met an omnibus whose driver remembered passing such a car a couple of miles or so after he had left Shorwell. Thus encouraged we pushed rapidly on and presently overtook a farm-labourer as we neared Brighstone village.

"We'll ask again," said the inspector. "He's had a chance of taking a by-road since we last inquired. Hullo, you, there!"

"Hullo, yourself," returned the labourer cheerfully.

"Has a car coming from the direction of Brook passed you recently?"

"There were one."

"A small, open car."

"Zo you might zay."

"There was a young man driving it?"

"Right you are."

"He was wearing a soft hat and a navy blue suit?"

"Zure enough."

"That was Rodd for certain!" cried the inspector.

"No, it weren't. It were Mr. Smith from Brighstone Old Farm," answered the labourer stolidly.

"Then why the devil didn't you say so at first?"

"Because you didn't ask."

The inspector and I looked at each other, and then, despite the annoyance we both felt, we burst out laughing. It was so manifestly a score for the labourer.

"Sure it was Mr. Smith?" queried the inspector.

"Ain't a fool. I works for en," was the answer.

"Well, drink his health to-night," I said, parting with a fraction of my fifteen shillings.

"The bus driver's information may also have referred to Smith," said the inspector gloomily. "Now we don't know where we are. Better push on, I suppose."

So we came through Brighstone and travelled on to Shorwell. Here we found that the news of the escape had arrived. A farm-wagon had been drawn across the road and the village constable stood on guard with an *ils ne passe-ront pas* air, taking no heed of the mingled prayers and imprecations addressed to him by the driver of a car which was held up by the formidable obstacle.

"You may be Smith and you may not be," the former was saying as we pulled up alongside the other car, "but you answer to the description, so here you'll stay. Here's Mr. Farrell. He'll decide it."

"This isn't the man," said the inspector. "There should be a later telephone message giving the number of the missing car. You can let this gentleman pass."

"Quite right to hold him up as you did," I added.

We questioned the constable, but he had no information of any likely car having passed through before the road was barred. I attempted to put myself mentally in the fugitive's position. His obvious aim was to escape from the island. He would know that all the steamboat routes would be watched and that long before he could hope to land at Portsmouth, Southampton, or Lymington, even if he succeeded in leaving the island, the telephone would have issued its warnings for the scrutiny of passengers. Clearly his only hope was to lie concealed during the day and after dark to make for the northern shores of the island, steal a boat from some secluded creek, and perform his crossing in that. I explained my ideas to Farrell and he was inclined to agree.

"It seems to me," I added, "that we should consider any likely hiding-places in the island. They should be searched before dusk, and the north coast of the island should also be patrolled and boat-owners warned to guard their craft."

"A very sound idea. I think I'd better go to Newport and make my report first. I've no doubt they'll give us plenty of searching to do afterwards."

It was midday when we drove into Newport. I could see that the news had spread. Several hands pointed to me, and I feared their owners regarded me as the culprit recaptured, which was a peculiar position for one who is a justice of the peace in his own county. Captain Bernard was seated in his office answering the telephone when we entered. He seemed quite pleased to see me.

"Is Arbuthnot with you?" he asked.

"No," I said. "He's exploring somewhere on his own."

"I see. Your friend Rodd seems a slippery customer. But he'll have his work cut out to get away from this island."

"Could it be done?" I inquired.

"I doubt it. From time to time convicts escape from Parkhurst Prison. They may remain at liberty for a certain time, but none has ever succeeded in getting clean away."

"I was very startled to hear that Rodd was implicated in the crime," I remarked.

"We don't know that he is, but there were sufficient grounds for arresting him."

"I've heard about the pistol," I said. "What else is there against him?"

"This is hardly the time to go into it," said the superintendent, "but his conduct all along has been peculiar. To begin with, his story of spending the night on the downs took a bit of believing."

"So I thought at the time," I admitted, "but later on I began to consider that he was the sort of happy-go-lucky fellow who would think nothing of it."

"Perhaps. Then the finding of his walking-stick in the hall-stand, though easily explicable in itself, begins to look very queer when associated with other points. There was his bicycle to account for."

"Ah!" said I. "Arbuthnot said he had a bicycle."

"Did he? I wonder how he tumbled to it? At any rate, Rodd bought a bicycle in Cowes on the evening that the crime was committed, and that bicycle was later found lying in a field near Newport. We traced the vendor, and his description of the purchaser tallied with that of Rodd, so he was taken to Freshwater yesterday evening to have a peep at Rodd, and identified him at once as the man who had bought the bicycle."

"I saw the fellow," I said. "He was looking through the window while we were at dinner. I was rather alarmed at the time, I don't mind confessing."

"Well, you see that Mr. Rodd's conduct takes a good deal of explaining. Now, inspector, let's hear your report."

Before Farrell had finished detailing our experiences of the morning the telephone bell was ringing. "This, I hope, indicates that our friend's brief spell of liberty is over," said Bernard, taking off the receiver.

The conversation that ensued was brief and Bernard's last remark was conclusive.

"Very well. We'll send along for him at once," he said, and hung up the receiver. "Captured at St. Helens," he told us. "That's at the eastern end of the island," he added for my benefit.

"Can't see how he got so far without being spotted," remarked Inspector Farrell.

"Nor I. Hullo! What's this?" The telephone was ringing again. Bernard promptly answered it.

"Confound it!" he cried, turning to us. "He's also been captured lurking behind some bushes in Blackgang Chine."

The inspector and I both burst out laughing.

"I don't believe that," I said. "No man trying to escape from the island would be found in that direction."

"I quite agree," said Bernard. "I must warn them to treat their captive with respect. He's probably some perfectly innocent person."

"Is a general search being conducted?" I asked, when the telephone conversation was over.

"More or less. The troops have turned out and are combing Parkhurst Forest, which is always a likely hiding-place.

All the outlying houses which are on the 'phone have been or are being warned. At four o'clock, when school is over, the Boy Scouts are joining in the search if the fellow hasn't been captured by then. I need hardly tell you that all passengers leaving the island are closely watched. I imagine I'd better run over to St. Helens and Blackgang and see which of the victims is Rodd. You can identify him most easily. Would you like to come?"

"Certainly I'll come," said I, and in a few minutes we were running swiftly eastwards.

I will be brief over the disappointments of that afternoon. The St. Helens capture turned out to be a peaceful botanist who, while pursuing his interesting hobby on the dover or spit there, which is noted for its plant life, was seized upon by three or four local lads and haled into confinement. The general description of Rodd fitted him, and as he spent most of his time crawling on hands and knees suspicion had been aroused. We apologized profusely and made all speed for Blackgang, only to be confronted with a formidable proposition in the person of Mr. Hiram K. Thacker, who had been collected from a secluded nook half-way down the chine, where he had been enjoying a quiet snooze after a morning's hard sightseeing. He had an almost ineradicable suspicion that the outrage upon him was in some way connected with the production of a humorous film. When he grasped the truth, however, he rose to the occasion magnificently.

"I've a car on the road," he announced, "and I'm at your service. Any low hound who goes around bloodletting in a wonder-show like this deserves all that's coming to him. I've a map right here, and I'll sure go wherever you tell me."

"Come along then," said Bernard tactfully. "The man is still at liberty and we're glad of all help."

It was three o'clock before we saw Newport again. Inspector Farrell, looking anything but pleased, was awaiting us.

"We were properly sold this morning," he said.

"You've had news!" I cried.

"I should think I have. I know now how we came to miss him this morning. The cheek of the fellow is beyond belief. You remember that when we found he had been seen on the road from Brook and yet had not passed the crossroads where we waited, we decided he must have gone to his right through Brighstone."

"Quite so," I said. "Didn't he?"

"Not he! He turned to his *left* and went into the grounds of Brook Manor. He was quick enough to guess what we should do and allowed for it."

"How was it he wasn't spotted there?" I asked.

"Spotted! He drove straight up to the door, rang the bell, and made himself out to be a representative of *Country Life* who wanted to see over the place with a view to writing it up in that publication!"

"Say, that young man's no fool," interpolated Mr. Thacker, who was still in our company.

"The family are away," continued the inspector, "and the servant on duty was easily deceived by Rodd's smart appearance and way of talking. Besides, he actually had a copy of the paper, which he must have found in the car he stole. He spent a quarter of an hour there choosing suitable subjects for photographic reproduction, as he alleged, gave the servant half a crown, and drove gaily away. No doubt while he was examining the beauties of the flower garden the telephone was ringing in the house."

"And nothing has been heard of him since?" queried Bernard.

"Not a word. This message only came half an hour ago, when the news of the escape happened to reach the Manor by word of mouth."

"He must be caught," said the superintendent. "Apart from his own conduct, which requires investigation, he is at present the chief hope we have of clearing up this case, since there is no information forthcoming at present about either Dalton Flyte or the man who was killed at Bouldnor Cliff."

"Since the number of the stolen car has been circulated I can't understand why he has remained unnoticed so long," I said.

"He probably had the sense to know that the car would eventually give him away and so abandoned it early in the day."

"Most likely. I wonder no one has come across it."

As I was speaking the tintinnabulation of the telephone began again, and the message that came through supplied a commentary to my remark. The car had been found in a field not far from Brook. A high hedge had screened it from the road, and the crop, which was oats, had partly masked it from the other side. Bernard left the telephone and went to a large local map that hung on the wall of his office.

"That, I hope, simplifies matters," he said. "Here between Freshwater and Newport, is the only considerable area of downland in the island. It is well cut up by valleys and partly covered by copses and furze brakes, the latter especially affording good hiding-places, as anyone who rides to hounds will tell you."

"And at night he would only have three miles or so to go to reach Newtown Creek, where he might hope to steal a boat," put in the inspector.

"So you think he took to the downs from the point where he left the car?" I asked.

"I do. It was quite a good idea of his if he did so, for one's first thought would be that he would use the car to get as far as possible from his starting-point," replied

the superintendent. He looked at his watch. "It is nearly
four o'clock," he added. "Thanks to fine weather and sum-
mer-time we can count on daylight till nine-thirty at any
rate. That gives us five and a half hours to catch him, and
I should not feel comfortable with a person of Mr. Rodd's
ingenuity at liberty all night."

"Could he swim the straits?" I asked.

"It would be courting death to do so at night. The tidal
currents are swift and treacherous."

Since the events I record I have found time to size up
on the map the area we set out to search that evening. I
estimate that the extent of the downland in which a man
could hope to lie concealed was not more than sixteen
square miles, which doesn't sound very much. In addition,
much of this was smooth chalk slopes where the short
grass would not have afforded cover to a rat. On the other
hand, there were many copses with undergrowth and, what
is more important, much furze. Men and dogs alike have a
rooted objection to the prickly advances of the latter.

There was no lack of help forthcoming. Stirred by various impulses, volunteers offered themselves in dozens.
After a considerable amount of telephoning, during which
the hands of the clock progressed at least an hour, the
disposition of the available forces was as follows. A party from Freshwater, under the command of our friend
Sergeant Rogers and reinforced by the golfer whose nose
had suffered by contact with the road in the morning,
and the other whose car had been stolen, was preparing
to move eastwards towards Brook. Contingents were being assembled in the villages of Brighstone and Shorwell,
and a strong party was mustering to explore up the valley
that runs south-westwards from Newport and carries the
road we had taken the day the boy shot himself at Brook.
Inspector Farrell, myself, and Mr. Thacker were detailed
as a motor patrol, for which the last-named offered his

car. It was our duty to keep running on the upper road to Freshwater in case the fugitive attempted to flee north-wards. We should have a good view of the north side of the downs, and if we saw a chase in progress we could travel swiftly to a position to head off the quarry. At half-past five, with four hours of daylight remaining, we moved off on our task.

"This is sure a great country," declaimed Mr. Thacker as we sailed through the suburb of Carisbrooke and came to the open country-side. "Fields the size of a kitchen tablecloth and hedges round 'em twenty feet thick! I guess I'll form a syndicate and buy the whole darned show as a rest-camp for broken-down millionaires."

"I fancy the inhabitants of the place might want a say in that matter," I observed dryly.

"Sure. They would need humouring some," he agreed, and conversing in this manner we drove into the village of Calbourne a few minutes before six o'clock and refilled our petrol tank. Continuing westwards, where the road runs more nearly adjacent to the downs, we were rewarded by the sight of half a dozen men strung out in a line across the down and working in the opposite direction to us. We were forbidden to use the whistles we had with us unless we had actually sighted Rodd, but Mr. Thacker produced a pair of powerful prism binoculars, with whose help we could see that one of the party was a policeman.

"That's the Freshwater party," said Farrell. "There's no point in our going any farther that way."

Hiram K. Thacker swung the car round.

"Seems to me we are missing all the fun of this Oregon trail business," he declared. "Can't we park the vehicle somewhere and draw cards ourselves. Never use your best brains on routine operations."

I was inclined to sympathize, but the inspector was adamant.

"It's good fun to you, gentlemen," he said, "but we mustn't forget that it's really a matter of life and death, and orders are orders. Besides, the sport might come our way in the end."

We drove slowly back to Calbourne, meeting one or two pedestrians, who gazed curiously at us, but seeing no signs of the hunt. It was already half-past six, and, although the day was still of noontide brightness, a coolness in the air betokened the approach of night. It was as if one could feel the shadows impending before their arrival. The inspector looked anxiously at his watch,

"Another three hours and he'll have the whole night to play about in," he vouchsafed.

"This gets my goat," said Thacker suddenly. "Can you drive a car?"

"I can."

"Then take charge of this Sister Anne show as a going concern while I stretch my legs. We'll meet again later at this same point."

Before I could utter a protest he was twenty yards away. Farrell looked at me and shook his head.

"He can't do any harm," I said.

"I'm not so sure about that," was his answer, as we watched our acquaintance progressing rapidly towards the spur of the downs that juts out towards Calbourne.

I started up the car and we ran slowly back towards Newport until we stopped at a little inn called the "Blacksmith's Arms" about three miles from the town. Perfect peace reigned everywhere. Hunted, hunters, and Hiram K. Thacker might have been conducting their affairs in another county.

"Might as well go back," I said, and the inspector moodily agreed.

We were not far from Calbourne on our return journey when we heard the first whistle. We had reached a stage when we had begun to believe that nothing was going to happen, and we both jumped at the sudden warning.

"Where did it come from?" I asked.

"From the down nearly due south of us. There it is again! Drive on a little way and we can look up one of the valleys that run south."

There is something peculiarly thrilling about the sound of a police-whistle, especially when heard under such circumstances. I pushed the car gradually along until Farrell bade me stop, and all the time I could feel my heart beating hard with excitement. Where we came to a standstill we could see up a narrow combe that ran well into the downs.

"There he comes!" shouted Farrell, gripping my arm. A little dark figure appeared on the hill-side and dived into the combe. The shrilling of whistles continued. Then four or five pursuers burst upon our view, and then more, strung out like a tired pack. They were probably a mile away at first and we had plenty of time to watch the chase. I snatched up the binoculars.

"He's coming this way!" cried Farrell. "Start up your engine!" I did so and hastily took up the glasses again. Then I flung them on the seat of the car with an expression more idiomatic than elegant.

"It's Thacker!" I cried.

"Good Lord! I might have guessed it," breathed the inspector.

Hiram K. reached us about ten yards in front of a man with a pitchfork.

"Say," he gasped, as he leaped for safety into the car, "the rush hour on the Elevated is nothing to this!"

"Serve you right," I said angrily, and turned to pacify as best as I could the furious members of the Brighstone patrol.

"I would have stayed to explain," said Thacker plaintively, "but I realized just in time that these chaps had never seen the wanted man and that my yarn would cut no ice. They were out for my blood."

"They still are," I returned. "You've probably upset everything."

Whistles were now sounding in all directions, and I pictured various parties converging towards the scene of the false alarm.

"I'd better go back with these fellows and explain things," I told Farrell.

"And I'll glue myself to the road," said Thacker repentantly.

Thus I led a very irritated and dispirited contingent back to the hills. As I feared, the search-parties were closing in from all sides. And it was nearly eight o'clock. The shadows seemed to grow longer as I watched them. On my suggestion men were detached to try and pick up the other parties and inform them of what had happened. The rest of us sat down on the hill-top and lit our pipes, and there were soon joined by the three other bodies. Bernard was there himself, and in none too good a temper. Apart from the abortive chase of our impulsive acquaintance no one had anything to report. Under the circumstances there was only one thing to do. Each party was to return home, making a thorough search as it went. By that time night would have fallen, and a clever man could have eluded a battalion of searchers on those downs after dark. I volunteered to return to the road and tell the car patrol what had been decided.

As might have been expected, there was no car visible when I reached Calbourne, but this was the less important as there was an inn at the cross-roads from whose window I could watch the road. It was nearly dusk when a dejected-looking Thacker drove slowly past. My shouts arrested him in his progress.

"My name is Mud," he said dismally as I came up. "The youth of the district will hoot at me in the streets. I shall be a byword and a reproach."

"You've certainly asked for it," I said brutally.

"I sure have," he said unhappily. Then he suddenly brightened. "Say," he remarked, "all those other fellows have beaten it back home by now. That's just the time when our shy friend, if he's hiding somewhere up there, will pop out to take the air and wave 'em *au revoir*. I'll make a proposition. You and I will take a stroll round way yonder. If we nail him, the honour and glory will sure be handed out to us, and I shall be able to hold up my head again."

"It'll be dark in half an hour," I objected, for I had no particular fancy for nocturnal perambulations in search of a wily and possibly desperate man.

"The very time when he'll be taking a peep to get his bearings before night," urged he.

I could see he was in deadly earnest. A great deal of discussion followed, in the course of which I eventually agreed to return to Freshwater by way of the downs. I had been sitting in a car nearly all day and was not averse to stretching my legs over a matter of six miles, but I resolutely declined to embark on a general search with an enthusiast who knew even less about the district than I did. He reluctantly agreed to accept my concession, and the inspector volunteered to take the car back to Newport. The semi-darkness of a May night overtook us as we strode up the road that crosses the downs from Calbourne to Brighstone, but in the north-west the sky was still pearly, toning to a pale saffron on the horizon. At the highest point of the road we should find a footpath leading to the right that would take us over the downs directly to Freshwater. I was keeping a look-out for this path when Thacker suddenly clutched my arm.

"There's some guy up there!" he said in a hoarse whisper, pointing to the slope that rose on our left. "I thought it was a bush at first, but then it moved."

Now to my dying day I shall firmly believe, in spite of what happened afterwards, that Thacker saw nothing on the down at that time and was merely using a fraudulent device to lure me into the search I had declined to share.

"I can't see anything," I answered, straining my eyes in vain to pierce the gloom.

"It went away over to that patch of bushes," he said. "I believe the fellow was coming down to cross the road when he got a sight of us. Come on!" Before he had finished speaking he was scrambling over a gate that led to the down. I hesitated, for I was vastly suspicious, but some irrational part of my mind told me that I could not leave him to go on alone. Inwardly cursing, I followed him over the gate. As we neared the furze it resolved itself into a fair-sized clump, including some high old furze near the centre that would have sheltered several men. Thacker, possibly being unused to the indigenous vegetation, thrust boldly in and recoiled with curses, quiet but hearty.

"There are generally little tracks made by foxes, rabbits, and such animals that run in and out of the gorse. Let's find one," I suggested in his ear. "Wading through gorse is unpleasant."

"No more Yale blues on a vegetable porcupine for me," he declared in an intense whisper.

"Here you are," I said in low tones, discerning with difficulty a little track of trodden grass that vanished into the gorse. The more I looked at it the less I liked it.

"Suppose I go round the other side and wait in case he dashes out?" I added, thoroughly believing that Thacker had drawn me into the search under false pretences.

"Fine," he said briefly. Then he dropped on his hands and knees, wriggled forward, and was lost to sight. I strolled slowly round to the far side of the clump, my feet moving soundlessly on the springy down turf, until I judged I was about opposite the point where Thacker had entered the furze. Here I sat down in the lee of an outlying bush and thought regretfully of a long-overdue dinner, cursing myself for being a weak-minded fool to yield to another man's whim. I must have been there nearly five minutes when my ear caught the crackling noise the old, dry furze makes when anything moves in it. The sound grew louder, and I realized that Thacker would reappear near where I sat, so I scrambled to my feet in order not to hurt his feelings by appearing disinterested in the hunt. It would be some consolation to me to hear his language when he came out. A little dark patch isolated itself from the rest of the clump and moved towards me.

"Had a rough passage?" I asked.

The patch made no answer. It moved on, and rapidly at that, but its direction was no longer towards me. In a second I realized what had happened. *The patch was not Thacker!*

"Thacker!" I yelled. "Come on! He's broken cover!"

"Hell!" said the voice of Thacker from the middle of the furze. There were sounds of violent tramplings and more expletives. I judged I had better not wait for him, and dashed forward in the direction the quarry had gone, blowing shrill blasts on my whistle as I went in case any of the retiring parties might hear them. The next minute I had stepped in a rabbit hole and was lying with my nose embedded in the turf.

"Where are you?" came in a shout from behind.

"Here," I cried, struggling up and fortunately finding myself little damaged.

"Which way did he go?" Thacker asked, coming up panting.

"Over there," I said, vaguely pointing into the darkness.

"Come on then!"

He dashed forward, and I followed, feeling nevertheless the futility of the whole business. The man had gone. He might be anywhere within a circle of half a mile radius. In the darkness we might have passed him within ten yards and never seen him. Even Thacker was forced to admit the justice of my remarks after we had devoted an unsuccessful hour to our task and completely lost ourselves in the progress.

"I'm going home," I said very definitely.

"I'll push on to Newport, where my car is," he answered. I directed him as best as I could by the stars, asked him to inform the police in the morning of what we had seen, and then turned westward at eleven o'clock to face a matter of nine miles, as I judged, to Freshwater.

As I walked I grew wearier and wearier, and I wished Thornton Rodd and Hiram K. Thacker every doom the savagery of man could devise. It was two o'clock in the morning when I trapesed past the dimly-seen bungalow where our trouble had begun and saw a light still shining from a lower window of the Stagrock Hotel. I quickened my steps. Hope revived. Probably Arbuthnot was staying up for me and had reserved some kind of stimulant for my famished body.

"At last!" I said as I flung open the drawing-room door of the hotel. Then I gaped and fell back in utter amazement. There was Arbuthnot sitting in an arm-chair and nursing the inevitable pipe.

Opposite to him sat Thornton Rodd.

7
Events of May 31st and June 1st

There is nothing more deplorable to my mind than the modern habit of falling back on coarse language as a medium of forceful expression, yet on this occasion I transgressed my own code in a most flagrant manner.

"You would appear to have had a trying day, King," said Arbuthnot soothingly.

"Yes, looking for that idiot," I stuttered angrily, indicating Rodd. "How long has he been here?"

"Quite a couple of hours, I should say. But I hardly think he deserves your last epithet. I gather that he gave you all a good run for your money."

"Your assistance wasn't exactly conspicuous," I answered hotly.

"Who captured him?" he returned with evident enjoyment.

"Nonsense," I said. "He surrendered himself when he realized that escape out of the island was impossible."

Rodd had been regarding us gloomily and in silence. He now rose. "I suppose I might as well go to bed. Good night," said he.

"Good night," answered Arbuthnot.

I said nothing. Rodd passed out.

"Is it safe to let him go like that?" I asked Arbuthnot.

"He has given me his word of honour to surrender to the police in the morning."

"The word of honour of a murderer!"

"That remains to be seen. Now, if you're not too tired, tell me about your day of adventures."

I had been very weary, but the amazing sight of the unspeakable Rodd sitting quietly at his ease while I had been marching dismal miles after an unavailing pursuit of him had given me the stimulus of anger.

"Very well," said I.

"There are some biscuits and cheese and beer on the table over there," remarked Arbuthnot.

I fell upon the food ravenously, and between mouthfuls I recounted the peculiar events of the day. He listened mostly in a silence which was punctuated by occasional amusement at the exploits of Hiram K. Thacker. Only toward the end of my account did he grow serious. Then he pulled his inseparable companion, the ordnance map, from his pocket.

"Show me exactly where you saw him," he said.

"Here," said I, indicating a point on the downs a little to the east of the road connecting Calbourne with Brighstone.

"At what time?"

"I should say a few minutes after ten o'clock."

"I see. Perhaps we'd better go to bed now."

It was three o'clock before I had carefully secured my bedroom door and got into bed, and even then I did not immediately sleep. The proximity of Rodd worried me. His sublime audacity in face of his guilty secret impressed me with a realization of his possibilities for evil. I recollected that I was a witness against him and felt none too comfortable. Eventually, however, sheer physical exhaustion led me to slumber. When I awoke it was bright day.

Stiff and heavy-eyed I arose, dressed, and found Arbuthnot alone at breakfast.

"Our friend has departed," he said. "In reply to my telephone message the police collected him at eight o'clock, and by now he is in the lock-up at Newport."

"Good," I replied. "Did he go quietly?"

"Like a lamb."

"What a fool to make all that fuss for the sake of a little liberty that he must have known could not be permanent," I growled. "How did he come back?"

"Quite openly."

"And gave himself up to you?"

"No, I met him on the stairs."

"On the stairs! Then he could have turned and run."

"He was coming down the stairs. But come, finish your breakfast as promptly as possible, for I want to go and see if Mr. Williams has heard any more of his prospective tenants. I expect by to-morrow at latest some report on them as a result of the inquiries I set on foot on Wednesday."

We found Mr. Williams in high fettle. He brandished a letter at us as we entered his office.

"The Parker is nosey, as you might expect," he cried, "but the gent who got his name from the pictures seems to have given in."

Arbuthnot read the proffered letter with interest and gave me a summary of the contents.

"Mr. Parker begins by pointing out very courteously the mistake over the address, which has made him aware there is another applicant for the bungalow. He renews his application. He has small means and an ailing wife, and it is only by the generosity of his late employers, for whose firm he worked thirty years, that he is able to take the holiday."

"What shall I tell him?" asked Mr. Williams.

"Reply that you regret that the bungalow has already been let. Point out that as a murder has recently been committed there it seems a very unsuitable place for a sick woman to live in. If he is a genuine applicant that will certainly finish him."

"Right you are."

"If there is any more correspondence about the bungalow I trust you will let me know."

"I will. Can you give me any idea of what's at the bottom of this business?"

"I can't at present. Later on I promise to do so. I owe you that much for your kind assistance."

As he left the office he remarked, "Now do you feel ready for a trip to Newport?"

"You want to be present when Rodd is charged?"

"Not at all. There will only be formal evidence of arrest and a remand to-day."

"What then?"

"I want to arrange for some supervision of that bungalow. While we may be prepared to concede that Mr. Parker is a perfectly innocent man, there yet remains Mr. Edginton to explain. He has apparently relinquished the idea of gaining possession of the bungalow by ordinary means. He may try other methods."

"I don't see why anyone should want to occupy the bungalow at present," I said. "It has been searched. There is nothing of special value left there, nor anything that might serve as evidence."

"I am not theorizing at present," he responded. "The fact remains that one person, if not more, wants the place for some reason. What he wants there we don't know, nor does it matter for the moment. What we have to do is to prevent his getting it."

"You would suggest a police guard?"

"No, I think we can guard it better ourselves if we are allowed. The police have many duties and there are never any to be easily spared for special work."

"Do you mean we should go and live there now?" I asked.

"That's exactly what I do mean."

"I'm not in love with the idea," I remarked.

"Nor I. But I think it our best chance of clearing up this unpleasant little affair we have become involved in."

The superintendent greeted us warmly.

"I was extremely glad to get your message this morning," he said. "I was roused in the small hours by a zealous American who had sighted Rodd on the down near Calbourne and I expected another day's search."

"What will happen to Rodd?" asked Arbuthnot.

"He'll be committed for trial. Of course all the present available evidence is purely circumstantial, but it is ample to send him up. There's plenty of time between now and the next assizes for fresh material to come to light."

"That's very true," said Arbuthnot. "For example, I know one thing at present that will take a deal of explaining."

"Indeed? What's that?"

"You remember that Dalton Flyte used three iron bars to protect the door between the hall and the kitchen. On Saturday last when we examined the place one bar was missing."

"I know. A very peculiar thing."

"On Monday evening when, with permission of your sergeant, I made a further inspection the bar had returned," continued Arbuthnot.

"Really! That's extraordinary. The disappearance of the bar and the return of the bar. What do you make of it?"

Arbuthnot shook his head.

"It seems to me that the bar was originally stolen to clear a way of getting into the house," I interposed.

"That way was not used," objected Bernard. "In fact we are still puzzling as to how the man did get in."

"He may have intended to get in that way and then been obliged to change his plans," I pointed out.

"To me the return of the bar is more significant," said the superintendent, "because presumably it was done by some one in the locality."

I stared at him. The same thought was in both our minds.

"Piling up suspicion against Rodd?" asked Arbuthnot genially. "May I make a suggestion?"

"Certainly."

"The bungalow should be guarded."

The superintendent looked thoughtful. "Do you think it worth while?" he asked finally.

"Somewhere in this district is, or was, a man able to go in and out of that place at will," answered Arbuthnot. "If it was Rodd, well and good—but supposing it wasn't. The unknown may return. I don't propose that you should employ any of your men on the job. I suggest that King and I should go there. Can it be arranged?"

"It can certainly be arranged," replied Bernard. "There will be no difficulty about that. But I doubt if you'll gain very much. However, I'll fix it up for you."

"Thanks very much. I suppose you know that Williams, the owner of the bungalow, has already had two applications to rent it since the crime occurred?"

The superintendent lifted his eyebrows. "I wasn't aware of it," he said. "It seems curious that anyone should want to live there just at present. I begin to see some sense in your proposed guard. When do you intend to begin?"

"To-night," said Arbuthnot cheerfully.

"Very well. I'll give you a letter to Sergeant Rogers, who has the keys." He wrote it out while we waited.

"By the way, you'll be required in court to-morrow," he said. "Both of you. At ten o'clock."

"It looks to me as if Rodd is in for a thoroughly unpleasant time," I remarked to Arbuthnot as we left.

"You sound vindictive, King."

"I had begun to like the fellow," I explained. "No one cares to be befooled by an artful scoundrel. The audacity of the man passes belief."

We spent that afternoon interviewing Sergeant Rogers, engaging the services of Mrs. Morris, who displayed some initial reluctance to return to the scene of the tragedy, moving our belongings to the bungalow, and settling in. The same evening marked temporarily the end of the fine weather. Clouds appeared, dusk set in earlier than usual with a strange yellow light impending over the west, and a variable breeze came in sudden little puffs that rattled the shutters of the bungalow. I was uneasy. The natural fears that anyone might have felt at our peculiar position were enhanced by those qualms which come over many people when a storm is approaching.

After Mrs. Morris had given us our dinner and departed homewards I mooted a suggestion for closing up the bungalow.

"With this system of shutters and our full complement of bars to the door we ought to be fairly safe," I remarked.

"Safe?" echoed Arbuthnot. "We didn't come here to be safe!"

"I don't understand."

"It is our business to welcome the intruder. We are here in the hope of finding out something. Beyond locking the outer doors and fastening the windows we shall take no precautions."

My back was towards a window as he spoke. I twisted round in my seat and saw that night was nearly upon us. No longer could I discern the dividing line between sea and sky. The waves below us that had been quiescent so long were making little whispering noises, and now and again a kind of moan would draw across the sea as if some aqueous spirit complained in its sleep. I got up and closed the drawing-room window.

"A gloomy evening," I said, and then added, "Aren't you afraid of being shot through a window? I should feel much more comfortable with the shutters closed."

"Who is going to shoot us?" he demanded. "If you stop to think it would be the most incredibly foolish action a person could undertake. If anyone retains an interest in this place he will not wish to draw attention to the fact."

"I'm very glad that Rodd is not about, anyway," I answered, "for it is quite possible to suppose that he is the one interested in this place."

"I'm going to bed at ten," said Arbuthnot, "leaving you on duty from then till one, when I will relieve you. That gives us half an hour. If you like, let us go over one or two peculiarities in the recent conduct of our friend Rodd that deserve some explanation."

"By all means carry on," I cried. "You haven't had much to say about things so far."

"I would refer," said he, "to the scene yesterday morning when Rodd was arrested. Did it strike you that at the beginning he accepted the position philosophically?"

"It seemed so."

"Then he changed his mind. Now can you remember the order of the conversation?"

"He asked us to look after his luggage," I said.

"Yes, and the police indicated that they would take it in their charge."

"Then he asked if he might go upstairs," I went on.

"And the reply was that he might do so if he were accompanied."

"Quite right. Then it was that he made his unexpected dash for freedom."

"That is where your phrase betrays you, King. He made no dash for freedom at all."

"I don't see what you mean," I answered.

"This is what I mean. His pretence at escaping was to divert attention from something else."

"What?"

"Something he had concealed in his luggage. He rightly judged that in the hue and cry after his person his belongings would escape attention for some time."

"Go on," I said excitedly, for a thought was rising from the back of my mind into startling prominence.

"He concealed himself at the least possible distance from Freshwater, and then, after dark, not too early for that would have been dangerous, and not too late for then the hotel would have been locked up, he returned, marched boldly in and went upstairs."

"And you met him coming down again!" I cried.

"Yes. And he very promptly and quietly surrendered himself to me," replied Arbuthnot.

"And then had all night to dispossess himself of whatever it was he feared the police would find. By Jove, Arbuthnot, it's a pity we didn't think of this last night!"

"What do you imagine it was he was concerned about," asked my friend.

"I have very little doubt as to what it was,* I said.

"Continue."

"Whoever murdered Flyte probably had a key of the bungalow. Whoever restored the bar also must have had a key. The bar was obviously put back by some one hanging about in this locality. I believe that Thornton Rodd sought to get rid of what would be the most damning piece of evidence that could be brought against him, that is—the key."

"We can't always be lucky," said Arbuthnot. "If your
idea is correct it should relieve you of some of the discomfort you felt at the prospect of living here. Now I am
going to bed. Call me at one and I will watch till dawn.
Put all lights out after eleven. I'm afraid you will have an
uncomfortable vigil, but we must not lose our opportunities. Naturally, if anything suspicious excites your attention you will rouse me at once."

Following these words he went off, and I set about being as comfortable as I might in the hour that remained.
The window-curtains were not drawn, and though they
were but flimsy white things I preferred them to the black
expanse of glass. As I pulled them together a shuddering
glare gleamed over the sea for a moment and was gone.
Lightning. I had counted twenty before the subdued roll
of thunder came to my ears. Some gimcrack ornament on
the mantelpiece vibrated in sympathy and a little wind
fluttered against the window.

Arbuthnot reappeared in his dressing-gown. "King,"
said he, "there is one little point that deserves your attention."

"Yes?"

"I had a few words with Rodd before he departed this
morning. He told me that no one had chased him on the
downs last night."

"Nobody chased him!"

"Funny, isn't it?" he remarked casually.

"The man was lying," I declared. "His statement was
dictated by some foolish pride that would not let him
admit he had been within an ace of being caught."

"Perhaps so. Still it's strange."

When Arbuthnot had retired again I also, somewhat
against my will, began to think it strange. There seemed
no reason in Rodd's denial. Had Thacker and I merely
flushed a poacher? It did not seem a very likely season for

a poacher to be active. What then? Imagination shrank from the answer. I sat down and tried to become absorbed in a novel until eleven o'clock should place me under the necessity of continuing my watch under sterner conditions. It was little use. The hero was one whose character burgeoned under the influence of a hundred carefully-recorded trivialities. It did not suit my mood.

Lightning again. The flicker behind the curtains caught my eye, which was only half-intent on the book. The roll of thunder that followed was more pronounced than the last. The rising wind made a kind of whispering around the bungalow. Within twenty feet of me, through a door I could not quite see from where I sat, was the spot where the soul of some strange recluse had unwillingly taken flight. I was far from believing in spirit forms and the rest of the paraphernalia of psychomancy, and yet I would not willingly have gone into that room.

When my wrist-watch indicated ten minutes to eleven I went off to my bedroom, which was the one opposite to the dining-room. Lightning gleamed at the window as I entered. I drew the ineffectual curtains and undressed. Then I extinguished my light and in the darkness hastily drew on a pair of plus-fours and struggled into a jersey. A dressing-gown completed my equipment for the two hours of duty that remained to me. Arbuthnot had forbidden lights. Even the striking of a match to light a pipe was interdicted. I felt quite alone, for Arbuthnot was capable of sleeping profoundly at a moment's notice, and I did not dare disturb him for nothing. With beslippered feet I shuffled from my bedroom into the passage. Opposite to me was the dining-room door. I did not choose to enter that room.

After consideration I worked my way along to the kitchen. A flash of lightning would occasionally light up the scene, leaving me in doubt as to what I actually had seen.

The glare would come to me by reflection from picture glass, and through the space between a door and its frame, and in all manner of unexpected ways, so that nothing assumed its familiar daylight shape and position.

Beyond the kitchen, I knew, was the scullery, and beyond that the coal-store. The latter naturally had a second door that communicated directly with the outside world so as to avoid any need of transporting coals through the kitchen. I sat on the kitchen table for perhaps five minutes. The lightning was becoming more vivid and more frequent. At intervals every object in the kitchen would leap suddenly into view, and I took advantage of one of the flashes to set a course towards the scullery door. It was devoid of bolts and operated by a simple latch, and after a little fumbling I got it open and passed on. I spent perhaps another five minutes in the scullery, and it was then that a brilliant idea came to me. The adjacent coal-store had no window, therefore if I got inside there I could smoke with impunity in between tours of inspection of the house. I was sleepy and yet at the same time nervy, and tobacco would be a distinct solace.

Treading softly and carefully, I worked my way back to my bedroom, groped around till I found my jacket on the back of a chair, and then collected pipe, pouch, and matches from the pocket. As I crept back a louder rumble than usual warned me that the onset of the storm was imminent. No sane person could condescend to be afraid of thunder and lightning, but it must be conceded that a storm has power to produce awe. Often on such occasions a pulse in my temple will throb persistently and the hair on the back of my scalp will bristle. Probably science can explain these things, but I am no scientist.

Back in the scullery I felt carefully for the latch of the farther door. For two or three minutes there was no lightning and my search was vain. Then I took an unlucky step

backwards and crashed against the very door I was seeking. I trusted the noise had not awakened Arbuthnot, for
did he investigate I was not sure that he would consider
I could perform my duties adequately in the coal-store. I
waited a couple of minutes, but all was still. Then I very
cautiously lifted the latch and pulled the door open. As I
did so a gust of cool air from outside smote suddenly on
my face and I stood frozen with amazement.

The outer door was open!

What I might have done in this emergency I don't know,
but fortunately for me, as I remained for the moment paralysed, the open doorway became instantaneously a rectan-
gle of dazzling blue, and the light of the flash enabled me
to see that the store was empty. Then the thunder broke
in a succession of staccato crashes, and under cover of the
sound I scrambled over the piled-up coal, pulled the outer
door towards me and hastily secured it with the heavy bolt
my fingers touched when I was manipulating the latch.

Then I absent-mindedly sat down on the coal and per-
spired with memory of a past panic. How on earth had
that door come to be open? Had it most carelessly been
left unfastened days before when the police and Mrs. Morris were at the bungalow? The breeze that had sprung up
with the coming storm might in that case have twitched it
open. I could not remember noting the door on the second
visit Arbuthnot and I had paid to the bungalow. Should I
rouse Arbuthnot and tell him what I had found? A thought
entered my head. Arbuthnot himself was perfectly capable
of leaving the door open to further some plan of his. However, it was now safely bolted, and if I had done wrongly
it was his fault for not confiding in me. I was about to
strike a match to see how much of my spell of duty remained, when an idea struck me cold with horror. Suppose
some one other than my friend and I were at present in
the house? Certainly it was only a bare possibility, but it

was enough to decide me to awaken Arbuthnot. Treading
with infinite caution I worked my way back into the scullery. Here I paused to listen, but to no avail. The wind
was making all kinds of disturbing noises outside, arid
frequently a peal of thunder would set all shaking. It was
comforting to reflect that the same sounds would mask my
own movements were an intruder actually there.

It took me an incredible time to traverse the passage
and reach Arbuthnot where he slept, door ajar, in the front
bedroom. His even breathing, denoting dreamless sleep,
gave me a feeling of pride, for it indicated his confidence
in my watchfulness. I crouched by the head of his bed and
touched him lightly on the shoulder.

"Arbuthnot!" I whispered.

"Yes," he said, almost instantaneously awake.

"Listen. I've found the outer door of the coal-store
open."

"What did you do?" he asked, going direct to the important point without comment.

"Closed it and bolted it."

"I see."

"Arbuthnot," I continued, "do you think anyone has
come into the house that way?"

"I don't. But we might be on the alert."

He sat up in bed, swung his feet to the floor, and stood
up beside me. As he did so the room was suddenly illuminated with a transitory radiance brighter than noonday.
Through the window I saw, for Arbuthnot had not even
bothered to draw his curtains, a momentary landscape in
which the grass looked an ugly grey and the sky a livid
blue. This I can write of now, but at the time it meant less
than nothing to me. For on the sward about twenty yards
or so from the bungalow stood a man!

He was between us and the flash and thus appeared a
black mass with a colossal shadow. Unconsciously I gripped

Arbuthnot's arm. On top of the flash came an ear-splitting roar of thunder, most like the sudden discharge of a machine-gun to one standing beside the weapon. While that crashed and echoed it was useless attempting speech. As the final reverberations died away I whispered hoarsely, "You saw him?"

"Of course."

"What's to be done?"

"Nothing. We can't rush out and seize a man just because he chooses to stand on the down in a thunderstorm. Besides, we should never get him in this darkness."

"I suppose you're right," I admitted, and my voice was not very steady as I said it. The silence of the doom-laden bungalow, the pudder of the elements without, and the sinister, lonely figure of the man defying the storm to maintain his watch combined to wreck the self-possession I would fain have shown.

"Quaint business," said Arbuthnot cheerily.

"Ah!"

My cry was purely involuntary. The flash was of almost inconceivable brilliance. It seemed to drown us in a pale-blue fire that ran everywhere and illuminated details that even day left plunged in gloom. The accompanying peal leapt out of the air immediately above our heads. In itself it was terrifying, but, my eyes focused on the vision revealed by it, I was almost indifferent to the natural phenomenon. The flash, no doubt a large one with the customary ramifications that modern photography shows, had lasted an appreciable fraction of a second. And there were now two men standing outside!

"My God!" I gasped. "It's an attack!"

My agitated mind pieced together the situation. Under cover of the storm two busybodies who had interfered with some evil scheme were to be quietly eliminated. The sudden fierce hammering of hail on the roof was the finishing touch. Under cover of that sound doors might be beaten in and shots fired without evoking any attention.

"Wait for the next," said Arbuthnot in my ear.

It was not long in coming, and, though less brilliant than the previous one, was sufficient for our purpose.

The down was bare.

8
Events of Saturday, June 2nd

Dawn broke when I had scarcely closed my eyes in sleep. I knew Arbuthnot was an immensely safe custodian, but whenever I closed my eyes my darkened eyeballs became suffused with a bluish glare in the midst of which stood two men, well apart from each other, and both, I felt, staring intently towards me. The rest of the night had been devoid of incident. The clatter of hail had given place to a gentle rain, the thunder had died away to a distant growling, and a perfect calm was restored. I got some sleep between four and eight o'clock, and then Arbuthnot made me get up, and I remembered that we had to be present at Rodd's committal that morning.

We had made an arrangement with the hotel before our change of habitat, and as we were on the point of leaving for Newport our letters were brought across.

"The invaluable Kaye has written," said Arbuthnot, looking up from the perusal of the first letter he had opened.

"Any luck?" I queried.

"He has established that Mr. Parker *is* Mr. Parker, for many years the cashier in the London office of Jute Products, Limited, and now pensioned off by his old firm. He is listed as an ardent devotee of natural history, complete with one wife, ailing."

"Good! That disposes of Mr. Parker," I said, in much the same tones that Alice in Wonderland must have used about the guinea-pigs.

"Mr. Edginton unfortunately had departed from the Bayswater Court Hotel before Kaye's man got there, having apparently left hastily on the receipt of the morning mail, which must have contained Williams's letter. Such a precipitate departure is surely significant."

"He must have been easily scared," I said.

"The address he gave in the hotel register has been found to be false," continued Arbuthnot. "The description of him speaks of a middle-aged man, bearded and bespectacled. I think the increasingly large proportion of the English race who keep their faces free of hair is a most hopeful augury for the future of society."

"How so?"

"Because a beard can hide a multitude of sins. The sensual mouth and the prognathous jaw equally disappear in convenient seclusion beneath it."

Before we left Arbuthnot addressed a few words to Mrs. Morris, the substance of them being that she was to remain in the bungalow during our absence and refuse admission to anyone but the police. I don't think the prospect pleased her altogether, but Arbuthnot got his own way as usual.

"It is quite easy to suppose that if Mr. Edginton disappeared from London to an unknown destination on Thursday he could have reappeared on Freshwater Down on Friday night," I remarked as we drove away.

"How well you put things, King," he answered in mock admiration. "And yet if my ideas are within a mile of the truth we are seeking to disinter, Mr. Edginton will not come to Freshwater yet. And when he does come—"

His words trailed off unfinished into silence, which was unusual in him, and he sat forward in the car, teeth clenched on pipe, and the look in his eyes that bade me not to interfere. So we came to Newport.

It would be traversing much familiar ground if I were fully to describe the court proceedings against Rodd.[1] He was represented by a solicitor who, I gathered, had been sent down by the firm he employed in London, but there was little the man could do for his client, and it was evident from the first that things were going to go hard with our erstwhile acquaintance.

The first witness to be put up was a Mr. Brown, manager of the Vectis Cycle Supply Company at Cowes, whose intent stare through the hotel window had caused me such alarm on a previous occasion. He identified Rodd unhesitatingly as the man who had entered his shop at about 7.30 p.m. on Friday the 25th, that is, the night of the crime. He stated that Rodd had purchased a bicycle for cash and ridden off on it immediately. He appeared to the witness to be in a hurry.

In his statement Rodd agreed with every word this witness had said. He had only arrived at Southampton from New York that same day and had decided to begin his holiday by a short visit to the Isle of Wight, where he had spent many pleasant days in childhood. He had reached Cowes by the 7.20 p.m. steamer. His original intention had been to walk to Freshwater, but he had varied this slightly by deciding to go to Newport first, and from there to get on the downs, which would provide a much more interesting way of reaching his destination. As the evening was already advanced and the road from Cowes to Newport not particularly attractive, he had thought of accomplishing the initial stage of his journey by means of a bicycle.

[1] Anyone further interested may consult a very full and accurate report which appeared in the *Isle of Wight County Press* dated June 9th.

He was asked whether it would not have been simpler for him to go to Newport by rail, seeing that there was a train running in connexion with the steamer which would have taken him there in eleven minutes. He replied that he had preferred the open air.

James Gale, a farm-labourer residing at Carisbrooke, deposed to having found a bicycle lying hidden in a field of growing wheat near Carisbrooke Castle. He was training a puppy and it had run away from him into the crop. If he had not entered the crop to look for the dog he would not have noticed the bicycle. He had handed it over to the police.

The manager of the cycle shop informed the court how by certain trade markings he had identified the bicycle in question as the one Rodd had purchased. Again Rodd concurred completely with the evidence. When he had reached a spot whence the downs were easily accessible he had discarded his bicycle, pitching it into the standing crop, where he might later on have found it again had he wanted it.

It was put to him that to buy a new bicycle and cast it away after half an hour's use was conduct at least peculiar. Rodd replied that he could afford to throw away a hundred bicycles if he liked. This point, of course, told heavily in his favour, for evidence was forthcoming that his means were so ample that it was incredible he should have assisted in a murder for pecuniary gain. Nevertheless, it was indisputable that he could easily have left his bicycle at a cottage adjacent to the field in which it was actually found. For a trifling consideration any cottager would have been willing to store it for him in safety. It was pointed out later on that the bicycle might easily have lain undiscovered in the crop until the latter was cut, and then, blistered by the sun and rusted by the rain, would probably have been unidentifiable.

Rodd's statement that he had lost himself on the downs excited less attention than I had expected. It appeared that such cases were not unknown, and records existed of individuals having been caught in snowstorms there and having perished miserably. Criticism was really aroused, however, when he sought to explain why he had chosen to settle down on the veranda of the bungalow the following morning. Arbuthnot and I in turn were subjected to a stiff examination as to the conduct of the accused on that occasion, without eliciting anything unfavourable to him. Rodd was asked why he had not pushed on the remaining few hundred yards that would have brought him to the comfort of an hotel. He answered that he was necessarily unshaven, untidy, and dirty after his night in the open and doubted whether any respectable hotel would have admitted him in that condition and without luggage, especially at early dawn. He had therefore stopped at the first house he had reached, hoping to be able to bribe a servant to allow him to shave, wash, and brush himself in the back premises. While sitting on the veranda he had dozed off to sleep until aroused by some sound which he later considered must have been Mrs. Morris's cry of terror after her gruesome discovery. The general feeling was that his explanation was not altogether convincing.

Inquiry then centred around the peculiar incident relating to Rodd's walking-stick. I had debated long with myself beforehand whether I should refer to the apparent alarm Rodd had originally shown at sight of the hall-stand with its quota of sticks, and had decided to keep silent on the point. Evidence of that kind easily creates an impression which may really be quite unjustifiable. As it was, the evidence of Arbuthnot supported by mine proved that Rodd had had a stick of the kind with him when we had first met him outside, although naturally we had not noticed whether it bore any initials. We also proved that he had had ample opportunity to effect an exchange of sticks before the hall-stand was examined by anyone. Moreover, there was no evidence forthcoming that a second stick of the kind had ever existed in the house.

Attention then concentrated on the pistol which had been found. Rodd frankly admitted that it might be his. This caused a momentary stir in the court which died away again when he went on to explain that he had purchased a weapon of the type when he was about to proceed to Canada, and had very carelessly left it in a table drawer in the bedroom of the Liverpool hotel where he had spent the night prior to embarkation. He had not missed it for some weeks and had judged it to be then too late to institute inquiries.

The defending solicitor made great play over the pistol incident. Certainly the bullet that killed Dalton Flyte could have been fired from the weapon in question, but the calibre was such a common one that the mere finding of the pistol near the scene of the crime was by no means conclusive. Moreover, the action of the village lad in discharging the weapon had effectually prevented any determination from the state of the interior of the barrel as to whether it had been fired on a previous recent occasion. The boy had fired one round, and three only had remained in the gun; but although it would hold eight when fully loaded, there could be no proof that it had ever actually contained that number. Arbuthnot later on criticized the solicitor severely over his attitude towards the pistol.

"Since Rodd's evidence was that he had lost the gun two years before it was none of his business to try and throw doubt on the probability of its having been used in the murder," he said. "He was too obviously preparing a second line of defence, suggesting that he did not believe the court would accept his client's story."

Rodd's attempt at escape naturally told heavily against him. He pleaded a mad impulse arising from the annoyance an innocent man would be bound to feel at seeing the prospect of an enjoyable and long-deferred holiday suddenly fade. The circumstances of his return had captured the public imagination. No one would accept for a moment that after a day's amusement at the expense of police and public he had quietly relinquished his hopes of escape and meekly surrendered. Every one scented a mystery.

Hiram K. Thacker and I were called to prove that we had unsuccessfully chased a man on the downs that night. If Rodd had been contemplating surrender he could have given himself up then. Rodd's answer was simply a denial that anyone had chased him on the down that night.

Then Arbuthnot recounted how that after every one else in the hotel had gone to bed that night he had stayed up to await the return of his friend, Sir Edmund King, who had gone out with one of the search-parties, how that after midnight he had heard footsteps approaching the hotel, had heard some one enter and walk upstairs without any attempt at concealment, and had judged it to be his friend. Five minutes later, thinking that his friend, not expecting anyone to be awaiting his return, had gone directly to bed, he had left the drawing-room and met Thornton Rodd descending the stairs. Rodd had surrendered at discretion.

Then it came out that Rodd's cabin trunk had still been in his bedroom at that time. In the excitement of the chase no one had remembered to have it removed. Sergeant Rogers, it appeared, had seen it in the morning, found it locked, and deferred its disposal until he had dealt with more urgent matters. Then he had not found time to see about it later, but in any case no one would have expected Rodd to return to the hotel. Arbuthnot, having been away from Freshwater all that day, had not been aware, he said, that the trunk still remained where Rodd had left it. Questioned as to whether Rodd was carrying anything when he met him on the stairs, he answered in the negative. The possibility remained, however, that the accused might have had some small thing concealed about his person. When the trunk had come to be examined later nothing incriminating had been found amongst its contents.

Rodd contented himself with a plain denial that the trunk had ever contained anything in the nature of evidence against him. He had gone upstairs to bed, intending to surrender in the morning. Then, feeling famished after an almost foodless day, he had come down again to forage for meat and drink.

From the point of view of the prosecution it could be said that Rodd had travelled to Freshwater as inconspicuously as possible; had disposed of his bicycle where he had good hopes for thinking it would lie unnoticed; had been in the immediate locality when a crime was committed by means of a pistol which had once been his; had been found on the scene of the tragedy without being able to give any good reason for his presence; had attempted to escape after arrest, and finally had courted recapture in order to return to the hotel for some unknown purpose. In the end he was committed for trial, bail being refused.

Arbuthnot and I had a late lunch after we had returned to Freshwater. He had very little to say, being obviously absorbed in his thoughts. My mind was also busy, and to be perfectly honest, I was feeling some half-stifled regret at the incarceration of Rodd. Apart from his impudence I had begun to find him a rather likeable fellow.

After lunch Arbuthnot suddenly lugged out his capacious wallet, withdrew a newspaper cutting from it, and handed the printed scrap to me without comment. I read with some surprise the following:

LINER'S COMING OF AGE
CELEBRATED BY RECORD RUN

The Cunard liner *Mauretania* berthed three hours early at Southampton on Friday as the result of a remarkable crossing during which she beat her previous best between Sandy Hook and Cherbourg. Although built as long ago as 1907, this grand old ship, since her conversion to oil-burning, seems capable of even more remarkable achievements than when she was first put on the transatlantic service so many years ago. She remains a semi-permanent tribute to British engineering skill and craftsmanship.

"Interesting," I said, "but—"

"What's it got to do with winning the war, you mean?" he asked.

"Quite so."

"I don't quite know myself. And yet I've a shrewd suspicion that but for the masterpiece of Clyde builders Thornton Rodd might still be a free man."

"I don't follow."

"We are honoured," remarked Arbuthnot. A knock had sounded at the front door.

"Gentleman to see you, sir," said Mrs. Morris entering with a visiting card on a tray. "There's a lady with him."

Arbuthnot passed me the card after he had glanced at it and I read:

Mr. Gervase Bellingham
280, Kensington Gore, S.W.7.

"Ask them into the dining-room," said my friend to Mrs. Morris, and as she left to execute his order he added,

"King, I shall be interested to hear your opinion of Miss Pamela Strode."

I jumped from my chair. He was grinning all over his face.

"What kind of game is this?" I demanded.

"Presently," answered he, and waved his hand towards the dining-room door.

Mr. Gervase Bellingham and his female companion were awaiting us when we entered from the drawing-room. I saw at a glance that he was a tall man with a soldierly bearing. Closely-cropped and almost white hair was scrupulously brushed back from a forehead already lined with age, but his eyes were bright and his air brisk. I should not exactly have put him down as a man of birth and breeding, but rather as one who by long association with people of a certain class had absorbed sufficient of their ways to pass under any but the closest scrutiny. And if Arbuthnot ever sees the preceding sentence he will guffaw.

As for the woman who was Bellingham's companion, she was of a type I have never professed to understand. I grant the charm of a slim and moderately tall figure. I can admire a hatless head covered with irresponsible curls of reddish-gold, severely disciplined not to exceed a certain length but otherwise apparently left to their own devices. I realize that unnecessarily large eyes of the blue that in certain lights would be violet and, one suspects, might on other occasions be almost green, have a certain attraction. And if Arbuthnot ever troubles to read the preceding sentence he will guffaw again. But I fail to appreciate the *raison d'être* for a cigarette-holder about a foot long, nor can I comprehend why anyone should wish to sit on the corner of the dining-room table and swing long, inadequately-clothed legs when there are perfectly good chairs in the room.

"Mr. Arbuthnot, I believe?" Bellingham was speaking.

"Quite right," said Arbuthnot, bowing.

"May I introduce Mr. Arbuthnot?" added Bellingham, turning to the girl. "Miss Strode—Mr. Arbuthnot."

"This is my friend, Sir Edmund King," remarked Arbuthnot in turn, and then Bellingham took up the tale. I remained well in the background. I realized that my attitude required a new orientation and I listened intently.

"I hope you will take our apologies for granted, Mr. Arbuthnot," Bellingham commenced. "I have gathered indirectly that you are not here as an investigator but have had a holiday interrupted almost as thoroughly as the unfortunate Mr. Rodd. Therefore it is rather an intrusion on our part to seek your help."

"Gerry puts it rather well, don't you think?" said the girl to me unexpectedly.

"Please continue," said Arbuthnot politely, relighting his pipe. "I will close the door that leads to the passage and we shall then be unheard." He did so as he spoke.

"I should explain," continued our male visitor, "that I am an old friend of Miss Strode's father, Sir Jervis Strode, whom you may remember as a permanent secretary prior to his retirement a few months ago."

The name was certainly familiar to me as that of a well-known public servant who had been the power behind the scenes in his particular department for many years.

"Hence in this very difficult position, Miss Strode has naturally turned to me. Her father has been no better than an invalid for the past few months, and she had the misfortune to lose her only brother, through ill-health resulting from war-service, not so very long ago."

"They don't think you're eloping with me," interjected Miss Strode, favouring me with what I half suspected to be the shadow of a wink. I felt rather disgusted. The subject did not seem to require flippancy.

"To be brief," went on Bellingham, "we are particularly concerned over the misfortune that has overtaken Mr.

Rodd. I may tell you in confidence that while an engagement cannot actually be said to exist between my young friend here and him, there is an understanding which in these somewhat unpunctilious days might be considered tantamount to a betrothal."

"The honourable member resumed his seat amid cheers," added the fair Pamela, extracting another cigarette from her case.

"It is rather a delicate subject, perhaps, but I should mention that Miss Strode's father did not altogether approve of Mr. Rodd as a suitor, as he was a man who still had to make his mark in the world. Recent financial events, however, might have removed the objection, but it is unthinkable that we should worry an invalid over affairs as they stand at present."

"Where do I come in?" said Arbuthnot bluntly, interrupting Mr. Bellingham's flow of speech.

"In this way. Mr. Rodd, in some way I, for one, entirely fail to comprehend, seems to have involved himself in what may prove a difficult and distressing situation. Naturally we are both convinced of his entire innocence. No one who knows him can doubt it. Nevertheless, we should both feel happier if we knew his affairs were receiving the attention of one who—er—is well known everywhere as a first-class intellect in the field of investigation."

"I see. Were you in court this morning?"

"No. We came to Freshwater yesterday as soon as we read in the London papers of the arrest, but I did not deem it advisable for Miss Strode to be present at the proceedings," replied Bellingham, passing a caressing hand over his firmly-outlined jaw as he spoke, in the manner of one who thought deeply.

"Might have put Roddy off his stroke if he'd suddenly seen me grinning at him," interposed Miss Strode brightly.

"I can imagine, Mr. Arbuthnot, that you are not tempted to take up a case by financial considerations," went on Bellingham suavely, "but you have my assurance that your—er—professional services will be very highly valued."

Arbuthnot waved aside the suggestion contained in the words.

"I've already got half my inquisitive nose into this affair," he declared. "I don't quite see how I can do more than I am doing."

"How does Thornton Rodd stand at present?" asked Bellingham.

"They can't hang him, if that's what you mean," replied Arbuthnot brusquely. "I take it you have been following the case ever since his name was first mentioned. The evidence against him is really very slender."

"The absence of motive in itself should be sufficient to upset the case," suggested our visitor.

"The absence of motive! It's fatally easy to give a possible reason why the accused should wish to abolish Flyte, but it's quite another thing to prove it."

Mr. Bellingham coughed discreetly.

"Might I inquire without giving offence whether, in the unlikely event of evidence apparently detrimental to Rodd—I say apparently—coming into your possession, you would feel bound to act on it?"

"Gerry!" cried the girl sharply.

"Forgive me, my dear," he answered deprecatingly. "You must remember that Thornton has already implicated himself by just the kind of innocent but foolish action I have in mind."

"I appreciate your anxiety," said Arbuthnot, "but I think you can trust me not to put a wrong valuation on anything I may discover," with which equivocal declaration his questioner had perforce to be content.

"We are staying at the Freshwater Bay Hotel," remarked Bellingham. "I hope you and Sir Edmund will dine with us some evening in the near future."

"Duties permitting, we shall be pleased to come," answered Arbuthnot gravely. Conversing on trifles they passed out of the room together, leaving me to follow with Miss Strode.

She stopped to light her third cigarette since she had arrived, swung her legs floorwards, and remarked cheerfully, "I've never had a *fiancé* in jail before. I call it thrilling."

"Not every one would bear it with your equanimity," I said maliciously.

"Oh, you fool! You utter damned fool!" she cried suddenly, drew her hand across her eyes with a childish gesture, and was gone before I had time to consider whether her display was genuine emotion or skilfully devised coquetry.

"I'm surprised that Rodd should have told you about his *fianceé,*" I said to Arbuthnot when we were once more alone. "I always fancied he was more friendly with me."

"He didn't mean to tell me. It was a slip on his part," responded my friend. "What do you think of his choice?"

"I don't know," I answered truthfully.

Arbuthnot sat silent, puffing at his pipe.

"I am waiting for realization of a very peculiar fact to dawn on you," he said at last.

"Indeed? I seem to have had a surfeit of such lately. What is it?"

"That a man should return to England with wealth after two years' absence overseas and, instead of rushing off to London to see the woman of his choice, elect to embark on a walking tour in the Isle of Wight."

I wrinkled my brows.

"He may have ceased to love her during his absence," I suggested. "Such things have been known to happen."

"Or—"

A light broke in upon me.

"He may have had something important and unpleasant to attend to here before he felt free for other things."

"King, if I have underrated your intelligence at times accept my apology. Yours is a very logical conclusion. The only drawback to it is that, like most of the logic of human beings, it probably isn't true."

"Confound you!" I said. "I'm going for a walk."

"You're not. You're going to bed."

"I prefer my own choice, thank you."

"Remember to-night's vigil. You will do well to get some rest while you can."

I hesitated. I recognized the wisdom of his remarks.

"How long is this look-out business going to continue?" I grumbled.

"Until one of two things happens," returned Arbuthnot lightly.

"What are they?"

"Either we shall eventually get the persons concerned in this affair—"

"Yes?

"Or else they will get what they come for, even if they inconvenience us seriously in doing so."

"Meaning?"

Arbuthnot shrugged his shoulders.

9
Further Events of the Same Day

About five o'clock I was awakened from the slumber to which Arbuthnot had consigned me by the sound of voices and the clink of cups in the drawing-room. Realizing that my chances of tea were in jeopardy, I hastened to join whoever might be there and found Arbuthnot dispensing hospitality to the superintendent of police.

"Bernard has this moment told me that they have fresh evidence against Rodd," Arbuthnot announced.

Bernard nodded genially to me. I returned his greeting somewhat gloomily and sat down to consider how Pamela Strode might take these tidings.

"Carry on," said Arbuthnot.

"It must have been apparent to you," explained the superintendent, "that the greatest weakness, in any case, against Rodd would be the lack of evidence connecting him directly with the man in whose murder he is alleged to have assisted. In other words, there has been so far no clue as to any possible motive he could have in doing such a thing."

"Quite right."

"Now a very remarkable piece of evidence has come to hand, linking him, in some way we do not yet understand, with the deceased Flyte. It reached me to-day just too late

155

to put into court although the intention of the sender was probably to make it available for the proceedings."

As he finished speaking he picked up a small attaché case that was lying on the floor beside him, opened it, and withdrew a large envelope. From the letter he then extracted with immense care a single unfolded piece of paper of irregular shape, whose edges I saw at a glance had been blackened by fire.

"I have to handle it very gingerly," he said, allowing it to lie flat on the palm of his hand, "for I am extremely afraid that it may crumble to dust. Just come round to this side of the table and look."

We hastened to place ourselves one on each side of him. What he had was well worth seeing. It was this:[1]

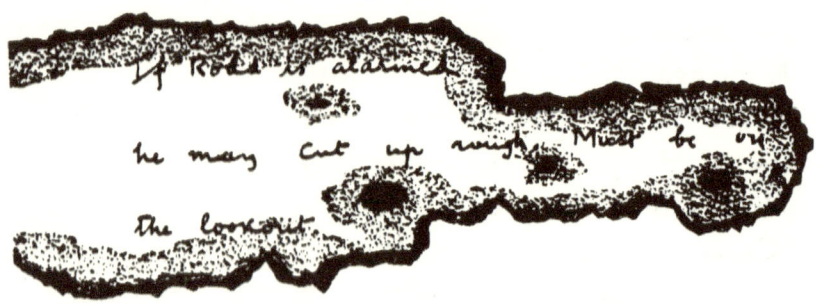

I felt a strange feeling of unhappiness come over me as I read the fourteen words that I already realized might secure the termination of the career of the gay young fellow who had ragged me not so many days ago.

"How did this come into your hands?" asked Arbuthnot briskly.

"It reached me by the second postal delivery to-day. The address on the envelope was hand-printed. The post-mark was Freshwater. There was nothing in the envelope

---

[1] Subsequently kindly lent to me by Captain Bernard for reproduction.

but this. The whole question that arises is whether those lines are in the handwriting of Dalton Flyte. If they are not, the affair may be the work of some misguided joker, but, if Flyte penned those words, Rodd will be lucky to get off under ten years. That's why I am here. I remember that Williams, the builder, had once been in written communication with Flyte, and to settle the handwriting question I want to see the letter of Flyte's that he has."

"Had."

"You don't mean he has destroyed it?" cried the superintendent, showing obvious signs of agitation.

Arbuthnot laughed. He pulled out his wallet.

"It is here," he said. "I took the liberty—or the precaution—of borrowing it."

"Good! Then we can settle things here and now."

As he unfolded it I felt fear clutch at my heart. It was none of my business to be interested in the fate of a devil-may-care youth and an impudent minx whose ways were beyond my comprehension, and yet I prayed inwardly that the two scripts might be dissimilar.

The white sheet and the charred scrap lay side by side on our tea-table.

"The same!" cried Bernard.

"I have made some small study of types of calligraphy in my time," said Arbuthnot quietly. "These, in my opinion, are undoubtedly the work of one hand. What do you think, King?"

I gazed dully at the incriminating documents.

"I'll take your word for it," I said.

"Now, as we cannot reasonably suppose that Dalton Flyte returned from the grave to manufacture evidence against Rodd, we are driven to presume that there was some connexion of an unfriendly kind between the two men," stated the superintendent, restoring his precious fragment to its envelope.

"Perfectly right. But what do you suppose has been the history of that bit of paper since it left the possession of Dalton Flyte?"

"I consider it to be the remaining part of a diary, or more probably a memorandum kept by Flyte. It was presumably in his safe and was stolen with the other contents the night of the murder. The thief would naturally have taken indiscriminately all he found rather than attempt to sort out his haul on the spot. Then by some fluke it escaped the general holocaust when the car was destroyed. A puff of wind may have carried it away before it was entirely consumed."

"That is quite possible. And then?"

"Then we must suppose that some person sightseeing at the scene of the car tragedy—there have been many such there—found it and retained it as a souvenir until the news of the arrest of Rodd made him, or her, realize that the paper was important. You are no doubt aware that a certain type of mind revels in relics of crime."

"Very true. I have been to Madame Tussaud's myself."

"The person concerned would naturally fear that if he sent in his find openly he would be in trouble for not having produced it before. Hence the anonymity of his communication," concluded the superintendent.

"Very ingeniously worked out," commented Arbuthnot.

"In addition to what I've told you there's other news," continued Bernard.

"More evidence against Rodd?" I asked.

"Not exactly. And yet nothing that is likely to tell in his favour. The identity of the man who was killed, in the car accident at Bouldnor Cliff has been established."

"That's interesting," remarked Arbuthnot.

I got up and wandered about the room. Things were developing at a rate with which it was difficult to keep pace.

"Before we buried the man in question," went on Bernard, "we naturally obtained a set of his finger-prints. These went up to Scotland Yard but were not found to correspond with those of any known British criminal. Very curiously, however, it happened that just after they received our inquiry a letter came in from the New York police enclosing particulars and finger-prints of a notorious criminal, rejoicing in the rather descriptive pseudonym of Jaguar Jim, who was suspected of having crossed to Europe. Comparison immediately showed that this criminal and the man who was killed at Bouldnor Cliff were identical. Naturally the communication from Scotland Yard contained few details, but I have found out some facts about the man."

"That's good," said Arbuthnot.

"It's a sort of hobby of mine," the superintendent explained, "to keep scrap-books of cuttings from newspapers and periodicals referring to crimes and criminals. They are not altogether dependable, of course, but they are often more accessible than official dossiers. I found I had this Jaguar Jim indexed. His record makes him out to have been a modern equivalent of the hired assassin of medieval Italy. He appears to have undergone imprisonment only once, having twice secured acquittal on capital charges through lack of sufficient evidence, but three or four of the most sensational unsolved murders of recent years in America have been provisionally placed to his credit by public opinion. These may be undeserved laurels, of course, but, judging from the newspaper article from which I got my information, he is supposed to have been the man who shot the State Attorney of Oklahoma on the eve of a scandalous oil-leases case, by securing admission to his presence as a poor old woman who had once been his mother's servant in Kansas City. Again, it is generally believed that he was the man employed to get rid of

Martin Plumer, the New York journalist who had worked as a bootlegger for three months and was on the verge of commencing a series of sensational exposures by means of articles to the Prohibitionist Press when he was murdered."

"And now you are occupied in asking yourself what could have brought Jaguar Jim to the Isle of Wight?" suggested Arbuthnot.

"Precisely. I am fully alive to the folly of speculating on an insufficient basis, and yet, judging by the past career of the man, he does not seem to have usually operated as a principal."

"Very well put. I think I see whither your thoughts are trending."

"To say anything more at present would be merely to give expression to a possibility that must also have entered your mind," said the superintendent apologetically.

"Never mind. Proceed as far as you can without actually contravening the facts as we know them."

"A great deal hinges on the character of Dalton Flyte. The mystery that still surrounds him suggests that his life may not have been one of uniform rectitude, to say the least."

"Perfectly reasonable."

"It is possible to suppose that Dalton Flyte if he had been in a position to harm Rodd would not have troubled to do so when the latter was poor. Rodd's suddenly acquired wealth might, however, have put a very different complexion on the matter. Flyte might have seen his way to a considerable share of it. It might also have occurred to Rodd that he could not hope to settle down in peace with his money while Flyte remained alive."

"This is all guesswork," I interrupted, rather rudely, I fear.

"Certainly it is," responded Bernard courteously. "I am only mentioning it at your friend's invitation."

"I'm sorry. Go on."

"We know that Rodd returned to England via New York. While at that place he may have arranged for the abolition of Dalton Flyte. Supposing he could get an American agent to do his dirty work, it would be a most suitable arrangement, for after the deed the man would naturally leave England as promptly as possible."

"Can well-known criminals travel from country to country as easily as that?" queried Arbuthnot.

"It is not easy, but possible. Judging from what I read, Jaguar Jim had considerable powers of disguise which might have helped him."

"Continue."

"It is possible that Flyte possessed in his safe some document by which he could have blackmailed Rodd. Jaguar Jim would be engaged to obtain this and hand it over to Rodd. Anything else the agent obtained would be his profit, in addition to whatever he was to get from Rodd. It is easy to suppose that Jaguar Jim's propensity for shooting led him to exceed his instructions. Rodd in his anxiety to see an end of the business might have stationed himself in the vicinity to receive the document at the earliest possible moment and then judged boldness to be the safest course and remained on the scene of the crime."

"On that showing," said Arbuthnot with a twinkle in his eye, "why did he return to the hotel?"

"Exactly. I'm afraid we slipped up badly there. It is credible that he thus gained the opportunity to destroy the biggest piece of evidence against him. However, I must be getting away. Have you had a peaceful time here so far?"

"Nothing to complain of," said Arbuthnot cheerfully.

After Bernard had left I established myself in a chair on the veranda that faced cliffwards. It was as pleasant an evening as one could wish, with a clear light that seemed to throw into relief at the same time the minutest details of the little bay and the hopeless sordidness of human actions. The radiance might have come direct from the eyes of God and filled me with a vast distaste for the imbroglio in which we were all concerned.

"What a gloomy old thing you are!" said a gay voice.

I looked up and Pamela Strode stood before me.

"Don't get up," she added as I struggled to rise from the depths of my deck-chair.

I relinquished the attempt and she characteristically perched herself on the veranda railing, lit a cigarette, and surveyed me with an assumption of interest.

"I hope you don't mind my butting-in," she remarked. "Of course Gerry is a nice old thing, but he's a fearful bore at times, especially when he's worried as he is at present. I felt I needed a change."

She had a trick of suddenly opening her blue eyes to their widest extent as if she would include one in an association from which others were debarred. The little breeze was making a curl beside her ear flutter irresponsibly and her lips on either side of the ridiculous cigarette-holder had a whimsical twist.

"You are lucky to have him helping you," I pointed out.

"He has nothing else to do," she said contemptuously.

"Then what does he generally do?" I asked.

"He used to be some sort of thing in the City," she answered vaguely. "He was in Calcutta for years and made pots of money. Now he just slacks. Like you."

"That's not fair, Miss Strode," I protested.

"I would let you call me 'Pamela'," she said with a bewildering smile, "if I could think of anything really suitable to call you. 'Eddy' would be unthinkable."

"It would," I agreed heartily.

"I could call you 'Mundy'," she suggested, "or 'Man Monday' for short. Chesterton wrote a book called *The*

Man who was Thursday. You would be *The Man who is Monday.* But perhaps as Monday is washing-day in some circles it would hurt your pride?"

"I would live it down," I declared.

"Edmund seems an intractable sort of name, doesn't it?" she complained.

"There was an Edmund, King of England, at one time," said I.

"And now there's an Edmund King of Kensington," she cried.

"How do you know where I live?"

"Gerry knows. His own hibernating quarters are in that region. It doesn't interest me."

"Edmund was a famous king," I stated. "He was called Ironsides."

"Oh, good! Then I might call you 'Tinribs'." Then, with a change of voice, "Have you any news for me?"

I shook my head. I thought that probably Bernard's information was confidential though he had not specifically made it so. In any case, I preferred not to be the one to bring fresh sorrow to Pamela Strode.

"Not the smallest bit?" she asked, and her lips took on a downward curve that worried me.

"Nothing," I said definitely.

She slid off her perch and came and sat cross-legged on the ground beside my chair.

"Is your friend in?" she inquired.

"He's about somewhere," I replied.

"Tell me. Is he really clever—I mean stinkingly clever like some people are stinkingly rich?"

"He is clever enough to make me look a fool pretty often," I conceded.

"And what does he think about things?"

"He's not saying anything at present."

"And what is he doing?"

"He doesn't seem to be doing anything either," I admitted.

"'They also serve who only stand and wait'," said a familiar voice from the window behind our heads.

"Good evening, Mr. Arbuthnot," cried Pamela. "Why aren't you out here enjoying the fresh air?"

By way of answer he left the window and a few seconds after appeared at the door.

"So you play a waiting game, do you?" said Pamela gaily. "Or is that merely a cloak for natural indolence?"

"The police are remarkably efficient," said Arbuthnot gravely. "I have had no opportunities to distinguish myself yet."

"How sad! So they are still hot on the track, are they?"

"Very much so. The police superintendent here is an exceptionally clever man. Almost invariably he makes good use of his chances."

"I suppose I mustn't be impatient," said Pamela, "but after not seeing Thornton for two years this business is pretty sickening."

"He would have been better advised to have gone to London to see you when he first landed, and so avoided his present entanglement," remarked Arbuthnot quietly.

"I'm sure he did," she said quickly. "But unfortunately I was obliged to be away at the time, and no doubt he came to the Isle of Wight to fill up the interval of waiting. Thornton wouldn't get any fun out of London unless I were there. Bye-bye now. I've got to take Gerry for a walk or he'll be liverish."

She scrambled to her feet, passed an ineffective hand over the wanton curls, lightly vaulted our veranda rail, and vanished.

I sighed.

"Really, King!" said Arbuthnot with assumed concern.

"She makes me feel so thoroughly Victorian," I explained.

"She seems to be addling your brain," he returned.

"What makes you say that?"

"Did you notice her reply when I expressed surprise that Rodd had not gone first to London to see her. She said, 'I'm sure he did', instead of saying 'He did'."

"What of it?"

"Do you mean to tell me that Rodd called at her home and never left a message of any kind, not even a card, by which she would know he had been there?"

"Now you put it that way—" I began.

"Moreover, if they are such a devoted couple as she would have us believe, surely he wrote to her while he was with us and explained how he was detained in the Isle of Wight to be a witness at an inquest. In that case he would certainly have referred to his visit to London if he had made it."

"He told me that he had gone to London first to see his solicitor," I interposed.

"He didn't tell that to the court. I have worked out from the time his steamer arrived that he would have had time to get to London and return to the Isle of Wight at the time we know he reached it, but precious little time to do anything in London."

"What do you infer?"

"I infer nothing at present. But it is clear that Miss Strode realizes her very existence is a menace to Rodd. For example, it would not take a very bright K.C. to inquire why he remained in Freshwater until Thursday when he was free to leave it on Monday after the inquest. Surely he ought to have hastened to her at the first possible moment?"

"All that is explained if we suppose that he has ceased to care for her," I pointed out.

Arbuthnot smiled.

"About last night's affair—" I said, changing the subject.

"Well?"

"It is obvious, even to me, that there is something concealed in this bungalow which certain unknown people very badly want in their possession."

"Continue."

"I can't understand why they didn't take it while the bungalow was unoccupied. Presuming that the power behind the scenes is this Cosmo Edginton, whoever he may be, he seems to have adopted very roundabout methods to achieve his end. It's practically established that some one is able to enter this place at will. Why didn't he accomplish his purpose before ever we came to live here?"

"A very shrewd inquiry. And where did Dalton Flyte's pince-nez go?"

"I wish you'd stick to the point," I said. "I'm afraid I haven't the panoramic mind."

"A good phrase. I thought I was keeping to the point," he answered meekly.

"I don't understand you," I replied shortly, "but it seems to me we are wasting time."

"How so?"

"If there is something hidden in this bungalow we ought to set to work to find it. It may be the solution of the whole mystery."

"Ah, there you run off the rails, King. The presence of this indefinable something in the house is our sole link with the rather mysterious individuals who come and go outside. If we drag it from its hiding-place we make it easier for them to obtain. If they fail in their enterprise through our discovery they have only to vanish to cause our trouble to begin all over again. We don't know any of them by sight even."

"I suppose you're right."

"Moreover, King, if we are known to have found what lies here we are marked men."

"That's a consideration," I said after a pause. "It's indubitably comforting to think that our would-be visitors have at present nothing to gain and everything to lose by attracting fresh attention to this place by an act of violence."

Arbuthnot surveyed me with his usual grin.

"I know what you're thinking," I said hastily. "On my own showing I should not have allowed myself to get into a panic last night."

"You'll have a chance of vindicating yourself to-night," he responded. "I propose you take the second watch, that is, from one o'clock onwards."

"Do you anticipate further attentions to-night?" I inquired.

"What more likely?" said he.

I was aroused from a comfortable slumber at one o'clock the following morning by the steady pressure of Arbuthnot's hand on my shoulder.

"Come, King, it's your turn," he said very quietly but distinctly.

"Anything happened so far?" I asked, sitting up in bed and rubbing my eyes.

"Nothing. The moon is near setting. You will have a dark hour before daybreak."

I got out of bed and groped around until I had secured enough miscellaneous garments to protect me from the chill that comes just before a summer dawn. I slipped my revolver into my dressing-gown pocket. No doubt we had no violence to fear, but were we lucky enough to seize an intruder he would probably require some tangible proof of the folly of resistance. Arbuthnot faded away silently to his bedroom, and soon afterwards I moved as cautiously as possible into the passage.

Aided by the declining rays of the moon, that was fast slanting seawards in the south-west, I made a thorough tour of inspection and satisfied myself that all the windows other than those of our bedrooms were secured and all the outer doors locked. Outside the June night was as calm as the seas of Paradise. Not even a murmur came up from the water below us. The only sounds were those of night, indescribable, almost imperceptible flutterings and sighings, as if some one were trying to brush the air with a feathered wand. Perhaps the ether was vibrating with messages beyond our ken. At times a subdued ringing, sounding of incredibly remote origin, would start up in my ears, as if another world than ours were calling. Night sounds are disturbing because they are inexplicable. And supposing we could track down all that are really of familiar origin, who can say that there would not be some residual whisperings to defy our commonplace explanations?

I considered where I should best place myself. Judging by past events it was a fair assumption that our unknowns were provided with a key of the bungalow. It therefore followed that they would probably enter by either the front door or the back door. Of the two I rather favoured the front entrance as their choice, as it faced seawards and a person entering that way would be screened from the observation of anyone who might be on the road.

I reflected that if I placed myself at the front door I could also command the back one, since the passage ran straight from one to the other, and the intervening door, which Flyte had so safeguarded, was now lying open. A further consideration influenced me. Whatever there might be in the bungalow that led to the mysterious activities proceeding around us, it was evidently situated on the inner side of the late tenant's carefully-constructed barrier, and therefore I could afford to neglect the kitchen department. Moreover, from the front door I could reach Arbuthnot in half a dozen steps.

With the intention of being as comfortable as possible under the difficult circumstances I sat down on the door-mat, leant my back against the door, and began to study possible courses of action in the event of an intruder's arriving.

Supposing he arrived at the front door I had only to slip into Arbuthnot's room and rouse him. If the unknown then entered the room we had him; if he passed by his retreat was cut off. So much was clear. But suppose he entered by the back door? In that case any precipitate action on my part might only lead to his hasty withdrawal before he had reached a position where we could intercept him. I judged that he would enter one of the four chief rooms of the house that opened on to the passage. In the darkness of the passage I was confident that I should be invisible. If the man came along and entered Arbuthnot's room I should leap on him from behind; the noise would inevitably arouse my friend and a capture could easily be effected. But if the man went into the dining-room, drawing-room, or my bedroom I should then rouse Arbuthnot and we should act together.

Above the door against which I sat was a fanlight of multi-coloured glass which gave but little light by day. Now, however, it was transmitting the rays of the setting moon to form what looked like a disarranged spectrum on the ceiling. One dark red patch in particular shone with a peculiar luminosity that suggested to my imagination the surface of a pool of blood. I resolutely set aside such disturbing thoughts, for I was really grateful for the presence of the fanlight, as the feeble illumination it would give after moonset would, I knew, only serve to accentuate the darkness beneath it where I sat.

The kaleidoscopic colours crawled along the ceiling with the certainty of doom. In ten minutes the moon would be gone. I fell to wondering what it could be that brought with it the necessity for our night watches. I had spent some part of the past evening after Mrs. Morris had gone home in going round the bungalow, tapping the walls and floors for possible hiding-places. I thought it possible that the thief's haul had not been complete and that Dalton Flyte's greatest treasures had been concealed against just such an eventuality as the robbery that had actually occurred. Arbuthnot had been vastly amused at my activities.

As my brain travelled hither and thither reviewing the curiosities of our immediate past the colours above me began to wane, giving that curious sense of withdrawal that comes with the dimming of light, as if one pictured the rays sweeping off to some incredibly distant bourn. Some far-away clock sounded three hours of the morning and a minute afterwards darkness muffled me.

Perhaps I had been sitting for another ten minutes, tense yet immobile, when I heard the click.

I sat up with a quick catch of my breath and strained my ears. There was little doubt as to the origin of the sound. It had come from the unlocking of the back door. The moment then had arrived, and I felt curiously calm. I found time to reflect on the advantage the stationary watcher has over him who seeks to move by night. I waited for another click denoting that the door had been closed, but it did not come. Evidently our visitor felt it safe to leave the door ajar, well knowing that no one would pass at that hour to take note of it. In that case my eyes ought gradually to become sensitive to the faint light of the summer night without, just as the long exposure of a photographic plate secures a record of the fainter stars. Against such a background I could hope to see the black shape of anyone moving towards me. But in any case I felt sure that no one, however silently he moved, could come beyond Dalton Flyte's inner door without my hearing him.

After the click had come a great stillness. I began to fancy that the far end of the passage looked less dark than before, but I could not be sure. No sound of any movement reached me. Could I possibly have been mistaken in the origin of the sound I had heard?

What was that? A faint rustling sound had begun. Was it the sudden stirring of a night breeze outdoors? Or was it some one stealthily shuffling along the passage towards me?

The sound ceased. Then it began again. It was a peculiar noise, hardly more than a whispering, and there seemed nothing inimical about it. Sometimes it seemed to me like the wind blowing over the June hay-fields. And again it might have been the stirring of a gentle gale in some leafy tree-tops. Perhaps six times the sound came and went and never another sound besides. Then I knew that the door was really open, for there came stealing into my nostrils some subtle aroma that must emanate from outside. It puzzled me for a moment, for it was but faint and I dared not even sniff. Then like a flash I realized the truth and, caution thrown to the winds, scrambled wildly to my feet.

From the kitchen came the rasp of match on box, a little spurt of light, the click of the closing door, and then, like the climax of a hideous dream, a vast flare of yellow flame.

10
Events of Sunday, June 3rd

For perhaps a second my tongue clave to the roof of my mouth. As in a nightmare I strove to utter words and could only produce a gurgle. Then the impediment suddenly left me.

"Fire!" I roared. I knew one shout would bring Arbuthnot from his sleep.

The fierce glare lit up the passage with a sinister light and shone upon the hall-stand by my side. With a wild idea of beating out the flames I grabbed a couple of walking-sticks and dashed towards the fire.

The kitchen was heaped high with a blazing mass of petrol-soaked hay. The heat seared my eyeballs. The fumes were almost asphyxiating and the smell of burning wood already added to the other odour.

"Arbuthnot!" I yelled.

Holding an arm before my scorching face I beat frantically at the flaming pile. As well have tried to subjugate Etna with a cup of cold water!

"Arbuthnot! For God's sake come!" I yelled again.

A hand caught my shoulder and twisted me out of the way.

"Get your bedding and soak it in the bath water," said his voice in my ear.

Out of the corner of my eye I saw that he was dragging a pile of sodden bedclothes with him. I dashed off to do his bidding, scrambled my bedding into an armful, bounded into the adjacent bathroom and plunged it in the water that Mrs. Morris, by order, ran in each night for Arbuthnot's cold tub in the morning.

When I got back to the scene of the fire I heaved a sigh of relief. The flames had diminished. Arbuthnot, reckless of burns, had flung his saturated blankets over the blaze, much as one would lay a tablecloth, but the kitchen table was still burning furiously and little tongues of flame were creeping here and there in the room. He seized my bedding and added it to the pile. Then we fell to beating the dwindling heap with sticks. Occasionally a flame would leap up at one point or another, but on the whole we were winning. The acrid smoke, mingled with the steam hissing from the sodden blankets where the flames met them, made the air a torture to breathe.

Arbuthnot left me to carry on, but soon returned with a jug of water with which he dealt with minor outbreaks in several spots. The worst was now over, but we made several more journeys for water to be on the safe side before we relaxed our labours. The kitchen was now in darkness and the first violent uprush of fire had destroyed the electric light bulb. Arbuthnot gingerly picked, his way across the floor.

"Our friend relocked the door before he departed," he remarked. "Come on. Let's see the amount of the damage."

He led the way to the dining-room. Fortunately the fire had not affected the connexions, and Arbuthnot switched on both lamps.

I gazed uneasily at the windows.

"Is this safe?" I asked.

"I imagine our visitor would prefer to admire his handiwork from a distance," he answered.

We surveyed each other. Arbuthnot's face was blackened and his hair and eyebrows singed. His pyjamas, fortunately for him not of an easily inflammable material, were scorched and in places actually marked by burns. Otherwise he seemed to have escaped damage. My left hand was rather badly burnt. This had happened in my first mad attempt to beat out the flames. All through the house was the horrible stench of the burning and the quenching, and I felt my mouth and throat to be as dry as a lime-kiln. Arbuthnot went to the sideboard and measured out two pegs of brandy. I gulped mine.

"Now for a bit of first aid," he said. He was never without some simple medical equipment, and in a few minutes my hand, which, now the excitement was over, was calling attention to itself by excruciating pains, was comfortably bandaged.

"I'm very sorry about this," I said frankly. "I never guessed what that devil was up to."

"It was largely my fault," responded Arbuthnot, "for not warning you that the man would most probably come by the back door."

With the help of an electric torch we examined the wreck of the kitchen. The floor covering was naturally ruined, the remains of the table had collapsed, the curtains had vanished, two chairs were charred skeletons of their former selves, and walls and ceiling were hideously blackened.

"A shock for Mrs. Morris in the morning," commented Arbuthnot with a chuckle. "It is no good making attempts at clearing up now. I'm going outside for a minute."

He produced the bunch of keys that had been lent to us, unlocked the kitchen door, and disappeared, taking the torch with him. After the lapse of a couple of minutes he returned.

"What have you been doing?" I asked curiously.

"Throwing the remains of a truss of hay over the cliff," he said. "The sight of it would otherwise have provoked inquiries."

"I think it time inquiries *were* instituted," I said. "Your thesis that no personal violence is intended to us seems to be at fault."

"Why, King," he cried, grinning at me, "you surely don't suppose that that individual meant to compass our deaths?"

"Why shouldn't I suppose so?" I demanded.

"It's difficult to burn people to death in a bungalow," he said. "I take it that our visitor hoped that the fire would be so far advanced before we woke up that we should have to make a dash for the open, leaving the place to be burnt down."

"Then there's clearly something in this place that has to be destroyed at all costs. Where can it be, though? I'll have a look in the roof when it's daylight."

Arbuthnot shook his head.

"I've already looked there," he said. "Now, King, cover yourself up as well as you can in the absence of bedding and get some sleep. I'm for a wash, but you'd better have a rest first."

"What about starting a hue and cry after this?" I suggested.

"No. We've nothing to trace him by. There are a hundred thousand people live in the Isle of Wight, besides the usual influx of summer visitors. Next time he comes here we must catch him red-handed."

"Are you going to inform the police?"

"Certainly. They will agree with me. It is no good scaring the man away by a local inquisition. He probably is posing as a seaside visitor and has quiet lodgings in one of the villages such as Brook or Brighstone. He may even be living in Freshwater. But that's no evidence against him. Now get to bed."

My eyes were still smarting with the smoke and my hand throbbed painfully so that I was glad to obey his injunction and forget my discomforts in sleep.

My rest was terminated by the loud outcries of Mrs. Morris on beholding the state of her beloved kitchen and the measured tones of Arbuthnot ordering her to observe secrecy. Under his orders the ruined furniture was thrown in on top of the coal pending final disposal. As it was Sunday nothing could be done that day to replace what had been destroyed. Mrs. Morris, however, dragged up the charred linoleum and washed the stone floor underneath before she set to work to produce what under the circumstances was a very creditable breakfast.

"Now remember, if you're asked, that the fire was an accident due to the dropping of a cigarette end," counselled Arbuthnot, as she brought in our bacon and eggs.

"Very well, sir. I hopes none of them kind of accidents happens to me," she observed.

After we had breakfasted and Arbuthnot had replaced my bandage by a fresh, spotlessly clean one, I took my pipe and strolled up the down in the warmth of the summer morning. It was a joy to be clear of the place that had produced such evil surprises. Arbuthnot went off in the opposite direction to the public telephone to talk to the police, for there was no instrument in the bungalow.

I walked slowly with eyes on the ground, musing on the amazing outcome of our intended holiday. The result of my meditations was a tentative conclusion that Rodd, whatever his guilt, must be dissociated from the people operating against us at present. Rodd might have employed an accomplice, but one could suggest no earthly reason for his being a member of a gang. The truth must be that the death of Flyte had set up another train of consequences to which at present we had no clue. At this point I looked up and saw an unmistakable figure coming towards me.

"Poor old thing," cried Pamela, flourishing a walking-stick as if to bar my progress. "Did it hurt its paw then?"

"It did," I said grimly.

"And what naughtiness was it up to?"

"We set fire to the bungalow," I admitted.

"Babies! All men are babies." Then, with the sudden change of tone I was becoming accustomed to in this lady, she added, "Is it very bad?"

"Good heavens, no!"

"So you say."

"Pamela," I said firmly, "what are you doing in Freshwater?"

She glanced at me in some surprise.

"Just being nosey, I suppose," she answered with a childish pout and a glimmer of mischief in her eyes.

"How many people know of your engagement to Rodd?" I went on, feeling that my manners were not above criticism but that the situation demanded plain speech.

"Only Gerry and one or two other pals."

"You realize, I hope, that your very existence as Rodd's fiancée makes his act in coming to the Isle of Wight appear peculiar."

"I'm not an imbecile," she remarked, walking on. I followed.

"Then why come here?"

"Gerry suggested it. He could see I was nearly frantic. We had seen Mr. Arbuthnot's name in the papers, and Gerry said it was better to try and get him to help Thornton if possible. Gerry knew your friend was very clever, and he said that if he found out about my being engaged to Thornton and I had kept it dark it would look very suspicious."

"There's a certain amount of sense in that," I agreed.

"When will they let Thornton out?" she queried, turning the wide blue eyes up into my face in a way I should have deemed theatrical in another woman. "It's maddening to be in a position when one daren't even ask to see him."

"I don't know when he may hope to regain his freedom," I said slowly, staring straight ahead as I spoke.

"But they've nothing against him except a lot of fluky coincidences. A clever barrister would make the whole thing look a farce."

"Look here, Pamela," I said desperately. "Things aren't so simple as you seem to think. The fact is—but I oughtn't to be telling you this."

I hesitated miserably. I thought she had a right to know what had been discovered. She was not the sort of girl whom it would have been a kindness to leave in a fool's paradise. She had better hear things from my lips than from newspaper reports of court proceedings. At the same time I was perilously near a breach of confidence in telling her.

"Edmund, you won't dare stop," she said firmly, but fumbling oddly to draw a cigarette from her case as she spoke.

"It is for your ears alone," I iterated.

"Of course." This was proudly spoken.

"Not even Mr. Bellingham must know."

"Gerry is too fond of me to split, but you needn't fear I shall tell him."

"I don't."

"Go on, then," she said, holding the match to her cigarette with fingers that first shook and then grew calm, as if their owner had ordered them to cease their foolishness. I was so engrossed as to have forgotten the customary act of politeness.

"The police have evidence that there was some bad feeling between Rodd and the man Flyte," I said bluntly.

Pamela stopped and faced me.

"What?" she said, with a catch in her voice.

I repeated my statement.

"What nonsense!" she cried. "What pure drivel!" But I could see that she had taken a shock. "It's a mistake of theirs," she added.

"I don't see that it can be," I remarked gloomily.

"What is it then?"

"They've obtained a scrap of paper that escaped burning in the motor smash. It's part of a memorandum in Flyte's handwriting to the effect that Rodd must be considered dangerous."

"Hold me a minute," she breathed.

I saw she was swaying on her feet. I supported her waist and felt very awkward there on the open down with some confounded golfers not a hundred yards away.

"I'm all right now," she said after a few seconds, with a long, shuddering sigh. "I'm sorry I was so silly."

We walked on in silence.

"Does Mr. Arbuthnot consider that conclusive?" she asked at last.

"I've no idea. He's not communicative in these days."

"I can't understand it, and I don't believe it," she asserted. I passed over the lack of logic in the remark.

"There's another small matter that's come to light," I said, feeling that it was better that she should know all I could tell her.

"Yes? Tell me. You needn't be frightened that I'll be silly again."

"It's not much. The police have found out the identity of the man who was killed in the car. It seems that he was a notorious New York criminal who is believed to have played the part of hired assassin on previous occasions."

"So they think that Thornton engaged a man to commit murder and then joined in himself," she cried scornfully. "Does it sound likely?"

"They surmise that Rodd was in the locality to receive something the other man was to get from Flyte," I explained. "They do not necessarily suppose that Rodd connived at murder. The other man may have committed that deed on his own initiative."

She nodded. She seemed to have recovered her self-control completely. "I can suggest a much simpler explanation," she remarked, "so far as Thornton is concerned."

"By all means let's have it."

"Which would you suspect first, Thornton whose record is known to everybody or this Flyte who seems such a mystery?"

"On first principles, Flyte, of course. But he didn't kill himself."

"Of course not. But you know Thornton had recently come in for quite a lot of money. Isn't it possible that Flyte was a man who lived by his wits and that he had a scheme for tricking Thornton out of some of his inheritance? His note might have meant that Thornton would be dangerous if he discovered the trick that was being worked."

"There are plenty of sharks always on the look-out for a young man with money," I said thoughtfully. "Do you suggest that Rodd was lured to the Isle of Wight, possibly by this American working as an accomplice of Flyte's, found that he had landed in a queer corner, and eventually had to shoot Flyte to get away?"

Pamela wrinkled her brows. "I didn't quite mean that," she confessed.

"If there's any truth in my suggestion," I continued, "it would surely have been the best thing for Rodd to have owned up at once. On a plea of self-defence he would probably have received the benefit of the doubt and got away with it."

During our conversation we had gradually approached the bungalow, and here we parted, I to seek Arbuthnot

and she to return to her hotel. I watched her going downhill with, I fancied, rather less than the usual joy of life
revealed by her step, and then turned to find Arbuthnot
standing at the back door regarding me with a broad grin.

"I'm afraid you're a butterfly, King," he said.

"I'm a blab," I answered as we went indoors.

"So you've been divulging our recent news to Miss
Strode?"

"Not our own affairs. Only what Bernard told us yesterday."

"How did she take it?"

"She seemed rather upset. Of course I made her understand that the news was confidential. Did you get on to
the police?"

"Yes. I told them about our recent adventure. They will
not intervene in that matter unless I ask for help."

"What did they think of things?"

"Bernard was naturally discreet on the 'phone. He said
that it probably meant they would have to revise their
opinion about Rodd and think he might have been as much
sinned against as sinning."

"That's rather my idea too," I said, and went on to give
him the gist of my discussion with Pamela.

"I obtained a couple of Sunday papers at the hotel. You
may find them interesting," said Arbuthnot.

They were lying on the dining-room table and I took
them up, and after a glance put them down again.

"They don't belong to that section of the Sunday Press
which I usually read," I remarked.

"That's a pity. But conquer your qualms for once and
look at this."

He took up one of the papers as he spoke, folded it
back at a certain page, and handed it to me.

"Third column," he said.

I read:

POLICE RAID DOPE DEPOT
ALLEGED CONNECTION WITH RECENT CRIME
(From our Crime Specialist)

Acting, we believe, on information anonymously communicated a detachment from Scotland Yard yesterday raided a house in the Brixton Road. The authorities are reticent concerning the nature of their haul, but it is alleged to have included considerable quantities of cocaine and other drugs which find a ready sale in the underworld. These, we are informed, were discovered in various cleverly-designed hiding-places about the building. No arrests have so far been made, as the occupants of the place had evidently taken alarm and decamped in time, but there were many indications that the house had been in improper use as a night club. In their craze for anything in the way of a new sensation we can quite believe that a certain section of Society found amusement in going so far afield from their usual haunts to visit this centre of degraded pleasure.

A thrill has been caused by the strong rumour that the police are aware that this den of vice was connected in some way with the 'mystery man', Dalton Flyte, whose murder under extraordinary circumstances has recently aroused such excitement in the Isle of Wight and elsewhere. The authorities have refused either to confirm or deny this report. Fresh developments are hourly expected, and all England is breathlessly waiting for news that may affect the fate of the brilliant young engineer, Thornton Rodd, whose daring escape

we recently chronicled and who now lies in
jail awaiting trial on a charge of complicity in
the above murder.

"It's no more than I expected," I remarked as I laid
down the paper.

"Quite so. No one supposed Dalton Flyte would turn
out to be a Sunday school teacher."

"This will tell in Rodd's favour," said I. "That is, presuming there is any truth in the report."

"It seems to be worth looking into at any rate," replied
Arbuthnot.

"Does that mean you are going to London?" I asked.

"Why not?"

"I was thinking of the watch on the bungalow," I said.

"I know. I shall go up this afternoon. The first available boat leaves Yarmouth at three-fifty-five. That will
mean one night in London, which I fear will entail some
loss of sleep for you. This you can recoup after my return."

"I'm not likely to sleep," I remarked.

"Not feeling nervous, King?"

"Not exactly. But I admit that I prefer a fight in the
open to the attentions of these individuals. Still, considering last night's events, they will probably be chary of
paying us another visit after such a brief interval. For all
they know, the whole island may be on the watch for them
by now."

"Notwithstanding what you say you should be on the
alert."

"Certainly I shall."

We had finished lunch and Arbuthnot was packing his
bag when Pamela and Mr. Bellingham arrived.

"We principally came to condole with you on what
might easily have been a disaster of some magnitude," said
the latter. "Pamela has been telling me that you were on

the verge of a serious conflagration last night. People will soon come to regard this bungalow as ill-fated and refuse to live here."

Arbuthnot laughed.

"I don't think the blame for King's carelessness should be visited on innocent bricks and mortar," he said.

"However, ill-fated or not, why not leave it for a couple of hours and give us the pleasure of your company at dinner to-night. It is very short notice, I know, but perhaps under the circumstances you will waive your right to a greater formality of approach."

"I'm very sorry," responded Arbuthnot. "I am about to leave the bungalow for longer than two hours."

"Surely you are not throwing up the case?"

"No. But circumstances have arisen which make it desirable for me to go to London. Have you seen to-day's papers?"

"Only the principal articles in the *Observer,*" replied Mr. Bellingham.

"Then you'll be interested in this," said Arbuthnot, handing him the newspaper folded so as to exhibit the account of the police raid. Mr. Bellingham scrutinized the page intently, while Pamela read from an angle at the same time.

"It is no more than one would have expected," he declared. "The mystery that surrounded the man Flyte boded no good. In a sense I think we may say that this scrap of information, if duly authenticated, will react in favour of our young friend."

"Possibly."

"You consider the news justifies your prosecuting inquiries in London?"

"It may do. We seem to be at a standstill here."

"Pamela, my dear, it appears that the little dinner-party you planned has vanished into the limbo of the impossible."

"Sorry I can't sob to oblige you," she answered, looking impudently at Arbuthnot.

"The loss is entirely mine," the latter said gravely.

"Why should we not contract our square into a triangle and ask Sir Edmund King to honour us?" suggested Mr. Bellingham.

"I doubt if Sir Edmund would care for a triangular existence," said Pamela, gazing up innocently at the last speaker. I smiled. "What you really need is a few angles rubbed off," she added, turning on me suddenly. This time Arbuthnot smiled.

I had been mentally busy manufacturing excuses that should sound plausible. Obviously I could not be away from the bungalow after dark. Unlikely as it was that there should be a raid that night, I dared not run any risk.

"My hand seems rather worse than I thought," I put in. "I'm afraid I should be very poor company at dinner."

"No excuse, King," said Arbuthnot genially. "Miss Strode, I perceive, has very kindly undertaken your reformation and the least you can do is to submit to the process."

"I'll take you in hand next," said Pamela mockingly to my friend.

Arbuthnot bowed. "I shall hasten my return," he declared.

I was standing in bewilderment. Surely Arbuthnot could not be so lightly contemplating leaving the bungalow unguarded during the evening hours? Perhaps he was only urging our visitors on to have the indecent pleasure of seeing me flounder amidst inadequate excuses. Then I saw that he was passing his pipe bowl around his right palm with a slow circulatory movement.

"I am at your service," I said to Pamela.

"Splendid!" cried Mr. Bellingham. "Perhaps I ought to mention that a short coat will be entirely appropriate."

"But long trousers," added Pamela, favouring me with a distinct wink. "And don't gape so," she continued, "it ruins your patrician aspect."

"I'm sorry," I said hastily.

"I will see that he has a protracted siesta," interposed Arbuthnot, "so that he will be sufficiently awake to profit by your instruction this evening."

"Good! Come along, Gerry. Sir Edmund King is going to hibernate."

She shot me a glance that made me feel prepared to tolerate her impudence, swept a bow to Arbuthnot, and had vanished before Mr. Bellingham had completed his more elaborate adieux.

"I'm surprised you should approve of my leaving here at night," I said to Arbuthnot when we were once more alone.

"Provided you return by midnight it will be all right," he answered. "I will leave you the back-door key and lock the front door, taking the key with me in case I may return when no one is in the house." He dissociated one key from the bunch and gave it into my custody.

"You can't say what time you'll return?" I asked.

"No. It will be some time to-morrow."

He left shortly after three o'clock and I took my pipe and a certain vague disquietude with me and sat on the veranda instead of indulging in the afternoon sleep that Arbuthnot had hinted at in preparation for my all-night vigil. At the back of my mind I fought shy of the prospect of returning to the empty bungalow at night. Our nocturnal visitors had a means of ingress, and the idea of possibly finding one or more of them ensconced indoors waiting for my return was not one to be faced with equanimity. However, Arbuthnot had said that everything would be all right.

Mrs. Morris brought me some tea and then departed homewards. I sat on until it was time to prepare to go out, watching clouds slowly banking up in the south over the sea. I judged that in spite of the moon it would be a fairly dark night with the possibility of rain. The pointer of the obsolete pattern barometer in the house was oscillating about the legend "Fair", but Arbuthnot's avowed contempt for the instrument had impaired my confidence in it. I dressed very deliberately, and yet found myself at the Freshwater Bay Hotel, a biggish building with adequate grounds, by a quarter past seven.

Pamela appeared radiant, defying superstition in a green dress with cunning traces of gold.

"Cocktail, of course?" she cried as soon as she arrived.

"Sherry for me," I said grimly. "I was well brought up."

"If you're going to be grumpy I'll develop a headache and leave you to the tender mercies of Gerry," she said menacingly. "He's keen on the economic dependence of the Irish Free State at present."

"Don't leave me," I said in alarm. "I'll drink all you give me—except cocktails. I belong to the Society for the Preservation of Abdominal Membranes."

"I thought you were going to say 'Ancient Monuments'," she observed. "Do you collect postage stamps by any chance?"

"*Your* hobby is obvious," I retorted.

"What is it then?"

"Ground-baiting for old trout," I said.

"Really, Edmund, you're coming on quite well. Given an opportunity you may become perfectly vulgar," she remarked critically.

"I should be very sorry to believe that Sir Edmund King could succumb to the modern craze for smartness at whatever cost in loss of gentility it may entail," said a familiar voice behind me.

"Gerry, you're like a large piece of damp rag," cried Pamela scoffingly.

"That's not original," I said.

"My dear boy, haven't you realized that we were born at least two thousand years too late to hope to be that?"

"Day by day the world offers greater opportunities to those competent to accept them," observed Mr. Bellingham.

"Day by day the world grows more bored with its own existence, so that it scrambles madly for any new sensation," said Pamela, dipping into a concoction containing a drowned olive. "Hurry up with your genteel drinks and come outdoors. I'm stuffy in here."

The five-minutes promenade on the lawn showed me the cloud-bank mounting. I decided that I should curtail my visit as much as I politely could.

"We dine at seven-thirty," proclaimed Mr. Bellingham. "Pamela has exerted her ingenuity in ordering the meal."

"He means," commented Pamela to me, "that he won't get any of the dishes that used to be hawked around in the baronial halls of old. Personally I think people were pigs in those days. Why, the ancient Romans even—"

"Pamela," said Mr. Bellingham warningly.

The gong cut short a possible dissertation on the gastronomical idiosyncrasies of Lucullus and his contemporaries.

"Talking of the Irish Free State—" said Pamela mischievously as she helped herself impartially to *hors d'oeuvres.*

"Pamela finds my conversation foreign to her interests," said Mr. Bellingham. "Nevertheless it cannot be denied—" And for the next half-hour we listened to a masterly analysis of the Shannon hydro-electric power scheme. When the speaker touched business subjects he was a different man, and he held my attention despite my preoccupation with my own far from pleasant thoughts. His face, slightly sallow, no doubt as a result of orient suns, set in unfamiliar lines as he traversed admirably and succinctly the economics of that ambitious undertaking. He was, *par excellence,*

the business man who had left no time in his working
life to acquire interests outside his own occupation. I am
always sorry for such.

"Bring me a large water," said Pamela abruptly to an
astonished waiter who was proffering champagne.

"My dear Pamela, this abstinence is abnormal," cried
Mr. Bellingham.

"I'm horribly dry!" she said.

Her companion looked at me as if he felt comment
were superfluous.

"Your friend, Mr. Arbuthnot, is an extremely interesting man," he said, abandoning the Irish Free State. "One
cannot imagine him discomposed at anything."

"His policy of masterly inactivity is only equaled by
the consummate lethargy of his associate," contributed
Pamela. "Gibbon ought to have written that."

"What do you know about Gibbon?" I inquired, rather
surprised.

"I know a bit about everything. That's why I'm the
most useless person in the world," she answered bitterly.
"People like me cut no ice nowadays. If I'd spent years of
research perfecting a tin-tack with an unbreakable head I
should now be reaping a fortune."

I twisted the stem of my wine-glass meditatively. This
young woman had more brains than I had supposed.

"Never mind," she continued more cheerfully as a fresh
dish appeared. "There is always the pleasure of seeing Gerry wrapping the asparagus round his ears."

All the events of that dinner bore then, and still bear,
an air of unreality to me. I have had a similar feeling when
returning from the trenches to some of the amenities of
civilization: a sensation that all my surroundings would
suddenly vanish and I should be hurled back into the confusion and danger from which I had just emerged.

Mr. Bellingham and I were alternate targets for Pamela's wit until about ten o'clock. In spite of the fact that she had drunk hardly anything, her eyes glittered and her speech was rapid. Her voice had the hard ring of those who find the world a farce, and a poorly-staged one at that. Only once, when my host made some passing reference to Rodd, did her chatter cease and the look in her eyes become momentarily wistful.

Shortly after ten, Mr. Bellingham, who for some little time had been straining his politeness to conceal a post-prandial lassitude, was guilty of an enormous yawn.

"Time you were in bed, Gerry," said Pamela promptly.

"I'm afraid I'm not the man I was," he said apologetically.

We were sitting outdoors under the now overcast sky. I rose from my chair.

"You're not to go," cried Pamela. "When Gerry retires I shall read you the lecture I have been preparing."

I submitted to remain.

"I am confident in Pamela's ability to entertain you," said Mr. Bellingham. "Perhaps on this occasion you will forgive an old man and permit me to leave you to her care."

I murmured acquiescence.

"I'll see that he goes straight home," Pamela remarked.

Mr. Bellingham waved a deprecating hand,

"My dear, I rely on your doing nothing of the kind. It would mean your returning alone, and that would worry me." With more courteous words to me he disappeared into the hotel.

The remaining two of us fell silent. I was watching the moon that was making but a feeble showing behind the flocks of fleecy clouds that covered the sky. In the half-light all the world was grey. I thought that possibly my

evening's amusements might not stop short at a dinner-
party. However, Arbuthnot had been confident that there
was no danger to be anticipated before midnight.

"This is a hell of a life!" burst out Pamela suddenly.

I mumbled something intended to be consolatory.

"One can do precisely nothing," she went on, mouthing
every word separately as if to challenge denial. I did not
answer, for her words were evidently true. Rodd, were he
guilty or innocent, had got himself into a fine mess from
which at the best he could only escape with a tarnished
reputation. I could not see any source from which clear-
ance could come. I anticipated a reluctant acquittal and
the voice of scandal heralding a poisonous future.

"You've forgotten your self-appointed task," I stated,
anxious to divert her mind to other things.

"What's that?"

"My reformation."

"Oh, you're a dear old thing," she vouchsafed.

"But that's exactly what I oughtn't to be according to
your principles."

"I'm not a reformer to-night," she answered. "Tell me
what you thought of Thornton."

"Everything?"

"Certainly."

Glad of a tangible topic, I embarked on a history of
the various happenings in which we and Rodd had been
involved.

"Good heavens, it's striking eleven!" I cried when I had
brought my rambling remarks up to the point of describing the great hue and cry after his escape.

"I'll walk back with you," she said.

"Mr. Bellingham wouldn't like that," I replied.

"Are you going to tell him?"

"Of course not."

"Then come on. I shall go mad if I shut myself up in a bedroom yet."

Together we strolled back towards my temporary dwelling. The world was asleep but for us. I felt acutely conscious of my companion's presence, as if the storms that must be agitating her mind stirred a sympathetic tide in my own. We were both silent as we passed the bay and mounted the farther slope. A greyish mass looming indistinctly on my right brought me back to my own troubles. I pointed out that our walk was nearing its end.

"Are you scared of sleeping in that place?" she asked.

"No," I answered, reflecting that my reply was perfect truth. I did not anticipate any sleep that night.

"I don't want to go back yet," she said. "Let's walk on a little way. My mind runs round and round like a mongoose in a cage."

I went on with her. After all, Arbuthnot had given me till midnight.

"Do people who are really suffering make a parade of their feelings?" I asked sharply.

"Of course not," she responded swiftly. "I'm only fifty per cent genuine. It's all my upbringing and style of life allow me to be."

I was nonplussed by such candour and strode on in silence. Presently we came to where the military road entered the cutting in the down. Pamela promptly mounted the bank on the right.

"Take care," I said. "You're not twenty yards from the edge of the cliff, and it's all downhill."

"Let's sit down a minute," she said. "This is a good place to feel how tuppeny-ha'penny one's own affairs really are."

I climbed up out of the cutting and sat down beside her. Before us lay a leaden sea whose fringe was making a sucking, gurgling noise among the rocks three hundred feet below. Behind us the black outline of the down cut the hardly less sombre sky in a convex curve.

"What would it be like to die that way?" she asked, and I felt rather than saw her point towards the cliff edge.

I shivered. An old antipathy of mine was aroused at the thought of that hideous downward rush through space. Away on our left the rotating beam from the great light-house at St. Catherine's swept over the sea towards us, vanished, reappeared, and continued its orderly movements.

"Arbuthnot tells me that that light is of fifteen million candle-power," I said, trying to edge the conversation on to safer ground.

"You fool!" she cried. "Where are your eyes? To me it's an angel with a flaming sword. No, I'm sorry. I shouldn't have cursed you. The truth is, I'm not fit to be with any-one to-night. Good-bye."

For one horrible moment I thought she had run towards the cliff. Then I heard her feet on the road and breathed a sigh of relief. I judged she was quite capable of returning home unescorted, and philosophically pulled out the pipe and pouch which had been making a bulge in my dinner-jacket all that evening.

"Poor Pamela," I said half-aloud.

The next instant a pair of strong hands fastened around my neck from behind, I gave an instinctive lurch forward, and in a flash my aggressor and I were rolling down the slope that led to the edge of the cliff.

11
Events of Monday, June 4th

There are times in a man's life when he may be forgiven if fear sends an icy hand to claw at his very heart-strings. Such was my state when my assailant and I rolled towards death. His initial grip had given him the advantage over me, and his hold he never relaxed even when my convulsive struggle for freedom had started us downwards to catastrophe. So the terror of my childhood's dreams was to have this ghastly fulfilment!

Suddenly I was on my back with the clutch still about my throat and my feet touching nothing. It was the end. I ceased to struggle for a second and then with the fury of despair, which is more than the strength of ten, I twisted myself round. The muscles of my neck cracked, but so furious had been my exertion that my adversary's grip momentarily relaxed. I had trusted to my knees to give me an instant's purchase and a last chance of life. But the slippery down turf was against me. My body slid outwards with a frightful acceleration. More by instinct than reason, for my brain had almost ceased to work and a red glow was suffusing my bulging eyes, I dug my fingers frantically into the treacherous grass.

A chalk down is not perfectly smooth. If it were this tale would never have been written by me. The surface is crossed by little parallel indentations which I call sheep-tracks, though Arbuthnot has quite a different and more scientific explanation of their origin. By the mercy of heaven one such ran at the very cliff's edge. The tufted grass that fringed it gave me something to grasp.

As my body straightened I thought my arms would be torn from their sockets. Then I swung with my feet kicking in space. The cliff overhung at that point and no foothold was possible to relieve the strain on my arms. I turned my face up to my attacker.

I wonder now whether I should have begged for mercy if I could. As it was, my tongue moved but no sounds came. Below me the surge and withdrawal of the swell was sucking at the rocks like some disgusting glutton expecting to be gorged. And I was still alive!

As the reddish mist before my eyes cleared a little I could see my enemy a yard or two away. He was down on his hands and knees inspecting me. His features were black and unreal and not like those of any man. I guessed he was wearing a mask. He moved carefully forward.

There was nothing for me to do. If I raised a hand to ward him off the other would fail to hold me. If by an enormous effort I swung myself up he could push me down again in the act. He approached.

So, after many vicissitudes, death had come to me at last! I knew by the shape of the cliff that I should not reach the water. My body would strike about half-way down and only a shattered mass of flesh would come to the maw of the sea.

There is something in the coming of death very different from one's anticipations. As soon as the inevitable was upon me the blind fury that had clouded my brain vanished as if by magic. I saw everything in a cold, clear, mental light while numbness crept over the limbs which had finished their part in life. The infinite littleness of human doings spread out before me like a problem solved. Some obscure cerebration even produced a kind of cold pity for my murderer. Arbuthnot would make him pay to the uttermost farthing and beyond.

My wrists were seized in a steel grip. I was strangely calm. I suppose I might have shouted for help, but my amazingly clear brain told me it would be useless. I might have threatened the man with the vengeance that would surely overtake him. I did neither. I was saying in my mind, "Fear not those who have power to destroy the body."

With a sudden heave my enemy dragged me upwards and forwards. I fell flat on my face on the grass. Some little breeze brought the scent of June meadows strangely to me at that moment when I had thought the sweetness of life was over. The relaxing of a strain is worse than the bearing of it. My head swam. I could not have risen. Then my foe stooped and swiftly dealt me a stunning blow on the side of my head.

Consciousness travelled slowly back to me through a monstrous, echoing void full of sounds like the crashing of waves on an iron coast. I opened my eyes and closed them again. There was an unnatural feeling about my head which gave me physical nausea. With immense labour I began to reconstruct the events that had gone before my downfall. I stopped with a kind of mental jerk. Then I was still on the edge of the cliff! I clawed fiercely at the turf and lay, not daring to move. Gone was the mood in which I had faced death with something approaching equanimity. Mysteriously enough, I had not gone to my doom. I did not at the moment stop to ask why. I was obsessed by the craving to live at all costs.

I realized that my head was above my heels in level. That was something, but the night was black and my vision was blurred by the racking pains in my head. An

inch at a time, prodding the air with my hands in case I
was mistaken in my direction, like one who essays to gauge
the temperature of a bath before entering it, I crawled forwards. It was a slow business. I was feeling horribly sick
and my damaged hand had received no benefit from the
night's work. I did not dare rise to my feet.

Gradually as my eyes became accustomed to the gloom
I could make out the slope of the down rising above me,
and I moved more quickly. Still I would not risk standing
up. At last, after what seemed hours of labour and may
have been about ten minutes in reality, I reached the edge
of the cutting and scrambled down into it. There I lay by
the roadside with my heart pumping as if I had sprinted a
quarter-mile.

Presently I regained some composure, but this only allowed a bleak realization of the truth to intrude upon my
anxiety for my own safety. I had no idea how long I might
have been lying on the cliff edge; it might have been a
matter of a few minutes or of a couple of hours. Probably
there had been ample time for my unknown adversary to
go to the bungalow and accomplish the purpose which we
had previously frustrated. Perhaps even now the house was
in flames. And I had failed in my trust. What a fool I had
been to go wandering on the downs with that girl when
I should have been mounting guard! Certainly Arbuthnot
had given me till midnight, but then he had obviously
not anticipated my undertaking a nocturnal stroll. The
watcher had not been slow in seizing his opportunity.
He had most probably already been aware of Arbuthnot's
departure.

I considered the sky. The opacity of the clouds was
such that it was impossible accurately to judge the position of the moon, which might have helped me to estimate
the time. I had naturally discarded my wrist-watch when
I dressed for dinner and had had no other one with me to

replace it. I knew that I had left the hotel about eleven. The attack on me must have been made about half an hour later. Then the time must be at least midnight.

I could form no plan. My only aim was to get back to the bungalow. I rose to my feet and found I was unsteady but capable of moving provided I did not try to hurry. I progressed about a hundred yards along the cutting and then giddiness obliged me to stop and rest. A thought of Pamela entered my head. How extraordinarily she had behaved! And how fortunately it had turned out for the man who had been watching his chance. Still, I could not blame her for that. I moved on.

Before I had emerged from the end of the cutting I felt assured that the bungalow was not yet ablaze or I could not have failed to see some reflection of the flames from the clouds above. A few large drops of rain were falling and a cool breeze brought some relief to my aching head. Then I came out of the cutting on to the open slope that led downhill to the bay and saw something which drove all thoughts of my personal discomfort from my head.

Away to my left front in a position I judged to be that of the bungalow shone a bright and steady light! For a fleeting moment I thought again of fire, but the steadiness of the light reassured me on that point. What I saw was the still radiance of electricity. In vain I told myself that the light could possibly proceed from a house on the far side of the bay. It was too far to my left for that, and beyond it could be only the sea.

The sight of the light was staggering to me. The sublime audacity of the individual who was thus going about his nefarious business in comfort was more disconcerting than any degree of stealthiness. Anyone seeing the light would naturally assume that it denoted my presence and so leave the intruder to work undisturbed. And what was his work?

A kind of blind rage came over me. This fellow had haunted the bungalow and attempted to destroy it by fire; he had brought me within an ace of death and then laid me unconscious by a savage blow, and now he was calmly carrying on his evil business unchallenged. I hastened my steps. In some way or another I would be even with him. But I must have a plan.

Presently I came to the disused, sunken road that ran to the cliff edge about two hundred yards from the bungalow. I dropped into it, and crouching on the farther side considered the position. The light evidently came either from my bedroom or from Arbuthnot's. Now my only entrance to the house was by the kitchen door. Then I remembered something. The electric light in the kitchen had been destroyed in the fire and there had been no bulb available to replace it. Could I but get into the kitchen unobserved I had a chance. So far as I knew the unknown would have to leave that way, and in the darkness he might easily fall into my hands. But I needed a weapon of some sort to give me the odds, and what could the bare down produce in that line?

Then I had an inspiration. A little farther along the road I was in was the post-and-rail fence I had seen on a previous occasion. I hurried to it. Fortunately for me the top bar was in sections and the securing nails had almost rusted to extinction in the damp sea-air. Anger lending me strength I wrenched off a section and then had a weapon in the shape of a wooden rail about four feet long and two inches or so square.

I moved outwards and to my right to reach the kitchen door by fetching a kind of semicircle so that I should not be under observation from the side windows of the house. With discretion I came to the door at last and listened, but could hear nothing. The rain was now falling fairly fast, pattering on the roof and even commencing to drip from the eaves. I welcomed it, for any noise would help to cover my own movements. I considered whether I should not do well to wait outside the door and take the chance of felling my man when he emerged. It was a safer course, certainly, but there were two things to urge against it: in the dark a blow might easily go partly or wholly astray and I might have no time to strike another; secondly, I was very uneasy as to what might be happening in the house while I stood outside in the rain.

Then I had the sudden assurance that there were still surprises in store for me. Maintaining a good grip on my weapon with one hand, I felt in my pocket for the key. *It was gone!*

I believe I was on the verge of tears. The pains in my head and hand were maddening, and this final disaster seemed to pass the limit of the endurable. Presumably the key had fallen from my pocket during the struggle. Perhaps it was even now lying for ever irrecoverable under the sea. But perhaps my assailant had seized the opportunity my unconsciousness afforded to dispossess me of it. I knew he had a key himself, so he could not want it to obtain admission to the bungalow. Rather had he taken it, and most likely hurled it away, in order that when I came to my senses I could not if I wished interfere with his devilment, or at the least I should lose valuable time through having to break into the house or seek assistance.

At that moment when all seemed black a ray of hope came. From far away beyond the marshes that lie behind the little bay sounded the chiming of bells from Freshwater Church. I held my breath. One! Two! Three! Four! I listened no longer, for it was clear that midnight was sounding. My spell of unconsciousness had been far less extensive than I had feared. Re-emboldened, I kicked off my shoes and stood on the wet ground. There was just a chance that my visitor had not bothered to lock the door.

He might be relying on my being knocked out for a considerable length of time and intending to lock it when he left. It was only a bare possibility, but I would try. I laid my hand on the knob and rotated it with infinite caution. Then in response to my gentle pressure the door opened!

With equal caution I gradually released my holding. I listened. The house seemed absolutely silent. Had the unlawful tenant already smelt a rat? Was he perhaps crouching behind the door waiting to deal with me? It was not an inspiring thought, but I could not leave the door open indefinitely. The sound of the falling rain would become more clearly audible through the opening, and this might attract attention. I stepped inside.

Nothing happened. The kitchen was in darkness and so was the passage, by which I judged that the door of the room where the light was situated was shut. With immense care I closed the door. Considering my shaky condition I felt that I had done well to achieve it with so little noise.

Then suddenly somewhere in the house a door opened; there were footsteps in the passage, a click, and the hall became faintly illuminated with light which I saw streamed out from the drawing-room. So the man was there! In the silence I had begun to wonder if the bird were flown. Well, he was going to get more than he bargained for this time. I didn't very much care how hard I hit him. It was my turn. I stepped back to be beside the door. From that position I could not see into the hall, but as the intruder was obviously exercising no caution I should have ample warning of his approach. My grip on the wooden bar tightened.

Footsteps.

They came along the passage. Then they stopped at the door leading into the kitchen. I thought that the thumping of my heart must be so loud as to be audible and my breath made a faint hissing like escaping gas.

A minute must have passed and nothing happened. I could not see the man, and equally I was sure he could not see me, but evidently something had aroused his suspicions. The strain was growing intolerable. I contemplated a wild dash, a risking of everything on a single blow.

Then, and my heart stood still, came a voice, and a familiar one.

"My dear King, wouldn't you be more comfortable in the drawing-room?"

My wooden bar crashed on to the stone floor.

"Arbuthnot?" I whispered, in disbelieving tones.

"He."

"Then how the devil did you manage to get back?"

"By the simple process of not going away."

"Good heavens!"

I staggered wearily across the kitchen floor and along the passage into the drawing-room, Arbuthnot preceding me. I hardly knew whether to be delighted at my friend's unexpected appearance or enraged at finding that my chance of retaliation on the enemy who had handled me so roughly was gone.

When I reached the drawing-room and stood blinking in the bright light I must have presented a sorry picture. My hair was dishevelled and plastered by the rain, there was a lump as big as an egg on the left side of my head, my tie peeped coquettishly from my right shoulder, my suit was garnished with chalky stains, and the bandage that should have covered my left hand hung in a foul festoon. My stockinged feet were caked with mud and one great toe peered out as if it disliked its habitation and meditated a change.

Arbuthnot burst out laughing.

"Peculiar effects of a harmless flirtation," he said.

"A flirtation with death," I answered.

The expression on his face changed.

"As bad as that?" he queried with his eyebrows raised. "But come—action before talk." With these words he marched me to the bathroom.

Arbuthnot had almost feminine skill in nursing. While I was gratefully drinking the peg he brought me, he swathed my aching head in a cool, wet bandage and redressed the burns on my hand. By the time I had shed my soiled garments, washed, and assumed a dressing-gown and slippers I felt moderately comfortable. We returned to the drawing-room and I sank into an easy chair and lit a cigarette.

"Now for your tale," said Arbuthnot. "I will take up the running afterwards." He listened with extreme care to all I had to say, making me begin my account from the very moment when he had left the bungalow the previous afternoon.

"Have I made everything clear?" I asked at the end.

"Very clear. I'm sorry you had such a dusting. Otherwise I am very pleased at the way things have turned out.

"Glad to hear you say so."

"This will interest you," he continued, thrusting his hand into his coat pocket.

Something spun in the air and alighted on my lap. I picked it up and gazed at it stupidly for a second. Then I sprang to my feet.

"Where on earth did this come from?" I cried.

It was the key of the kitchen door!

"All in good time," he answered, smiling. "Let us do everything decently and in order."

"Hurry up then," I said, my pains and fatigue forgotten as I regarded the little scrap of metal in my hand.

"I would first draw your attention to the localization of everything in this case," he began deliberately. "This district has been the scene of action the whole time. That in itself was enough to make me indisposed to leave it.

The account of the police raid we read in yesterday's paper immediately aroused my suspicions. Whence did the police get their information? So far as I could see it must have been communicated by one of the gang who evidently used the place as head-quarters. The death of the man whose name to us was Dalton Flyte had probably caused a break-up of the gang; judging by his affluence one might suppose him to have been the leader. The old headquarters were of no more use except in one way: they would serve as a bait to draw me to London out of the way of whatever was intended here."

"Some outside person who had merely used the place as a night-club or as a source of drug-supply might have informed the police," I suggested.

"In that case why the delay? Flyte was killed on the twenty-fifth of May—to-day is the fourth of June. Why should anyone wait a week before sending an anonymous letter? No, there was a strong probability, to say the least, that the revelation was just one more move in the game."

"Well?"

"My obvious line of action was to appear to fall into the trap. Some one no doubt would be watching to see if I departed for London, and I should not know him for a watcher if I saw him. Hence I went through all the routine of departure, not even confiding in you."

"You might have done that," I suggested.

"No, it would only have given you one more thing to worry about. It was not possible to concert a plan of action beforehand or there would have been some point in telling you."

"Go on."

"I made my journey as far as Lymington, being careful, however, to purchase a ticket to Waterloo in case I were overheard while at the booking office. I hung about in Lymington for the rest of the afternoon and re-crossed to

Yarmouth by the last boat, arriving at seven-fifty. Anyone who had previously watched me depart would know that I could not get back from London that night. I did not leave Yarmouth till dusk, and then came cross-country to the bay. By half-past ten I had got into position behind that clump of furze on the other side of the road about two hundred yards from us. It was darkish, but my eyesight, as you know, is pretty fair, and I judged that I could see anyone approaching or leaving the bungalow."

"Of course, I see now why you were so indifferent as to what time I returned from the dinner-party," I said.

"Exactly. The later you were the better chance it gave me of catching our visitor unawares. The place was dark when I took up my post, so I knew you had not returned. Shortly before eleven a man came on to the down. He did not come from the bay but by the road that leads to the down from the landward side and terminates near the first tee of the golf-course, about fifty yards from where I was hiding."

He paused to relight his pipe.

"The fellow went straight across to the bungalow," he continued when the pipe was drawing to his satisfaction, "then skirted it on the east side and disappeared. I knew he must be on the veranda awaiting the return of the reveller."

"Curious he didn't go straight in," I muttered.

"That is a subject for speculation. I continued my watch, revolving varying plans of action in my mind. A few minutes later my friend King and his fair companion appeared in sight coming from the direction of the bay. I knew that the watcher by looking out from the west side of the veranda could see their approach. It was the time to act. You and Miss Strode stopped on the road midway between me and the bungalow. I supposed that she would turn back at that point and you would cross the grass to the back door. Rather to my surprise you both walked on. Perhaps you had gone a couple of hundred yards—at any fate I had lost sight of you—when the man emerged from the veranda. I expected him to enter the house, but he did not. Instead he made a wide sweep to reach the higher ground on the left of the road and disappeared. This was the second unexpected incident of my watch.

"In turn I made a sweep to my right where the slope kept me below the skyline and so arrived at the veranda of the house. I opened the front door and went in, taking up a position at your bedroom window. If you returned first I should know you because you would have Miss Strode with you. I have never learnt enough to allow fully for the eccentricities of women. If some one came alone it would be my quarry."

"I had a narrow escape there," I said meditatively.

"You did! About twenty minutes after I had entered the bedroom I caught the sound of hasty footsteps on the road."

"That, of course, was Pamela," I interposed.

"Undoubtedly. But how was I to know that? The sounds came from a solitary person. They passed by. The person had gone on. I was puzzled. The footsteps might merely have been those of some belated but perfectly innocent individual. Things were not turning out at all as I had anticipated. But the next occurrence was more exciting."

Most irritatingly he stopped to bring out a match and relight his pipe.

"I had opened the window a little in order to hear better. Three or four minutes after the first person had passed my ear caught the sound of some one running. The down turf makes no sound, but this individual must have got on to the road, from which I judged speed was more important than silence. He came from the direction in which you had gone."

"I can quite see the need for his haste," I cried, leaning forward eagerly. "He didn't know how long it would be before I recovered consciousness."

"I felt sure it wasn't you," continued Arbuthnot, "for surely you would not have run away and left Miss Strode on the down alone. I went swiftly to the back door and was only just in time. The key grated in the lock, the door was flung open without regard to caution, and a man sprang inside and slammed it after him. Then he stooped to lock it and I hit him a blow behind the ear which sent him over like a falling chimney."

"Then you've got him?" I shouted, leaping to my feet.

"He is at present lying unconscious and securely tied to your bed.

"Oh, well done! Let's have a look at him."

"Let me finish," said Arbuthnot.

"All right. Go on."

"I dragged him into the passage and there left him while I switched on some lights in the house. I thought the sight of them would hasten your return. Then I lugged my captive into your bedroom in the dark and bound him hand and foot. And there he is now. Come and see."

"Don't switch on a light until I have closed the shutters," he added as we entered the bedroom.

I waited while he did so; then under the glow of the electric light I bent over the recumbent figure on my bed.

"Like the look of him?" queried Arbuthnot.

I shook my head. He was a tallish man, dressed in a very ordinary grey flannel suit. He had quantities of black hair, a sloping forehead, eyes very closely set together, distended nostrils, and thin lips. He was breathing stertorously and his eyes were closed. The mask he had been wearing still rested on his hair.

"He looks a nasty customer," I said. "I suppose you'll hand him over to the police in the morning?"

"I don't know," said Arbuthnot slowly. "I principally want to identify him."

"How can you hope to do that?" I asked. "It's obviously a police job."

"We shall see," was all that he would answer as we left the room.

I remembered that the kitchen door was still unlocked. We were unlikely to have any more visitors that night, but I was taking no risks. When I returned to the drawing-room I held up the key before Arbuthnot.

"Had he only the one key on him?" I asked.

"Only the one."

"Then he must have thrown mine over the cliff."

"If he ever possessed it."

"Certainly it might easily have fallen from my pocket," I mused. "I'll have a look in the morning."

"Better go to bed, King," said my friend. "You're pretty well exhausted."

"Where?" I asked, for the prisoner was occupying my bed.

"Take my room. I must remain awake in case that gentleman comes to his senses."

"That's not fair," I argued. I was at the absolute nadir of my forces, but I protested against my friend's taking all the work on himself.

"I'll sleep after dawn," he said. "I've plenty to think about."

Rather reluctantly I accepted his offer. Covered with a motley assortment of coats, waterproofs, and dressing-gowns that were doing duty for our incinerated bedding, I lapsed into a dreamless sleep. I had feared horrible dreams, but mercifully none came. When I awoke the morning sun was streaming in through the window and Arbuthnot stood at my bedside with a cup of tea in his hand.

"Half-past eight," said he.

I sat up in bed. My head ached and my hand still pained me, but the rest had given me new strength and vigour. I drank the tea thirstily.

"What about the prisoner?" I asked.

"He's gone to sleep again," said Arbuthnot grinning.

"How?"

"He seemed very dazed when he came to and couldn't get his bearings at all, so I gave him a couple of aspirin tablets quite innocent of acetyl-salicylic acid, with some tea, and now he'll sleep a good bit longer."

"Why don't you hand him over to the police?" I inquired.

"I told you I want to identify him."

"I don't see how you can hope to."

"Perhaps last night's rain will help."

"Footprints, eh?"

Arbuthnot burst out laughing.

"You'll have to square Mrs. Morris," I said.

"I have done. She now takes everything that happens to us as a matter of course. Breakfast will soon be ready."

I rose, bathed and dressed as rapidly as I could with the handicap of a damaged hand. After the meal Arbuthnot took himself off for a well-earned rest. I looked in on the prisoner. He was sleeping heavily, with his arms and legs still securely bound together. Arbuthnot was taking no risks.

I went out to the veranda. The air was delightfully fresh and cool after the rain, and on the east side, sheltered from the north-west breeze that was blowing, I settled to enjoy the sunshine and a pipe. Things were looking much more roseate than they had done for some time. One of our opponents was safely in our hands at any rate. I remembered that on the night of the storm I had seen two men on the down, so I did not flatter myself that our troubles were over. Still, events were moving in the right direction.

My thoughts went round to Pamela. How were things coming out for her? Was she wasting her affections on a scoundrel? In any case the tension for her must be terrible. I had seen how the simulated gaiety could break down; I had had some glimpse of the fires that raged beneath, of the bitterness that hurt me doubly coming from one to whom life should have been gay. How amazing her conduct had been last night!

My meditations were interrupted by the appearance of Mrs. Morris with the morning papers. Their transit from London to that remote corner of the Isle of Wight took some time and we never expected them until the middle of the morning. I took up one. Possibly there might be some further news of the raid on Dalton Flyte's alleged headquarters. I found a brief notice of the affair, which, however, gave no additional information, merely stating that "the police were prosecuting their inquiries".

Then I suddenly sprang from my chair as if galvanized. My hands shook as they held the paper and my eyes eagerly—nay, feverishly—scanned the little paragraph that had leapt all at once into my vision.

This is what I saw:

STOP PRESS
ISLE OF WIGHT TRAGEDY
RODD CONFESSES
Winchester, *Sunday*

Information has just come to hand that Thornton Rodd, who is at present lying in the county jail on a charge of being accessory to the recent murder of Dalton Flyte at Freshwater Bay, Isle of Wight, has made a full confession to the police of his share in the affair.

That was all there was.

"Pamela, God help you," I whispered.

Savagely I crumpled the paper into a ball and flung it on the ground.

"So I suppose your horse is still running?" said the subject of my thoughts with a gay laugh.

12
The Same Continued

She had come round the corner of the veranda unnoticed by me and was now staring in grave concern at my still bandaged head.

"Did you fall out of bed?" she asked.

"I just bumped myself," I answered hastily. "It's really all right now. I'd forgotten that the bandage was still on."

I hurriedly unfastened it, rolled it up, and pitched it through the open window of Arbuthnot's bedroom, which was behind me.

"The side of your head is all green and yellow. It must have been a great crash."

"It was," I replied briefly, swinging myself over the veranda railing to the ground beside her. "How about a stroll?"

"I'd love it."

"Come on, then."

My real object was to get away from the proximity of Arbuthnot; it was not fair to rouse him after his sleepless night.

"Was I very horrible last night?" she asked as we wandered off.

"I can easily find excuses for you," said I.

"You're sure you didn't bash your head against the wall with rage after you got home?"

"No, I simply cracked it to let in a little sense."

"I don't think you're really very cheerful this morning," she said critically. "Perhaps it aches."

"I'm not a bit happy," I answered, jumping at things.

"I'm sorry. Somehow being with you last night bucked me up quite a lot. I feel lots better this morning."

"I don't," I said. "Can you stand bad news?" I added abruptly.

For a moment her fingers fastened on my arm. Then she withdrew her hand and laughed—the kind of laugh that conveys no sense of merriment.

"Try me," she said simply.

I looked at her doubtfully. It was no easy task I had given myself.

"I know what you're thinking. You're expecting me to faint or do something silly of that kind. I promise you I won't. I'll keep a hold on myself if it tears me to bits to do it." The expression was peculiar but easy to understand, especially when I heard it in her choking tones.

"Rodd has confessed," I said bluntly.

"Thank God for that!" she cried, and turned a tear-stained but defiant face up to mine.

"What do you mean?" I asked, honestly bewildered.

"Mean? Do you think any woman who really loved a man would care a tuppenny damn whether he had killed a worm like Dalton Flyte or not?"

In his *Pilgrim's Script* Sir Austin Feverel had written, "I expect woman will be the last thing civilized by man." Perhaps for the first time in my life I grasped his meaning. Through the flippancy of this twentieth-century damsel had suddenly risen something elemental which left me agape.

"A difficult attitude to maintain," I murmured fatuously.

"Of course I can be sorry about it," she said, "but it makes no difference."

"You're very brave."

"It's not bravery. I don't know what it is. Tell me—exactly what did Thornton confess?"

"I don't know. There was only a bare statement in the papers this morning."

"How can we find out? Can Mr. Arbuthnot do anything? Oh, I forgot. Of course he isn't here at present."

I hesitated. I had really no right to divulge that Arbuthnot's trip to London was nothing but a myth.

"He is sure to have seen the news in the papers," I remarked. "The chances are that he will get the full details before he returns here. Could you come round, say, by about six this evening?" I judged that Arbuthnot when he heard what the papers contained would immediately get into touch with Bernard to ascertain the facts of the case.

"I'll come. Do you want Gerry? No, I can see you don't. I'll give him the slip. Anyway, he'll be as miserable as sin when he sees the news. If he comes poking around here to find out if you have heard any more you needn't say that I am coming back this evening."

I readily promised, having no particular wish to hear Mr. Bellingham enlarge on the situation; in his own particular field I felt that he was nearly a genius, outside it he was nothing but a pompous old bore.

"I don't really care a hoot," remarked Pamela suddenly.

"About Mr. Bellingham?"

"No, stupid. About the confession."

She dragged off the hat that was crammed on her head, masking the wanton curls, and began kicking it along the turf. "That's all I care for what people think," she cried.

"You cared very much yesterday when I told you there was fresh evidence against Rodd," I pointed out.

"You don't understand women," she said.

"I don't," I replied sadly.

"Women are like that. They worry and fret all the time. Then when the crisis comes they're hard as nails."

"I am learning," I said humbly. "I wish you strength to maintain your attitude."

"You're a nice old thing," she responded. "Now I'll run back. Gerry having by now—er—perused the daily press will be hunting everywhere for me with a face as long as a mooring-mast."

She ran off down the hill as lightly as a child skipping to school and I scratched my head and returned into the bungalow. I took a look at the prisoner and found him still asleep. Then I considered whether I should wake Arbuthnot. He had only had a couple of hours sleep. On the other hand, he might be extremely annoyed if I left him to sleep on in ignorance of this fresh development. While I was still undecidedly pacing the veranda Mr. Bellingham appeared, immaculately dressed, hatted, and gloved.

"Pamela has just called my attention to the news," he said heavily. "It is appalling."

"Pretty bad," I replied, "though we must await further details before we can say exactly how bad. Miss Strode seems to be bearing it rather well. I imagine she thinks that Rodd's guilt in the matter will turn out to be more technical than real. It seems quite likely that he fell among thieves."

"A very plausible hypothesis. But while I concede that Pamela is not likely to waver in her allegiance to Rodd if such turns out to be the case, she is still less likely to marry him."

"Indeed! Why?"

"You do not know her father, Sir Jervis. He is a man who seems to have conserved in his person all the public and private probity more characteristic of the past generation than of the present. To him the idea of becoming connected with a man who is bound to remain notorious at the best would be abhorrent."

"Parents must stand aside sometimes," I suggested.

"He is an invalid. He spent all his strength in the service of his country. His years are numbered, his sands of life are fast running out. To bring undeserved distress upon him in his last days would be an act of cruelty of which Pamela would never be capable."

"That rather alters things," I admitted.

"It does. But do I perceive you have damaged your head, Sir Edmund?"

"My own carelessness. We have no light in our kitchen since we had the blaze there on Saturday night, and I collided with the corner of the dresser."

"Most unfortunate. I am positive this bungalow is ill-fated. What does Mr. Arbuthnot think of this business of Rodd's confession?"

"I shall know when he returns," I said. "Probably he will have collected the whole story."

"I trust I may hear something from you then?"

"I shall let you know at once any news that is available."

"Many thanks."

He turned to go. I had not asked him to enter the house; it held too many secrets. I watched him pursue his dignified way towards the bay.

"You're much too posh," I growled unconsciously aloud.

"Who is much too posh?" inquired a voice, and I turned to see Arbuthnot looking at me from the drawing-room window.

"Bellingham," I said. "I can't imagine why a man should march about on a morning like this with gloves and an umbrella. I'm afraid our talk woke you up, but I was going to rouse you in any case."

"King, I smell news."

"You are right. Thornton Rodd has confessed."

"Confessed to what?"

"I don't know. Only the bare fact is given in the 'Stop Press' column of the morning papers."

"Then I must find out."

"I thought you would wish to do that at once. In fact, I have rather committed you in advance."

"You are altogether too susceptible, King," he said, grinning, having grasped my meaning very easily.

"I suppose I am. At any rate, I told her that if she came here at six o'clock this evening—alone—there might be some news for her."

"I will do my best," said Arbuthnot, and his voice had the peculiar ring which I knew from experience indicated that he had some inward source of amusement. "Run down to the Stagrock Hotel and get the car if it's available. Meanwhile I'll dress. If I can have the car I'll slip into Newport by the military road and return in time for tea. Probably Bernard will tell me all there is to know."

"Very well."

"You'll be in charge of the prisoner. No need to make a pet of him. He's not really a nice man. An electrician, a painter, and some kitchen furniture will be arriving presently. I have sent Mrs. Morris into Freshwater to see about things. Make sure that no one has a chance of entering that bedroom."

I obtained the car without any difficulty, and Arbuthnot, after snatching a meal of bread and cheese and tea, drove away, looking as fresh as if he had just slept the clock round. A remarkable man.

Mrs. Morris returned and gave me my lunch soon after one. I had barely finished when a rumbling outside betokened the approach of a furniture van. Cautioning her that no one was on any account to go beyond the door that led from the kitchen into the passage, I entered the bedroom where the prisoner lay. The shutters naturally remained fastened and the room in darkness. I switched on the light and found the man still dormant. The more I looked at him the less I liked him.

I pushed a chair against the door, sat down and smoked. Sounds came to me of the transport of furniture, and instructions from Mrs. Morris *re* "minding the paint" were clearly audible. Ever and again my thoughts came back to Thornton Rodd. I recollected my early suspicions of him, how they had first waxed, then waned and disappeared, only to be suddenly renewed, and how after meeting Pamela I had hoped against hope that Rodd had only been involved in the affair by a succession of coincidences. Now hope and fear were equally out of the question.

Sounds of activity continued from the kitchen. I fetched a novel from the drawing-room and then returned to my post. Once the light went out and I presumed the electrician had cut off the supply while he carried out his repairs. It was nearly five o'clock when I re-entered the kitchen and found the renovations complete. I guessed that it was owing to our friendship with Mr. Williams that things had been put right with such promptitude. Shortly after five Arbuthnot returned.

"Any luck?" I questioned.

"Everything," he answered briefly.

Mrs. Morris bore in tea.

"This room strikes me as very damp," he added to her.

"It is, sir. It smells fair mouldy to me. That's after the rain."

"No doubt. I think we'll have a little fire. Use some of Mr. Flyte's coal. I doubt if he'll ever feel cold again."

Mrs. Morris, looking a trifle shocked, hastened to carry out the order. After the rain the day had not been particularly warm and the air of the room struck me as being chill and clammy. I was quite pleased to see a few lumps of coal presently burning away merrily in the grate.

"Bernard saw Rodd in prison yesterday morning," began Arbuthnot after we were alone, "and told him of the important new evidence there was against him. I believe he went in hopes of getting Rodd to make a clean breast of things. If he did his intentions were fulfilled. Rodd seemed very down, according to Bernard's account. His night in prison had apparently shaken his confidence. As soon as he realized that a definite connexion between him and Flyte was established he volunteered a confession."

He paused.

"Go on," I said anxiously.

"Your friend will be here in a few minutes. Why not wait?"

I agreed that that was the reasonable thing to do, although secretly I should have liked to have known the story before Pamela came to hear it.

"What about the prisoner?"

"I think he will go to the lock-up to-morrow."

"Then who will identify him?"

"Miss Strode," said Arbuthnot, "is at the door."

A moment after Pamela burst into the room.

"Sorry I didn't knock," she cried. "I saw you through the window looking ever so comfy, so I just rushed in. Imagine a fire in June!"

"Old bones soon grow chill," remarked Arbuthnot.

"More likely lack of exercise causes it," she answered swiftly.

I pulled forward an easy chair.

"Not for me, Edmund. I'm going to sit on this jolly little stool by the fireside."

It was all very well done, and had I been meeting her for the first time I should have been deceived. But she threw me one look from eyes that seemed all the bigger because of the mournful light at the back of them, and I prayed heartily that Arbuthnot's story might not bear too hardly upon her.

My friend was engaged in lighting his pipe.

"I can tell you what you want to know," he said, tossing the burnt match on to the hearth. Arbuthnot wastes no time on preliminaries. Both his listeners leant forward. Save for the flickering of the fire there was not a sound in the room.

"Rodd," he said slowly, "has confessed that he killed Dalton Flyte."

Pamela was fumbling in her bag. I knew her desire and passed her a cigarette.

"Thank you, Edmund," she said, and her voice was as steady as anyone could wish. I lighted the cigarette for her after two attempts, the first having failed through my own shakiness. One does not like to see a fellow being in the pillory.

Arbuthnot was gazing steadily into the fire.

"He did not confess to murdering him," he added.

He was silent for quite a minute. It looked like intentional cruelty, but I knew it to be due merely to his habit of very careful arrangement of his statements.

"Another long instalment next month, I suppose," broke in Pamela, biting her lip. I guessed that she was on the verge of hysteria.

"It began in Canada," continued Arbuthnot deliberately, "that is, according to Rodd's account. You are well aware that he recently inherited quite a lot of money. People who have no money may quite easily be ignorant of certain dangers lying in wait for those who have." He paused again.

I nodded encouragingly to Pamela and she sent me a wan sort of smile.

"Soon after the news of his good fortune was published he says he had occasion to make a trip to Montreal on the firm's business. It was a matter relating to some concrete blocks."

I glanced sharply at Arbuthnot. Was he intentionally straining Pamela's endurance to the utmost by introducing these irrelevant details? Surely not?

"There he says he met a man, a stranger to him, who went by the name of Curtis Schnitzler. It was the ordinary sort of acquaintance that men from the backwoods, with no friends to visit, make when they are staying in great cities for a little while. One evening, Rodd says, he was induced to join in a poker-school. He had always steered clear of gambling, he states, because he had never had the money to throw away."

"Perfectly true," put in Pamela.

"He was rather excited at the prospect of gambling without having to bother about a possible loss of a couple of hundred dollars or so. As it turned out he actually won about that amount. The party consisted of him and this Schnitzler and two other men he hasn't seen since. Schnitzler and he became quite friendly."

Another pause.

"Under the urge of loneliness men may make friends with individuals who normally would have no attraction for them," Arbuthnot continued, filling himself another pipe.

Pamela had already finished her cigarette and crushed the stub to extinction in the ash-tray on the table beside her. I gave her another and she thanked me with her eyes.

"Rodd told Schnitzler that he was hoping to go on leave to England shortly. Curiously enough, Schnitzler was entertaining the same expectation. Perhaps they might meet again on some occasion. The latter hoped so, for he had practically no friends in England. His firm were giving him leave to study English methods in the fine cotton trade. Apart from an old acquaintance now retired and living in the Isle of Wight he really knew nobody."

"It sounds very ingenious," I interpolated.

"Very. Rodd was naturally interested in the Isle of Wight. He had spent boyhood holidays there. He intended to go there again. Schnitzler's friend, Dalton Flyte, who had a charming little bungalow on the cliff at Freshwater Bay would be delighted to welcome Rodd. Schnitzler himself would be there during the month of June. What more pleasant than a reunion at some time during that period? Rodd explained that he hoped to cross by the *Mauretania* and the new friends parted with a general sort of understanding that they would meet again."

"The thing's as plain as daylight," I said.

"Now we come to recent events," went on Arbuthnot, disregarding my comment. "Rodd arrived in England in gorgeous weather. He naturally thought of a visit to the Isle of Wight. He makes no mention of you in this part of his statement, Miss Strode. I presume he went to London first and found you were out of town."

"Had to be," said Pamela, discarding the end of another half-smoked cigarette.

"There was no need for him to drag your name in," proceeded Arbuthnot. "At any rate, he went to the Isle of Wight. From that point he adheres for a while to his original story. His explanation of the bicycle incident remains the same. When he reached the bungalow the sole occupant was Flyte, but while he was engaged in explaining the cause of his visit Schnitzler came in, having apparently been out for a walk."

"And having really been engaged in shadowing Rodd from Southampton, of course," I cried.

"So it would seem. Flyte apologized for the unusual absence of his housekeeper. However, they would do their best to make him comfortable. A meal was got together and there was plenty to drink. After supper they washed up their own plates and dishes to conceal from the housekeeper the primitive nature of their repast and then in hilarious mood sat down to poker."

Pamela reached out for another cigarette.

"For perhaps the first half-hour Rodd says that he prospered. With only three players there was naturally a great deal of early 'showing-down', but on balance he was about twenty pounds to the good and Schnitzler was joking him about his regular luck. They had another drink and continued the game. Then the luck appeared to be changing. In a few minutes Rodd had lost all his winnings. Naturally that didn't worry him. Play went on."

We sensed that the climax of the story was approaching. Pamela added the remains of another ill-treated "gasper" to the little collection in the ash-tray. She had taken the hearth-brush in her hand and was absent-mindedly sweeping the ashes in the grate into a tidy condition. My teeth gripped the stem of an empty pipe as I listened. Arbuthnot was staring intently into the fire; he had not altered his pose since the beginning of his story and seemed absolutely unmindful of our presence.

"After another quarter of an hour or so Rodd was a hundred pounds to the bad. Still he wasn't worried. They had another drink. Play continued. By eleven o'clock Rodd was losing a thousand pounds. At that point Flyte suggested that the sums involved were getting too large for a friendly game. Supposing they continued their game the next night to give Rodd a chance of his revenge? Schnitzler agreed. Rodd admits that he had had more than his usual amount of drink. He declared boastfully that a thousand pounds was nothing to him, and insisted on writing out a cheque on the spot for that amount. They laughed at him. Flyte pooh-poohed the idea and went to the sideboard to mix more drinks. Rodd followed him, folded the cheque and tried to thrust it into Flyte's coat pocket."

I spared a glance for Pamela. Her eyes were shining with excitement.

"Flyte rebuffed him," went on Arbuthnot, "causing him to withdraw his hand sharply from the latter's pocket. His sleeve-link caught in the edge of the pocket, he gave a jerk—and the ace of spades and the ace of diamonds fluttered to the floor."

Arbuthnot unkindly choose to make one of his pauses at this point. Pamela and I were looking at each other with wide-open eyes.

"Rodd was sufficiently sober to realize the situation. He knew he was in the hands of crooks. First of all, he thought of making a dash for it. Then he saw Schnitzler was in position by the door that led to the passage and Flyte barred his retreat by the door to the drawing-room. At this crisis he put his hand in his pocket and pulled out his pistol. Till that moment he had forgotten it was with him. He had become accustomed to carrying it in the backwoods and had got into the habit of transferring it from coat to coat as he changed, so that it happened to be still with him. He had even forgotten to declare it at the customs on landing, for which I have no doubt he will be called to account."

"Never mind the customs," I cried.

"It was a peculiar position. Both men apparently had looked on him as a bit of a greenhorn and had never dreamt he would be armed. They were unprovided against the situation. Flyte tried to argue and attempted a bluff, but Rodd had had enough of bluffing for one night. While Flyte was talking Schnitzler suddenly feinted a rush, Rodd turned on him, reluctant to shoot unless obliged, and at that moment Flyte ran in. Rodd swears he never shot to kill. The man was on him; if it came to a grapple they were two to one, and something had to be done. He fired,

N. A. Temple-Ellis

intending to wing his man in the shoulder. Not unnaturally under the circumstances his aim was bad. Flyte recoiled and dropped like a stone. It was not difficult to guess that he was dead."

The brush Pamela had been wielding fell from her hands with a crash.

"The situation was very awkward for both survivors. Each in a way had the advantage of the other. Eventually they came to terms. Flyte's death had not been intended, and anyway he was a precious scoundrel and no loss to the world. Rodd was to take his cheque and go. Each man was to observe silence over the night's doings. Rodd guessed that the other man would not exactly go empty away. He left Schnitzler to his own devices and made tracks to get away from Freshwater by the least frequented route—the military road. When the night air had calmed him a little he thought of the pistol. He wished to get rid of it, not because he ever imagined its possession would be a danger to him, but because with it he had committed manslaughter. In the dark he thought he had hurled it over the cliff."

"Why did he come back?" I asked.

"In the darkness he lost himself. After a good deal of wandering he found himself back near Freshwater again when day broke. Then after much consideration he decided that the boldest course was the safest. He judged that Schnitzler would take all he could with him when he left. That would immediately make it a crime of robbery with violence in the eyes of the police, and Rodd could never be suspected of that. Had the pistol gone to the bottom of the sea as he supposed he would have been perfectly safe."

Arbuthnot commenced to load another pipe.

"When Rodd heard of the motor-car tragedy on the cliffs he was not exactly displeased, you can guess. The one witness against him was dead. Every one would suppose that Schnitzler had murdered Flyte and the case would come to an abrupt termination. He says that he several times considered the advisability of confession, but could not see that it would serve any useful purpose. Both men had been thorough villains. That he had unintentionally killed one of them was not likely to lie heavily on his conscience." For a minute after he had finished his narrative we sat silent. Personally I felt that an immense burden had been lifted from me.

"You're wonderfully kind to have explained everything so clearly," said Pamela to Arbuthnot at last. "Let me ask one question."

"You want to know what will probably happen to Rodd?"

"Please."

"Very little on that showing. He is by his own account technically guilty of manslaughter. A plea of self-defence might be set up, but there is no evidence to corroborate his own on that point. His excellent record will be in his favour, whereas of the other two men one was certainly, and the other probably, a blackguard of the deepest dye. He will escape with a nominal sentence of imprisonment. The presiding judge will address a few scorching remarks to him on his previous attempt to defeat the ends of justice, and he will be invited to write his life-story for the Sunday press. That's all."

"And when may I hope to see him?"

"Probably quite soon. If the authorities give credence to his story I don't think a renewed application for bail would be refused. Excuse me one moment. I must speak to the housekeeper."

He passed out through the dining-room.

"You're marrying a remarkable man," I said to Pamela. "If he translates his audacity to domestic spheres you need never know a dull moment."

"We're not married yet," she answered gravely. "I've got to wangle round Dad, if I can without upsetting him."

We both stood silent for a minute, each busy with his or her own thoughts. Then Arbuthnot re-entered from the hall.

"I'm going," said Pamela. "By the way, can I tell Gerry all the news?"

"I see no objection," replied Arbuthnot. "There will no doubt be a full account of it in to-morrow's papers."

"Then I'll tell him. It'll keep him from thrusting in here."

"Thank you," said Arbuthnot dryly as he escorted her to the door.

"Not at all. It is I who should thank you."

"What for? I've done nothing for you so far."

"You and Edmund gave me a feeling of confidence through the worst time." She paused at the front door.

"A very easy form of service. By the way, Miss Strode, I think you are forgetting your stick."

"I didn't bring one with me," Pamela answered.

"No? Then you must have left this on the occasion of a previous visit."

"I don't think so. Let me see it."

Arbuthnot withdrew a walking-stick from the hall-stand and presented it for her inspection.

He was just in time to catch her as she fell over in a dead faint.

13
The Same Continued

I was so staggered by the occurrence that I hardly had wits left to assist Arbuthnot to carry Pamela back into the drawing-room and lay her on the couch.

"How the deuce did that happen?" I asked him.

"Get some water," said he.

I dashed into the dining-room and returned with a carafe from the sideboard. Arbuthnot sprinkled a few drops on her forehead and regarded her critically. "She'll come to in a minute or so," he said.

I looked at the tumbled curls on the cushion, the half-closed eyes and parted lips, and the cheeks drained of all vestige of colour. It was no doubt a case of the reaction after a strain being worse than the strain itself.

"A pretty domestic scene, is it not?" remarked Arbuthnot.

"What is?"

"The sparkling fire, the ash-tray with its quota of ends from Virginia cigarettes, the carefully-swept hearth."

"I don't follow."

"Does it stir no response in your memory? Sarah Battle, you remember, 'loved a clean hearth', but I never came across a bachelor who cared a hang about the condition of his."

Recollections of the day when Dalton Flyte had lain dead in the adjacent room flooded in upon me.

"Arbuthnot!" I cried. "Surely you don't think—"

"Get on to the veranda, King, and give me warning if Bellingham appears in sight. He might be disposed to be inquisitive."

I saw the necessity for the precaution and promptly obeyed. The state of my mind was chaotic. I was like a man one moment comfortably pacing a liner's deck and the next moment precipitated to a hungry sea. Then my ear caught the sound of voices and thought was suspended.

"Roddy?"

The voice was shaky.

"I'm afraid not."

"Who are you then? Oh!"

There was a pause.

"I suppose I fainted?"

"You did."

I was craving to come to the window and look in on the scene, but I dared not relax my watch. It was only too likely that Bellingham would descend upon us.

"What are you going to do?"

Pamela's voice had the weariness of one broken beyond hope.

"For the moment, nothing."

"Aren't you dying to enjoy the fruits of your cleverness?"

"I don't bully women who are at the point of collapse."

"And afterwards?"

"I give you an hour. If you return within that time prepared to tell me all you know of the truth I promise you the fairest deal in my power. Otherwise it may go hard with you."

"And if I put myself beyond your power?"

There was a certain flat finality about the tone of her voice that made me shiver.

"Then Thornton Rodd shall hang."

"That's an empty threat."

"Far from it. He has confessed to killing Flyte. It will be my business to prove his real motive."

I stole a glance into the room. Pamela was standing up, swaying slightly and holding on to a table with both hands.

"One hour," said Arbuthnot.

"I suppose so," she answered listlessly.

I saw Arbuthnot cross to open the door and a moment later she appeared on the veranda.

"Pamela," I said.

She shook her head and walked on with unseeing eyes. I burst into the house.

"Arbuthnot! This is a hell of a business!"

"Would you like to hear about it?"

"Like to hear about it? I'm not made of iron, like you."

"Then just have a look at the prisoner first, will you? It's about time he was waking up."

Hastily I went to my bedroom, flung open the door, and switched on the light. The prisoner was standing in the middle of the floor. His wrists and ankles were still secured, but evidently by his flushed face he had been working feverishly to free himself. He blinked at me with a most evil light in his deeply-set eyes. Then I did something which even now brings a flush of shame to my face when I record it. I stepped up to him and struck him with all my force on the point of the jaw. With a grunt he collapsed on the floor, the back of his head coming to the ground with a ghastly thud. Then he lay still. I gathered him in my arms and flung him back on the bed.

I have never quite been able to see why I acted as I did on that occasion. In a normal state I could never have brought myself to strike down a man incapable of defending himself. True he had knocked me out when I was similarly situated, but that did not supply the motive for my

action. It all arose in some way out of the scene between
Pamela and Arbuthnot, and if I were a psychoanalyst I
might be able to explain why.

Ruefully regarding my bruised knuckles I returned to
the drawing-room.

"All right?" inquired Arbuthnot.

"He was standing up," I said.

"What have you done?"

"Knocked him down. I think he'll go on sleeping for a
bit."

I fancied that Arbuthnot raised his eyebrows slightly at
this piece of information, but he said nothing.

"Bring out your secret," I continued. "Never mind how
bad it is."

By way of answer he made a journey into the hall and
returned bearing a common ash-stick, rather the worse for
wear, which he placed in my hand.

"You spent long enough looking for it. Now you have
it," he observed.

"Then this—"

"Is the second stick."

"It doesn't matter much now Rodd has confessed," I
said.

"It doesn't! Have a good look at it."

I did so. Then it nearly fell from my fingers as I sprang
back in amazement. Just below the handle it bore the following legend roughly carved:

T. R.

P. S.

"I think Miss Strode might be excused for fainting,"
said Arbuthnot very casually.

"But what's the history of this?" I cried. "The other
stick also carried initials. He can't have had two with him."

"Sit down and light your pipe and I'll try and explain things."

"Hurry up," I said, "that old fool Bellingham may turn up at any moment."

"True. I'll be as quick as I can. You were the one to put me originally on the track."

"How so?"

"When you and Rodd and I searched the bungalow together the morning after the murder you surprised him looking horrified at something he saw in the hall."

"Go on."

"You came to think it possible that his shock was due to his having seen his own walking-stick in the hall-stand."

"Yes."

"You afterwards reversed that opinion because while we were in other rooms he had an excellent opportunity to effect an exchange, whereas his own stick was actually found in the stand later by Sergeant Rogers."

"Quite so."

"King, he did effect an exchange. He took out the stick which you are now holding and put in his own. Do you see now?"

I rose and paced the room.

"Then I take off my hat to him for that," I said.

"Well said. Now we must inquire what he did with this stick before he came forward and claimed his own. He had no alternative. There was only one possible way out of it. When we re-entered the house with the police he loitered outside for a moment. His own excuse was that he was finishing a cigarette. In that moment he flung this stick over the cliff, leaving him free to claim his own from the hall-stand."

"Pretty risky," I said.

"It was Hobson's choice. Moreover, the eastern end of the beach is very little used indeed. At that hour of the morning it would be deserted. Remember he was no stranger to Freshwater."

"Did you guess all this at the time?" I asked.

"Not quite. But my suspicions were thoroughly aroused. Hence when Rodd took a walk along the beach that morning at the earliest possible moment, I followed him, you may recollect, with my binoculars."

"Yes, yes."

"We saw him drop his stick. I believed, though I could not actually see, that when he picked it up he picked up another one with it. What did he do then? Something surely no sensible person would have done without good cause. He crossed to the foot of the cliff and continued his walk over the big stones that lie there and are unbelievably hard to the feet, as you know."

"There were people on the down above. He didn't wish to be seen with two sticks," I suggested.

"Exactly. Then his knowledge of Freshwater stood him in good stead. He went to the corner of the bay, entered one of the caves, and concealed this stick in some crack in the rock above high-water mark. It was the best available hiding-place."

"Very true."

"The caves are accessible only at or near low water. The tide was rising when he returned. Therefore I had to wait till the evening for a chance to verify my surmise. That was why I asked you to go for a walk with him not earlier than seven o'clock."

"I remember your insistence on the time puzzled me exceedingly," I said.

"I made my journey, found the stick, noted the initials, and replaced it in its hiding-place. From that moment there was only one possible theory to account for Rodd's conduct. He was shielding some one; some one who had been in this house on the night of the murder, and that some one a person closely connected with him or they would not have had their initials on the same stick."

"Continue," I said grimly, feeling that perhaps I was meant to accept a certain implication in his words.

"Nothing more happened until last Tuesday. Then Rodd received a cabin trunk from Cook's at Southampton. It was big enough to hold this stick, which you notice has been a little cut down. I expected him to go out and fetch the stick, taking advantage of the low tide shortly before midnight. He didn't go. I had thought he would choose to get away from the place as quickly as possible once he could remove his precious stick in secrecy within the trunk. I had to suppose that he was waiting another day, because on receipt of his trunk he had written to some one making an appointment at a certain time and place and thus had to allow a day for the letter to reach its destination. On Wednesday night I stayed up and, unperceived, saw him fetch the stick. On Thursday morning, as you know, the police came to arrest him. They naturally sent on word to me first of their arrival, relying on me to arrange for the thing to be done with as little fuss as possible. That was a pretty situation to face."

"I don't quite see."

"I had rather got to like the young devil. If the police found this stick in his belongings it was the beginning of the end for him. I asked them to wait in another room for a few minutes while I fixed up things. Then by a little device that you did not at the time fully appreciate I secured possession of Rodd's keys, raided his bedroom, collared the stick, pitched it into my own trunk, and locked it up. There it lay until I brought it out this afternoon."

"Good heavens!"

"Then came the only piece of real luck we have had so far. When the hue and cry after Rodd began I did not, as you know, join in. Instead, I took the hotel car and quietly slipped away to Yarmouth. I was working on the assumption that Rodd was intending to meet some one that day. I had planned to follow him when he left. There was a good chance that the 'some one' was none other than the unknown 'P. S.' Where would they meet? If in London I was wasting my time. But surely in that case Rodd would have gone up by the first train in the morning. He was bound to be anxious to get away from Freshwater as soon as possible. His choice of a later train suggested that he was meeting some one travelling down from London. The local train from Lymington connects with the Waterloo express at Brockenhurst, which lies, as you are aware, in the heart of the New Forest. What better spot for an assignation?"

"Plausible," I said, copying Arbuthnot's own familiar remark.

"Quite so. I got out of the train at Brockenhurst, and the first person I saw was a rather attractive-looking girl walking up and down the platform and anxiously scanning those who alighted. In her hand was a leather bag and on it was embossed the monogram 'P. S.' That was the piece of luck. Certainly there were several other ways in which I could have eventually tracked the owner of those initials. Knowing they denoted a woman was itself a great advantage."

"How could you know that the initials indicated a woman?"

"Otherwise Rodd would have destroyed the stick. Still it saved an enormous amount of trouble to stumble upon her in that way."

"What happened?"

"Ten minutes later the Waterloo express came in from Bournemouth. Very reluctantly she got in. Evidently she had been told that if Rodd did not arrive by that train she was on no account to wait. I also got in. The rest was a matter of mere shadowing. When I had established who she was I returned to the Isle of Wight. I knew that Rodd would certainly come back to get this stick if he had not been previously captured, so I waited up for him—and for you."

"What did he say to you when he found the stick gone?"

"Nothing. Once or twice I fancy he was on the verge of tackling me on the subject, but his nerve failed him. It must have been a crushing blow to him."

"He had a chance that night of getting a letter off to Pamela informing her of his loss. Why didn't he do so?"

"Because he feared it would drive her to some precipitate action, probably in the way of confession. Evidently Rodd is a judge of character."

"It's an amazing tangle," I said, walking the room feverishly.

"Which is now well on its way to being unravelled. The next hour should see us make two good steps in that direction."

"May I come in?"

Pamela was standing beside the window. Her face was dead white and her eyes seemed to be set in a stare. Her voice was a dull monotone. Oddly enough, I thought of Clara Middleton, whose respite had also been for an hour. I feared Pamela had not been so fortunate as she.

I opened the front door. As Pamela entered she glanced up to me for a moment with the look of a child who has been unexpectedly struck, touched me lightly on the sleeve, and walked on to face the music. Arbuthnot brought forward a chair.

"I've had no time to think," she said, dropping into it wearily. "I ran into Gerry as he was on his way here, and I had to tell him all about Thornton's confession to prevent his coming on to you."

"A work of art," said Arbuthnot.

"I'm telling the truth," she answered in the tone of one beyond gibes.

"I mean Rodd's confession."

"I suppose it was. Why couldn't you leave it at that?" she asked bitterly.

"A passion for the truth."

"Then you shall have all that is in me."

"I believe you, Miss Strode."

She looked up at him in some surprise. "Of course you must know that I was in this house the night Flyte was killed."

"Of course. Why not begin at the beginning?"

Pamela passed her hand across her brows.

"It began with Winton," she said.

"Your brother?"

"Yes. In the war he was very badly shell-shocked. He never got over it till the day of his death. He was three years older than me, but we'd been a lot together as kids. He was delicate when he was little and couldn't go to a prep. school."

She broke off and shivered.

"After the war he was always strange. Sometimes he would be in a hell of his own and at others he would be wildly excited, and making all sorts of plans. But he never stuck to anything."

"Evidently the effects of drugs," remarked Arbuthnot, as if to help her past a difficult point.

"Yes, though it took me a long time to guess it. If you've played together as kids it takes a little while to realize these things. As it was, I found out suddenly."

She checked and caught her breath.

"You know my father was in his way a very important man till he retired. His safe used to contain at times papers that only he and the Secretary of State knew of. One day I caught Winton opening it."

I turned and looked out of the window. The telling of this tale was cutting Pamela like a knife. She did not require my gaping to increase the strain on her.

"Of course I stopped him. I couldn't *do* anything more. I daren't tell my father. Even then the doctors were saying that it was touch-and-go with his heart. But I made Winton tell me the truth."

Arbuthnot silently proffered a cigarette. She took it gratefully.

"He admitted that he was in league with this man Flyte, who called himself Hunter then. I never heard him called Flyte till after the murder. He was in Flyte's debt for drugs. We aren't a wealthy family. My mother left me some money, but all Winton had was an allowance. Flyte offered him a lot of money if he would rob my father. He gave him a narcotic to slip into my father's coffee after dinner so that he could get the key from him when he was in his study, where he generally went to read last thing at night. Do you want all these details?"

"Better tell me everything."

"There was some document Flyte thought my father had. I don't know what it was. The trouble was that Winton had obtained an advance of money from Flyte by signing a paper admitting his intentions. Fortunately—I say fortunately—Winton died soon after."

She choked over her words.

"Then Flyte began on me."

"Unfortunately he also is dead," I said, and was surprised at the sound of my own voice. "Some people are allowed to escape out of life much too easily."

"It didn't take him long to get what little I had. I couldn't tell my father. Thornton, I knew, was saving hard towards what we hoped for. To ask him for money would be to smash his hopes. And although I'm very fond of Gerry I couldn't bring myself to take money from him. I've no doubt he would have given me thousands for the asking, but—"

Pamela, beneath all her rowdiness, I guessed had a very sound idea of the things that could be done and the things that couldn't.

"Then I had the news of Thornton's good fortune. It was the first ray of hope. I trusted him to be willing to help me out. Then, soon after, Flyte began to press me for all he was worth. It was strange, for if he had had any inkling that Thornton and I were engaged he would surely have waited. I wasn't going to tell him, anyway. Do you blame me?"

"Not at all," said Arbuthnot, rather to my surprise.

"Flyte broached a plan. Being my father's daughter I knew a good many people. He wanted me to get him certain information of a confidential nature. In return I should have the document Winton had signed. He gave me four days, that is to say, the time expired at noon on Friday, the day he was killed." She was speaking more confidently now she was dealing entirely with her own affairs.

"I expected Thornton in London on Friday afternoon, so when things were getting desperate I asked Flyte to give me at least another few hours. I had to see Thornton. It wasn't a matter I could explain in a radiogram. In any case, I thought he couldn't send me money from on board ship. Flyte wouldn't allow another minute. I thought he must be mad. In my despair I told him he had only to wait till Thornton landed and I could give him almost anything he asked. It made no difference at all. He wouldn't budge an inch."

"An interesting point," said Arbuthnot. "Tell me, where were you accustomed to interview Flyte?"

"At the house in the Brixton Road which the police raided on Saturday. He was generally there at some time or other every day I think, except during week-ends."

"I see. I want to know whether he ever took any interest other than financial in you."

"Never. Thank God, I was spared that."

"Good! Continue your story."

"At noon on Friday I went to the house in the Brixton Road. Flyte was there, as well as a beastly rat of a man who used to act as a sort of bodyguard to him."

I stared at her in astonishment. We knew perfectly well that Flyte had arrived in Freshwater on Thursday. Surely Pamela hadn't the audacity to be emulating Rodd and treating us to a bogus confession? Apparently Arbuthnot was taking no notice of the remark. Then I realized that owing to the absence of Mrs. Morris from work on that Friday Flyte could easily have returned to London for the day without our finding out anything about it.

"Before Thornton went to Canada" she continued, "he had given me a little pistol as well as the old walking-stick that had gone with us so many times on the days we stole from the world for ourselves. I took both—one for protection, the other for luck.

"Flyte was in a peculiar mood. He didn't seem at all himself and would hardly have a word to say to me. Then I went the limit. I'm not always a fool, and I knew that in a blackmail action the evidence as to the hold the blackmailer has on the other person is not required. I said definitely that I should make a clean breast of everything to the police."

"Good!" I cried.

"Flyte got badly rattled. He knew that I was my father's daughter and that my remarks would receive some attention from the authorities. Finally he suggested that if I would sign a promissory note for five thousand pounds he would hold things over until I had seen Thornton. Of course I saw through that easily enough. I told him he could have his note in exchange for the letter of Winton's that he held. He hummed and hawed and said that the letter wasn't with him. He told me he had sent it out

of London to be posted back to my father so that there
should be no clue to the sender."

"Excellent," said Arbuthnot, leaning forward with a
smile on his keen features.

"I'm glad you're enjoying it. I told him I could easily
intercept the letter. He laughed and said my father always
had a big mail and that I should not dare open all his letters to find one. We came back to our original position.
Then he offered to get me the letter back if I would come
with him for it and give him the note in exchange. I knew
I was running some sort of risk, but I chanced it. By the
first possible train from Waterloo we went off to the Isle
of Wight, Flyte and myself and the assistant blackguard."

"Before that, I take it, you were unaware that Flyte had
a home here?"

"Quite unaware. They wouldn't tell me even at the time
exactly where we were going. At Southampton we waited
a bit, and they got a car from somewhere. It was a weird
position, for at some point on that journey I might easily
have run into Thornton. Goodness knows what would
have happened then! When we drove up the pier to the
little steamer that goes across to Cowes I could see the
four red funnels of the *Mauretania* where she lay at the
landing-stage. From Cowes we drove out into the country,
taking things very easily. You can guess we weren't very
conversational."

Pamela had regained her hold on herself. She was
speaking almost cheerfully of her drive with that couple
of scoundrels, but I could imagine what an ordeal it must
have been.

"It was after dark when the car pulled up. As soon as
it got dark they had bandaged my eyes, and I had no idea
where I was, but now I know we were in that little sunken
road outside here which leads to the cliff. I had to stay in

the car with the rat while Flyte disappeared into the darkness. Presently he came back and led us to this bungalow. We came in by the front door into this room; Flyte waited a bit, then said he would fetch the document and went off into the dining-room, closing the door after him. I sat down by the fire."

"And swept the hearth," put in Arbuthnot.

She glanced at him. He looked meaningly at the fireplace.

"You seem to have set the stage very well for me this evening," she cried, taking in the situation.

"Please go on," said Arbuthnot, smiling.

"It's no good my describing the state I was in. You can guess I was feeling awful, and as soon as Flyte had gone out the rat-man began looking at me in a certain way. I was worked up to a pitch."

She hesitated.

"Then," said Arbuthnot quietly, "only a minute or so after Flyte had gone out you heard the sound of a voice or voices in the next room, a pistol shot, and then the fall of a body. Go on from there."

"It finished me," she said. "I suppose my nerves had been gradually wearing away all that day. I made a wild rush for the front door. The rat-faced man seemed too scared himself to try to stop me. The door was locked! I turned and bolted down the passage like a rabbit. As I passed, some one slammed the door between the dining-room and the passage. I rushed through the kitchen, bumping myself on this and that. The back door wasn't locked, and in a second I had run out on to the down. It was dark, and anyway I was too scared to look where I was going. Before I knew what had happened I had fallen over a bicycle lying on the turf."

There was a silence in the room. I was trying to avoid looking at Pamela.

"I am telling everything," she said, and despite her bravery her voice sounded as if the words had been torn from her heart.

"Quite right. It's the only thing you can do. Please continue," said Arbuthnot.

But I hardly had ears for the rest of her story. I could guess whose bicycle it had been. I pictured Rodd either in London or Southampton catching sight of the trio. Heaven knows what he had imagined. To arrive in England after two years' absence only to see his fiancée disappearing in the company of two men whose very appearance portended no good! What blind rage must have filled his heart! I saw the pursuit of the slow-moving car by the bicycle; I saw Rodd by chance finding the back door unlocked and entering to confront Dalton Flyte. Then the fatal shot. And finally Flyte's accomplice, Jaguar Jim, "the rat-faced man", collecting everything of value in the bungalow and stealing away, only to meet his doom at Bouldnor Cliff.

"I can ride a man's bicycle after a fashion," Pamela had been saying. "I used to ride—Winton's when I was a girl, and there was no one to stop me. I pulled my skirt up round my waist, scrambled on somehow, and dashed off with no light. I might have gone over the cliff. As it was I luckily struck the road where you and I walked last night, Edmund. Then when I'd gone some way I thought of my pistol. I didn't fancy having it about me after what had happened, so I got rid of it. I believed I had flung it over the cliff."

"Then the pistol found was yours?" I cried.

"Yes, of course it was."

"Another theory upset," murmured Arbuthnot to me. I had no answer ready.

"Some way farther on I remembered my stick and where I had left it. I dared not go back. Besides, I had no reason then to be alarmed for anyone but myself. I went on. When I guessed I was getting near a fair-sized town I abandoned the bicycle and hid it as well as I could. I walked on most of the night, missed the way to Cowes, and finally caught the first boat from Ryde in the morning."

"Are these facts known to anyone but those present?" asked Arbuthnot.

"Not to a soul."

"Good! Please continue to be silent. I am afraid this recital is rather taxing your strength, but I should like to know what has happened since. Having trusted us so far there is no point in withholding anything."

"No. When I returned home on Saturday I was very surprised to find Thornton had not been there. I was still more startled when he didn't come on Sunday. On that day the crime was briefly reported in the papers. There had been no time for much detail to come to hand, I suppose. On Monday you can guess I had an appalling shock when Thornton's name first appeared. I looked at the papers first and my letters second that morning. Then I found I had a note from him. It's destroyed now, of course, but I know it by heart:

> "'I was there on Friday night. I will come to you when I can. On no account try to communicate with me. All will be well. Ever loving you,
>
> "'T.'"

"On Wednesday I got another:

> "'I have your stick. Meet me at Brockenhurst at twelve on Thursday. If I do not arrive then, return to London immediately. All is well.'"

"I went to Brockenhurst, but Thornton never came. The evening papers told me why. I think I should have gone out of my mind that night but for one thing, a very strange incident indeed. As I was sitting in the Waterloo train at Brockenhurst waiting to start back home again, some one passing on the platform flipped a folded scrap of paper on to my lap."

"Quite so," said Arbuthnot. "It had a message on it: 'T. R. cannot come. His interests are being watched. Say nothing. Do nothing.' And in spite of that you came to Freshwater the very next day."

Pamela and I were staring at him in astonishment.

"Perhaps you're not quite the beast I thought you were," she said slowly. "It was Gerry who suggested coming here. I ought to have known better."

"You ought. For a couple of intelligent young people you have behaved throughout like a pair of arrant fools. You have spent a week in a specially-selected hell of your own, each believing that the other was guilty of murder."

Pamela was weeping. I turned and looked out of the window, pondering over the mist on the glass, produced, I supposed, by the chill of evening.

"And I regret to notice that in spite of that fact you were both prepared to continue your attachment, and that one even attempted to defeat the ends of justice by confessing to a crime he never committed in order, as he thought, to shield the other."

"And I could do nothing for *him!* Anything I could say or do would only have made things worse," Pamela said between her tears.

"Precisely. I knew you understood that. That is why I had to adopt unpleasant means to extract a confession. Now I think there is only one thing more required of you."

And there, for the first time in this story, Arbuthnot was wrong.

14
The Same Concluded

"Of course *we* are only too willing to believe you when you say Rodd is innocent," I remarked to Arbuthnot. "But have you any evidence on that point that will convince a court of law?"

"You must take my word for it at present," he answered, "unless you choose to use your brains instead."

"I would accept your word if you told me I looked pretty when I was crying," declared Pamela, achieving half a smile. "I can't say more."

"Feeling pretty fit now?" inquired Arbuthnot.

"I can't say yet how I *do* feel."

"Well, come along. I want you to meet an old acquaintance. That will cheer you up."

"My face looks awful."

"Never mind your face. Come with me."

He led her through the dining-room, and I followed, inwardly perplexed. We stopped at my bedroom door. Arbuthnot opened it, went in, and switched on the light. The prisoner was sitting on his bed with his head sunk on his chest. He looked a miserable object; no doubt his recent severe treatment at my hands had completed his discomfiture.

"Get up when a lady comes into the room," shouted Arbuthnot.

The man had not looked up at our entry; now he sprang to his feet and gasped.

The recognition was mutual. Pamela was staring with wide-open eyes.

"Have you ever seen him before?" Arbuthnot asked her.

"Of course I have! He was the man who came here with Flyte and me," she cried.

"You may see me again," said the prisoner, casting a savage glance at us.

Pamela flinched. I don't know whether she regarded him as a horror of the past or a danger in the future.

"Yes. In the dock," said Arbuthnot curtly. "Lie down on your bed," he added sternly.

The man hesitated a moment and then complied. Arbuthnot bent over him and tightened his bonds. Then we returned to the drawing-room.

"When did you catch him?" asked Pamela.

"Last night."

"Then Edmund caught him! Is that how he got his bump?"

"Not exactly," said Arbuthnot with a laugh. "It's too long a tale to tell now. But don't worry. I know you are thinking that he has it in his power to recount some strange things when he appears in court. We still have your father to consider, but this fellow can't do any harm."

"I'm not very much afraid of him," she answered. "Since Flyte's papers have all been burnt there would only be the man's word for anything he said. Perhaps he doesn't even know very much. I never said anything in front of him."

"One more question," said Arbuthnot, "and I won't worry you any more. On the night of the murder was this man wearing a brown tweed suit?"

"He was!" she cried. "How on earth did you know?"

Arbuthnot left the question unanswered.

"I am going to telephone to the police," he said. "May I offer myself as escort if you think of returning to the hotel? It may be that your self-appointed guardian will be puzzled by your absence. It is nearly dinner-time."

"I can't make you both a speech of thanks, but you ought to know—" Her voice trailed off into nothingness and her eyes had a suspicious brightness as she turned to go.

"Miss Strode, I think you are forgetting your stick." It was the Arbuthnot touch.

She took it, choked over something, and ran out of the house.

"Look after the prisoner, King," growled Arbuthnot as pipe in mouth he wandered off. "We'll have him in the lock-up to-night."

Left to myself I leaned my arms on the drawing-room window-sill and watched the blue Channel ceaselessly rising and dipping, with little white crests curling off as the waves raced shorewards. Behind me Mrs. Morris was laying the dining-room table, and the quality of the sounds from the cutlery she manipulated breathed faintly of the disapproval with which she regarded our conduct. Pamela had gone away into the sunshine. Nevertheless, I was conscious that much remained to be done before we could put the Freshwater tragedy into the category of finished inquiries. I did some hard thinking in the next few minutes.

The discovery that our prisoner had been present in the bungalow at the time of the crime put a very different complexion on things. What had he done after the murder? Had he been terrified by Jaguar Jim into submission? Or had he fled for his life, taking the car by which Pamela had arrived? The car had certainly gone and nothing had ever come to light concerning it. No one had ever dreamed there had been a car other than Flyte's there that night.

Of the chief actors we knew that neither Rodd nor Pamela could have taken it, and Jaguar Jim had chosen another conveyance for himself. At that stage in my meditations Mr. Bellingham hove in sight.

"I don't know whether to be elated or depressed at what Pamela tells me you have learnt," he said gravely as I admitted him. "By the way, I half-expected to find her here?"

"She has returned to the hotel," I said.

"Ah, then I missed her by coming the other way. I have been absorbing a little of this wonderfully pure atmosphere before dining."

"Things might have turned out much worse," I said shortly, for I was not feeling exactly in a conversational mood.

"With respect to Rodd, you mean? I agree. His action was nothing more than a youthful folly. And yet the scandal, my dear Sir Edmund, will be considerable. I think his friends should use their influence with him to persuade him to return overseas until the clamour has somewhat abated."

"Why shouldn't he face it out?" I asked. I had to keep a close watch on my tongue in order not to reveal by mischance what Arbuthnot had decreed should for the present be secret.

"That would be laudable but hardly politic. If I may be permitted to skate over thin ice, I should say that I fear my dear old friend, Sir Jervis Strode, cannot be spared to us much longer. It would be a thousand pities to embitter his last mundane moments by any act of undue precipitancy, and, after all, Pamela and Thornton are young and liable to hasty actions they would later regret. A little patience might clear the way to everything."

"I should not dare to offer advice to either of them," I declared.

He chuckled.

"Ah, this modern generation! Well, I must hurry away and do my best to console Pamela. She is even more distressed than I should have expected."

I surveyed his departing back with satisfaction till he went out of sight. Then I revisited the prisoner, who was lying on the bed with his face set in a sullen stare. His eyes watched me malevolently, but he kept silence. I was glad to leave him. Presently Arbuthnot returned.

"Bernard is coming over himself," he said. "He seemed to find my news rather startling."

"I can quite believe it," I replied.

"You've certainly made a mess of your knuckles, King."

I flushed. "I deserve it," I said.

"In a way you do. Let's have a look at the prisoner."

"I've just been there," I said.

"Never mind that; I should like to see him."

The man had not moved since my previous visit. Arbuthnot bent over him and rolled him on to his face. "Have a look at his knuckles," he said.

Feeling some surprise I inspected the prisoner's hands, which were securely pinioned behind his back. They were not the hands of a manual worker; in fact, they were rather white and effeminate in appearance. Then I looked up at Arbuthnot in amazement. The man's knuckles bore no trace of any abrasion! Together we went back into the drawing-room.

"That's an amazing thing!" I cried. "And he wasn't wearing gloves, for I felt his hands on my wrists when he pulled me up. He must have struck me with a weapon."

"If he had had a weapon he would have used it at first instead of trying to throttle you."

"Then—then—" I stuttered.

"Your aggressor and our prisoner are different men."

I sat in silence for a moment.

"They both had masks," I argued.

"Who wouldn't?"

"I don't understand you."

"Who would willingly embark on business of this kind without some concealment? You might just as well say they were one and the same man because they were both wearing trousers."

"There were two men on the down on the night of the storm," I cried. "I see it now. One had to deal with me while the other went to the bungalow. I suppose he didn't dare go so far as to kill me, but was content to knock me out."

"Have you ever seen a fireman working on a railway engine?" Arbuthnot asked unexpectedly.

"Of course I have. But what on earth—"

"A strenuous life. King. Monotonous, heavy toil in an uncomfortable position, and a restricted space. Grimed with the black dust, he toils on with rhythmic regularity at his essential task. Have you no sympathy for him?"

"Not particularly," I said. "I suppose he's paid to do it. Badly paid, I've no doubt, but probably as well as he would be in any other occupation he could hope to secure."

"Your remark epitomizes a common attitude which is doing incalculable harm at the present day."

"I'm open to conviction," I said.

"Well, I may try to persuade you to see the error of your ways."

"In the meantime—" I began.

"In the meantime here is Bernard arriving. He can hardly have loitered by the way." There were sounds of a car outside.

"You're an extraordinary chap," said the superintendent of police to Arbuthnot as he entered. "We spent half this afternoon talking, and you never said a word about this bird you'd caught."

"An oversight," said Arbuthnot, grinning. "There will be another kind of bird appearing on the table shortly. Will you stay and share it?"

"I've got Farrell outside in the car," said Bernard. "He can take charge of your prisoner and escort him to Newport, and then the car can come back for me. I very much want to hear all about this capture of yours."

"Good! Sit down. King will be only too pleased to deliver our man into the clutches of your inspector. He isn't fond of him."

Five minutes later the car drove off with the rat-faced man sitting securely handcuffed beside Inspector Farrell. He had preserved his reticence to the last. I returned to the drawing-room, to find Arbuthnot and Bernard deep in conversation. To retail it would be to cover much familiar ground. Bernard gummed up the facts very well at the end, which did not come till we had nearly completed dinner.

"To put it briefly," he said, "on Friday night you saw two men watching the bungalow; on Saturday night one or more entered the kitchen and tried to set fire to the house, and last night one man attacked your friend King on the cliff, while another came into the house and was captured."

"Quite correct."

"It's a fair assumption that these men were connected with Flyte in some way. That doesn't speak any too well for him."

"Perfectly true."

"Of these men at least one remains at large. Do you want protection? Shall we institute local inquiries?"

"No. That might result in scaring him away. I suggest you wait a day or two to see if we are lucky enough to catch him ourselves."

"I'm inclined to think that would be best. I'll send out help at a moment's notice if you telephone me."

"Thanks."

"The great point is, what do these fellows want here? I take it you have found nothing in the bungalow that they might wish to secure or to destroy."

"Nothing."

"I must be getting away. This affair needs a good deal of thinking over," said Bernard, rising.

"What will happen to Rodd?"

"He will probably get out on bail if he applies. We should not oppose an application, especially in view of this last development. It's beginning to look as if Flyte was the ringleader of a very cheery set of scoundrels."

"It would be an excellent thing if Rodd's release were deferred till Wednesday, the day after to-morrow," suggested Arbuthnot.

"Why so?"

"He has a knack of getting in the way," said my friend.

"Very well," answered the superintendent. "I'll see that he isn't free to bother you till the day you mention."

With that he departed in the car, which had returned five minutes previously. It was then long after nine o'clock and I was feeling thoroughly tired from my various experiences.

"Bernard is no fool," said Arbuthnot.

"Certainly not."

"He can put two and two together as well as most people."

"He can. What are you thinking of particularly?"

"Of the fireman."

"Confound the fireman! Can't you be more explicit?"

"Presently. I'm going to write a letter."

I lolled in an easy chair and stifled the yawns of pure fatigue while Arbuthnot sat at the bureau writing in his deliberate, methodical style.

"Read this," he said after five minutes' silence, passing me a sheet of notepaper.

I read:

> "Dear Rodd,
> "I believe you are likely to be released on bail. Do not, however, assume that your troubles are entirely over. Your obvious popularity in certain quarters may be offset to some extent in other directions by an impression that you have cleared your reputation rather at the expense of others.
> "When you come to the bungalow telegraph me in advance and I will arrange that you are suitably greeted. It would not be unwise to arrive after dark. I know that you can afford to purchase a bicycle.
> "Yours sincerely,
> "Montrose Arbuthnot"

"I don't quite see the need of this," I remarked as I wrinkled my brows over the singular epistle.

"Neither do I—quite. But I am disinclined to run risks. Now, King, are you fit?"

"Fit for bed," I answered. "I think I'll take the second watch to-night if you're agreeable."

"We'll see how you feel by that time. Will you help me to close the shutters?"

"All of them?" I asked in surprise.

"I think so."

I complied with his wishes at once, feeling an odd disquiet. Surely Arbuthnot's steel nerves were not at last showing a flaw?

"You appear somewhat perturbed, King," he said as I returned from my task. "Let me assure you there is no need for alarm—at present. I will explain things a little."

"Do so," said I.

"A week ago to-day," he began, "we came here and found that some one had entered the house previously and restored the missing bar."

"I'm still puzzled about that bar," I said.

"Never mind it now. What matters at present is that we learnt that some one in the district retained an interest in the place. Later we found that that person was not Rodd. On Tuesday last our friend Williams received two unexpected applications to rent the bungalow. The one from Mr. Cosmo Edginton, coupled with his subsequent behaviour, necessarily aroused our suspicions. Although he admitted to awareness of the crime he addressed his letter in a degree of detail which indicated previous acquaintance with the area."

"True. He wrote 'Lilac Villa', a name which had not appeared in the papers."

"We had scarcely taken up our residence here when we had unmistakable evidence that the interest of some persons in the place had not abated. That presented a puzzle. If there was something in the bungalow either so valuable or so dangerous as to render its removal essential, why had it not been taken away long before we came here? There were only two answers to that. It was either too bulky or too inaccessible to be removed in a hurry. Of the two possibilities the first was negligible."

"Very reasonable," I concurred.

"We know now that Flyte's nefarious activities included the gentle art of blackmailing," continued Arbuthnot. "I would ask you, King, of what a blackmailer's stock-in-trade consists?"

"Of letters, documents, and similar articles, of course," I said.

"True. Now the blackmailer is unique amongst tradesmen. He does not as a rule need to dispose of his goods in order to secure his profits. Once in a way he may sell an article outright, and very occasionally he may part with one to bring about an exposure *pour encourager les autres.* But as a rule he does not even need to take stock from time to time. A few names and addresses and some coded memoranda in a pocket-book serve his need. For his real wares he requires only such safe concealment that, in the words of the poet, they may 'dry-rot at ease till the Judgement Day' if not previously brought into use."

"You put things clearly, as usual," I said.

"Good! It is a very reasonable assumption that Dalton Flyte kept his merchandise somewhere in this bungalow. He would not keep it in premises that might fall under police suspicion at any moment. Therefore I rule out the Brixton Road head-quarters. He certainly would not keep it at his hotel. We cannot imagine that he would be such a fool as to carry it to and fro with him on his journeys. That would be courting disaster. Neither, surely, would he leave it in his dining-room safe at the mercy of the unhampered operations of a burglar in a house that was always empty at night for half the week."

I jumped to my feet in alarm.

"Then Winton Strode's letter still exists!" I cried.

"Presumably. Now, at this point we derive some help from the incendiary activities of the gentleman who was recently conveyed away. He was willing to burn the house down. Then if my theory is correct, Dalton Flyte's documents cannot be above ground. If his efforts had been successful we should have been obliged to abandon the remains of the bungalow, leaving him much freer to pursue his object."

"That's plain as day," I agreed.

Arbuthnot smiled.

"I gave some consideration to the floors of the rooms," he went on. "Those in this part of the house are naturally wooden and would burn. The back premises, however, as usual, have stone floors. It is within your recollection no doubt that you once found the outer door of the coal-shed open?"

"By Jove, yes!"

"A well-arranged affair. A person's act in removing coal to the outside of the house would give the appearance of an attempt at a common and rather trivial theft, but what would one think if one found coal had been transferred to the scullery? Dalton Flyte kept a good stock of coal, even in June. I estimate there may be nearly three tons there."

"A remarkable hiding-place!" I ejaculated.

"Very clever. Who, considering Flyte's obvious defences against burglary, would think for a moment that his chief treasures lay outside his barriers? I don't suppose he needed to unearth them more than once every six months, if as often. You may remember his occasional kindness in giving Mrs. Morris a holiday without her asking. No doubt those were the times when he wished to examine his wares. Provided he maintained a good stock of coal he was as safe as man can ever be. One thing remains."

"Yes?"

"Bernard, now he has the facts, or at least most of them, is quite capable of reaching a similar conclusion."

"Do you think so?"

"I am sure of it. You would prefer that a certain document should not come into the hands of the police?"

"Of course."

"Then you must shovel coal."

"Try me!" I cried, walking backwards and forwards.

"Good! It is now quite dark. Unfortunately I cannot allow you a light for your labours as it could probably be seen through cracks in the outer door. I don't anticipate interference to-night, but I shall take post outdoors to prevent any suspicious person approaching within sound of the shovelling. I will relieve you when you are tired."

Together we made a journey to the coal-store. The quantity of coal there was impressive.

"It must be moved into the scullery," said Arbuthnot. "Heaven only knows what Mrs. Morris will say in the morning if we don't get it put back in time."

Our first task was to remove the scullery furniture into the kitchen to clear room for our operations. Then Arbuthnot disappeared outdoors, leaving a couple of lights burning in the house as a hint to possible intruders who came near enough to trace a glint here and there through the shutters. I stripped down to singlet and trousers, seized a good-sized coal-shovel that lay by the door and set to work. Heavens, how I toiled that night! I had very little room, for I had to work standing in the doorway and to make a half-turn each time to throw my shovel load behind me into the scullery. Perspiration started from every pore in my body, my damaged hand objected to the strain I was putting upon it, and the bruise on my head began to ache in a dull, irritating fashion. From time to time my inexperience caused me to sustain knocks from my tool and from the door frame, and occasionally large lumps of coal from the upper parts of the pile, unstabilized by my encroachments beneath, descended swiftly and found my none too well protected feet.

"Have you no sympathy with firemen?" asked a voice. Arbuthnot had come into the scullery and was chuckling to himself in the dark.

"I'll give a hundred pounds to their union when I've finished this," I growled.

"Good! Now I'll take a turn. Do you wrap yourself up well after your exertions and take post outside."

I was nothing loath, and pulling on an overcoat over my other garments I went out into the moonlight. The time was after eleven o'clock and hardly a light shone in the scattered houses around the bay. I started a pipe and, despite an incrustation of coal-dust on the stem, enjoyed it. To the passer-by I was nothing but a lover of fresh air taking a brief breather before turning in. Time flowed on insensibly and nothing occurred demanding my notice. When the sounds of midnight rang silvery clear from the inland tower I went in to Arbuthnot.

"Take over," said he, climbing out over the enormous accumulation of coal that had grown up in the scullery and was faintly revealed by the moonlight without. "There's not a great deal left to do. Is all clear outside?"

"Quite."

I fell to my task again without further words. I am physically strong, but in such work experience is everything, and that I lacked. I felt as if a rift had suddenly developed in my back. Arbuthnot came in just as I was finishing.

"That's fine. Now I must prise up these flagstones. I shall be obliged to use a candle, so perhaps you'd better continue the guard outdoors."

I don't suppose I had spent more than half an hour walking up and down in the utter solitude outside when a low whistle brought me back to the door.

"Got it!" whispered Arbuthnot in my ear. He swiftly locked the back door behind me and led on into the dining-room. Then I saw clearly why he had insisted on the closing of the shutters. Behind their cover we were free to examine our haul in safety.

"So that's it," I said, as he switched on the light. Under his arm was a massive steel box about the size of an ordinary attaché-case. He laid it on the table and I examined it eagerly. Despite a certain covering of dirt I could see that it was exceptionally strong and well-constructed.

"Open it," I cried. "The key will be one of those on the bungalow bunch."

By way of reply he drew out the keys that had been given into our care, selected one, opened the safe that stood in the corner, placed the box inside, and locked it in.

"Aren't you going to open it?" I asked in disappointed tones.

"King, I invite your attention to the state of the scullery."

There was wisdom in his words. I could picture Mrs. Morris at sight of it bursting into tears and departing for ever from our service. I have no language to describe the rest of that night. Dawn was breaking as the last shovelful of coal went back into its usual abode, and my back was in a similar condition.

"I'll sweep the floor when it gets a bit lighter," said Arbuthnot in matter-of-fact tones. Extraordinary man, he had had no sleep the preceding night and yet he seemed as alert as ever and ready to carry on indefinitely.

"I'm for a wash and a few hours' sleep," I said, "since you are not prepared to open the box at present."

He looked at me curiously and said nothing. I took myself off to the bathroom, shed my disgustful garments in a heap, and took first go at Arbuthnot's morning tub, chuckling to myself over his impending discomfiture. Despite my exhaustion I was in high spirits, and the cold water stimulated tired brain and body. Another stage accomplished! Flyte's box was in our hands. Soon the terror of Pamela's life would be shrivelling in the flames. Let the rat-faced man tell his tale then and be laughed out of court. I pulled on my dressing-gown and sauntered into the dining-room just as Arbuthnot returned from his business with the broom.

"I have achieved a semblance of order," he said.

"You must be thoroughly tired," I answered.

"Not I. I'm sorry if I appeared to be churlish over the question of opening the box." He went to the safe as he spoke, withdrew the subject of his remark, and laid it on the table. "Here are the keys," he said, passing me the bunch as he spoke.

I took it and one by one I tried all the keys of a suitable size on that obdurate box. Not one would fit it. Silently Arbuthnot removed the box and restored it to the safe.

"We are not out of the wood yet," he said as he took himself off.

15
Events of Tuesday, June 5th

"This affair may be said to have possessed a certain degree of complication," said Arbuthnot as we sat at breakfast a few hours after the events recorded in the last chapter.

"You speak in the past tense," I remarked.

"Do not misunderstand me. I do not suggest that nothing remains to be done. That is far from the truth. But we have now sufficient threads in our hands to weave a fairly satisfactory pattern."

My reply was prevented by the entry of Mrs. Morris with a fresh supply of tea. Her face was a mask of silent indignation and had been so ever since our first sight of her that morning.

"I'm afraid you may have found the scullery a little untidy this morning," hazarded Arbuthnot, winking at me.

"Untidy!" She became speechless.

"There was a rat in the coal-store and we had a great hunt for it last night, in the course of which some coal probably found its way into the scullery."

I thought "found its way" was distinctly good, especially as I still ached in every limb from my unwonted labour.

The good lady sniffed.

"Then it was the liveliest rat I ever heard tell of," she remarked with some asperity. "Did it roll up and down the curtains, may I ask?"

Arbuthnot laughed.

"It was no ordinary rodent," said he, and fell silent over a letter that had just arrived by the morning mail.

After breakfast I unashamedly sought to make up some arrears of sleep on the drawing-room couch. Arbuthnot disappeared, and I guessed he had gone to send his letter to Rodd. I still felt disconcerted over our inability to open Flyte's box. No doubt he had devised some particularly safe hiding-place for the key, and where that might be I saw no hope of discovering. The box had looked as if it would offer a stout resistance to forcible treatment, and in any case I chafed at the delay. I was aroused from slumber by Pamela, who was leaning through the window and tickling my nose with a piece of grass. I sat up bewildered.

"What have you been up to now to be so lazy?"

"Digging," I said briefly.

"The grave of lost hopes?"

"No. Coal."

"If I weren't so grateful to both of you I should call you a comical pair," she said.

"This is confidential," I said hastily, becoming fully awake.

"Trying to earn an honest penny, I suppose. When do you think Roddy will be let loose?"

"Very soon, I should say."

"Will he come here?"

"Why not?"

"Why not, of course? Gerry may be a bit stuffy, but then he doesn't know the whole truth yet."

"Neither do we."

"I suppose not. I expect Mr. Arbuthnot knows."

"He's like an oyster," I said.

"And you're an old crab. Bye-bye, coalie."

She was gone. I slept again. When I woke up Arbuthnot was nursing his pipe in an adjacent chair.

"I presume Rodd caught sight of Miss Strode with her escort at Waterloo, having arrived there earlier than expected," he said, as if he were continuing an already initiated conversation. "It must have been rather a shock to him to see her departing from London in such company on the day of his return. No doubt the sight of the stick she was carrying assured him of her continued fidelity, and he followed. While they were making their arrangements in Southampton he must have managed to equip himself for an ostensible walking-tour by purchasing a rucksack and some oddments of kit. I don't suppose that when he had succeeded in following them here he entered the bungalow. He probably lurked on the veranda trying to gather, despite the shutters, some inkling of what was proceeding within. What must he have thought when he heard the shot? Most likely he also heard the back door open. He may have been near enough to glimpse who it was who was thus escaping. I think he did and that decided him to stay in the locality to keep in touch with developments even at some risk to himself. When the pistol was found he would know that he could only clear himself from suspicion by one method, and that one that would be unthinkable to him. So he invented a distinctly ingenious confession as the best way out of an apparently hopeless position."

"He isn't cleared yet," I pointed out.

"Quite so. What would you say was the best defence to a charge of being concerned in a murder?"

"A complete alibi, I suppose."

"That certainly won't do here. We must try what else we can do."

"We also want to open that box," I said anxiously.

"A tough proposition, I fancy. Why not defer the pleasure for a day or two in the hope that the key may become available?"

"Is that likely to happen? It's very difficult to imagine where Flyte may have kept it."

"Not at all. He had no special need to hide the key, seeing how well concealed the box was. I've no doubt Flyte kept it in his trouser pocket, which would have been the very best place for it."

"Then why isn't it on the bunch now?" I demanded.

"That's very simply answered."

"Yes?"

"Because it has been taken off."

"A very edifying reply," I remarked, a little nettled.

"It is, if you would but consider it properly. Hullo! That must be Bernard."

There were sounds of a car outside.

The superintendent entered with a little air of excitement about him. "I've been thinking a lot about this affair," he said. "I'm driven to the conclusion that there's something in the bungalow we don't know about. No other hypothesis seems possible."

"I agree with you entirely," said Arbuthnot.

"Then we must search for it!"

"Are you sure that you want to find it—yet?"

"Why not?"

"By finding it you remove the attraction the bungalow has for at present certain unknowns. There is at least one of them left. You don't know him, and he may quite easily without arousing suspicion find out that investigations are proceeding. Then he will vanish."

"There's some sense in that, and yet perhaps we have the whole secret of Dalton Flyte's past life lying here under our very hands to be had for the finding."

"Wait another forty-eight hours, and maybe in that time it may be found for you."

"By you?"

"Not necessarily.

"I see. You would make this remaining individual a catspaw."

"Doesn't it appeal to your sense of justice?"

The superintendent laughed. "Have your own way," he said. "I must see the landlord to get permission to knock his place about a bit if necessary, and we shall be along here on Thursday morning if fresh developments have not by then rendered the search superfluous. Good-bye."

Even Arbuthnot, man of iron as he is, retired for a brief rest on that pleasant summer afternoon. I drowsed in a deck-chair, watching the play of sunshine over the bay and the gulls wheeling and plunging beyond the edge of the cliffs. Chance had served us up some very peculiar holiday fare; no doubt it still had one or two piquant dishes in reserve. Pamela's affairs were not finally settled, Rodd's official exculpation remained to be secured, and the murder of Dalton Flyte still preserved most of its mystery to me. Still, all for the moment was at peace. Then my siesta was abominably truncated by the appearance of Mr. Bellingham with a neatly-folded newspaper under his arm.

"I hesitated to disturb you," he said affably as he mounted on to the veranda, "but at last my curiosity got the better of me. I see by this morning's paper that the police have made another arrest."

Without awaiting my comments he opened the paper and read out sonorously:

THE BUNGALOW TRAGEDY
SURPRISING DEVELOPMENTS

"The first part is all about our young friend Rodd's confession," he said. "I needn't read that, but listen to what follows."

"'Public interest has been further stimulated by the news that the police have just effected another arrest in connection with the case. As Thornton Rodd's statements reproduced above necessarily lack corroboration at present, it is hoped that this fresh development may serve to throw some fresh light on the baffling mystery of the late Dalton Flyte's identity.'

"I am surprised you failed to notice it," he added as he finished reading, "but I imagine you supposed that the whole column dealt with Rodd's affairs and that therefore you did not bother to read it."

"Quite so," I replied.

I did not choose to tell him that I had been far too tired all that day to care to open a newspaper.

"It would be interesting to know if your friend Mr. Arbuthnot had any hand in securing the arrest," said Mr. Bellingham tentatively.

"I have come to believe he has a hand in most things," I responded guardedly, for I did not know how much I ought to tell this old busybody. Quite possibly he had seen or heard something of Bernard's visits to the bungalow of the night before and that morning.

"It's beginning to be abundantly clear that the late Flyte was the leader of some body of unprincipled men," he continued. "One cannot grieve over the accidental removal of such a menace to society."

I should have welcomed the accidental removal of Mr. Bellingham at that moment; as it was, I had to endure his platitudes for another ten minutes.

"I see that the papers already report the arrest of the man whom the police took away last night," I said to Arbuthnot as we sat at tea.

"Yes. I telegraphed the news to London myself when I went out with Miss Strode yesterday evening."

"Why such urgency?"

"We haven't much time. Bernard is dying to pull the bungalow to pieces. The news I sent is calculated to accelerate the arrival of Mr. Cosmo Edginton."

"Probably he has been in the locality for some time," I suggested. "Remember we once saw two men."

"Perhaps."

At the back of my mind I recollected a remark Arbuthnot had made on the day Rodd was committed for trial. He had said, "Mr. Edginton will not come to Freshwater yet. And when he does come—" He had not finished his sentence. I was puzzled.

"I want you to take the second watch to-night, beginning at one," continued Arbuthnot. "I shall spend that part of the night outdoors. Listen carefully to your instructions."

"If anyone should come will he have a key?" I interrupted.

"Almost certainly. Keys are easy to duplicate, and no doubt a replica of the one we captured was made long ago as a precaution. Now your job is a fairly easy one. If anyone enters the bungalow you have only to give the alarm as loudly possible. You have a revolver. Fire off a couple of shots at random, provided you don't shoot the visitor."

"Have I to make no attempt to capture him?" I asked in surprise.

"None at all."

"Very well."

"I suppose," he added casually, "you have no belief in the supernatural?"

"I've never admitted to any," I said, "but I'm not mentally alert enough at present to defend my attitude. Natural phenomena seem to have been taking up most of my time recently."

"I would not question your attitude," he answered. "It seems an admirable one from my point of view. We shall be dining out to-night, Mrs. Morris," he added, as she appeared to remove the tea-tray.

"Very well, sir."

"I want you to stay in the bungalow till we return. We shall not be late."

"I'll put in the time doing a bit o' cleaning," answered Mrs. Morris grimly, and we both laughed.

"Where are we dining?" I inquired with some interest when we were once more alone.

"At the Stagrock Hotel, if you will condescend to be my guest for the occasion."

"With pleasure. I've no quarrel with their cuisine at all, but you'll hardly persuade me that we are going for the joy of banqueting."

"Not exactly. I had a letter from Kaye this morning. He's dug out a little information that arouses my interest."

When we arrived at the hotel I found that a table had been reserved for us, which was more a gesture of welcome than a necessity, since I knew from Arbuthnot that the hotel was temporarily empty of guests. The little waiter, of that alleged Swiss extraction that covers a multitude of nationalities, beamed at our return and served us assiduously. The meal did not take long, and in little more than half an hour Arbuthnot had paid the bill and the waiter had returned with a plate whose load of silver coins of varying denominations enabled the diner to exercise a nice discretion as to the appropriate reward he should grant for the services he had received.

Arbuthnot appeared to hesitate.

The waiter stood with the air of one to whom the idea of a *pourboire* is abhorrent.

I awoke suddenly to the fact that something interesting was about to happen.

"I am going to ask you a question," said Arbuthnot in that particular tone that often half won him the battle before it had really begun.

"Yes, sir?" The waiter looked astonished.

"No doubt you remember the chambermaid who left here last Thursday week? Her name, I believe, was Sarah Tuson."

It was my turn to look surprised.

"Oh, yes, sir, quite well do I remember her."

"Was she a friend of yours?"

"Oh, sir, I had for her the most respectful admiration. But she—she was what you call stand-offish."

"I want to know all you can tell me about her."

The waiter hesitated. He clasped his hands in a kind of agonized way and shuffled his feet.

"I see," continued Arbuthnot, tracing the little man's distress to its source. "You are reluctant to speak. I give you my personal word of honour that I intend no harm to the young lady. I promise you further that no one shall touch her in any way. Do you believe me?"

People have a habit of believing Arbuthnot.

"Yes, sir, of course."

"Continue."

"Only one month had she been here, giving every satisfaction. Very quiet she was—like a lady. Then one day she tell me she is not happy. The manageress is too stern. Next day she tell me she cannot stand any more and will go. I am very sorry. Then I say, 'At least give to me your address,' and she give it and laugh. The next morning there is a terrible rumpus with Madame and she pack and go and I—I have wept in the pantry." In his distress he was almost dignified.

"Continue," said Arbuthnot.

"The next day there was a telegram. I took it. That night I stay up late and write what is in my heart. My letter and the telegram I send together. Alas, to-day both come back from what you call the Dead Letter Office. She is not there at the address she has given to me."

"Have you still got the telegram?" asked Arbuthnot sharply.

"Yes, sir. Now I do not like to return it to the post office."

"Fetch it."

The little man gasped, received a look from Arbuthnot, and fled to obey.

"What strange trail is this you follow?" I asked, my voice betraying some excitement.

"A short one, I think," he answered in sombre tones.

I could make nothing of the answer. The waiter re-appeared. His hand was shaking as he passed the orange envelope to Arbuthnot, who took it and placed it in his wallet without a word. Then he rose from the table.

"The address to which you wrote was, care of Mrs. Price, 67, Stormont Road, Lavender Hill, S.W.," he said, more in the tone of one who makes a statement than of one who frames a query.

"Yes, sir." The waiter was hopping about in a state compounding bewilderment and alarm.

"You have my promise," said Arbuthnot curtly and strode out of the room. I followed. The glittering array of silver coinage lay untouched on the table, and I glimpsed the little waiter drawing his sleeve across his eyes.

"There's a strain of brutality in your nature," I remarked as we set off back to the bungalow.

"The man's a fool," he answered brusquely, and I said no more.

Back in our sitting-room Arbuthnot pulled out his wallet and extracted the missive he had so unceremoniously seized from the unfortunate Swiss.

"I was almost certain there must have been a telegram," he said, half to himself, "but I never expected to get possession of it quite so easily as this."

I was silent. I could make neither head nor tail of the business, and Arbuthnot was not in a mood to have much consideration for those less mentally agile than himself. With a penknife he methodically slit open the envelope, withdrew its contents and unfolded them.

"Handed in at South Kensington at eleven-thirty a.m. on May 25th," he said.

I saw him scan the message, raise his eyebrows and contract them again as if his brain was working furiously. Then he laughed and I shivered. I expect Sanson in the days when he was busy feeding Madame la Guillotine sometimes heard a laugh like that one.

"Read that, King!" he said, tossing the telegram on to the table.

I picked it up and saw that it contained only four words:

Previous instructions cancelled Juproli.

"Juproli!" I cried. "An Italian! What on earth does this mean, Arbuthnot?"

"Mean? Can't you see what it means?"

"I haven't an idea," I said frankly.

"It means a man's life. And now get away to bed and rest. There may be no room for mistakes to-night."

"What about the shutters?" I asked.

"Leave them open."

I went to bed, but hardly to sleep. I was unnerved by a sense of climax. Arbuthnot saw something approaching. I was none the happier for failing to see it myself. When circumstances permit I am fond of having cats about me, and yet there are times when the presence of a cat is no

comfort. One glances over one's book and the cat is looking. There is nothing particular to look at in the silent
room, but that strange animal that was once worshipped
by the sons of men stares and stares and by and by the hair
rises along its back. Nervous people will say that it sees
something not within the range of our vision.

The uncanny feeling induced by the cat was with me
that night intensified a hundredfold. It was not yet dark
when I got into bed and I watched the light fade gradually
away. There was a moon to come, but it was past the full
and would not rise till later. The rest of the world was at
peace, but the air in that place that had once shrouded
horror seemed to throb as if the violence of human passions had given it an eternal agitation. After an hour or so
I think I must have dozed off.

I awoke with a start and realized that some sound had
called me back to consciousness. Moreover, I knew, though
how I knew I could not say, that the noise had had a metal-
lic quality. Then I became aware that in some room in the
house a light was burning, for as my eyes became more
accustomed to the darkness a faint glimmer showed through
my bedroom door.

I lay still, feeling some alarm. I had no idea what the
time might be; I might have slept for one hour or for four.
For a moment a cold sweat broke out on my brow as it
struck me that Arbuthnot might have called me to my duty
and I might have dozed off again instead of getting up.
I rejected the idea, but it left me uncomfortable. Surely
the light could not be due to Arbuthnot? Maintaining a
light would be a very strange way of attracting the man we
wished to capture.

Then my ear caught the sound of a faint and inter-
mittent scratching. It was a peculiar noise, hardly more
distinct than the scraping of a defective pen-nib on rough
paper. That settled it. I slid out of bed determined to

investigate things and satisfy myself that nothing was wrong.

My bedroom door was ajar. As soon as I reached it I could see that the light proceeded from the dining-room opposite. The door of that room was also open to the extent of about a foot. I paused to feel sure that I had a good grip on myself and then tiptoed across the passage.

The scratching noise continued. With the utmost caution I applied my eye to the narrow chink between the door and its frame, and what I saw made my blood run cold. There was a man in the room. His back was towards me, but I could see very well what he was doing. On the dining-room table lay the box that we had dug all the previous night to secure, and the man was busy with a piece of wire trying to pick the lock.

The unexpectedness of the sight and the audacity of his action made me gasp audibly. The man lifted his head sharply as if listening and then turned it towards me. It was Arbuthnot!

"Go to bed, King," he said in low but penetrating tones.

I complied, feeling more than a little hurt. I could not see any reason for his secret attempt to deal with the box. He must know that I should covet the opportunity of being present at the opening of it. To set about picking the lock at dead of night in a brilliantly-lighted room with not even a curtain drawn to cover the window struck me as an action that, coming from any other person, I should have deemed folly. It was almost inexplicable.

Presently I heard the sound of the closing of the safe. The light from the dining-room vanished and a moment later a patch of yellow appeared in the black shadow of the bungalow outside my bedroom window indicating that the light in the adjacent room had been switched on. Five minutes later it disappeared and then I heard a sharp whisper from my bedroom door.

"King, take over, will you?"

"Right," I answered, jumping up from my bed.

"I think our visitor is about," he continued, never raising his voice above a whisper. "If, as I hope, he has seen me with that box he will know that it's a case of now or never for him."

I could have kicked myself for misjudging my friend. I might have known there was method in his apparent insanity.

"Is it likely he has a key of the safe?" I asked.

"It is possible. You will need to be alert. I wish this cursed moon wasn't so bright."

"Are you going outside now?"

"Soon. Of course, if I'm seen the man will run for it and our work will have to be done over again. But I think it's worth the risk."

"How can you manage to escape detection?"

"Only in one way. I believe the man, if he comes, will enter by the back door. I shall therefore go out by the front and make a dash for it. There's just a bare chance that if I'm seen I may be attacked. I'll leave the front door unlocked when I go and you can watch me from the drawing-room, only be careful to stand well back in the room. If you see the fellow after me it's up to you to rush out and warn me in time."

"I get you." I moved out into the passage in my stockinged feet and stood there while Arbuthnot went silently from room to room. I guessed that he was trying to glimpse from the various windows whether there was anyone in the vicinity of the bungalow. Probably nearly half an hour had elapsed before he had satisfied himself as to the advisability of making his exit.

"I'm off," he whispered at last as he passed me in the passage on his way to the front door.

I immediately moved to the drawing-room and took up my position where I had a good view of the narrow moon-lit strip of ground lying between the front of the bungalow and the edge of the cliff. I never heard Arbuthnot either open or close the front door; he had all the stealth of a cat when he liked. Suddenly something crossed my line of vision. It moved like a flash across the turf, and its shadow raced along at its left hand like some attendant demon. Then form and shadow vanished as if instantaneously destroyed. I stood thunderstruck. Had that been Arbuth-not? If so then he had surely gone over the cliff!

It took me a few seconds to realize what had happened. Then I glimpsed some small, round object moving at the edge of the cliff. I drew in my breath. That daring man had dropped over the cliff edge and now, hanging by his hands, was working his way along to my left to a point—I guessed it would be the end of the sunken road—where he could pull himself up under cover and at some distance from the bungalow. It was a feat requiring a good deal of physical strength and an iron nerve. Had some piece of the edge treacherously yielded he must have been precipitated on to the great stones that lay on the beach below.

My mind flew back to my own terrible position two nights before. Supposing our adversary had seen what he had done? Nothing was easier than for him to dash across the grass and push Arbuthnot off into space before he could scramble up to safety. Now I knew the reason why I had been set to watch. I glued my eyes to the scene in front of me long after I had lost sight of the curious trav-elling object that was really Arbuthnot's head, and I don't know to this day what it was that finally caused me to turn my head and look through the open door behind me into the dining-room beyond.

Then I stood frozen to the spot, while disbelief and panic fear strove for mastery in my disordered brain. My scalp tingled, my throat contracted as if some clammy, evil hand had suddenly gripped me there, my eyes distended as if they would burst from their sockets and my jaw dropped. For there, standing where the westering moon sent its slanting rays through the uncovered window into the darkness of the dining-room, was the ghost of Dalton Flyte.

It stood there not a yard from where Flyte himself had collapsed to death. Its neck was thrust forward at an ugly angle and its face was white as paper. The pince-nez, most horrible element of all that ghastly vision, glittered in the lunar rays. Its body was an indistinct silvery grey that merged insensibly into the shadows of the room.

Like most men who were of an age to answer the call to war I have seen some odd things in my time, but never before had I been called up to combat the powers of hell. The thing stood there with its neck protruding and its eyes half-turned in my direction. I gazed paralysed. A kind of numbness was creeping over my limbs. All my old comfortable beliefs in the strict limitations of a corporeal world were smashed to atoms. I felt my tongue shrivelling between my parched lips like a dry leaf in heat. Some remote corner of my brain had withdrawn itself to an enormous distance and was calmly witnessing the collapse of the system it had once directed.

Arbuthnot's remarks have a habit of living longer in the memory than most. But for that I often wonder in what state I might have finished. What had he said that very evening? Something about the supernatural. The little corner of my brain went on unconcernedly working it out. "I suppose you have no belief in the supernatural?" That was it! He had seemed pleased when I had disclaimed any faith in that direction. Arbuthnot rarely talked to no purpose. What had he meant! Heavens! *Had he anticipated this!*

In my excitement I must have made some sound. The head moved sharply. Some enormous surge of feeling from unplumbed depths swelled up over me, body and soul. I found my tongue move.

"To hell with you, ghost or no ghost!" I shouted and sprang forward. The apparition spun round, knocked against the dining-table, and vanished.

So it was flesh and blood! I did not stop then to marvel, but flung out after my flying foe. He might have waited and struck me down, for in my blind passion I looked neither to right nor left, but for all he knew he had two against him, so he ran.

Not five yards separated us when we passed through the kitchen door. How the man ran! But I gained on him. I had dropped my revolver in the rush, but I cared not for that. This, though only God knew how, was Dalton Flyte, whose evil deeds had dragged Winton Strode to ruin, cast Rodd into prison, and brought hell into the life of Pamela, and all I wanted was to get to him with my fists. He made away up the down along the military road, drawing away from me for a few seconds by an immense effort.

"I'll kill you! I'll kill you!" I was shouting, and never knew till afterwards that I had uttered a single word.

I gained ground. I was almost within touching distance. Suddenly he turned and aimed a blow at me. I could not check my rush and I took it on the point of the chin. Had he been less exhausted it would have served his purpose. As it was it sent strange lights into my eyes and made my head ring. Before he could strike again I had given him a reply full in the teeth, a little higher than I had intended. He gasped, wavered, and then turned to run on. I grabbed for his collar, missed it by an inch, stumbled, and came down on hands and knees among the loose flints on the road. I was up again like a flash, but the slip had given him twenty yards. We had passed the junction with the sunken road and there was still no sign of Arbuthnot. I shouted his name again and again.

My breath was giving out. The man in front ran remarkably well. He had some incentive, I thought grimly. We neared the hill-top and plunged into the cutting. Then I glimpsed something that sent a red-hot stab of despair into my heart. At the beginning of the downward slope was a car with its back towards us. It was touch and go whether I could get there in time to stop him moving off. He had only to get his hand to the brake and the car would rapidly slide downhill. Then I stumbled again. That had ruined it. Still I ran on, though now with no hope.

Flyte reached the car. Then, uncanny in the silvery light, arose a black figure from the back seat. I saw Flyte hesitate, and then I got near enough to hear the voice I knew so well.

"Put up your hands Mr. Flyte or Hunter or Orsini, as I think you originally were," it said.

Then Arbuthnot, revolver in hand, climbed leisurely down on to the road. Flyte was finished. He made no more show of resistance. His breath came in shuddering gasps that seemed to tear his body, and he dribbled blood and teeth on to the ground. I leant against the car and struggled to regain my wind and my composure both.

"Come along, King," said Arbuthnot sharply. "You've left the bungalow unguarded. Get this fellow into the back seat and we'll be moving."

I half-pushed, half-carried the wretched Flyte into the car, Arbuthnot took the wheel, and, progressing backwards, we had reached the bungalow again within five minutes.

"Shutters," said Arbuthnot briefly to me. "I'll keep him here in the kitchen till you've fixed them."

I hurried off to obey. I had recovered my equanimity and my mind was a mass of questions tumbling over each other. Arbuthnot had no intention of allowing any of them. Together we marched Flyte into my bedroom, lashed his arms and legs together, and bound him securely to the bed. He made no demur. His desperate bid for freedom had apparently exhausted his resources and he lay silent. Only his pale-blue eyes glanced incessantly here and there. Arbuthnot bent over him and searched his pockets. Then with a little cry of satisfaction he stood upright and held up for my inspection a little key. The prisoner's lips moved and he spat at us.

"Come along, King," said Arbuthnot. "I dare say you want a drink."

We went into the dining-room.

"I'm utterly lost," I said as I eagerly gulped a stiff brandy-and-soda. "I thought he was a ghost."

Arbuthnot laughed.

"I understood you had no belief in the supernatural," he said. "I questioned you on that very point because I anticipated the possibility that Mr. Flyte would appear as his natural self. After all," and as the comical side of it struck us we both smiled, "he's the rightful tenant of the bungalow till the twenty-fourth of this month, there is no charge against him, and we have been guilty of assault and illegal detention. Perhaps he contemplated attempting an enormous bluff if he were unlucky enough to be caught here. Under different conditions it might conceivably have succeeded. And of course a mask wouldn't fit in very well with his pince-nez."

"You can imagine I'm rather staggered over this business," I said. "I've suspected every one from old Bellingham down to Mrs. Morris, but never did I guess there were two Flytes."

"This isn't the time for talk," answered Arbuthnot briefly. "I am not quite sure yet who these Flytes used to be, but I think they were the Orsini Twins, who were really successful acrobatic performers in the music-halls of twenty years back. Then there were one or two unsavoury incidents in which they were concerned and they vanished from the public view. It was generally believed that they had been acting as secret agents. I'll tell you more later. At present you'll have to stay in charge here."

"What are you going to do?"

"I am going to take our friend Flyte to Newport and let Bernard have a look at him."

"Now at once?"

"Yes. Flyte dead was a comparatively harmless person, but Flyte *redivivus* is an individual I would prefer to have off my hands at the earliest possible moment."

"He seems very broken at present," I suggested.

"Dangerous for all that," said Arbuthnot, looking at me queerly. "I'll go at once so as to have him disposed of before dawn. One other thing."

"Yes?"

"There is no justification whatever for any relaxation of vigilance."

"All right," I answered. My faculty for being surprised was temporarily atrophied. I welcomed a stretch of solitude, as an opportunity to marshal my scattered ideas into some sort of coherence and order. Five minutes later the car slid away, its engine startlingly loud in the hush that comes before any eastern light touches the world's rim, and I went to the bathroom to remove the few fragments of sock that were still with me and to cleanse those wounds which the flinty road had inflicted on my unprotected feet.

16
Events of Wednesday, June 6th

Arbuthnot returned at dawn and promptly sent me to bed when I would fain have questioned him. My body after my various recent experiences was a medley of bruises, burns, and cuts; nevertheless I slept the sleep of reaction. I woke to bright daylight. Then like the swift transit of a wave the memory of some astounding occurrence welled up from the subconscious, and in a second I was wide awake and scrambling out of bed.

My friend sat at breakfast as spick and span as if his quota of slumber had never been denied him, and with his familiar, the teapot, close by his elbow. He grinned when he saw me.

"I want to know all about this affair," I said, pouring myself out a cup of tea.

"Better get dressed first, hadn't you?" he suggested, smiling.

"I suppose so," I admitted.

I fear my toilet that morning was devoid of that care which I generally choose to bestow on it. Outside my bedroom window stood the car which Flyte had used and which had brought Arbuthnot back from Newport. Probably the same car had played a part in this tangle once before in bringing Pamela to the bungalow. It had been an amazing business. Now I had come to the unveiling.

I returned to the dining-room. Arbuthnot had finished breakfasting and, shoulders propped against the mantel, was filling his pipe.

"What on earth did Bernard say?" I asked.

"I wish you had been there. His remarks deserved a place in your note-book. They were singularly apt. I gave Flyte in charge and then insisted on coming straight back here, for one is in no mood for explanations at three in the morning. They can wait. After all, my dear King, you certainly have first claim to know what there is to be known, for, in a sense, if you have not borne the burden and heat of the day you have certainly coped with the terror that flieth by night!"

"What did you charge him with?" I asked.

"With being unlawfully on private premises at night. That serves the present purpose of keeping him locked up."

"But he was in his own house!"

"Officially he is dead. If the police choose not to realize that the man I charged is Flyte they can hardly be blamed."

"I see," I said, laughing. "Now let's be serious. My curiosity is entirely beyond control."

"Certain points still require elucidation," said Arbuthnot slowly. "An investigation into crime is not like a proposition of Euclid. The gathering up of loose ends may never be finally completed, and human motives can never be as accurately assessed as points in a problem. However, barring a certain amount of the necessary spadework of verification, I can present you with a fairly coherent tale."

"Do so," I said. "You sound like a Gifford lecturer."

He laughed.

"There are two methods of laying bare the past," he went on. "One can either reconstruct events into a continuous story or one can detail the steps by which one

was led gradually to a solution. The second way takes too
long, for I am likely to have a busy day. Be content with
the first, and admire my modesty in sacrificing some of my
dramatic effects."

"I've had quite enough drama, thank you," I said.

"Good! We will now inquire into the circumstances
preceding and following the murder of Dalton Flyte's
brother, who, like the dark member of a double star, seems
to have assisted the motions without possessing the brilliance of his twin. To avoid confusion I will call him Flyte
Number Two. On the night of May the twenty-fifth he was
murdered by an American called Jaguar Jim, who, we now
know, specialized in the art of speedy removals."

"How was it done?"

"Patience, King. About two months before the crime a
new servant-girl came to the Stagrock Hotel in answer to
an advertisement. She was well recommended, for bogus
testimonials are not difficult to manufacture, and efficient, but not disposed to fraternize. As you know, she
suddenly quarreled with the manageress and left on Thursday morning, May the twenty-fourth. The morning after
the crime I picked up one of my own visiting-cards on the
floor of Dalton Flyte's dining-room. Where had it come
from? And why had it arrived there? To say the very least,
it was unlikely that anyone should have considered using
such a thing *before* we left London. It was a reasonable
conclusion that the card had been annexed during our stay
at Freshwater. Then it was nearly safe to say that one of
the hotel servants had taken it. On principle, suspicion
attached to the one who had left. Certain other facts in
addition led me to frame a theory which has only recently
been substantiated."

"What was that theory?"

"That the murderer of Flyte Number Two masqueraded
at the hotel as the chambermaid, Sarah Tuson!"

"Then there was a dreadful irony in your assurance to the little waiter," I said with a shudder.

"Yes, it was quite a stage situation."

"But I don't see the grounds for your belief yet."

"Of course you don't. Assume for a moment that she, or he, was here to compass the murder. Having chosen a moment to act he picked a quarrel with the manageress and left the hotel, but not the locality. What did he do with the luggage he must have had with him to maintain appearances? He might either have sent it to some accomplice, if such existed, or dispatched it to a fictitious address, trusting that the slow process of inquiry by the railway company or agents would not materialize until long after he had vanished. He showed his intelligence by choosing the latter course, for if the luggage were eventually traced back to Miss Tuson at Freshwater Bay it proved nothing, whereas the other plan, if available, might have eventually extended the sphere of inquiries. I put Kaye on to worry the Southern Railway. His letter of yesterday told me that a trunk consigned 'luggage in advance' by a Miss Price from Yarmouth, I.W., on May the twenty-fourth to 67, Stormont Road, Lavender Hill, S.W., had not been delivered by the railway company as no one of the name of Price was known at that address."

"So far so good," I remarked.

"Still assuming that this person Tuson was the murderer, let us consider his possible plan of campaign. We know Flyte was a suspicious man. We guess he was not likely to leave his doors unlocked at night, and yet Miss Strode, you remember, found the back door in that condition when she fled. There was also no trace of the house having been broken into. I suggest Tuson had a key of the back door. How was it obtained? I refer you to the peculiar burglary at Mrs. Morris's cottage when nothing was taken—except an impression of the bungalow key!"

"That would only admit him to the kitchen," I argued.

"Very true. I have no doubt that the defences of Flyte's domicile were a matter of local gossip and that the murderer was well aware that the key would only be serviceable by day, and then only if Mrs. Morris and her niece, who sometimes acted as a substitute, were both prevented from being there."

"What then?"

"I believe steps were taken to ensure that Flyte should be alone on that Friday. I think Tuson, having disposed of his luggage, purchased crabs, a highly flavoured article of diet in which the taste of a foreign substance would easily pass unnoticed, treated them with some drug to produce violent symptoms of illness for a short time—a drop or so of croton oil[1] would have served the purpose—and returning to Freshwater at dusk on Thursday evening sold them to Mrs. Morris's niece by tempting her with their unusual cheapness. An illness arising from eating shell-fish would hardly excite suspicion later on."

"It hangs together," I said.

"So far. I consider that Tuson, having probably anticipated Rodd's later procedure and spent a night on the downs, in the course of which he may have managed to effect some alterations in his personal appearance, since by Bernard's account female disguise was no new thing to him, appeared at Flyte's bungalow at some time on Friday with the back-door key as evidence that he was acting for Mrs. Morris, she and her niece both being ill. The sight of the key would be necessary and sufficient to convince Flyte. Tuson would choose to defer his act till the last possible moment at night when Flyte was about to close his

---

[1] The name of the actual substance my friend mentioned has been deleted by request.

inner door. The shutters would be in position to deaden the sound, the down would be deserted at night, and the darkness would cover his retreat. He could count on at least nine hours before Mrs. Morris arrived to discover the crime."

"I'm with you so far," I agreed.

"What exactly happened then we may be able to get out of Flyte later on. I think that Flyte Number Two and his party from London arrived just at the moment when Dalton Flyte was about to shut his inner door and the apparent housekeeper was on the point of killing him. The fact that Miss Strode found a fire burning in the house when she arrived should have led you to see that there was already some one there when the party from London turned up. Flyte Number One no doubt hustled Tuson out of the house when the others arrived. He would have no love for eavesdroppers. Tuson was probably staggered at seeing his plans miscarry at the last moment by this most unexpected occurrence. We know he was a desperate character, and he was no doubt aware that Flyte himself was no angel and that visitors who came to him at night were probably in the same category and would think twice before they raised a hue and cry. There is no knowing to what rash lengths such a man may proceed when he sees a cherished plan suddenly go wrong. I think Tuson returned to the house determined to accomplish his purpose. Meanwhile what had happened? Flyte Number Two had brought Miss Strode to the bungalow and had gone into the dining-room waiting to change places with Flyte Number One, who would then proceed to interview the visitor. That was where my visiting-card would come in useful, for if Tuson failed to find his victim alone he could represent that he had returned because a person was waiting outside to see Flyte, and in all modesty I think the name on the card would have caused a certain flutter in the dovecotes."

"But Tuson could not anticipate that use for the card."

"No. I think he originally took it to bluff with if Flyte detected the imposition."

"I see. Go on."

"Picture Tuson re-entering the house, card very prominent in one hand and the other holding a pistol concealed in his pocket. In the dining-room, which was obviously the first room he would go to, he sees Flyte Number Two, whom he naturally mistakes for Flyte Number One. Probably they had a system by which they always dressed alike, for clearly, by Miss Strode's account, they were accustomed to exchanging positions. Tuson shoots, kills, and turns to flee. Meanwhile I guess Flyte Number One was in his bedroom, the room you are now occupying. His suspicions were aroused, either because he heard the opening of the back door or by voices in the dining-room. He rushes out, hears the shot, grabs one of the iron bars from the recess in the passage just outside his bedroom door and strikes Tuson down with it as he emerges from the dining-room. Whether the bar was merely bent or had a flaw and so broke in the process we don't know, but evidently it was damaged in some way, so that when the bungalow was evacuated they took it with them. The act of replacing it later would have been a good move if I had not previously noted its absence."

"What happened then?"

"The escape of Miss Strode. The two survivors of the double tragedy were probably very relieved that she went when she did. It is no enviable position to have a couple of corpses left on one's hands. It was not sufficient simply to disappear from the spot, for the nature of the crime would not deceive an investigator into thinking the dead persons had destroyed each other, and the last thing Flyte would want would be a sustained inquiry into the affair. Now Flyte, as you have already realized, has a brain, and

with the aid of the remaining man he put into operation
a remarkable scheme. Since apparently people were out to
murder him it would be an excellent thing if he became
theoretically dead. Then if it could be shown that his murderer had met an accidental death while making his escape
no further inquiries would, in all probability, be made.
On this basis they set to work. They stripped Jaguar Jim's
body of its female garb, having undoubtedly already recognized that that was nothing but a disguise, and dressed it
in the brown tweed suit that the accomplice was wearing.
To leave it in woman's dress would assist its identification
with the supposed Miss Tuson and stimulate fresh interest
in the crime. Moreover, the attire of a servant would not
harmonize with the other details of the plan they had in
view, while the use of one of Flyte's suits would be even
less desirable. You remember that when we inspected the
corpse of the man who was brought from Bouldnor Cliff I
remarked on his ill-fitting suit."

"What did the accomplice wear then?"

"Presumably one of Flyte's own suits. Mrs. Morris's
statement about his clothes, you recollect, makes that possible."

"Quite so."

"The next step was to stimulate the appearance of a
robbery. They cleared the safe, that is, if there was anything in it at all, and made a packet of old copies of the
Morning Post, which, when burnt, would quite well suggest that they had once been its contents. They removed
from Flyte Number Two any signs that he was not Flyte
Number One, and even went so far as to equip him with
the latter's diamond ring to make identification doubly
sure. That was cleverness to excess, for it threw a doubt on
the robbery motive. Also they forgot the box of cigarettes
in the sideboard, a trifling matter in itself, but significant when considered with other things. Evidently the two

Flytes had not the same taste in tobacco. Having, as they thought, made everything safe they drove away, using both cars, Flyte's own and the one from Southampton, and taking with them the dead man, his female clothing, the keys of the house, the key that Jaguar Jim had possessed, the bundle of newspapers, the damaged bar, and the pince-nez that Flyte Number Two had worn. It was the absence of the latter article that was the real hinge on which I hung my since-confirmed theory."

"How?"

"Why should anyone steal pince-nez? They are only of use to the person for whom they are made. We know that Flyte was so blind without them that they were always on his nose, so there was no value in the suggestion you made that they had been stolen prior to the crime. I couldn't see how it could have been done. And if Flyte had found that his pince-nez had disappeared you may be sure he would have smelt a rat and disappeared also. No, the pince-nez were taken away because otherwise they would have revealed that they had not belonged to Dalton Flyte. If once one was forced to that conclusion the dead man ceased to be Flyte. I presume that Flyte Number Two had perfectly good eyesight, but used pince-nez containing plain glass in order to counterfeit his brother."

"Events have justified you," I said.

"Very well. This interpretation enabled me to see Flyte's apparently blameless life from a new angle. It is reasonable to suppose that when Flyte Number One travelled to London he went to his Brixton Road headquarters, while at the same time Flyte Number Two moved from the Brixton Road to the Brompton Palace Hotel. This gave Number One a perfect alibi in case of need.

"We now draw near the end of this phase of the affair. We must suppose the two cars went by the main road as far as the beginning of the little side lane that leads to Bouldnor

Cliff. There the accomplice remained in charge of the
Southampton car, while Flyte took the other one on and
sent it over the cliff. Probably he set fire to it in advance
to make doubly sure. Then he rushed back and drove away
in the second car, and in due course they crossed from
Cowes to Southampton by the first boat that morning and
disappeared. The car outside at present is probably the
one they used, and Bernard of course wants it back at
once, for there is clearly some reason to suppose that the
owner may be connected with the Flyte gang."

"Your theory had only a lean backing of facts to begin
with," I suggested.

"Then there was the hat, or rather the absence of one,
to consider," Arbuthnot continued, disregarding my comment. "A person engaged in the commission of crime will
ninety-nine times out of a hundred wear a hat, partly because it shields the face to some extent, but chiefly because
a hatless man is noted and remembered long after his more
conventional brethren have been forgotten. It was a grave
error on Flyte's part not to drop a hat somewhere near
the scene of the supposed accident, thereby suggesting it
had blown off when the car plunged downwards. Naturally
he understood that he couldn't put it on the head of the
corpse, for what man would put on a hat after having had
his head smashed in? And Flyte knew that if the blow had
been received by a man wearing a hat, the hat should bear
traces of it, as no doubt the woman's hat Jaguar Jim would
have been wearing did. He wished us to believe that the
man's head had struck the upright of the windscreen, and
for all I know it may have done, unless Flyte had the nerve
to daub the upright with the blood that was found on it.
Still, he should have provided a hat."

"One question I want to ask," I said.

"Fire away."

"What happened to Jaguar Jim's pistol?"

"A very shrewd question. One would naturally have expected to find it in the vicinity of his corpse. Flyte cheerfully sacrificed the bungalow keys to make certain that people should believe what he wished them to believe. Why didn't he throw in the pistol, which would have furnished proof beyond doubt? Very likely Flyte and his assistant were in a deadly funk. One of their number had been slain outright that night, and they had no guarantee that that would be the end of it. Flyte probably always went in fear of his life from one person or another. If the man from London had not brought a pistol with him, and I don't see why he should have done so, then when the cars separated each man would want to have a weapon available. But only Flyte can solve that mystery."

"Subsequent events are now fairly easily explicable," I suggested.

"Yes. Flyte and his friend went away with the backdoor key that Jaguar Jim had possessed. It was the only one of interest to them, seeing where Flyte's treasure lay. He obviously had no time to disinter the box on the night of the crime and relied on its remaining safely hidden till he could get at it. When he failed to rent the bungalow under the pseudonym of Cosmo Edginton he set his minion on to obtain the box, preferring not to risk a visit to the Isle of Wight himself. Only when we captured the other man did he feel impelled to act personally, with what results we have seen. And another point arises over the conduct of Flyte, as Edginton, when he received the letter with the intentional mistake. He disappeared like a shot. Why? Surely he did not fear our friend Williams? No, the 'mistake' showed him that there was another person after the bungalow, and he concluded that the name of Parker shrouded the identity of some one who inspired him with panic fear."

"But Parker was innocent," I urged.

"Very true, King. There are a whole battalion of 'buts' to be met and overcome."

"First of all," I said, "it is now clear that Jaguar Jim was only an agent in the affair."

"Right. As the girl Tuson he left the hotel before Flyte arrived in Freshwater that week. Therefore he had information from some one on the point or he would not have acted in advance. That that some one was a principal in the affair is now proved by the telegram we obtained yesterday."

"That telegram baffles me," I admitted.

"We are bound to take it that the 'previous instructions' refer to the murder of Flyte. Suddenly, for some reason, the order to murder Flyte was countermanded, but too late for the cancellation to have effect."

"That's all right so far. Now another point. If the papers burnt in the car were only a few issues of the *Morning Post,* how do you explain the scrap of paper that was found with Flyte's note about Rodd on it?"

"My dear King, that was a wonderful bit of evidence. That such a thing should come to light after I and others had most carefully quartered the vicinity of the burnt-out car in vain is enough to humble the spirit of the proudest investigator. That the only shred that survived the fire should actually mention Rodd's name, and yet that the discriminating flames should have obliterated the latter half of the first line which would otherwise have told us the subject of Rodd's possible alarm, is a coincidence that reduces the brightest efforts of sensational fiction to the merest commonplace."

"What do you mean?" I exclaimed.

"I mean that if we use our imaginations we can finish the incomplete first line, 'If Rodd is alarmed', very neatly by adding 'about Miss Strode'. Knowing what we do, can we suggest any other subject over which he was likely to become alarmed at the time? I think not."

"Well?"

"I feel obliged to suppose that the scrap of paper was a fragment of a letter written by Flyte to some other person and used by that person to manufacture evidence against Rodd."

"The devil!"

"Some approximation to him. But time flies! 'The sermon is upon the paragraph that is toned to awaken the clerk.' Listen."

"Carry on," I said eagerly.

"Flyte knew of the existence of Rodd and of his relation to Miss Strode. That scrap of paper proves it. We may be sure that a man who had been making his living by Flyte's methods would not fail to note the Press announcements of Rodd's sudden wealth. Yet at this juncture Flyte begins to force the girl to do some impossible piece of dirty work for him on the threat of immediate exposure if she fails to do it. Her period of grace is timed to expire a few hours before Rodd is due to arrive and Flyte will not extend it. He even goes to Freshwater unusually early that week, as if to prevent her making a final appeal. What are we to make of such conduct? For a moment I thought that Flyte might have been attracted by the girl's person, but she has assured us that that was not so. Yet did Flyte really meditate an exposure when he would thereby lose the large sum he might hope to extract from Rodd? It isn't sense when you look at it that way."

"What other way is there?"

"Only one. Flyte had another use for the document instead of keeping it to put the screw on Rodd. There was no way in which he could use it profitably himself, so we are driven to suppose that he had arranged to dispose of it to another person."

"What!" I shouted. "Do you mean that that paper is still loose somewhere to do evil?"

"That is a possibility. There was no more money to be got out of Miss Strode, and therefore Flyte had no further interest in her; but that is not to say that no other person had an interest. When she was at her wits' end on that Friday morning she would probably have welcomed the intervention of anyone who could assure her that it was no longer in Flyte's power to do mischief. There would be a price to pay, of course."

I shuddered.

"But there was no such intervention!" I cried.

"No. That is the puzzle. In place of that the girl rounded up Flyte Number Two, who took her to Freshwater, either acting under orders or because he didn't know what else to do under the circumstances. Therefore the next thing for us to do is to—"

"Open the box!" I cried.

"Precisely." Without more words he unlocked the safe and pulled out the receptacle which might or might not contain the document that had been the root of all our troubles.

"Let us go into your bedroom," he said, "and we shall thereby avoid possible interruptions."

The box lay on my bed while Arbuthnot fitted the key and threw back the lid. We bent eagerly over the contents. There were several smallish bundles of papers neatly clipped together, but varying from the merest untidy scrap to portentous-looking documents,

"Let us first satisfy ourselves on the point at issue," decreed Arbuthnot.

"Of course."

Methodically he went through the various bundles, now raising his eyebrows over some item, now bringing them down over another. It was a motley assortment. There was a ball-programme with a message scribbled in pencil on it, a pawn ticket, several hotel bills, a passport and some photographs, besides letters and legal-looking papers.

"Here we are," said my friend.

He loosened the clip of one of the bundles and withdrew a single sheet of innocuous appearance.

"Thank God for that! Let's get rid of it at once."

"Would you deprive Miss Strode of the pleasure?"

"It would hurt her to see it."

"No doubt. But to put it to the flames with her own hands would convey such a realization of security as far to outweigh that. As a rule I defer to your knowledge of women, King, but I do know that they value concrete assurances."

I conceded his point and he folded the incriminating paper and slipped it into his wallet.

"A bonfire for the rest?" I suggested.

"Not at all. Don't suppose that all Flyte's dealings were with high-souled damsels. There may be material here to secure the conviction of a dozen scoundrels. I will do a bit of weeding out if necessary and let Bernard have the rest. He deserves all we can do for him."

"And I'll leave you to it," I replied.

Mrs. Morris met me at the door with a telegram addressed to Arbuthnot. He read it and passed it to me. It contained these words:

> "*Legal delays. Arrive to-night. Please warn all concerned. Rodd.*"

"Don't mention this to anyone," he said as I returned him the slip.

"All right."

I drifted out to the veranda. Arbuthnot's explanation had taken a long time and noontide was past. Then

I caught sight of Pamela in a deck-chair. She jumped up when she heard me.

"Where have you been? And how much longer is Mr. Arbuthnot going to make me stay in Freshwater?"

"I had no idea he was keeping you," I said.

"Of course he told me to stay. Otherwise I would have been at the prison-gates waiting for Roddy to come out."

I had to laugh. "He isn't completing twenty years' penal servitude," I remarked.

"It's been a jolly long time, anyway," she answered, pouting, and then vouchsafing a half-smile.

"I'll fetch Arbuthnot," I said, "and then you'll know your orders."

"You're awful when you try to be humorous," was all the reply she made.

We went indoors and met Arbuthnot in the drawing-room. Without a word he handed her the telegram that had arrived.

"Oh!"

The simple comment as spoken by her needed no amplification.

"Rodd is still a suspect in the eyes of the law," Arbuthnot pointed out. "His arrival must be kept secret. It would not be fair to worry Mr. Bellingham, for as a friend of your father's he could hardly approve of your meeting a man so situated. But I believe he generally retires early, and probably you could manage to come here after ten to-night. King would be a very adequate chaperon."

Pamela laughed.

"I'll risk it cheerfully," she declared, and her eyes were dancing. "Will he be wearing the broad-arrow?" she asked.

It was our turn to laugh.

"I have something to give you," said Arbuthnot in matter-of-fact tones. "I obtained it from Dalton Flyte."

The shock struck all the colour out of her face.

"From Flyte! I don't understand. How could you since he's dead?"

"He was very much alive when I took him to the police station this morning," answered Arbuthnot soberly.

I thought she would have fallen and hastened to her side.

"That's not funny," she said with an effort.

"It won't be funny for Mr. Flyte, I can assure you," said Arbuthnot solemnly, "but I don't see that you have anything to fear. He left this for you."

Arbuthnot had opened his wallet and now proffered her the fatal paper without comment. I turned my head away as she took it. Arbuthnot with studied deliberation felt in his pocket, took out a match-box, extracted a match, and struck it.

"Ashes to ashes," he said gently.

Pamela was standing rigid, with all the tension of a steel rod the moment before it snaps. Without a word she held the corner of the paper in the little flame that burnt so feebly in the summer sunlight. A greater flame leaped into being, soared up and sank, and a shrivelled grey film went floating earthwards.

"If I erred in thinking that you would like to be present at this act of destruction, forgive me," said my friend.

"Forgive you!" she cried, and could get no further.

"How about some lunch?" I said fatuously.

"Oh, I couldn't! Some time you must tell me all about this—but not now."

At the door she paused, turned, and sent us a gallant smile, as if she sought to draw a mental shutter over the tragedy that had darkened the past. Arbuthnot put a finger to his lips. She nodded and was gone.

"I'm afraid your knowledge of women is only skin-deep after all, King," said my friend, shaking his head. With this comment he returned to his labour of classifying

Dalton Flyte's legacy of mischief. After a moment's thought
I followed him.

"Since the paper was in the box, how does that affect
your theory of Flyte's actions?" I asked.

"We must believe he changed his mind, or that all
along he was playing what our American friends call the
'double-cross', while at the same time some other person
was trying the same game on him. Flyte would not fail to
see the chance of putting up his precious document, as it
were, to auction between Rodd and another."

"This Juproli!" I cried. "Flyte also was really an Italian
you said."

"Only on the stage perhaps. But I certainly think you
have guessed the truth there. Flyte was expected to get the
document on Thursday and send it to London to arrive before Rodd did. Actually he never intended to do anything
of the sort. How do we know that? Because in that case
he would have told Mrs. Morris on the Thursday night
that he would not require her the following day. He would
have wanted to be free to fish up his box. Juproli, as you
call him, had decided that Flyte, who knew a great deal
too much, would be better dead as soon as he had delivered the goods. Jaguar Jim had orders to act any time after
Thursday. When the document failed to arrive on Friday
the telegram was sent to stop the murder, but it arrived
too late, as we know. Now let me get this job finished."

We lunched late that day after Arbuthnot had dealt
with the contents of the box. I was in a mood of alternat-
ing exultation and bewilderment and withal haunted by
the sinister figure of the unknown Italian.

"It is well known," said Arbuthnot, applying himself
to the tea that he always demanded in place of the more
usual narcotic, "that Indian civil servants rarely live long
after entering upon the retired leisure they have so richly
earned."

"The point has escaped my notice," I said, wondering how his mind could busy itself with so many things at once.

"They die because the one great interest of their lives is withdrawn and they have no adequate substitute. It is the man with the single aim who makes the world. He achieves either triumph or tragedy. And the wicked man who has learnt to concentrate on a single end makes half the world's great criminals. Beware, King, of such men. It is your multiplicity of interests that makes you such a harmless individual."

"Thank you."

"Don't mention it. I present you with the fact as a subject for meditation while I'm away."

"You're going?"

"At once. Bernard is probably raging. He has been most decent throughout, and now I've got to get down to brass-tacks with him. He has two prisoners there on remand, and naturally he wants a full statement of evidence against them—and lots of other things besides. To-morrow this place will be humming with reporters. I'm taking the box and the back-door key I obtained from Flyte. Here are the others. If I should be late and Mrs. Morris has gone when I return I can let myself in."

"You don't anticipate any danger?" I asked, with the thought of Juproli at the back of my mind.

"Not to you. And very little chance of it to anyone. Good-bye."

Day waned. A rising wind fluffed the curtains as I sat alone at dinner, and over the sea crept up a long smudge of neutral-hued cloud. I was vaguely uneasy. Somewhere or other Rodd was on his way to the bungalow, even as on another night not so long ago. In the big hotel on the far side of the bay Pamela, I guessed, was torn between joy and questionings. Arbuthnot had not returned.

On the pretence of considering him I directed Mrs. Morris to leave some cold provisions on the sideboard, for I thought it unlikely Rodd would have dined. As I watched from the drawing-room, the cloud-bank grew and rose out of the sea, menacing like some doom that creeps towards fulfilment. The sea was darkened now, but little patches of white glimmered where the cat's-paws were flicking off the crests of all the little waves hurrying shorewards. By ten o'clock it was quite dark.

I sat in a blaze of light in the drawing-room, making a pretence of reading. Mrs. Morris had gone. Soon I might be expecting arrivals. I went to the window. The clouds now towered like some vast impending figure of fate, and my mind reverted to that evil influence which had come in to disturb our calculations at the last moment—the Italian who pursued his aim without regard to human life. My imagination for a moment let me see Pamela in his clutches, and I shuddered.

"Edmund!"

She was there. Her face showed wan and elfish in the darkness outside the window. I hastened to admit her.

"I'm not late? Good! Gerry's been grumpy with lumbago all day. Fortunately it sent him to bed early."

I helped her to a cigarette.

"I've got my balance back," she said quietly, taking up a characteristic position on the edge of a table. "I want to know everything."

"Then you must wait for Arbuthnot," I answered. "He may know everything. I certainly don't."

"Is he not here?"

"He had to go to Newport."

"I see. I wish I could thank him—and you. But there are no words made for occasions like these."

She suddenly slid from her table, crossed the floor with a rush, and before I quite knew what was happening had reached up and kissed me. I think of it now sometimes. The curious thing is that she didn't do the same to Arbuthnot. I know, for I asked him.

Perhaps five minutes had elapsed when we heard a faint tapping at the front door. Without a word I went to open it, leaving Pamela standing in the centre of the room, her hands nervously clenching and unclenching.

"Is that you, Rodd?"

"Yes. Surely it's King?"

"Come in," I said. He stepped over the mat and silently pressed my proffered hand.

"The door on your left," I added, and pushed him in.

Then I strode off down the passage. Only before I had gone two steps I heard one cry of "Roddy!" Then I went into my bedroom, sat on my bed in the dark, and waited till I could decently reappear. It is only on such occasions that a bachelor questions the wisdom of his own ordering of life. These two had emerged triumphantly from the doom that had threatened to overwhelm them. They saw their haven. Well, I would give them ten minutes, and then I would return to congratulate Rodd.

Time slipped away, and I was just on the point of moving when I heard the sound of a key in the back door. I chuckled. That was Arbuthnot returning. I would sit tight and let him walk in upon them. That would fulfil all the requirements of drama. Arbuthnot had saved them; it was only right that the curtain should fall with him in the centre of the stage. I was ready to join in the applause.

Footsteps passed my bedroom door and went along towards the drawing-room. I waited for a loud outburst of voices. None came. Surely Pamela and Rodd had not gone outdoors during my absence? I left my bedroom, crossed the passage, and went through the dining-room towards the drawing-room. What was happening? Then I looked into the lighted room and my heart gave one enormous jump and checked as if it would never beat again.

Pamela was standing near the doorway with her back towards me. On my right was Rodd, his face the colour of the ash of a fine cigar and his eyes half-glazed with the stare of one who sees death. Opposite to him and near the door that led to the passage, with his eyebrows arched in a paroxysm of uncontrollable rage, his lips drawn tightly back from wolfish teeth and a pistol gripped in his right hand, stood Gervase Bellingham! And not one of the three was saying a word.

There are situations in life which are beyond speech. Some of the scales fell from my eyes as I stood there frantically and vainly striving to devise any means of averting the catastrophe that threatened.

"What's all this?" said my tongue suddenly without my having willed it to speak, and to myself the sound of my voice was far away and foolish. But the spell was broken. The presence of a fourth person in the room brought the actors back from marble to life.

"No!"

It was Pamela's scream. Before anyone else could move she had sprung forward and with her nearer hand, the left, had grasped the muzzle of Bellingham's pistol.

There was an explosion. I have often debated with myself since whether he had actually been on the point of firing or whether Pamela's act had jerked the weapon and caused an unintentional discharge. We shall never know.

Bellingham uttered an exclamation that mingled rage and horror. The pistol clattered to the ground. Without seeking to retrieve it he turned and fled out into the night.

Pamela spun round, holding up her left hand, and I saw with a sudden cold sickness that the third finger from the lower joint upwards was gone!

"A hundred per cent genuine at last, Edmund!" she cried, laughing exultantly to me over the stump that was pumping blood in a stream along her hand and arm. Then Rodd was just in time to catch her as she collapsed.

I left him to it. It was his job. I fancied that mine lay outside.

Events take longer to record than to occur. I don't suppose that Bellingham had more than a few yards start of me, but the night was overcast and seeing was almost impossible. Outside the bungalow I paused, listened, and heard the clink of flints on the road. He was making towards the down! With a bound I was after him. The thinking part of my brain was still dulled by amazement, but some lower part of the organism directed my feet. I rushed along by the side of the road, where, on the turf, I made no sound.

Then the long ray of a powerful electric torch leapt into being from a hundred yards away. It shone straight in my eyes, wavered up and down, and finally fastened on a black object in front of me. That was Bellingham! He swerved to his right, and the ray followed him. I ran on. Roughly speaking, Bellingham, I, and the man with the torch formed the three vertices of an equilateral triangle. And the triangle was getting smaller!

The torch flashed from Bellingham to me and back again.

"Is that you, King?"

Heavens, it was Arbuthnot!

"We've got to get him!" I yelled.

Now Arbuthnot and I were nearly together. Barely twenty yards separated us from Bellingham. So wildly excited was I that I never sensed what was coming and only most narrowly avoided catastrophe. Only ten yards remained. And he was unarmed.

Suddenly there was no Bellingham!

Arbuthnot grabbed my arm and arrested my progress. "Listen!" said he. I dropped panting on the turf.

There came floating up as it were from beneath us a scream the like of which I pray God I may never hear again. It is said that those who fall from heights are plunged into merciful unconsciousness in their descent. I know better. The sound ceased, there was a sudden rattle of small stones, and then silence.

"You're within two yards of the edge of the cliff," said Arbuthnot dryly.

"Did he intend to do that?" I asked in a shaken, husky voice. There is something terrible in that kind of death, even when it is a bad man who dies.

"I can't say. He should have known the cliff was there. He acted like a man bewildered by some unexpected occurrence. What has he been up to?"

"He came to the bungalow when Pamela and Rodd were there and shot her."

"Badly?"

"Blew off one of her fingers."

"Might have been worse. You were surprised to see him, eh?"

"Of course I was."

"It was one of those happenings it is impossible to provide against. You see what it means?"

"I see nothing," I said wearily. My head was burning as with fever, and if I had been a woman I should have wept.

"It means Sir Jervis Strode is dead. But say nothing about that to-night."

"A thousand pities you were late."

"The car that was bringing me back broke down and so I had to finish on foot. I started to ran when I thought I heard a shot fired."

"How do you know Strode is dead?"

"To-morrow will do for that, King. Let us get back to the bungalow."

Pamela lay on the drawing-room couch, very white and with her eyes closed. Rodd was kneeling beside her. She opened her eyes when we entered.

"Where is he?" she cried.

"That is entirely a matter for conjecture," said Arbuthnot, "but be assured he will not return here."

The clearing up after a feast is an anticlimax, and in the same category must be placed the addenda in which a chronicler records details relating to the actors after they have quitted his stage. Let me therefore be brief.

Dalton Flyte and his "rat-faced" accomplice went away to respectable terms of confinement at the public expense on various charges arising out of the events I have described. The activities of the police also resulted in bringing into the net some smaller fish, including the gentleman at Southampton whose car was available with such suspicious readiness on two occasions. Flyte in his evidence went to extreme lengths to try to prove that he had been nothing but the tool of Bellingham in the affair. Those statements deserve only a limited credence. On the other hand, it was independently established that Bellingham had paid a visit to New York two months before the events here recorded, and one can hardly be mistaken over the purpose of that journey.

Rodd and Pamela had to stand the glare of publicity for as long as the law required their assistance. Then Pamela received a wedding ring on the wrong finger, and she and her husband departed for the Laurentian wilds, for, as Rodd, who turned out to have more sense than I had originally thought, put it, "a man, married or not, must finish his job!"

But long before these things happened, and in fact the day after the final tragedy, Arbuthnot favoured me with an explanation of what remained to be cleared up.

"The essential clue," he said, "was the application of Mr. Herbert Parker to rent this bungalow. He was ignorant of the crime; in fact we may assume that he was the type of man who would never read a newspaper report of such an occurrence, yet he wrote to the address the newspapers gave in their descriptions of the affair. Then we found that he was a pensioned employe of the London office of Jute Products, Limited, and had been promised a holiday by his old head. What more likely than that he was being put into the bungalow to prevent some one else getting possession of it—was being used as a dummy, in fact? We can picture a certain person suggesting to the worthy Parker the charms of a seaside bungalow in the Isle of Wight and offering to pay the expenses of taking the ailing wife to what would be an ideal spot for an invalid. If Parker had arrived and found out what had previously happened in the bungalow, a simple soul like him would never have suspected his patron of knowing the truth, and fear of incurring the displeasure of his benefactor would probably have kept him there. But by whom he was being used did not at first appear. Still, you should have smelt a rat when you heard that Bellingham had made his fortune in Calcutta, which is the centre of the world's jute trade. Actually he was, prior to his retiring from business, the chairman of Parker's old firm. Now, as soon as we begin to ask why Bellingham wanted possession of the bungalow the whole plot becomes apparent at once. Bellingham was, *par excellence,* a man with a single idea. When he turned from business he concentrated on getting Miss Strode. Doubtless he loved her after his fashion or he would not have been so aghast at what he did last night. He won her father's favour easily enough, but realized that he made no progress otherwise. Then, perhaps not for the first time, he became connected with Flyte. Together they hatched the scheme for putting pressure on the girl to drive her into Bellingham's arms before Rodd could intervene. Neither trusted the other. Flyte secretly planned to go back on his bargain, and Bellingham went one better and imported a scoundrel to abolish Flyte as soon as the latter ceased to be useful. As you know, both schemes went wrong and Bellingham never got his document. But he did not relinquish hope. He managed a plausible excuse for coming to Freshwater; he surveyed the bungalow on the night of the storm when we saw two men, but not together, and both promptly disappeared at sight of each other; he manufactured evidence against Rodd out of a letter Flyte had written him at some time; he attacked you on the cliff and knocked you senseless. He was no weakling despite his fifty years or so. When you commented so adversely on his gloves the following morning I suppose you hardly thought that one of them probably concealed a set of scarred knuckles. That night he pulled you from the edge to take your key, which he used to enter the bungalow last night; he most probably inspired the police raid on the house in Brixton to get me out of the way, and in fact he kept on trying for what he guessed the bungalow must contain until a telegram last night told him the game was up, for the last obstacle to the union of Rodd and Miss Strode had been removed by the sudden death of Sir Jervis. That was a possibility I could hardly allow for, although I had sensed a certain danger to Rodd and arranged for his visit to be secret. No doubt the telegram announcing the untoward event was sent to Bellingham in order that he might break the news to Miss Strode. He may have held it up some hours while he racked his brain for a method of dealing with the new situation. As you know to your cost, his retirements to bed were sometimes more apparent than real, and last night must have been another example of that. Then he lost his head and you know the rest."

"But where did Juproli come in?" I asked.

"Ah, yes, Juproli. A prearranged code. The single idea again." He took a sheet of paper, wrote busily on it for a moment, and then passed it to me. Here it is as it lies before me now:

JUPROLI
JU PRO LI
JUte PROducts LImited

The Author

N. A. Temple-Ellis was the pseudonym for Neville Aldridge Holdaway (1894-1954). He taught for many years, including in the Isle of Wight and in India, and was deputy head master at a boy's school in Surrey at the time of his death. During World War I, he earned the Military Cross. He authored ten mysteries, published between 1929 and 1941. His first mystery novel, *The Inconsistent Villains,* won first prize in the $2,500 Dutton-Methuen detective mystery contest, judged by A. A. Milne, H. C. Bailey, and Ronald Knox.

THE EDINGTONS

THE HOUSE OF THE
VANISHING
GOBLETS

THE
DESERT LAKE
MYSTERY

KAY CLEAVER STRAHAN
Author of THE DESERT MOON MYSTERY

THE STUDIO
MURDER MYSTERY
THE EDINGTONS

DEATH
ON THE CAMPUS
ADDISON
SIMMONS

Coachwhip Publications

CoachwhipBooks.com

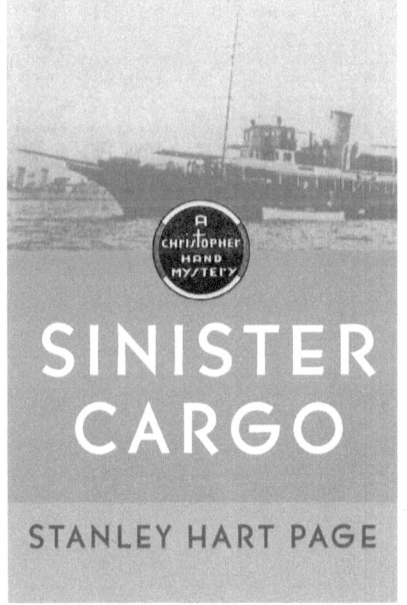

Coachwhip Publications

CoachwhipBooks.com

CLUES OF THE CARIBBEES
being certain original investigations
of Henry Poggioli, Ph.D.
T. S. Stribling

MURDER
IN A WALLED TOWN
KATHERINE WOODS

THE CASE OF THE
UNCONQUERED
SISTERS
A THIRD HUGH RENNERT MYSTERY
Todd Downing

LOUIS F. BOOTH
THE BANK VAULT MYSTERY
BROKERS' END

Coachwhip Publications

CoachwhipBooks.com

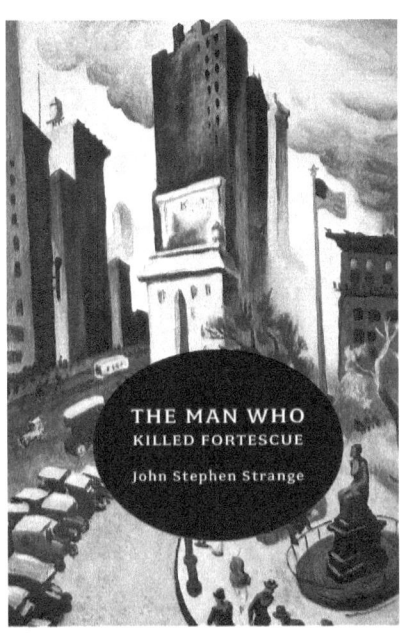

THE MAN WHO
KILLED FORTESCUE

John Stephen Strange

POISON CASE | MURDER CASE
NUMBER 10 | NUMBER 33

FROM THE FILES OF
THE MICHAEL JOYCE AGENCY

LOUIS CORNELL

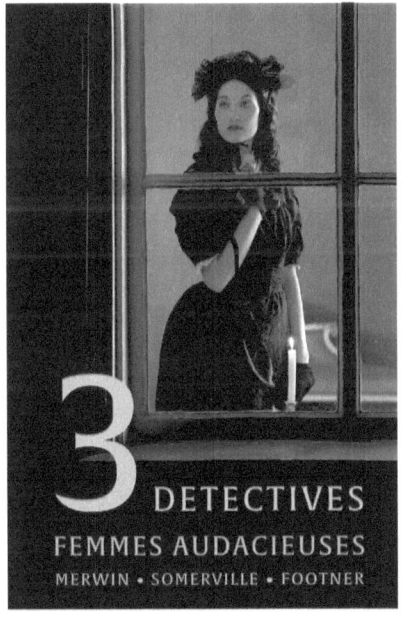

3 DETECTIVES

FEMMES AUDACIEUSES

MERWIN · SOMERVILLE · FOOTNER

MEDORA
FIELD

WHO KILLED
AUNT MAGGIE?

Coachwhip Publications

CoachwhipBooks.com

THE HOUSE WITH
THE BLUE DOOR
HULBERT FOOTNER

The
Jekyll-Hyde
Murder Case
MADELON ST. DENIS

VIRGINIA RATH

DEATH AT
DAYTON'S FOLLY

THE 5.18
MYSTERY

J Jefferson
Farjeon

Coachwhip Publications

CoachwhipBooks.com

THE
BEACON HILL
MURDERS

∞

THE
BACK BAY
MURDERS

THE ROGER SCARLETT MYSTERIES
VOL. 1

THE
SARA ELIZABETH
MASON
MYSTERIES

MURDER RENTS A ROOM

THE CRIMSON FEATHER

HELEN BURNHAM

THE MURDER OF
LALLA LEE

THE TELLTALE
TELEGRAM

THOMAS KINDON

MURDER
IN THE
MOOR

Coachwhip Publications

CoachwhipBooks.com

THE MYSTERIOUS WAYS
OF WANG FOO

SIDNEY C. PARTRIDGE

MURDER
ON THE
BLUFF

ESTHER TYLER

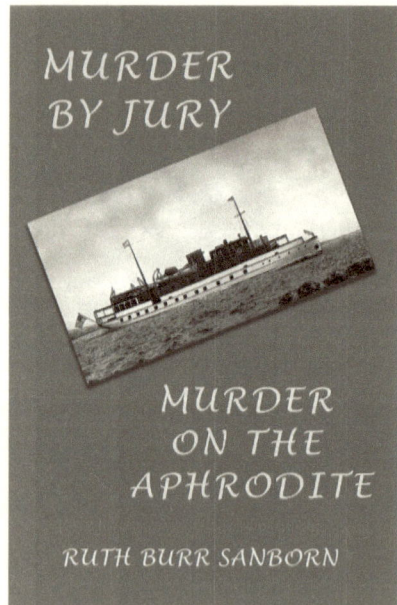

MURDER
BY JURY

MURDER
ON THE
APHRODITE

RUTH BURR SANBORN

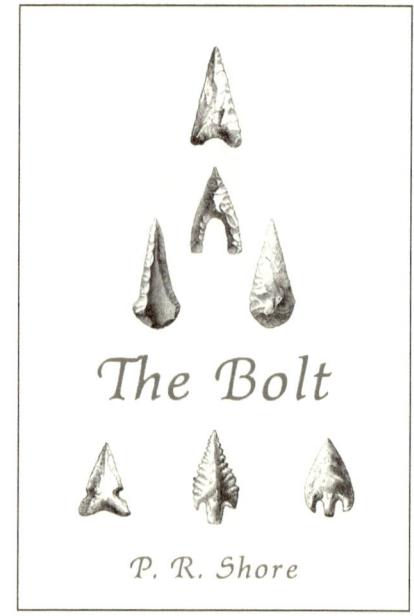

The Bolt

P. R. Shore

Coachwhip Publications

CoachwhipBooks.com

HIDE AND GO SEEK

with, GOING TO ST. IVES

COLVER HARRIS

A JUDGE MASSIE MYSTERY

THE CORPSE IS INDIGNANT

DOUGLAS STAPLETON and HELEN A. CAREY

hot tip JACK DOLPH

THE MAY DAY MYSTERY

OCTAVUS ROY COHEN

Coachwhip Publications

CoachwhipBooks.com

www.ingramcontent.com/pod-product-compliance
Lightning Source LLC
Chambersburg PA
CBHW031107030726
47496CB00002BA/429